The Speakeasy

STRAIGHT UP

K. EVAN COLES AND BRIGHAM VAUGHN

Straight Up
ISBN # 978-1-83943-896-7
©Copyright K. Evan Coles and Brigham Vaughn 2020
Cover Art by Erin Dameron-Hill ©Copyright June 2020
Interior text design by Claire Siemaszkiewicz
Pride Publishing

STRAIGHT UP

Dedication

For my husband, who is patient with my endless scribbling.
For my son, who makes me laugh every single day and gives me all kinds of fun ideas.
For the people in and around my life who inspire me, let me be weird and make me feel brave.
And for Brigham Vaughn, who endures my questions and rants, indulges my humor, and is nearly always willing to put pen to paper when our stars align. Frustrating as the co-writing can sometimes be for both of us, it's a blast.
— *K. Evan Coles*

This book is for my friends who were patient when I was too busy writing or editing to spend time with them. For the people who cheered me on and had faith in my writing long before I did. For my parents, who are the best patrons of the arts a writer could ask for.
And, mostly, for K. Evan Coles, who got me into reading and writing gay romance in the first place. I wouldn't be here without you! It's been a wonderful — and occasionally frustrating — journey. There's no one I would rather have done it with.
— *Brigham Vaughn*

K. and Brigham would also like to thank their patient beta readers: Shell Taylor, Rebecca Spence, Allison Hickman, Jayme Yesenofski and Sally Hopkinson. You've helped us mold six books over the years. Truly, we could not have done it without you. Also, our thanks to Lisa Bailey and Melissa Johnson for helping us choose the name of one of the cutest dogs we've dreamed up.

And the speakeasy crew who just won't stop talking — Jesse, Kyle, Will, Malcolm, Carter and Riley. Those boys have got a whole lot more company these days.

Chapter One

March 2016

Malcolm Elliott stared at the contents of his mother's refrigerator. Or lack of contents, to be more accurate. His mom, Kim, lived alone. Surely, she needed more nutrients than could be gotten from cottage cheese, celery, baby carrots and bottled water. Knowing the pantry would be similarly bare, he worried his bottom lip between his teeth.

"Mom," he said, "you need to tell Jack and me when you're running low on food."

"I'm not running low, silly." Kim flashed a smile when Malcolm glanced her way. "My doctor said my cholesterol was on the high side at my last appointment, so I cut back on junk food."

Malcolm watched her for a beat, unnerved by her ability to lie with a straight face. He doubted his mom's cholesterol levels were off. She'd eaten well for years and, at fifty-seven, was more active than women half her age. The half marathons she ran several times a year were a testament to her discipline.

Diet and lack of exercise weren't a problem. Kim's wallet was, though, because it was just as empty as the refrigerator.

"Good thing all the stuff I picked up is healthy." Malcolm stepped back so the refrigerator door swung shut and turned to the counter where he'd set several bags of groceries. Kim moved to Malcolm's side and reached for one of the bags.

"I love you for doing this for me, Malcolm, but I wish you wouldn't. I'm capable of shopping for myself. Not to mention you came all the way out here on your birthday!"

Malcolm's tension ratcheted up several more degrees. "I don't mind. I like seeing you on my birthday. I like grocery shopping, too."

His mom had always hated grocery shopping, but these days, she avoided it for very sobering reasons. Not that Kim or her sons spoke about those reasons. That she'd been laid off and never told anyone. Burned through her entire savings before Malcolm had accidentally found her out. And that even with the part-time job she'd found at a local college, she was so broke her sons had to support her.

Malcolm and Jackson bought her groceries. They filled her gas tank and paid her utility bills, as well as tackling the endless list of small repair jobs that needed doing around the old house. Malcolm didn't mind doing any of those things. He loved his mother and would do anything for her. He just wished he knew how the hell to help her get out of the financial hole she'd dug for herself, short of handing over the bigger part of his paychecks. He really, really wished he had a way to call her out on her epic levels of denial. Malcolm knew he needed to draw a line in the sand with his mom, but he simply couldn't seem to get there. He couldn't bear the idea of shaming her.

Malcolm shook himself. "I gassed up your car," he said. "That should tide you over until Jack comes out next weekend. Unless you go driving up to Maine to see your boyfriend."

His mother gave a delicate snort. She'd started an online relationship with a man named Scott who lived in Kennebunkport, Maine. From her descriptions, things with Scott were progressing, but they hadn't yet arranged to meet in person.

"You know me better than that," she said. "If Scott wants to meet, it's on him to come to New York. I'm still a bit old-fashioned when it comes to dating IRL."

Malcolm stopped, two boxes of spaghetti in one hand and a jar of pasta sauce in the other. "IRL, huh?"

"I know how to use Urban Dictionary too, sweetheart." Kim tossed her honey-blonde hair at him and they shared a laugh. Her expression turned fretful when Malcolm set the boxes and jar of sauce on the counter. "Why didn't you buy fresh tomatoes and herbs for sauce?"

"The Roma tomatoes looked a bit old," Malcolm replied. He hadn't looked at tomatoes, Roma or otherwise. Produce prices were higher this time of year and fresh pasta and tomatoes hadn't fit into his grocery budget. At least not at a high-end market like Clark's, the nearby supermarket his mother favored. He'd been tempted to visit the discount market down the road from Clark's, but Kim disdained the place and he knew she'd spurn the food if she found out that was where Malcolm had bought it.

You're just as bad as your mom, a voice in Malcolm's head whispered, *acting like nothing is wrong instead of dealing with the mess in your life.*

"I grabbed some thyme," he said. "You can pop some of that into the jarred sauce and dress it up. There's a chicken and some potatoes, too, and you can use the thyme there."

"A whole chicken?"

"Yes. A smaller one. Roast it for Jack when he comes out to visit."

Malcolm turned toward the refrigerator with several containers of yogurt. His mother would let go of the topic if he didn't engage. He had bigger fish to fry and they were wilder than fresh produce and jarred sauce. He waited until everything was put away before he went for broke.

"Do you have your tax documents ready?" Without looking at Kim, Malcolm headed out of the kitchen and for his father's old office, a tiny space located off the family room. "Jack and I are sending ours in this week and I can get yours ready, too."

"Goodness, I haven't even thought about taxes yet."

Malcolm halted mid-step and counted backward from five before he turned around. "Mom, Tax Day is a month from now."

Kim rolled her eyes. "I know that. I've been filing taxes for longer than you've been alive, honey, and the date has always been the same."

"Yeah, hah. Well, let's do it now while I'm here and can help."

"I appreciate that, but we both know you've got plans tonight and it's almost four o'clock." Kim cocked her head. "I have plans, too. My friends and I are taking Rose out for dinner, then over to a paint and sip place in Elm Park." She grinned. "I've never painted under the influence before. It sounds fun."

Malcolm's stomach knotted. Paint and sip parties typically started at over forty dollars a head, money his mom didn't have. Not to mention dinner and a birthday gift for Rose. "Sounds fun. You, um, have a designated driver, right?"

"Of course. Rose's husband organized a shuttle to get us there and home. You worry too much, Malcolm. Watch out you don't go making yourself old before your time."

Too late.

Right or wrong, Malcolm had worried about his mom since his parents' divorce, especially after he found out she'd lost her job. Kim had no family apart from Malcolm and Jackson. As the oldest son, Malcolm felt an obligation to support and protect his mother, even if it meant his own inconvenience. Was that more than a little dysfunctional? Maybe. Unfortunately for Malcolm, he didn't know any other way to be.

"What time do you need to get back to the city?" Kim asked him now.

"Soon." He felt just like a little boy as Kim stepped forward and looped her elbow through his. Any hope he'd held of talking about tax documents died. "I'm meeting the guys at Under around seven."

"Is this the monthly party you've told me about?" Kim led Malcolm away from the office with measured steps. She'd never been to the speakeasy in Morningside Heights co-owned by two of Malcolm's friends, but she delighted in his descriptions.

"No, those happen on the third Thursday of the month, barring holidays." Malcolm hoped his smile looked natural because God knew it didn't feel like it.

Coming out here would leave him drained for days. "We're just getting together to hang out. I'm not sure why, but we've never needed an excuse."

Kim's bright brown eyes sparkled. "Well, I'm glad. You deserve to relax, honey. You've been working so hard on that fundraiser."

"Busy comes with the job. And everyone helps out, Carter included." Malcolm worked with Carter Hamilton at Corporate Equality Campaign, an organization dedicated to ensuring the rights of LGBTQIA employees in the corporate workplace. Carter and his partner also happened to be two of Malcolm's dearest friends. "He and Ri came up with a lead on a restaurant we may hire since the original caterer canceled, actually. I'm meeting with the chef later this week."

"That's great! Maybe Carter and Riley can come up with a lead on a nice girl for you, too. Or boy!" Kim threw in when Malcolm made a noise of protest. "Whatever works for you."

"I meet people, Mom," Malcolm murmured as they walked back into the kitchen, though guilt flared in his gut at the lie.

Of course, Malcolm met people in his day-to-day life. As Social Coordinator for Corporate Equality Campaign, meeting people was a big part of his job. Interfacing with other humans wasn't the kind of 'meet' his mom was talking about, however. Kim wanted Malcolm with someone, paired up like everyone else in his life, and that wasn't happening, no matter how many people he met.

Malcolm hadn't been on a date in almost a year, a fact that didn't bother him in the least. He just wished he knew how to explain that to his mom and how his own weird wiring was the cause.

In truth, Malcolm was still coming to terms with the words he'd found to describe his identity. They'd come to him by chance, really, during a conversation with Carter after that fateful last date, an evening that had held all the right components but gone nowhere, like every date Malcolm'd had in recent memory.

'*I don't know what's wrong with me,*' he'd said while Carter had paid for their lunch at a hot dog cart near the office.

Carter had frowned. '*What makes you think anything is wrong with you at all?*'

'*Well, for starters, I think it's clear I'm a complete failure at dating.*'

'*Do you think that because Tessa's the one who asked you out?*'

'*No, that doesn't bother me.*' Malcolm had bitten into a dog and chewed for a moment. '*It didn't occur to me to ask her out at all, now that you say that.*'

'*Maybe you weren't interested in her,*' Carter had replied.

'*Maybe.*' Malcolm had sighed. '*Tessa's cool and I like hanging out with her and Kyle after yoga class. We had a nice time on the date, too. We saw a movie and grabbed a drink afterward, then I walked her home. But when she kissed me goodnight, it was like…nothing. Just blank. And I know I'm supposed to feel fireworks. Or something?*'

Carter had smiled. '*I don't know about fireworks, babe. That kind of thing doesn't happen as often as people like to think. Kisses should feel nice though, if you're attracted to a person.*' He'd chewed for a moment and his gaze had lost focus before it sharpened again. '*Are you attracted to Tessa, Mal? Sexually, I mean.*'

Dread had filtered through Malcolm. No one had ever asked him such a thing straight out. Malcolm had never considered it, either. And now that he was…well. Malcolm wasn't sure what he was supposed to be feeling around the women he dated. And that didn't seem right.

Now and then, something passed over Malcolm when he looked at another person. A frisson of energy that made his skin heat and his heart pound a little faster. That energy felt good. Those moments were rare, though, and Malcolm knew from the way other people spoke that such feelings should be his norm and not his exception. Even odder, the feelings only happened around people he knew well.

He'd known that energy sometimes around Bethany, a high school girlfriend, and regularly around Liz, a young woman he'd dated during college. Malcolm had cared about Liz and she'd cared for him, too. He'd seen it clearly in her eyes and felt it in her touch. Liz had also loved having intercourse and they'd had sex often. While Malcolm had enjoyed getting off very much, making Liz happy had far outweighed any real urge of his own.

He'd been drawn to Liz, almost pulled, like iron to a magnet. Unfortunately, Malcolm felt a similar pull around Carter, which only added to his confusion. Because that meant Malcolm could be bisexual, right? Except he didn't think that fit either. Malcolm had kissed a guy once during college. The guy was handsome, all dark eyes and a wicked smile, and they'd been out dancing. They'd both been loose on a lot of drinks when the guy had leaned in and laid one on Malcolm. Malcolm had kissed him back, but there'd been nothing deep about it. Just the mechanics of mouths sliding together. There'd been nothing deep with Tessa, either, only a weird, blank disinterest that unsettled Malcolm enough to make him want to stop.

'*Mal?*' Carter had prompted, his voice gentle.

'*I'm not attracted to Tessa. Or anyone, really.*' Malcolm had pursed his lips, his lunch turning leaden in his belly. That might not have been entirely true, but he couldn't tell his friend that. '*That's weird, right?*'

'*I don't think so. Or not in the way I believe you mean, at least.*' Carter had folded up the wax paper that had been wrapped around the hotdog and tossed it in a trash can as they passed. '*Have you ever considered that you could be ace?*'

Something in Malcolm had clicked in that moment, like a key sliding home in a lock. He'd started researching asexuality and talking with Carter about the things he'd learned, and the more Malcolm had talked, the more things he'd recognized about himself.

He rarely checked people out. Flirting was a language he neither spoke nor understood. Outside of his family and friends, he'd never been much into being touched, Liz being a notable exception. While being with Liz had been satisfying for Malcolm, he suspected the flashes of energy — the pull — he sometimes experienced around Carter meant something, too.

Malcolm wasn't interested in changing anything about himself — he didn't see why he should. And that set him apart from the people around him. They didn't just like having sex — they actively wanted it, while Malcolm thought about it very seldom if at all. Understanding as much through the lens of asexuality soothed him in ways he hadn't known he'd needed. And while he was still learning where he fell on the ace spectrum, he did belong there, somewhere.

Unfortunately, Malcolm had yet to figure out how to talk to anyone except Carter about his journey.

Kim beamed at him now. "If you fold up that bike of yours and put it in my trunk, I'll give you a ride to the ferry terminal."

"You don't have to do that, Mom."

"I want to. Plus, we can make a stop at the café on Bay Street."

"The café that sells used books?"

"That's the one!" Kim gave Malcolm's arm a squeeze. "I've been dying to find a new book series to start. The café also makes the best smoothies and I swear I've had the worst craving all week."

More money you can't afford to spend.

Malcolm didn't give voice to the thought. He couldn't bear the idea of hurting his mom, no matter how frustrating these visits became.

* * * *

Between the ferry ride and a stop at home to leave his bike and change clothes, Malcolm didn't board a train uptown until close to seven and he spent most of the ride messaging with Jackson about their mom and how not ready she was to file her taxes.

She'll blow me off next weekend, Jackson wrote, words that made Malcolm sigh.

So we try again the weekend after, he replied, *and the weekend after that.*

Until she files an extension. Like last year and the year before that. Wtf knows.

Malcolm could imagine his brother's snort perfectly. Jackson's next message made the weight in his chest press even harder.

Should we get Dad involved?

Malcolm's thumbs flew over the phone's screen.

We can't do that. Let's just get Mom to 4/15 and go from there.

As the train's intercom system announced its approach to Morningside Heights, happiness surged inside Malcolm for the first time that day. He signed off with Jackson and the tension knotting his insides melted as he exited the train.

Minutes later, he was inside Lock & Key, a homey, ordinary pub staffed by bartenders and servers who knew Malcolm by name. He exchanged greetings on his way past the bar, then walked through a plain door and into a hallway with an old-fashioned wall phone beside a blank door at its end.

A smile crossed Malcolm's face as he ran his fingers along the right side of the blank door and pressed a catch release that revealed a secret staircase. Under had been in business for over six months when Malcolm had first descended those steps, and his friends had already built a loyal client base. He'd felt immediately at home inside the speakeasy's confines and Under had gained a special place in his heart. The friendships Malcolm had formed with the men who gathered behind its door had made him love it even more.

Under's door swung open at Malcolm's knock, and the rattle of ice in a shaker and the murmur of voices filled the air. Jim Taylor, who headed security for the speakeasy, gestured Malcolm inside.

"Hey, man. What took you so long?"

Malcolm shook Jim's hand. "Eh, ferries and trains — you know how it is."

"You know I do." Jim closed the door behind them with a smile. "I was back up in Boston to see my family earlier this week and the transit system there is even worse."

They chatted as they walked toward the long bar that ran the length of the room, and though Malcolm had been inside Under dozens of times, he admired his surroundings regardless.

Under's low-key luxury imparted both comfort and sophistication. House music throbbed through the speaker system, running like a heartbeat beneath the customers' conversations, and sleek leather seating areas dotted the wide, open space. Shelves lined the wall behind the bar, backlit with an amber glow that highlighted bottles of high-end liquors, as well as the bartenders who mixed the craft cocktails that put the speakeasy on every *Top Ten Bars To Visit* list in the city.

A cluster of familiar figures in the center of the bar turned and the bright expressions that greeted Malcolm sent a flush of pleasure through him.

"You made it!"

Co-owner Kyle McKee smiled at Malcolm from behind the bar. He extended a hand over its top, his touch sending a pleasant jolt along Malcolm's arm, while the others around them patted his shoulders. Those small contacts deepened the warmth growing in Malcolm's chest.

"About time." Kyle's business partner, Jesse Murtagh, eyed Malcolm with a grin. Jesse sat beside his ginger-haired partner, Cam Lewis, and both swiveled their seats Malcolm's way. "I was starting to think we'd need to send out a search party."

Cam's lips curved in a smirk. "He'd have done it, too. You know how much Jes likes to make a scene."

Jesse poked Cam in the ribs and made him squirm. "You're one to talk."

"He's got you there, Cam." That from Will Martin, who sat on Cam's right. "You're the one who DJs under a spotlight three times a week."

"Says the professor who's shacked up with a senator," Malcolm teased. Will's boyfriend, Senator David Mori, was the most progressive member of the GOP in New York's State Senate. As a gay republican, he drew considerable media attention and he and Will appeared regularly in the society section of the city's papers.

Malcolm's words drew a fist bump from Kyle's boyfriend, Luka Clarke, who leaned against the bar beside Will. Luka and Kyle had just spent a week in Nicaragua on vacation, and while Kyle's sunburn had already faded, Luka's golden dark skin was still beautifully browned and made his eyes appear extra blue. Even the tight coils of his hair seemed tipped in gold.

"Kyle mixed up something special for you." Luka picked up a rocks glass Kyle set down and handed it off to Malcolm. "It's a Tequila Mockingbird and so delicious."

Malcolm laugh-groaned at the terrible pun. "What's in it?" he asked.

"Don Julio Silver tequila, Aperol, basil and grapefruit," Kyle said. He tapped the silvery scar on the right side of his chin with his index finger. "Nothing too complex that you lose track of the tequila flavor."

"Sounds great." Malcolm spotted Senator Mori walking toward them from the back of the room and smiled.

"I'm sure everyone's already given you crap about running late, so I'll skip it." David shook his hand with an answering grin. "Carter and Ri are on their way out—they ordered food from the kitchen upstairs and wanted to make sure it got down now that you're here."

Heck yes. Malcolm's last meal had been a jar of overnight oats with his morning coffee and his stomach rumbled so hard he wondered that no one heard it over the music. The idea that he'd kept his friends waiting pricked at his conscience, though.

"I didn't realize seven o'clock was a set time, guys. I would have left Staten Island earlier if I'd known."

"No big thing, babe." Riley Porter-Wright leaned up to buss Malcolm's cheek, then stepped back so his fiancé could do the same. "We're just glad you could make it."

Malcolm smiled. "I wouldn't miss it." Riley's and Carter's easy affection gave him a lightness he loved, and he basked in the sensations. Outside of his family, only they and Kyle made Malcolm feel like this. "What's the occasion anyway?"

Carter smiled so the corners of his pretty hazel eyes crinkled. "We're celebrating your birthday. Which, lucky for us, falls on a Saturday this year." He accepted a fresh drink from Kyle and held it up, the others mimicking his actions. "Happy Birthday, Malcolm, and many happy returns."

Malcolm's face blazed as the whole bar toasted his health. "Holy crap. And thank you. I'm gonna kill you guys later." He couldn't fight his grin. Or his delight at putting Staten Island behind him — at least for a while — so he could let go in the company of his favorite people.

Chapter Two

"I know this is a rush job, so you should refer to the plan I've made." Stuart Morgan nodded at the sheets of paper clipped to the ticket rack above the workstation. "The recipes you're familiar with—the plating will be a bit different, however. I need small portions, no more than two bites, and everything tidy. We don't want food landing on the designer dress of a woman who wants to write a fat check to Corporate Equality." Everyone laughed softly. "Three key words for these passed hors d'oeuvres are small, simple, neat. You got that?"

"Yes, Chef," the small cluster of men and women arranged in a semi-circle in front of him choroused.

Stuart nodded, dismissing them, and they scurried to retrieve the serving dishes and pull prepped ingredients from the walk-in cooler across the kitchen. He'd asked them to come in early to prepare the tasting menu for a last-minute job he'd agreed to do, and this would be a long day for all of them.

"You don't mind me taking this on, do you?" he asked the dark-haired woman to his right. She was surveying the kitchen like a ship's captain, and the comparison wasn't so far off, given how orderly the space was and the way it ran like a well-oiled machine.

Marisol King, executive chef and owner of the Tribeca restaurant where Stuart worked, let out a little scoff. "Why would I? I've never minded you doing these catering gigs. You pay for the supplies and the equipment, along with a wage to my staff, so we all make a nice bit of extra money. It's a good deal for everyone."

Stuart chuckled. Marisol was more than a boss. She'd taken Stuart under her wing after he'd arrived in New York eleven years ago from the small town in Utah where he'd grown up. Stuart had worked as a dishwasher and a cook and had always wanted to go to culinary school but, once there, found he was woefully unprepared for the rigors of the Culinary Institute of America. He'd almost quit half a dozen times. As one of his instructors, Marisol had seen something in him and helped Stuart gain confidence. He'd graduated with the skills and grades that allowed him to get his foot in the door at his first fine dining restaurant.

After opening her own restaurant, Marisol had hired Stuart as her sous chef. And if she was King's captain, Stuart was the first mate. He oversaw everything for the food preparation and cooking. When Marisol was away, he took charge.

"You've worked with Carter Hamilton before. Gave him some private lessons, if I remember right." She waggled her eyebrows at Stuart.

"Private cooking lessons, yes — not any other kind. The man wanted to learn to cook to impress his kids and his boyfriend. Besides, I'm not in contact with Carter on this. I've been talking to someone he works with named Malcolm Elliott. "Speaking of which…" Stuart glanced at the wall clock. "He'll be here any minute. I better put on a fresh uniform." He signaled James, the *garde manger* chef in charge of salads and appetizers. "You got this?"

"Absolutely, Chef."

This side catering was a delicate balancing act, forcing some flexibility into the typically rigid hierarchy of the kitchen. People were pulling double-duty and stepping outside their typical roles, things Marisol saw as opportunities for the staff to learn skills they wouldn't otherwise. Not every executive chef would have felt the same.

Stuart walked down the hall toward the cramped office he shared with Hugh—the other sous chef there at King's. The rest of the staff had a locker room they shared but Stuart was grateful to have this space. It was a small oasis of calm after the loud, chaotic kitchen. A desk took up the majority of the space and behind the desk were two even tinier closets. Stuart's held his uniforms, clogs, aprons and knife kit. With a small smile, he reached for one of his black chef's coats.

Stuart was proud of his uniform. He'd worked his ass off to earn it. He liked managing the staff of chefs, cooks and kitchen workers at King's, as well as helping create dishes for the restaurant menu. While many chefs hoped to work their way up to an executive position, Stuart wasn't sure he'd ever want to own his own place. Becoming an owner would push him into an office, away from the noise and energy of the kitchen where he thrived on the challenge of keeping the people under him working like a well-oiled machine.

Marisol had asked Stuart about owning his own place once and he hadn't known how to answer. A part of him liked the idea of total creative control. But Marisol wasn't the sole owner of King's — she had other investors to answer to. There was always someone else to answer to.

When Marisol had opened her place, she'd chosen her investors wisely and deliberately created a different type of atmosphere that did away with many of the traditional unspoken rules of the restaurant business. She paid everyone, from her sous chefs down to her dishwashers and waitstaff, a living wage and gave them more reasonable working hours.

Most restaurateurs easily worked eighty-plus hours a week and most sous chefs like Stuart worked at least seventy. The hours took a toll on Marisol's relationship with her wife, too, and Stuart's own schedule had strained the few relationships he'd attempted over the years.

Her unorthodox approach was a risky move in a field that had incredibly tight profit margins. Creative marketing that appealed to people willing and able to pay top dollar for ethical business practices had ensured a steady stream of customers. So far, it had paid off and Stuart was grateful to work for someone like her. Whether or not he ever attempted to open a business like that himself someday...well that remained to be seen. For now, he was happy at Kings.

Stuart buttoned his black uniform jacket, rolled the sleeves halfway up his forearms and stepped back to eye himself in the mirror. He smoothed his thick, dark hair back from his forehead.

Hair neat, beard trimmed, tatts on display. Check, check and check.

He had no idea what Malcolm looked like, but he had a damn sexy phone voice and Stuart wasn't about to go into this meeting by putting anything less than his best foot forward. Besides, he represented King's and respected his job, the restaurant and his boss too much to let them down.

* * * *

"Stuart Morgan." He held out a hand to Malcom, who gave it a firm shake. He wasn't sorry to see that the rest of Malcolm matched his voice. *Damn sexy indeed.*

"Malcolm Elliott."

"Nice to put a face to the great voice I've been talking to on the phone," Stuart said with a smile.

Malcolm's blue eyes widened almost imperceptibly. "It's, uh, a pleasure to meet you as well."

"Please, follow me." Stuart ushered Malcolm into the restaurant and toward the table he'd prepared.

He wasn't here to flirt. At least, not *just* to flirt.

With hours to go before the restaurant opened, it was peaceful inside the front of the house. Wood floors, brick walls and black ceilings gave the place a modern rustic vibe. Black metal lanterns hung from the ceiling, lighting the polished white plates on the long wooden tables and making the flatware and crystal gleam.

"Everything has been prepped for your tasting, so why don't you have a seat and look over the contract I've prepared." Stuart handed Malcolm the sheaf of paperwork. "I'll be back shortly."

Malcolm smiled at him. "Sounds great."

Stuart gave Malcolm one final glance before he walked into the kitchen. Delicious.

Malcolm was not at all what Stuart had expected. For one, he was tall, at least an inch or so taller than Stuart's six feet. And while Stuart had assumed anyone working for Corporate Equality would be clean-cut and well dressed, he hadn't expected Malcolm's square jawline or how well he wore his tailored blue suit. It wasn't a stuffy look — he hadn't worn a tie, and his shirt collar was open. Malcolm still looked buttoned up.

And Stuart liked buttoned up.

Maybe it was a throwback to growing up around Mormon men in black suits, crisp, starched white shirts and ties. Fucking well-dressed men felt dirty. Corrupting the incorruptible was a very enjoyable pastime.

In his time off, Stuart loved to go to a nice bar and pick up businessmen looking to unwind at the end of a long day in the corporate world. In turn, they seemed to enjoy his rougher look. Black jeans, a tee and a leather jacket made his bearded face and tattoos edgier. The look put a lot of men off, too — he'd noticed the sideways glances from some who seemed to be wondering if he were going to pick their pocket — but there were always a few who responded favorably. Whose glances lingered. Who slipped Stuart business cards in the hallway leading to the bathroom or tucked one under his cocktail napkin as they got up to leave.

Mostly, they met at hotel rooms or went to Stuart's place. Discretion was key with these closeted and/or conservative guys. Oh, it turned Stuart on to suck off a guy in a suit. Shove his pants to the floor and bend him over a desk or bed and fuck him. Stuart liked watching in a mirror — seeing the guy sweat and lose his cool — and damn, if the image of watching Malcolm Elliott coming apart didn't pop into his head right then.

Working for Corporate Equality didn't guarantee that Malcolm was gay, of course. It guaranteed he was at least open-minded. And Stuart had a hell of an urge to find out if Malcolm swung that way himself.

In the kitchen, Stuart gave the tray a final critical glance and nodded. The food arranged on it was small, simple and neat. Exactly as he'd asked.

"Looks good." Marisol scrutinized the plating. "Not that you need my approval, of course."

He knocked elbows with her. "I still like to hear it."

She snorted. "Your ego doesn't need any more inflating, hot shot. Go knock his pants off."

Stuart lifted the tray. "I think the phrase is 'knock his socks off.'"

Marisol grinned at him. "Yeah, but I know you."

Many people considered Stuart remote or serious. Marisol was one of a few who brought out his lighter side and made him laugh. He was still laughing when he stepped back into the dining room, and Malcolm looked up and smiled, his solemn expression lightening, as if Stuart's laughter was contagious, though he hadn't heard the joke.

"Had a chance to look over the contract?" Stuart set the tray on the section of table he'd cleared before Malcolm's arrival.

"Yes. I have a few, very minor notes. Overall, it looks great." Malcolm gestured to a notepad in a leather-bound folio to his right. The notes were written in blue ink, marching neat and tidy across the lines of the paper. Very unlike Stuart's slanted scrawl that decorated the myriad papers in the office.

"Glad to hear we're in agreement on the terms. I'm happy to discuss any tweaks." Stuart took a seat across the table from Malcolm. "For now, let's focus on the food. This is a duck confit bruschetta." He pointed to one of the hors d'oeuvres. "The focaccia toast is layered with triple crème brie, a slow-simmered duck breast and julienne apples."

Malcolm lifted the food to his mouth and took a careful bite. He chewed slowly, his face expressionless at first before a small smile bloomed across his face. "Oh, I like that."

With a nod, Stuart gestured next to a mini stemmed cordial glass. "Red snapper ceviche marinated in citrus and cumin seed and topped with avocado crème."

Once again, Malcolm seemed to savor the food, taking his time over it. Stuart liked that.

"Mini profiterole buns," he said as they moved on. "Stuffed with New England lobster salad dressed with Meyer lemon and herb aioli."

"Now this Carter is going to love." Malcolm offered a small shrug when Stuart shot him a questioning glance. "He and Riley went to Harvard together and they're obsessed with New England seafood."

"Ah."

Despite Carter's impressive pedigree and social standing, Stuart had found him very approachable and easygoing during their cooking lessons. He'd been quite aware that he worked for Carter and wasn't his social equal, of course, but Carter had never treated Stuart as anything less than an equal, and Stuart couldn't say that about many of his upper echelon clients.

He led Malcolm through the remainder of the dishes and Malcolm sampled them with a studious thoroughness that Stuart enjoyed watching. He even liked that Malcolm nixed two dishes and made intelligent suggestions for others, too.

"Maybe another vegetarian option, something low carb. And something else gluten-free, too."

"Our kitchen is not totally gluten-free," Stuart warned. "There are always trace amounts on equipment and we can't certify anything."

"Understood," Malcolm said. "We'll be sure to include a note on the menus and that the waitstaff knows."

"Good."

"And you can arrange all of this in time?"

Stuart grinned. "I wouldn't have agreed to it if I couldn't."

Malcolm flushed. "Yes, of course. I apologize. The last-minute cancellation was a nightmare and—"

"That was bad luck," Stuart agreed. "Although I'm not sorry it led you here instead."

"Yes. I think this is exactly what we have in mind for the fundraiser." Malcolm's tone was friendly but bland. As if he were ignoring Stuart's flirtatious tone.

"Are you satisfied with the options, then?"

"After you make the modifications we discussed? Absolutely."

"Great, I'll revise the contract and send it your way. Email all right?"

"Email's perfect." Malcolm slid a business card across the table to him. "You have my address already, and I'll keep an eye out for it."

Stuart leaned forward. "You said you have bar service covered, but our sommelier and head bartender would be happy to work with you on your options."

Malcolm laughed. "Are you familiar with Under?"

Stuart had heard of Under. He'd never been in the place but knew its name and reputation as top-notch, so if they were serving drinks for the event, Stuart trusted they knew what they were doing. He nodded.

"Two of Carter's best friends own the place and they'll be working with us," Malcolm continued. "Trust me. We have drinks more than covered."

"Excellent."

"I'd like to set up a meeting for all of us in the near future, actually. To coordinate drinks with the menu and discuss logistics."

"That sounds great to me."

"I'll pull together some possible dates and get back to you shortly with details." Malcolm tidied the stack of paperwork and tucked it into his leather folio.

"Perfect. I think we're all set then, unless there are any other questions you have."

Malcolm scrutinized him. "Will you be there the night of the event?"

"Would you like me to be?" Stuart injected a flirtatious note into his voice again, to see if Malcolm would take the bait.

"It would be nice to know you're there to take care of any issues that arise." Malcolm's tone was decidedly not flirtatious. It was almost impersonal.

"I can be, if you'd like."

"That would be great."

Technically, Stuart should charge more if he was on-site for the event, but he liked Carter — and Malcolm so far — and it would be a good way to advertise King's and his own personal brand. Whether he ever opened his own restaurant or not, he wanted to have the option if he chose to go down that road someday. And in this industry, it was all about who a person knew. Besides, this event was a fundraiser for a non-profit that he was enthusiastic to support. Waiving the fee was his way of contributing.

Unfortunately, Stuart was having trouble getting a read on Malcolm. Usually, he could tell if a man was interested in him. Plenty of those buttoned-up businessmen had been closeted — maybe cheating on their unsuspecting wives, in fact, though Stuart had never asked — but even with them, Stuart had known. With Malcolm? Nothing.

There had maybe been a small hint of something for the briefest second. Not enough to be sure, however.

"Thank you again." Malcolm stood with a smile and Stuart followed, taking Malcolm's offered hand and allowing the handshake to linger a little longer than necessary. An expression of surprise flickered across Malcolm's face before he let go.

Stuart wouldn't mind getting to know more about the man who stood in front of him. Malcolm intrigued Stuart, and few people did. Maybe, if Stuart played his cards right, he could peel Malcolm out of that very nice navy-blue suit.

Stuart was a professional, but he didn't mind mixing business with pleasure.

* * * *

Pushing open the restaurant's back door, Stuart stepped into the March night, tired and content. The air outside was pleasantly cool after the heat of the kitchen. A Thursday evening wasn't the worst by any means, but there had still been a hundred and fifty covers — guests — and they'd easily cleared ten thousand dollars in sales. His feet hurt and his back ached and he was still buzzing with the adrenaline from the steady rush of orders on top of the meeting with Malcolm that morning.

Nearly everyone else had trickled out of the kitchen after closing — or rushed out in a few cases — but since Stuart had opened, Hugh, the other sous chef, would close. Hugh would be there at least another hour, making sure everything was in order for tomorrow.

"Drinks?" Danny, the P.M. prep cook, asked.

Stuart went out with the line crew fairly often after shift or sometimes wandered off on his own to pick someone up. Tonight, he craved solitude and shook his head. "Nah, I'm beat."

He walked down the block and around the corner to where he'd parked his bike and he patted the leather seat of the Suzuki C90T before he climbed on. Until recently, Stuart hadn't been in the market for anything more extravagant than the full-face helmet he slipped over his head. However, when he'd paid a visit to the dealer to buy the new helmet, the simple, classic style of the cruiser had spoken to him, and after a test drive, he'd traded in his old ride and walked out with a new helmet and bike. Now, he twisted the key in the ignition and the long-stroke V-twin engine roared to life, the vibration settling into Stuart's bones as he accelerated slowly onto the street.

The trip from the restaurant to his place in Little Italy took less than ten minutes, but after a long day in the kitchen, it got Stuart's blood pumping again. He turned left onto Greenwich Street, leaning into the turn and smiling at the feel of becoming one with the bike. He needed to get out for a longer ride soon. He'd been craving it for a while.

Unfortunately, his joy was short-lived.

By the time he found a rare spot in his neighborhood that hadn't been taken already, Stuart's mood had soured. He parked the bike at an angle to the curb, anchored it with a heavy-duty chain lock and crossed his fingers he wouldn't get a ticket. He'd paid for more parking tickets than he cared to count over the years. Parking regulations were convoluted in the city and the parking enforcement officers were all too happy to slap a ticket on the windshield at the slightest provocation. There were days he swore he'd just sell the damn bike and take the subway like everyone else. In the end, he never went through with it. To Stuart, the bike meant freedom.

He'd left Utah and his ex-wife riding a used motorcycle he'd bought on the fly, the saddlebags empty but for the money he'd stashed away and a few personal items. He'd traveled two thousand miles of road, just him and the bike. With the face shield down, no one had seen the turmoil or fear in Stuart's eyes. Or the tears on his cheeks as he'd left everything behind, shedding his past like layers of clothing.

Elijah Stuart Morgan had been an upright Mormon citizen. A man who didn't drink or smoke. Didn't wear tattoos. Married a woman who had their whole lives planned out. Temple on Sundays. Children as soon as possible. Fulfilling their duties to God and family.

In New York, Stuart had become someone new. Elijah hadn't fucked men. Stuart did. Stuart also drank like a fish, and he screwed around a lot during that first year of freedom to make up for lost time. He'd worked hard, too, using the carpentry skills his father had taught him to make enough money for culinary school and cover his body in ink. And they were more than rebellion.

They were a reminder.

Like the bike, the tats were a signal to himself as much as to the rest of the world that Elijah Morgan was dead. Stuart Morgan, on the other hand, was very much alive.

Now, he unlocked the door between the beauty salon and the dry cleaner, then walked up the steps to the fifth floor to an apartment that was—in Marisol's words—a shithole. The three-hundred-fifty square foot studio had a bathtub in the kitchen for Christ's sake and she'd been horrified when she'd seen it.

Still, it was home. Stuart set his helmet on the dresser and dropped his keys beside it. His place was quiet. Safe. Private. No risk of anyone poking and prying into his personal life or his belongings. So what did it matter if he stared at the stove while he bathed or that the curtain never quite protected the refrigerator from the spray of the showerhead?

Stuart squatted down, then pulled open the bottom drawer of the dresser and stared down at the tangle of silky fabrics. He itched to take the lingerie out. It had been a while. Wearing them always brought up such weird feelings, unfortunately. Shame mostly.

Despite his upbringing, Stuart had reconciled his feelings about being gay. About wanting to be a chef instead of a carpenter. Even about walking out of a disastrous and short-lived marriage. But this? This went deeper.

Every time he'd brought up his kink to guys he dated, in the hopes they'd accept it—even if they didn't embrace it—their reactions had shoved him further down that spiral of shame. No one understood why it turned him on. And they sure as hell wanted nothing to do with Stuart after they discovered that truth.

K. Evan Coles and Brigham Vaughn

Stuart couldn't just enjoy it the way he wanted to. And he'd given up hoping that he'd be able to share it with anyone.

Chapter Three

"Crap, crap, crap." Malcolm took the subway stairs two at a time, muttering under his breath.

He'd arranged the Thursday meeting with Chef Morgan at Lock & Key, expecting forty-five minutes would be plenty of time to commute up from Midtown. However, a mechanical problem had plagued his train and he'd spent the crawling ride exchanging messages with his mom, trying to get her to apply for job openings he'd found in the neighborhoods around Staten Island. Now Malcolm was nearly fifteen minutes late and almost sprinting along Broadway in his loafers and business casual duds, messenger bag bumping his hip.

Malcolm hated being late, particularly when it came to his job. He'd texted the chef with a heads-up he was running behind but still felt wretched and unprofessional. He also knew this would make a poor impression on a man who had high expectations of the people around him. Stuart had been friendly—even charming—when he'd introduced himself to Malcolm, tattoos peeking out from beneath the chef's white jacket. His demeanor had changed the moment the talk had turned to food, however, shifting into a thorough confidence that was reflected in the quality and plating of the food he'd put in front of Malcolm. Everything had been luscious — both aesthetically and in taste — and Malcolm had known from the first bite that the chef and his staff at King's would do impeccable work for the CEC fundraiser.

The steel in Stuart's expression as he'd spoken about food and his work had reassured Malcolm. He understood how to interact with a man who was all business. He'd been less sure of how to handle the moments when Stuart had smiled at him, however, and the way that warmth had made his brown eyes dance. The chef's touch had tingled against Malcolm's skin when they'd bid each other goodbye, too and...well. Malcolm really didn't know what to make of that.

He caught sight of a huge motorcycle parked by the curb as he neared Lock & Key and slowed to a walk. It was a beautiful machine, gleaming black and chrome in the late afternoon light, and Malcolm could imagine the kind of man who rode it, clad in a leather jacket with tattoos on full display.

I'll bet Stuart Morgan wears a leather jacket.

Malcolm nearly tripped into Lock & Key's door. Where the hell had that come from?

Seconds later, his errant thought literally came to life and Malcolm blinked at the sight of the chef seated at Lock & Key's bar, a tall glass of water in hand and motorcycle helmet by his elbow. Stuart wore a black leather jacket, just as Malcolm had imagined, and a scowl so mighty he looked almost like a stranger. Malcolm's stomach flipped.

"I'm sorry I'm late," he said in a rush. Moving quickly, Malcolm waved hello to the bartender, then pulled the strap of his bag over his head and stepped up beside Stuart. "I meant to be here to meet you, Chef, but the train—"

Stuart cut in, his voice gruff and grumpy as Malcolm had expected. "I get it. Public transportation sucks."

"It's unpredictable," Malcolm replied. "Anyway, Under's head bartender is waiting for us downstairs."

"Downstairs?" Stuart waved at the room around them with one hand. "Downstairs from here?"

"Um, yeah. This is Lock & Key. Under's located in the basement."

"I thought you said the event would be happening on the roof?"

"I did say that. Under and Lock & Key will be part of it, too. Sort of." Heat flashed over Malcolm's cheeks when Stuart rolled his eyes. "Sorry, let's..." He blew out a breath and squared his shoulders. "Let's start again."

Stuart's expression softened by a degree. "Okay. I'm listening."

"There are three areas in this building suitable for hosting events. This floor, Lock & Key, has the only functioning kitchen. So your staff will prep the food in Lock & Key's kitchen." Malcolm frowned at Stuart's scoff.

"I hope the kitchen's more impressive than what I've seen so far."

"I... It's always seemed adequate to me. I'm not a cook, though," Malcom hastened to add when Stuart's right eyebrow rose. "If you have concerns, we can look into how to address them." He licked his lips. "Under, the speakeasy, is located in the basement and will provide beverage service for the event."

Stuart nodded. "And the new venue you mentioned last week is on the roof?"

"Yes. There's a service elevator, so getting things up and down between levels shouldn't be a problem."

"I'll be the judge of that if you don't mind," Stuart muttered. "Though I suppose there's something to be said for the building only being three levels total." He furrowed his brow. "What's the roof deck called?"

"The Over Under." Malcolm tried to smile. "It hasn't officially opened for business yet. It's set to happen on Memorial Day weekend."

"Under, Lock & Key and The Over Under, huh? Precious." Stuart rolled his eyes again. This time the corners of his lips tugged upward.

"My friends like puns."

"Sounds like they're not concerned about accuracy, considering The Over Under is, in fact, over Lock & Key. Not my problem, though."

Stuart drew a noisy inhale through his nose then stood, moving quickly enough Malcolm couldn't quite get out of his way. Something about him creaked as he moved and Malcolm had a second to notice that the man was wearing leather pants too, before Stuart's shoulder made contact with his chest. Malcolm's face went up in flames once more.

"Sorry. I'll, um, grab Matt from the back and we can head down." Malcolm nearly jumped when a familiar voice spoke from behind Stuart.

"I'm right here, kid."

Jesus, Malcolm hadn't seen Matt coming at all. His stomach fell when he noticed Matt looked cranky as hell, no doubt because he'd heard Stuart's dismissive remarks about Lock & Key, an ordinary pub to be sure, but the residents of Morningside Heights liked it just fine. The place had even undergone a makeover earlier in the year and Malcolm thought the new butcher block tables and white metal seating looked nice, especially on the sidewalk patio area outside.

"Hey, Matt." Malcolm kept his tone light. "Chef Morgan, this is Matt O'Hearn, General Manager of Lock & Key."

Stuart extended his hand even before Malcolm had finished speaking. "Stuart Morgan," he said. "I cook under Marisol King at her restaurant in Tribeca."

"Malcolm and Kyle briefed me last week." Matt shook Stuart's hand. His expression remained tight and he jerked his head toward the back of the bar without offering any other pleasantries. "Let's go see the man downstairs before the dinner rush starts."

To an outsider, the next ninety minutes would have appeared to have gone smoothly, with all three arms of food and service for the CEC event team getting to know each other. Stuart was clearly charmed by Under and its hidden door and staircase, and he responded at once to Kyle McKee.

Kyle took obvious pleasure in introducing Stuart not only to the speakeasy but his philosophy of serving the highest quality craft cocktails possible, and the two men fell into easy conversation about sourcing local ingredients. In many ways, Kyle's dedication to his craft reminded Malcolm of Stuart's passion for his work in the kitchen, and while cookery and mixology were wholly different art forms, Malcolm recognized a connection forming between bartender and chef.

The same could not be said of Stuart and Matt, however, who continued to eye each other warily. Malcolm suspected Stuart harbored some regret for his earlier harshness, because he was both polite and professional during the kitchen tour. He deemed it more than adequate to serve the needs of King's staff.

While Matt answered every inquiry without hesitation, his stony demeanor didn't crack.

Malcolm swallowed a sigh. He really hoped everyone was getting the information they needed. The fewer awkward sessions he needed to orchestrate between Stuart and Matt, the better.

"How will you manage serving your customers on the night of the event?" Stuart asked Matt as they approached the service elevator.

"We won't." Matt tapped the elevator's up button, his gaze trained on its doors. "We'll close after lunch and most of the kitchen staff will clear out so we're not in your way."

"Matt'll be upstairs with me. I thought Lock & Key's waitstaff could work the event, too," Kyle said, then frowned. "Or do you bring your own servers, Chef?"

"That depends on the event," Stuart replied. Everyone filed onto the elevator car and Kyle hit the button for the roof. "King's provides waitstaff for catering events, but there's often room for additional bodies. That said, everyone, including King's staff, is required to attend a briefing beforehand so we can run through the menu and make sure everyone understands what they're serving and to whom."

"Of course," Matt muttered.

The edge in his voice made Malcolm swallow and Stuart parted his lips as if to speak. Thankfully, the elevator's chime cut him off and Malcolm stepped toward the doors.

"The Over Under," he said with a gesture for Stuart to exit.

He watched Stuart run his gaze over the wide-open space. The sun had set, and the sky hung purple above, stars just beginning to peek through the twilight. Then someone hit the lights, filling the space with a beautiful, golden glow, and a faint smile crossed the chef's face.

"This isn't bad at all," Stuart said, voice soft.

Malcolm agreed. The Over Under had been set up in the style of a French bistro with a black-and-white tiled floor and the vibe it carried was both elegant and welcoming. Wrought-iron chairs and striped cushions had been paired with glass-topped tables, with lamps fashioned like antique gaslight posts rising over them. A bar situated at the far end of the roof stood beneath a shelter open on three sides, with a gleaming bar top, ample seating and open, backlit shelves of bottles.

Malcolm glanced back for Kyle and Matt and saw them talking by the elevator, their expressions serious. No doubt Stuart having acted like a pompous ass was hot topic number one.

Crap again.

Malcolm hated that Matt was so obviously irritated. Stuart's shift in behavior from cold to hot made Malcolm's awareness prickle in ways he didn't understand, too. The man seemed so much bigger than life. His questions and observations showed his confidence in how he wanted the event catering to play out, but he commanded Malcolm's attention even when he fell silent. He'd stuck close throughout the tour, too, which heightened Malcolm's nerves even more. On several occasions, the smell of black leather had filled Malcolm's nose, and he'd nearly walked into a door when he'd noticed Stuart's leather pants were in fact chaps with shiny silver zips running up the inside of each leg.

"I thought you said the place hadn't opened yet?" Stuart asked, appreciation plain in his gaze.

"It hasn't," Malcolm replied.

"Certainly appears to be."

Malcolm clasped his hands together. "Kyle, Matt and their partner, Jesse, have had a few parties up here for their friends. Trial runs that act like a soft launch with easy critics, if that makes sense. That gives them a chance to find and work out any kinks before they go public. They know none of us will hold mistakes against them. Not that they make many at this point."

"Smart. Based on its looks and Under's reputation, this place should do well." Stuart's gaze landed on Malcolm. "So these guys are friends of yours, too? I thought you only knew them through Carter."

"Long story short, I do know them through Carter, but yes, they're my friends." Malcolm stuffed his hands in his pockets as he and Stuart moved toward the bar. "I met Kyle and Jesse after Carter got to know them, back when we both worked at his family's firm."

"I had no idea you and Carter had known each other so long." Stuart grimaced. "Shit, things at the office must have been awkward when he quit and came out of the closet all at the same time."

Malcolm shifted in his seat. "You know about that, huh?"

"My boss reads the society columns. She also knew Riley from cooking class and went a little bit bananas over the news. She liked talking about the Porter-Wright and Hamilton dramas while we prepped for dinner."

"Ah." Malcolm nodded. A lot of people in Carter's life had gone very bananas after he'd come out and quit, Malcolm included, though his upset had been at losing a great boss who'd started to become a friend. "It was a hectic time."

Stuart chuckled. He set his helmet on the bar and slid onto one of the stools, the creak of his leather pants so loud Malcolm rubbed the back of his neck with one hand.

"I imagine it was a lot more than hectic, but you're a good guy for not gossiping." Stuart waved at Malcolm to join him. "I know Carter and Riley weren't even dating at the time. Marisol told me that, too."

"Your boss was right." Kyle passed by them both on his way behind the bar, and the smile on his face didn't warm his dark eyes. Kyle was nothing if not loyal and protective of his friends. "Carter was at loose ends for a while before he and Ri got together. We all took good care of him, though." His gaze shifted to Malcolm and softened. "Hell, Malcolm left the ad business to keep a better eye on his old boss."

"That is a lie." Malcolm set his bag on the bar and sat beside Stuart. "I wanted out of advertising, yes, and the CEC had a position that worked for me, so I took it. I started hanging out with these guys more," he said with a wave toward Kyle. "Kyle and Jes had opened Under earlier in the year and made a point of hosting get-togethers for friends and family, so I tagged along and they let me stay."

Kyle aimed a droll look over the bar at Stuart. "He says this like it's a chore enduring his presence. Like he's not the easiest person in the world to get along with."

"You're confusing low-maintenance with easy," Malcolm replied and laughed when Kyle reached over the bar and mimed strangling him. "Did Matt go back downstairs?"

"He did," Kyle said. "Lock & Key's starting to get busy and he figured you and I could handle any questions the chef here might have."

Stuart drew his eyebrows together. "I have none. The kitchen looks adequate for my needs and if Under handles the beverage service—"

"We'll more than handle it," Kyle said, his lips curling into a smirk that made Malcolm bite back another laugh. People didn't doubt that cockiness once Kyle set a cocktail down in front of them. "I'd like to curate a special menu for cocktails, so you and I should coordinate."

"Sounds good." Stuart met Kyle's smirk with one of his own. "Something tells me you won't have trouble keeping up."

"How about I mix some drinks right now?" Kyle glanced from Stuart to Malcolm. "I took the liberty of stocking the bar with one of Mal's favorite tequilas after he told me he'd be bringing you by. There are plenty of other things to choose from, however, if you're not a tequila fan or staying sober."

"Tequila's fine," Stuart said at the same time Malcolm asked if he'd be okay to drive.

"Not that you don't know your own limits, of course," Malcolm hastened to add. The irritation he expected from Stuart simply didn't come.

"One or two won't hurt me," the chef said, "and today's my day off so I have plenty of time to metabolize any alcohol I put in my system."

"Great," Kyle said, amusement clear in his expression. He set out three shiny silver cups and filled each with crushed ice. "There was a run on mint and blackberries at the market I hit on my way here, which work perfectly for the cocktail I've got in mind."

"And what kind of magic are you mixing up?" Malcolm asked.

"Blackberry Mint Julep Margaritas," Kyle replied. "That may sound strange, but tequila and citrus flavors mix well with mint and honey."

He measured tequila into a shaker, then followed it with blackberries, mint leaves and fresh lime, and topped it all with a thin golden syrup. After muddling the contents the shaker, he added more ice and capped it and rattled the mix with a flourish. Kyle was smiling as he poured the deep purple cocktail, and he winked at Malcolm before he set about garnishing each drink with fresh berries and mint sprigs.

Stuart let out a low whistle when Kyle set a julep cup in front of him. "These are beautiful. You weren't kidding about paying attention to details."

"You said earlier that you've never seen the point in doing a half-ass job," Kyle replied. "I feel the same about my own work. And Malcolm looks like he had a bit of a day, too, so I hoped one of these might turn his frown upside-down."

Malcolm chuckled and ran a finger through the frost on his cup. "Thanks, babe. I haven't had reason to doubt your magic yet." He raised it in tandem with Kyle and together they turned to include Stuart, who mimicked their movements with a smile.

"Here's to magic and blackberries," Stuart said, "and the end of a not-awesome Thursday."

By eight, Malcolm and Stuart had moved back down to Under so Kyle could go on duty, and Malcolm was feeling the effects of the tequila on an empty stomach. Besides breakfast, he hadn't eaten, and while part of him was tempted to order something cheap from the kitchen upstairs, he felt loathe to do so in Stuart's company.

"I can see why you like hanging out with Kyle," Stuart said. "He seems like a good guy. Doesn't hurt that he's hot, too, and has that Indiana Jones vibe with the scar on his chin."

Malcolm's whole body tensed. "Kyle and his boyfriend were gay bashed late last year," he said. His flat tone and blunt words chased the humor from Stuart's expression in an instant. "Kyle was beaten badly trying to pull three guys off Luka. That's where the scar came from."

"Shit. I'm fucking up all over the place tonight." Stuart heaved a sigh. "Are they okay? Aside from the scar, I mean."

Malcolm nodded, though he knew the movements were stiff and jerky. "They're getting past it. Things were hard for them earlier this year. Kyle says he and Luka are in a better place now."

"I'm glad. And I apologize," Stuart said, voice low and earnest. "I didn't mean to offend you. Or poke at your friend. Or screw things up with the guy from upstairs, either. I'm sure his pub is a nice enough place—"

Malcolm cut him off. "Lock & Key is a nice place. Not at the same level as King's but the place is practically an institution in the neighborhood. Lock & Key is full for lunch and dinner every weekday and stuffed to the gills for brunch both Saturday and Sunday. They serve great food and affordable drinks, and some people need that option more than they need fine dining."

"You're right. I'm not incapable of enjoying pub or street food, or even fast food," Stuart added. "I like it all. I was…in a mood earlier today and my attitude got away from me. My afternoon was shot and you were late, and I knew it was stupid to get angry, but I took it out on you and Matt. So again, I'm sorry." He aimed a crooked grin at Malcolm. "Not apologizing for saying Kyle's hot, though. Because he is."

The mischief in his face melted Malcolm's irritation. "You're not the first person to say that," he said over the rattle of a shaker.

"What, you don't agree?"

Malcolm shrugged. "Kyle's one of my best friends. I never really thought about it."

Malcolm glanced down the bar to where Kyle stood, pouring what looked like Manhattans into cocktail glasses. From a purely aesthetic perspective, Malcolm could appreciate the lean figure Kyle presented and the way his dark clothes set off his very fair skin and black hair. He knew his friend was more than just average on the attractiveness scale. Malcolm also loved Kyle dearly, and he was one of very few people Malcolm felt almost completely comfortable around. Regardless, detached admiration was as far as he got when it came to Kyle—nothing about his friend had ever sparked any kind of physical interest, before and after they'd grown close.

Not that Malcolm would admit any such thing to the man beside him. He imagined Stuart would find his utter lack of interest odd if not plain wrong.

That idea didn't sit well with Malcolm at all.

Stuart shifted back in his seat when Malcolm pushed away his julep cup and reached for his wallet. "You outta here?"

"Yeah. I have a couple of meetings tomorrow morning and if I don't get myself home soon, no way I'll make it out of my apartment on time." Malcolm went still when Stuart laid a hand on his arm.

"I'll get this." Stuart drew his own wallet from his pocket, a slim black billfold attached to a chain clipped to his belt loop. "It's the least I can do for being such a bear when you walked in today."

"I was just going to leave a tip for the waitstaff," Malcolm said. "Kyle and Jes say my money's no good in here and they wouldn't charge you as my guest, either. But you switched to water even before we left the roof — doesn't seem fair you'd be the one to leave the tip."

"I don't mind." Stuart laid several bills on the bar top and slipped his wallet away again. "Besides, now I can say you owe me a favor."

"I owe you?" Malcolm frowned. "Um. Okay. But —"

"I'm going to cash it in right now, too."

Malcolm stood when Stuart did, his tired, slightly tipsy brain limping along but failing to catch up. "I don't understand. What do you want from me?"

"I want you to accept a ride home." He held the black helmet out to Malcolm and gave him a positively wolfish smile. "On the back of my bike."

Chapter Four

Stuart cruised into the currently empty loading zone near Malcolm's building in Koreatown, turned the bike off, flipped up his visor, then fired off a quick text.

Here. Parked by optical place.

On my way down.

Stuart slid the helmet off and raked a hand through his hair so it wasn't sticking up wildly. A businessman in a suit walking by paused for a fraction of a second and swept his gaze over Stuart. Stuart didn't smile, but he did wink and enjoyed the hitch in the man's step as he hurried by.

Stuart dismounted the bike and retrieved a helmet from where it had been stowed in the pannier, then returned his focus to Malcolm's building. He hadn't paid much attention the other night when he'd dropped off Malcolm. It was nice. Not luxury, but nicer than Stuart's. Built of brick, it rose maybe ten or twelve stories and was mixed use with the optical place and what looked like a clothing shop on the ground floor.

A few minutes later, a smiling Malcolm stepped out. That smile wavered when his gaze dropped to the helmets in Stuart's hands.

"We're taking the bike again?" he asked, his voice rising a little.

This time, Stuart smiled. "Yes. I don't own a car and you said you don't, either. How did you think we were going to get there?"

"I thought we were going to hike in the Ramble in Central Park."

Although it had lessened over the years, the Ramble had a reputation for gay men cruising and using it for a hookup spot. He had a feeling that wasn't what Malcolm was angling for. "That's not a hike. It's a stroll in the park. We're going into the woods."

"I know there are hiking trails where I grew up on Staten Island, but I've never gone. I guess I've never really hiked. Not...like that."

"There's a first time for everything."

Malcolm glanced down. "I see why you suggested long pants and sturdy shoes."

"Good for the ride and the hike." Malcolm's clothes were more appropriate for the gym, but they'd do. "Be careful not to burn yourself on the exhaust. The polyester in those pants will melt and make the burn infinitely worse."

"Right." Malcolm cleared his throat. "So where are we going?"

"Surprise Lake, New Jersey. It's about an hour ride if we don't get stuck in traffic." Forty-five or fifty if Stuart was riding alone but he didn't want to scare the shit out of Malcolm; he already seemed nervous enough. Presumably about the bike, though Stuart wasn't sure.

For the life of him, he still couldn't get a read on Malcolm.

During the meeting at Under, Stuart had sworn an undercurrent of energy had passed between them. Malcolm had climbed on the back of his bike afterward, apprehension clear on his face, and wrapped himself around Stuart like a starfish. He'd kept his hips as far from Stuart's ass as possible. His tight grip on Stuart's ribs could certainly have been chalked up to fear of falling off the bike, but the way Malcolm had responded to Stuart during the ride had made him question if there was more to it. The noise of the engine and the helmet had made it impossible to talk. At every stoplight, he'd reached up to pat Malcolm's hand and reassure him. Each time, Malcolm had softened a little, relaxed. Maybe it was sheer trust as he'd realized that Stuart was a skilled, controlled rider, but Stuart had hoped maybe it was something more.

He'd thought Malcolm would ask him up to his apartment and he'd be able to suss out Malcolm's interest more. Instead, Malcolm had merely handed him his helmet, thanked him, and disappeared through the door without a backward glance.

So, Stuart had tried again. He'd asked Malcolm if he wanted to go for a hike and Malcolm had said yes. Malcolm had even taken a day off work. He assured Stuart he was doing Malcolm a favor because he had more vacation time accrued than he ever took, and his manager was always on him to use it up. But then nothing in the texts they'd exchanged since indicated this might be a date or whether Malcolm was straight or just plain not interested.

Stuart wasn't going to push. He didn't mind going for a hike with a friend. He couldn't remember the last time he'd felt so off his game with anyone though. Damned if he wasn't frustrated but enjoying the challenge, too. Which was probably why he kept coming back for more.

"How'd the fit on the helmet feel last time?" he asked.

Malcolm shrugged. "Okay? I'm not sure what I'm looking for."

"I want you to try both of them on." Stuart had brought his new helmet and an old one. He handed Malcolm the new one and Malcolm put it on with the visor up. His eyes looked wide and blue as Stuart reached out to fasten the chinstrap, tightening it until it was snug but not digging into his skin.

"How does that feel? Is it squeezing your temples or painful anywhere?"

Malcolm seemed to consider that. "No."

"I'm going to jerk it around on your head to see if it comes off." He grabbed the rear of the helmet, pulling up forcefully as he tried to roll it forward and off Malcolm's head. It stayed on, though Malcolm looked startled. "That's a good sign. Try the other one."

The older helmet seemed looser, so Stuart handed the new one back to Malcolm. "You can wear that one."

"You're very thorough." Malcolm's voice sounded muffled as he pulled the helmet back over his head.

"I don't fuck around with safety on my bike or in the kitchen."

Stuart settled the older helmet on his own head, mounted the bike, then glanced over at Malcolm. "Ready to go?"

"As ready as I'll ever be." Malcolm continued to stand a few feet away, however.

"You remember the hand signals I taught you the other night?"

"One quick tap means stop when you can, several quick taps means stop immediately. If you touch my thigh, you're checking in with me, and it's a thumbs-up for I'm good, a thumb down for I'm not, and thumb sideways for neutral."

"Excellent." Stuart raked his gaze over Malcolm, who wore a heavy canvas jacket. "You think you'll be warm enough in that? I could swap you my leather, if you want." The wind on the highway would be numbingly cold if he wore canvas since he'd be taking the brunt of the wind even with the windscreen, but he didn't want Malcolm to freeze either.

"I'll be okay."

Malcolm sounded confident enough that Stuart didn't argue. Stuart's torso should block the worst of it. If they rode together on any kind of regular basis in the future, Stuart would make sure he brought an old leather for Malcolm.

"Then get on the bike. New Jersey awaits."

Malcolm let out a quiet snort. He approached the bike and swung a leg over, then settled behind Stuart. He wrapped his arms around Stuart's chest. Stuart had told him last time that he could hold on to his hips, but Malcolm said it didn't feel safe. And Stuart wasn't complaining that Malcolm seemed to prefer having his arms around him.

He checked in several times throughout the ride to make sure Malcolm was okay and got a thumbs-up every time. Malcolm seemed a lot more comfortable riding pillion than last time, so Stuart pushed the speed limit, and it wasn't long before they reached the parking lot near the trailhead.

"You warm enough?" Stuart asked.

Malcolm nodded. "I'm fine."

Stuart stripped off his leather jacket and stowed it in the pannier before locking his bike. He'd been to Surprise Lake before. On a sunny April day with temperatures reaching the high sixties or low seventies, the hike would be pleasant. After a quick check to be sure everything was safely secured, they struck out on the trail. It wound through a rocky, wooded area and the path wasn't wide enough for them to walk side by side in most places. Stuart took the lead and Malcolm didn't protest.

The trees were beginning to leaf out, and the air was noisy with birds. In the summer, it was a heavily trafficked trail, but at this time of year—and on a Tuesday at that—it was quiet. Not many cars had been parked at the trailhead, so Stuart didn't expect to see many other hikers.

"You didn't grow up in New York, did you?" Malcolm asked when they'd walked a few minutes.

Stuart shot him a glance over his shoulder. "No. How'd you guess?"

"I don't know any native New Yorkers who'd willingly drive to New Jersey to hike."

Stuart laughed. Not many people made him laugh, but Malcolm had managed it a few times now. He liked that. "There was a lot of wilderness near where I grew up. I love the city, but I like to get out in the fresh air when I can."

"It is nice here," Malcolm said, and Stuart was inordinately pleased with the compliment.

The first three-quarters of the hike took them up a steep elevation that became a more gradual ascent before they reached a ridge overlooking the lake. Surprise Lake was small but pristine looking with blue, sparkling water and ringed by wooded areas and a rocky shore.

They stopped at an overlook to catch their breath and take in the view. Stuart knew from talking to Malcolm that he was active and studied yoga and assumed he'd be able to handle the moderately challenging trail.

Right now, Malcolm's face was pink from exertion, and while his breaths had quickened, they weren't too heavy, so Stuart thought he'd judged it well. "You doing okay?"

"I'm good." Malcolm smiled. "That was invigorating."

"Yeah, it gets the blood pumping." Stuart shrugged off his flannel shirt then knotted it around his waist. When he looked up, Malcolm was staring at the tattoos revealed by Stuart's short-sleeved T-shirt.

"You have any ink?" He would have been shocked if Malcolm answered yes, but sometimes people surprised him.

Malcolm shook his head, still looking intently at Stuart's arms. Stuart held one out, turning his palm up so Malcolm could see some of his favorite designs.

"You can look more closely if you're curious."

"I wasn't sure if that would be rude or not."

"Some people find it rude. I don't."

Malcolm stepped closer. He reached out, trailing his fingertips through the air over Stuart's skin as he traced across a skull wearing a toque with a crossed chef's knife and honing steel overlaying it. He didn't touch

Stuart's skin, but the motion made Stuart's arms pebble with goosebumps anyway.

"Like skull and crossbones, right?" Malcolm glanced at him with a curious expression. "For chefs."

"Yes." Stuart held out his other forearm to show off the butcher's diagrams of cuts of meat for cow, pig, chicken and fish.

"I take it you'll never become a vegetarian."

Stuart smiled. "Unlikely. We're heavy on meat at King's and I have no argument there. I enjoy charcuterie too much to give it up, but you never know."

"Charcuterie are prepared meats, right? Like salami and prosciutto."

"Yes. Exactly. Bacon, ham, sausage, pâtés, confit…" Stuart continued. "Although, I do think if a chef can't make a vegetable taste every bit as good as the cut of meat it's next to, he's failing at his job."

"You're really passionate about it. You must be, anyway, to cover your body like this."

"I am." Stuart paused. "The tattoos go farther than my arms. I could take off my shirt if you'd like to see the ones on my chest and back." Somehow, he felt disrobing without asking first would be rude to do in front of Malcolm. He wouldn't have thought twice with anyone else.

Malcolm hesitated for a second before nodding, and slowly, like he might spook Malcolm if he moved too fast, Stuart removed the black T-shirt. Malcolm's eyes went wide.

Stuart spun in a slow circle, deliberately giving Malcolm time to take it all in. Stuart's chest and abs were tattooed, as was most of his back. They were intricate pieces, many food-related, with a few designs woven throughout relating to his love of New York, bikes and other interests. The main piece was a detailed cluster of ingredients that stretched from his left hip, up his back, across his right shoulder and down his right arm. Spiky artichokes mingled with a wedge of melting brie cheese while delicate herbs wove around them before segueing into bumpy kale, vine-ripened tomatoes and split pea pods with curling leaves. Honey spilled onto a halved peach before flowing onto a hunk of crusty baguette. There was far more than that — more than Malcolm would be able to study now — and it had taken numerous sittings to get it all inked onto Stuart's skin.

Stuart stopped when he was facing Malcolm again. Malcolm appeared fascinated, drinking in everything with his gaze as he stepped closer. He hovered his fingers across the words by Thomas Keller tattooed over Stuart's heart, stretching across his chest from shoulder to shoulder. Stuart didn't have to look down at them to know what they said.

When you acknowledge, as you must, that there is no such thing as perfect food, only the idea of it, then the real purpose of striving toward perfection becomes clear: to make people happy, that is what cooking is all about.

"Is that why you do it?" Malcolm looked him in the eye.

"It's a big part of it, yeah." Stuart's voice came out a little husky.

"What else?"

"It's who I am."

Their gazes met and held for a long moment before Malcolm shivered, as if he were the one without a shirt.

There was something very unusual about the way he looked at Stuart.

It wasn't childlike—Malcolm was a grown man—but innocent maybe. Like he was assessing him at a distance. It was…different. Not unpleasant, just different.

Stuart wondered if perhaps Malcolm was closeted. It seemed strange—from what Stuart understood of the crowd at Under, most of Malcolm's close friends were gay or bisexual, so why would Malcolm not be comfortable coming out? Unless maybe his parents were conservative. Stuart certainly understood that. If Malcolm was closeted and trying to avoid his family's suspicion, why would he work for a company like Corporate Equality? There was such a thing as hiding in plain sight, but that seemed risky and Malcolm didn't strike Stuart as the risky type.

Which left the conclusion that maybe Malcolm hadn't figured it out himself. Which was equally baffling. How could Malcolm not have figured it out? He spent all day working on LGTBQ+ rights issues and hanging out with gay and bi friends. How could he not have put the pieces together?

It was intriguing to say the least.

Stuart slipped on his shirt again. The sun felt good on his skin, but he didn't like to expose the tattoos to the sunlight unless he'd slathered them with sunscreen. He wanted to keep the vibrant colors bright for as long as he could. "Shall we get going again?"

"Sure."

They walked along the ridge for a while before the trail began to descend again. There was a rocky face where Stuart had to get down low and scramble over it. When he'd made it down, he turned back to see how

Malcolm was doing. He'd made it about halfway down and had paused, as if assessing his best route down.

"You see that dip in the rock to your right?" Stuart called out to him. "That'll give you solid footing. Don't be afraid to get on your butt and scoot down. There's no shame in that."

Malcolm did as Stuart had instructed, though he didn't quite need to scoot to make it. "Sorry," Stuart said when Malcolm was standing beside him. "I should have warned you what this was going to be like."

"No worries." Malcolm brushed his hair away from his forehead. "I like the challenge."

Stuart glanced down at Malcolm's footwear. "If we do this again, you might want to think about investing in a good pair of hiking boots."

"Maybe." Malcolm sounded a bit skeptical.

Stuart wasn't sure if the hesitation was because Malcolm wasn't enjoying hiking, didn't want to go out with Stuart again, or something else entirely.

Now Malcolm looked at Stuart's feet. "Yours aren't hiking boots, are they?"

"They're tactical combat boots from a military surplus store," Stuart admitted. "Practical and they look good on the bike, too." He flashed a grin at Malcolm, who gave him an enigmatic half-smile in return.

A man Stuart had once dated had teased him about caring so deeply about his appearance. That guy hadn't understood how much it signaled to the world who a person is or who they wanted to become. Then again, the man he'd dated wasn't a straight, married Mormon carpenter turned gay atheist biker-slash-chef, either. People from Stuart's past wouldn't recognize him now. Which was really the point.

"You ready to keep going?" Malcolm asked.

Stuart nodded and turned away. Malcolm fell into step behind him, and for a while, they hiked in silence, with only the sounds of nature accompanying them. Ten minutes down the trail, they passed an older couple who greeted them before resuming their conversation about birdwatching.

Stuart nodded at a signpost as they walked by it. "This segment we're on overlaps with the Appalachian Trail. In a bit, we'll curve around to go to the Greenwood Lake overlook. If you keep going straight, you're heading south on the Trail."

As they continued along, a rocky stream cut across the path with a boardwalk over it. Some boards were rotted, and the water was running fast from the recent rains. Stuart stopped on the other side of the boardwalk and held out a hand to Malcolm who hesitated—just long enough for Stuart to notice—before he took it.

Stuart frowned as they started to walk again. Malcolm seemed to be avoiding touching Stuart if he could help it. Like when he'd examined Stuart's tattoos. His fingers had been a mere fraction of an inch away from Stuart's skin but never made contact. Another thought popped into Stuart's head. What if Malcolm wasn't so much trying to figure out his sexuality but had an aversion to being touched? Could someone have hurt him?

That didn't quite fit either. Malcolm didn't seem afraid of Stuart or nervous to be around him. He'd touched Stuart readily enough on the bike and hadn't hesitated to come out alone to the woods.

Malcolm was an enigma, that was for damn sure.

They ascended again, and the next time they reached a rocky slope, Stuart paused and looked at Malcolm.

"Would you rather go first so I can help spot you? Or do you want me to go so you can watch what I do?"

"You can go first."

Having hiked the trail before, Stuart had already gotten a feel for how to navigate it and he scrambled up the face quickly. He waited at the top, watching Malcolm's more measured ascent. Malcolm moved carefully, but he wasn't tentative.

"Ever gone rock climbing?" Stuart asked.

"At a gym a few times. I enjoyed it."

"Maybe we should go sometime. It would be good for another da—" Stuart cut himself off. "Day out."

He'd nearly said date, but he was even less sure that this was one now that they were out on it.

* * * *

"Thanks." Malcolm took a few sips of the water bottle Stuart had packed in the saddlebags before he handed it back to Stuart. "For the water and the hike. That was fun."

Malcolm did appear to have had a good time. He seemed even more relaxed than he had before and there was a quiet contentment on his face.

"I'm glad you enjoyed it." Stuart guzzled water, then handed it back to Malcolm. "You finish it." He shrugged his leather jacket back on. "You ready to head out?"

"Sure."

"I'm pretty hungry. I know a nice place around here where we could stop if you want."

An uneasy expression crossed Malcolm's face. "I could eat. My budget is tight right now though."

"My treat," Stuart offered. When Malcolm hesitated, Stuart gave him another option. "Or, go to my place and I could throw together a simple meal."

That seemed to relax Malcolm. "You don't mind cooking on your day off?"

"Not if I have someone to cook for."

* * * *

"Wow, this place is small," Malcolm said as he stepped into Stuart's apartment. "Like, really small. It makes Kyle's old place look huge, and the speakeasy crew always referred to it as the shoebox."

Stuart chuckled and shut the door behind him. "Speakeasy crew. That's great. And yes, this place is small, but I value privacy over space."

Malcolm let out a small sigh. "I have a roommate. My brother, Jackson."

"Oh? What's that like?"

He shrugged. "We get along fine. It would be nice to have more privacy, though. Jack's girlfriend used to be over a lot, but she moved to a new apartment and now they stay there instead. It's just weird because I'm always wondering when they'll stop by so it's hard to fully relax."

"That doesn't leave anyone with much privacy."

"When they are there, I try to clear out periodically so they can have some time alone."

"Are they respectful when you have dates over?" Stuart asked. He kept his tone casual as he stowed the old bike helmet in the closet by the door. He took the other from Malcolm and placed it in its usual spot on the dresser.

"Dates? Uhh, no, I've never brought anyone back to that apartment." Malcolm shrugged out of his canvas jacket and handed it to Stuart without meeting his gaze.

Damn it, Stuart had hoped that would clear up a bit about Malcolm's orientation, but no such luck. Once the jacket was out of the way, he unclipped his wallet chain from his jeans. "Come on in. Make yourself at home."

There wasn't room for a couch and a bed, so Stuart had gone with a bed, which, thankfully, he'd made that morning. He'd even changed the sheets, in case this had been a date and had gone well. Whatever it was, he was sure he and Malcolm weren't going to be having sex tonight. He'd had a nice time anyway.

Malcolm took a seat on the edge of the bed. "Toilet's that way." Stuart pointed to a door across the room. "I'd offer to let you shower, but, as you can see, the rest of the bathroom's here in the kitchen."

Malcolm's eyes widened. "I'm good."

"Just as well." Stuart rapped his knuckles on the wooden butcher block countertop he'd built and installed over the tub. "This functions as counter space."

Malcolm stood and examined it. "Clever."

"Thanks. I was pleased with the way it turned out. Rather brilliant, if I do say so myself."

"You made it?" Now Malcolm sounded impressed.

"I did. I'm handy with wood and tools." *Shit.* He hadn't meant for that to sound like innuendo. "I mean, I grew up doing woodworking. My dad's a carpenter and he owns his own business. I started in his workshop when I was small and even worked for him when I was old enough."

"But you decided to become a chef?"

Stuart hesitated. That was a whole lot of history he didn't want to delve into right now. "I've always loved cooking. I decided to strike out on my own and make it a career."

Malcolm nodded but didn't ask any further questions. Stuart liked that about him. He also liked that he felt comfortable bringing Malcolm here. He didn't bring a lot of people over, in part because of his fear of people snooping. Stuart trusted Malcolm, however. If he went in the bathroom and shut the door, Malcolm wouldn't poke around his dresser or pry into Stuart's personal belongings.

Which was a good thing because if Malcolm was closeted or otherwise unsure about his sexuality, he really wasn't going to be able to handle what Stuart had stashed in the bottom drawer of the dresser.

Stuart rolled up his sleeves and washed his hands, then opened the refrigerator door. "Okay, I don't have a lot of food right now, but I always have eggs on hand. How does a cheese omelet sound?"

"Perfect."

Stuart turned his attention to the ingredients in front of him. In the words of Thomas Keller — the ones he had etched into his skin — there was no such thing as perfect food. But hopefully his cooking would make Malcolm happy.

Chapter Five

Despite every effort, Malcolm had trouble keeping focused in the days following his New Jersey hike with Stuart. He stared at his computer monitors now while the words in front of him blurred and melted into swirling shades of dark and light that were both familiar and strange.

He'd traced designs like those with his gaze as he'd followed the graceful lines of black ink etched into Stuart's olive-toned skin. A tiny smirk had crossed Stuart's face as he'd slowly spun to show off the designs. And why not? His body made for a beautiful canvas, planes of muscle gleaming with perspiration in the sun. Malcolm remembered how good he'd smelled, too, like wood and spice and sweat, the scents rising up in a heady mix that had filled Malcolm's senses.

Malcolm swallowed. His thoughts wandered further, recalling the heat of Stuart's skin and the way it had made Malcolm's fingertips tingle. The wonder that had grown inside him. The steel in Stuart's brown eyes and how they had softened as if he'd enjoyed being the object of Malcolm's attention. Malcolm suspected Stuart would have smiled if Malcolm had actually touched him.

You wanted to touch him.

Malcolm's focus snapped back to reality as that errant thought rattled around his brain like a pebble in an empty soda can.

Holy shit. He had wanted to touch Stuart. To get closer to that heat and explore the contrast of soft skin and fine hair.

Malcolm's hackles rose. He'd been struck by Stuart from their first meeting, a thing that didn't happen to Malcolm very often. On the rare occasions it did, he usually made friends with the person and even grew close. Malcolm and Liz had started dating that way. It was how he'd become friendly with Kyle, too, and the other guys in the speakeasy crowd.

This…thing with Stuart was different, however. Malcolm knew it in his bones, even if he didn't fully understand what it meant. The pull was there, much like the intrigue he felt for Carter, a fascination that had held steady for years.

A thick crinkling sound caught Malcolm's attention and he stared at the white paper bag that was set down before him.

"Beef brisket sandwich."

Malcolm looked back up at Carter. "Say what now?"

"I brought you lunch. I had to pick up a couple of things from the café over on Tudor City Place," Carter said, "and I grabbed a sandwich for you, too. Besides, you've been killing it here at work and glued to this desk all day. Someone's got to feed and water you if you're not going to do it yourself."

Malcolm's stomach growled at the luscious smell of smoked beef. Beyond his oatmeal, he'd been eating spaghetti with sliced zucchini squash and olive oil since Tuesday night and the idea of something meaty made his mouth water. He couldn't hide his frown, however. Carter buying lunch was nothing new. He did so frequently, and Malcolm knew he expected nothing in return. Malcolm liked treating Carter back, though, and right now, he simply didn't have room in his budget.

"Thank you," he made himself say. "What do I owe?"

"Don't worry about it. Like I said, I was already there, and I remembered how much you liked the brisket." Carter's expression shifted under Malcolm's gaze, becoming uncertain, and a beat passed before he spoke again. "Everything all right? You look distracted."

Malcolm almost laughed. Oh, he was distracted all right, by the situation with his mom and his dwindling bank account, not to mention thoughts about Stuart that didn't make any sense. Feelings, too. Unfamiliar, almost scary feelings Malcolm had no idea how to interpret or talk about, even with a friend he trusted. So he forced a smile instead.

"I'm okay," he said to Carter. "Lots going on and not enough time. The usual."

Carter slid his hands in his pockets. "How can I help?"

Warmth filtered through Malcolm. Carter might have been the head of communications for the CEC, but he never hesitated to pitch in when needed, no matter how mundane the task. He'd always been that way, even when Malcolm had worked as Carter's assistant back in their advertising days.

"I could use a hand cross-checking the RSVPs for the fundraiser and proofing some social media posts," Malcolm said. "Are you up for that?"

"Of course." The uncertainty in Carter's face disappeared. "Link me the docs and I'll look them over while I eat."

Forty minutes later, Malcolm's belly was pleasantly full and his focus somewhat better, plus he'd gotten through most of Carter's notes on the fundraiser's guest list. Unfortunately, any hope he had of finishing the day without drama went right out the window the moment his mom called.

"I need you to promise me not to freak out." The odd strain in Kim's voice had Malcolm sitting up straight in his chair.

"That is so not the right thing to lead with, Mom." He ran a hand over his head. "What's wrong?"

"Nothing," she said, her reply too quick.

"Mom—"

"Okay, okay." Kim sighed. "I fell. On the steps out back," she added. "The boards must have been rotted inside because my foot went right through like they were made of paper."

"Crap," Malcolm muttered. The sun porch his family had added to the back of the Staten Island home was almost twenty years old. "Are you okay?"

"I'm…at the Emergency Department at the hospital on Seaview Road."

"You're what?" Malcolm could feel the gazes of his coworkers on him.

"I sprained my ankle but it's no big deal!" Kim exclaimed. "I have a walking cast and some crutches and ibuprofen and I'm all ready to go home. I'm fine,

Malcolm, and, like I said, there is absolutely no reason to freak out."

"Yeah, I'll be the judge of that." Malcolm closed the documents he'd been working on and shut the laptop's lid. "How did you get to the ED? You didn't drive, did you?"

"Of course not. I know not to drive with an injured foot." Kim's haughty tone pricked Malcolm's conscience. He drew a deep breath in through his nose, then nearly choked at his mother's next words. "Your father drove me here, actually."

While Kim and Stephen Elliott were on civil terms since their divorce, a veritable minefield of resentments and emotion remained between them. The tensions had worsened after Malcolm's father had remarried and Malcolm hadn't seen his parents together in the same room in almost two years. He counted to five in his head before he continued speaking.

"I'm sorry. Did you say Dad drove you?"

"Yes. He was out at the house when I fell and insisted on bringing me when he realized I'd been hurt."

"I see." Malcolm rose from his chair. "Why was Dad at your place?"

"He was in town on business and stopped by to say hi."

"Oh. I didn't know you guys were hanging out on the regular again."

"We're better at it now than we used to be." Kim's tone soured. "He stepped out to make a call, probably to his wife, and I figured this was as good a time as any to reach out to you and Jack."

"Right." Malcolm turned in the direction of the workbench where his manager had set up to work. "Have you talked to Jack?"

"No, I called you first."

"Okay. I'll call him, then, um, head your way."

"You don't have to do that—"

"Pretty sure I do," Malcolm replied. "You live alone, and you just told me you're in a cast. Is Dad cool to give you a ride home?"

"Of course." Kim chuckled. "He wouldn't leave me stranded here. Your father may be in the throes of a mid-life crisis, honey, but he's not a bad person."

Malcolm already knew his dad was a good person. He also believed Kim was mistaken about Stephen Elliott's alleged mid-life crisis. If that was how she needed to rationalize the breakdown of her marriage, however, Malcolm wasn't going to argue with her. And regardless, he smiled at the sight that met him several hours later as he parked the car he'd borrowed beside his father's Lexus. His parents were seated in the shade of a red oak in matching lawn chairs, with Kim's foot propped up on a third. The day had been unseasonably warm, and now, at three o'clock, both Kim and Stephen looked rosy-cheeked and relaxed.

"Well, damn. Non-profits must pay a lot better than I thought," Stephen called after Malcolm had closed the car door behind him. He set the tall glass in his hand on the grass and stood, squinting at the gleaming black Tesla Model S. "How the hell much did that run you?"

Malcolm smiled. "This is Carter's car." He hefted his duffel and messenger bag higher onto his shoulder and crossed the lawn toward his parents. "He loaned it to me so I could get back and forth more easily. You know he doesn't need to rely on any salary to get by."

"Good point." Stephen drew Malcolm into a hug as soon as he'd set down his things. "How long did it take you to get here?"

"Over an hour." Malcolm shared his father's chuckle. "I appreciated the gesture anyway." He clapped his father's back with one hand, then drew back to regard Kim, who was watching them with a smile of her own. "How's the patient?"

His mom rolled her eyes. "I'm fine, Mr. Worrywart. I told you, it's only a sprain! And perfect timing, too, because your father needs to go before the traffic gets bad."

Stephen grimaced. "I hate to leave you guys in the lurch like this. Genifer and I are having...people over for dinner tonight. I promised I'd pick up some wine on my way back."

Malcolm nodded. He knew from his father's split-second hesitation over the word 'people' that there was something he wasn't saying. "Okay. I'll just put my stuff inside and you can give me a rundown of what happened at the ED."

"I'll walk you in." Stephen stooped to pick up his glass. "You want some more iced tea?" he asked Kim.

"No thanks." She held up her own glass and gave her ex a crooked smile. "I'd appreciate a hand, though, because it's high time I heeded nature's call."

Between Malcolm and Stephen, they helped Kim into the house and let her go when she claimed she could make it around the ground floor unassisted. Though his mom seemed hale enough, she made slow progress, and worry curled in Malcolm's gut. He turned to his father the moment she was out of sight.

"Is it really just a sprain?"

Stephen nodded. "Honestly, I'd say her pride hurts more than the ankle right now. She's bruised from the fall and that's no doubt slowing her down, too." He rubbed a hand over his chin. "She's lucky there weren't many steps to fall through or it could have been worse."

He gestured to a brown pill bottle on the table that sat beside several rolls of elastic bandage. "The doc at the ED said she should apply ice several times a day and keep it elevated and staying off the ankle is key. We already talked about her using the sofa bed in the living room until her follow-up appointment on Monday. Not having to go up and down stairs would be best, and a lot easier to manage."

"Got it." Malcolm licked his lips. "Maybe I'll put one of the lawn chairs in the shower so she can sit if she needs to. Is that weird?"

"Not any weirder than bringing the crutches into the shower." Stephen laughed. "If your mom plays by the rules, she should be off the crutches by the time you head back. Did you call Jack?"

Malcolm nodded. "He'll be here Saturday—he offered to come sooner. I told him not to bother since I'd be here and I can stay through early next week. He said he'd call once he knew I'd made it out."

A rueful expression crossed his father's face. "Of course, your mom hasn't been grocery shopping, so I'm afraid the fridge is barren. I noticed when I was making the iced tea." Stephen looked around the little kitchen. "I offered to go after I'd brought her back here, but you know how she is."

I know her a lot better than you do, Dad, Malcolm thought. Stephen didn't know that Kim hadn't had a full-time job in over a year, for example, or that Malcolm had enrolled her on his own health insurance because she'd been unable to buy her own after her unemployment benefits had run out. Which meant Malcolm was stuck paying for the deductible and additional costs of today's trip to the ED and any follow-up visits, too.

"No biggie." Malcolm covered the sinking sensation in his middle with a smile. "I can find enough in the cabinets to throw together for tonight, then deal with a shopping trip tomorrow."

The corners of Stephen's mouth twitched upward. "You boys take good care of your mom. I'm glad she's got you in her life."

"I'm glad you were here to help her out," Malcolm replied. "For what it's worth, I'm happy you guys can talk to each other again without yelling."

"I guess we've both mellowed with age," Stephen said, his smile growing wider. "Though, I'm still not allowed to talk about Genifer without getting the death glare."

Malcolm laughed. "Sorry about that. Is everything okay with you and Gen? You seem...I don't know, weird."

"I spent several hours with my ex-wife in my ex-house, kid—I'm allowed to be weird."

Stephen paused as Kim re-entered the kitchen and the next several minutes were spent on goodbyes and wishes for a speedy recovery. His expression had sobered by the time he and Malcolm were back outside by the cars, however.

"You asked if Gen and I are all right and the answer is sort of," Stephen said, his deep voice quiet. "We've been talking about hiring a surrogate. A candidate and her wife are coming over tonight for dinner. We both know it's the right thing to do, but Gen wanted to have a baby herself. She sees it as a failure on her part and there's not a lot I can do to convince her otherwise." He sighed. "Sorry. I'm sure you don't want to hear your old man complain. Or deal with a baby brother or sister at your age."

"Oh, shut up," Malcolm said. "Of course, I want to hear it. Jack and I are down with more siblings, too."

"Really?"

"Of course. We care about you and Gen, Dad, and we want you both to be happy."

He drew Stephen into another hug, holding on more tightly this time and for longer, heartsore to know Genifer was struggling with something so many people took for granted. Petite and pixie-haired, Genifer was closer in age to Malcolm than her own husband, but the brothers liked her. She had a cheerful personality and an open heart to go along with her pretty face, and Malcolm knew she made his dad happy. He felt sad and helpless as he watched his father drive away, and his mother's frown when he went back inside told him that his mood showed on his face.

"What's wrong?" she asked from her seat at the kitchen table.

"Nothing." Malcolm stooped and kissed her cheek. "Dad and Gen have stuff going on. But don't fuss — they're handling it."

"Oh." She turned her gaze on the door Malcolm had just come in. "Your father didn't say anything to me about her this afternoon."

"Dad knows the topic of Genifer is off limits where you're concerned," Malcolm said, keeping his tone light. "Are you good for right now? I want to take a look at the steps."

"Yes, of course." Kim waved him off. "Be careful out there, please. I hate to think that the rest of the porch is about to go."

Malcolm hated that idea, too. The small sun porch was a simple screened-in space with a single-sloped roof, but his mother was fond of it and spent many evenings on it during the warmer months. Hiring someone to tear it down wouldn't be cheap. Malcolm thought he and Jackson could manage on their own, if it came to that.

He'd just closed the door behind him when his phone chimed in his pocket, and Malcolm's insides did a funny kind of swoop at the sight of Stuart's name on the screen.

Hike tomorrow? Stuart had asked. *I'm off and we can do the Rambles if you sneak out early.*

Can't – I'm at my Mom's, Malcolm replied. *She's got a bum ankle and needs help.*

He'd hardly tapped 'Send' when the phone rang in his hand. "Hey."

"What happened?"

Awareness zigged up Malcolm's spine at that deep voice in his ear and made him smile. He appreciated Stuart's straight-to-the-point approach to everything. "She fell down the steps attached to a porch at the back of the house."

"Is she okay?"

"She seems to be. Outside of the sprained ankle, she got a clean bill of health at the hospital and should be up and around in a few days." He crossed the sun porch and opened the door leading outside, then frowned. What had been five steps was now three with a collection of broken bits of wood at their base. "Can't say the same for the porch steps, though. They look totally trashed. Mom said her foot went through the wood without any effort, which is kind of strange given the rest of the porch seems sturdy enough."

"Wait. Are you on the porch?"

Malcolm went still at Stuart's sharp tone. "Yes. Why?"

"Get out of there right now," Stuart said. "You have no idea if the rest of it is structurally sound. It may not be safe to stand on and you need to get your ass away from it ASAP."

"Yeah, okay." A warning tingle crawling through him, Malcolm headed back toward the door leading to the kitchen. "I'm going inside right now."

"Good." Stuart's relief was audible. "I didn't mean to bark at you, but—"

"No, you're right. I don't know if the rest of the porch is safe." Malcolm paused in front of the closed door and sighed. "Damn. I should cordon it off until I can find someone qualified to give us an idea of how bad the damage is. Maybe the neighbors know someone local—"

"I'll do it."

For the second time in only minutes, Malcolm froze at Stuart's words. "You'll—wait, what? No, no, I can't ask you to do that."

"You didn't ask. I offered." Stuart sounded amused. "I'll come out tomorrow morning after rush hour. I told you, I have the day off, and we both know I wouldn't offer if I didn't want to."

Despite himself, Malcolm smiled. "Yeah, I know." And he did. Stuart would be honest with him about the cost of repairs or a demo, too.

Malcolm let himself back in and glanced at Kim, still seated at the table and now immersed in a book. The idea of Stuart inside the white Colonial-style house was almost amusing, particularly here in the kitchen, which was filled with quaint little touches that were on the opposite end of the spectrum from tattoos, leather chaps and hipster aesthetics. Malcolm's smile grew wider. Damn, his mom was going to have a cow. Still, Stuart had a background in carpentry, and knowing he was someone Malcolm could trust…

"Okay," Malcolm said. "If you're sure it's no trouble, then yes. I really appreciate it, Stuart."

"No problem. I'll be there by ten or so."

"Who is Stuart?" Kim asked once Malcolm had hung up.

The questions in her bright gaze made Malcolm's head spin, as did the number of things he needed to do before Stuart set foot on Staten Island, like get his mother set up on the ground floor and fill the empty refrigerator, not to mention circling back to the CEC work he'd left unfinished. He'd already had to reschedule three different planning committee meetings today.

"Stuart's a friend," Malcolm said without hesitation, and *friend* felt right.

Stuart's contradictions had drawn Malcolm in, what with the hot-and-cold behavior and reluctance to talk about his private life, despite the scowls and badass-biker vibe. Those moods had mellowed the more he and Malcolm worked together, though, and morphed into a rapport that was surprisingly easy.

Malcolm liked that Stuart appeared comfortable around him. Why else would he have invited Malcolm hiking? Or back to his tiny apartment, so spartan there'd been nowhere to sit but the bed? Stuart had shared a meal and a bottle of wine with Malcolm that night and talked a little about himself. He hadn't once pressured Malcolm to return the favor. That, more than anything, had made Malcolm feel comfortable, too, and he'd looked forward to the text messages he and Stuart had exchanged since the hiking trip.

"And how did you meet?" his mom prompted.

"Working on the fundraiser, if you can believe it," Malcolm said. "And as luck would have it, he also knows carpentry. He offered to come out and take a look at the porch, then help us figure out what to do next."

Kim's face lit up. "Oh, great! Call him back and ask him to stay for dinner. We should place an order with Clark's and have it delivered, by the way. I don't even have enough to feed you right now."

"I'll do a grocery run tomorrow, Mom, and I can pull a meal together tonight."

"Really?" Kim cast Malcolm a doubtful look as he moved toward the pantry. "It'd be a lot easier to order takeout, if you ask me."

"Okay. I'd rather cook in, if that's okay," Malcolm called back with all the gentleness he could muster. Checking the canned goods, he actually smiled when he spied chickpeas. They would go well with the package of frozen spinach he'd bought on his last shopping trip. "I'm, um, trying to watch what I eat anyway, and cooking at home makes that a lot easier."

"Oh, Malcolm, do not tell me you are on a diet. There's not an ounce of fat on you!"

"That's because I'm watching what I eat," Malcolm lied. "Besides, I'm not dieting—I'm eating clean." He aimed a smile his mother's way. "Wait until you try the tapas I've got planned."

Chapter Six

Stuart debated between the two tools in his hands before deciding to pack both. *Who knows? Might need them.* He slipped them into his canvas tool bag, grasped the leather handles and stood. He made a mental inventory of everything he might need to assess and maybe repair Malcolm's mom's porch, then nodded to himself. *Yep, that should do it.*

After securing the storage locker where he stored his own personal tools, he walked toward the entrance to the woodshop.

Unlike a lot of workshop spaces in the five boroughs, The Co-Op Shop wasn't owned by an outside company. Instead, all the members had a stake in it. Being a member gave Stuart access to a full woodshop and tools, plus the use of a truck. Yesterday, he'd called the minute he got off the phone with Malcolm, but thankfully, no one else had already claimed it for today. The co-op had recently purchased a second truck, so Stuart was comfortable taking it out of town.

Earl, one of the workshop's coordinators, word-lessly slid a sheet of paper toward him. He was a grizzled old guy whom Stuart respected the hell out of. He had decades of experience and skills Stuart could only dream of. Earl, in turn, seemed to respect Stuart's knowledge. It had taken no time at all for Stuart to pass the workshop certification required to be a member and Earl had joked that Stuart might even be able to teach him a thing or two.

"Where are you headed?" Earl asked. He had the kind of gravelly voice that made Stuart wonder if he'd been a heavy smoker.

Stuart looked up from the sign-out sheet. "Staten Island. A friend's mom needs some help with a construction job. She fell through the steps yesterday."

"Must be more than a friend if you're driving way the hell out to Staten Island," Earl said with a snort as he handed over the truck keys. Stuart just laughed and thanked him.

Stuart walked to the truck he'd already loaded with the bigger tools he might need. *Is Malcolm more than a friend?* he wondered.

The phone call from Malcolm yesterday had worried the hell out of Stuart. When he found out Malcolm had been standing on a potentially rickety sun porch with no concern for his safety… Stuart shook his head. He'd had visions of the porch collapsing on Malcolm and crushing him beneath the roof's weight.

Stuart knew he'd surprised Malcolm by offering to take a look at his mother's sun porch. Frankly, he'd surprised himself. But he felt protective of Malcolm in a way he couldn't remember feeling with anyone before. Not with his ex-wife or with anyone he'd dated before. And he wasn't even dating Malcolm. He didn't think. He was still fuzzy on that one.

Stuart was no closer to knowing that answer than he had been when they first met.

He felt strangely okay with that.

* * * *

Stuart pulled into the driveway of 250 Roswell Avenue and parked behind a shiny black Tesla. Damn. He wondered who that belonged to. It was a nice piece of machinery and no doubt cost a pretty penny. Malcolm used public transit and his mom's house wasn't particularly luxurious.

I'm here. Stuart sent a quick text to Malcolm before he hopped out of the truck. He looked the house over as he walked up the sidewalk. It was just as Malcolm had described. A small Colonial with a light blue front door.

From the front, the house looked solid enough. The roof appeared to be in good shape, and he didn't see any obvious issues with the foundation at a quick glance. The shingles could use a good power washing and there was paint peeling from the front door and the columns on the small portico over the front steps. Thankfully, that appeared to be the worst of it and the steps were concrete. He'd give the columns a closer inspection before he left for the day, though. No point in fixing the sun porch on the back if dry rot made the front collapse on top of Malcolm or his mom.

Before Stuart's booted foot hit the front step, the door opened. Malcolm looked tired and stressed, but his face brightened. "Hey, thanks for coming out. How was traffic?"

"Not too bad. I got hung up on the bridge for a bit. Other than that, it was fine."

"Malcolm! Don't keep your friend waiting out on the steps. Let him in." A small blonde with a bright smile peeked her head around Malcolm's arm.

Malcolm stepped back and Stuart followed him inside the house.

"Mom, this is my friend, Stuart Morgan. Stuart, my mom, Kim Elliott."

Kim's gaze traveled up Stuart's arms, her eyes wide at the sight of the tattoos under his rolled-up sleeves. He'd left off the leather jacket this morning in favor of a plaid shirt, but he probably looked a bit different from what she'd expected.

"I'm glad to meet you, Mrs. Elliott. I was sorry to hear about your accident." He kept his voice soft, and he offered her a smile. Marisol had once commented that rather than resting bitch face, he had resting pissed-off face, which worked in concert with the tattoos and stern expression to keep people away. While Stuart liked that most of the time, they sometimes gave the wrong impression to people he didn't want to scare off and he tried to be mindful of that.

"Oh, I'm doing all right now." Kim's wary expression lightened. "It wasn't too serious of an accident and I'll be back to normal soon enough. It was very nice of you to come out all this way to take a look at the steps, Stuart. Would you like some coffee before you get started?"

"That would be nice."

A short while later, Stuart sat at a banquette in the small eat-in kitchen across from Malcolm and his mother as they sipped their coffee. The house was on the small side and slightly dated, but it was clean, well laid out and homey. He approved of the gas stove across the room, too, because he couldn't stand electric.

Kim chatted away, talking about Malcolm's childhood, and her obvious affection for him made Stuart smile. Predictably, Malcolm looked like he wanted to be anywhere else, and after Stuart drained his cup, he took pity on his friend and changed the subject.

"Thank you for the coffee, ma'am. I'll go ahead and take a look at the porch now."

"Of course," Kim said. She reached for the crutches. Before she could grab them, Malcolm had handed them to her. "Please, call me Kim."

Stuart nodded. She turned toward the back door and Stuart was on his feet in an instant. "Not that way. We should go out through the front."

Malcolm immediately nodded. "We can't go out there until Stuart makes sure it's safe, Mom."

"Oh, right, yes—you told me that." Kim let out a little laugh. "How silly of me. I'm glad I have you around, Malcolm. And that you have Stuart." She smiled at him now. "You'd make someone a good husband. You aren't married already, are you? Or have a girlfriend or boyfriend at home?"

Stuart raised an eyebrow. Clearly, she'd gotten over the first impression she'd had of him.

"No, I live alone. I am gay, however."

"That's a shame you haven't found anyone." She gave Malcolm a pointed look. "I keep telling my son he should get out and date more but he's always working and taking care of me."

Malcolm opened his mouth as if he wanted to say something, then closed it again.

"Well, let's see if we can't get these stairs fixed so you don't take any more tumbles," Stuart said. "That way Malcolm worries less."

Half an hour later, Stuart crawled out from under the sun porch and stood, then brushed the dirt off his clothes.

"Well, I think you're in luck. The porch seems solid and there are no signs of termites or dry rot. I'd like to add more support in the center... Whoever built it originally skimped a bit so your floor is beginning to sag. Some bracing should do the trick. I can also build a new set of steps for you."

Kim, who had been sitting in a lawn chair watching him work, clapped her hands. "Oh, that's wonderful news, isn't it, Malcolm?"

Malcolm, who had been standing nearby with a worried frown on his face, let out a relieved-sounding sigh. "It is."

"I'll have to make a run to the home improvement store for some boards and hardware, but I have all the tools with me that I'll need. Would you like me to do the work today?"

Malcolm stepped forward, the crease over his eyebrows returning. "How much is that going to run? The materials and labor, I mean."

Stuart smiled at him. "Well, labor's free. Keep me company while I work and we'll be even. The materials? Couple hundred, tops."

Malcolm's jaw tightened before he nodded. "Okay."

"You're always worrying about money, Malcolm," Kim said, her voice light.

Malcolm, who was still facing Stuart, had a look in his eyes that made Stuart want to reach out and pull him into a hard hug. Something was clearly stressing him out and Stuart remembered the conversation they'd had about Malcolm's budget being tight.

If Stuart had to lay bets, he'd guess it had to do with Kim Elliott, though he wasn't sure what exactly.

"You want to come with me?" Stuart asked. "Or do you need to stay with your mom?"

"Oh, go on," Kim said with a wave. "Just bring me a book and my cell phone. I'll sit here in the shade and enjoy the nice weather while you two go off and do manly things at the hardware store."

Stuart had to smother a laugh. He doubted the image that popped into his head at that statement was what Kim had intended. Or, maybe it was. While he worked, she'd made several comments about Stuart and Malcolm getting together, all of which seemed to make Malcolm deeply uncomfortable.

"Are you sure, Mom?" Malcolm asked. "What if you need to use the bathroom?"

"Oh, you won't be gone that long. I'll be fine right here for an hour or so, and I have my phone in case of emergencies."

Stuart wandered toward the front of the house as Malcolm and his mother talked, and after a few minutes, Malcolm appeared once more.

"Give me a minute to get her situated before we head out," he said as he passed Stuart.

"Sure. No rush."

Stuart inspected the entryway columns while Malcolm went inside and returned a short while later with the book and cell phone, plus water and medication. He seemed more worried than the situation warranted but Stuart appreciated what a thoughtful, caring guy he was.

"Everything okay?" Malcolm asked after he'd rejoined Stuart at the front of the house.

"Yep." Stuart brushed the peeling paint from his hands. "The columns and door need some sanding and a coat of paint that's all. I could take care of that, too, if you want?"

Malcolm hesitated. "Maybe. It'll depend on what the other materials cost. Like I said, my budget is tight right now. My mom's having some...financial difficulties and I've been trying to help out but—"

"Does that have anything to do with the Tesla parked in the driveway?"

"No." Malcolm let out a surprised laugh. "The car is a loan from Carter. I was at work when my mom got hurt and he wanted to make it easier for me to get out here and back."

"That was nice of him. I'm disappointed, though," Stuart joked. "I was hoping I could ask to take it out for a spin."

Malcolm's expression eased. "If there's time before you head back into the city, I could take you for a drive. It's not quite the same but—"

"No, that sounds nice."

Away from his mother's house, Malcolm seemed much more relaxed, even when the time came to buy the lumber and supplies. Stuart was able to keep the budget for the steps low thanks to a sale in the millworks department and his contractor discount, and Malcolm said he'd wait on the paint, in case his mom had any on hand from the last time the exterior had been painted.

They returned to find Kim in good spirits and she directed Malcolm to the garage where the cans of paint were stored. Stuart gave him a few tips on prepping for painting, then tackled the job of demo-ing the rotted steps. With that cleared away, it was simple enough to add some additional bracing.

Stuart lost himself in the smell of fresh cut lumber and the feel of the drill vibrating in his hand. He'd stripped down to a T-shirt and was beginning to sweat in the late April sunshine when Malcolm appeared with a tray containing bowls and two tall glasses of what looked like iced tea.

"Want to take a break? I made lunch. Nothing fancy, just a taco salad."

"That would be great. Thanks. Are you going to eat with me?"

"Sure, if you can give me a few minutes. Mom ate already and I'll see if she wants to lie down."

"Of course."

Stuart took the tray from Malcolm and set it in the shade under a tree. Using a hose attached to the house, he washed the grime off his hands and wet his face. He was sprawled out on the grass under a red oak by the time Malcolm returned, his tired expression easing into a smile when Stuart gave him a lazy wave.

"You look comfortable."

"I am. Starving, though." Stuart sat up and leaned against the tree's trunk. "Thanks for lunch."

"Sure." Malcolm sank onto the ground beside him with a sigh.

They dug into their salads and Stuart had to compliment Malcolm after just a few bites. "This is good. I like the black beans and the lime dressing. A pinch of cumin might be nice, too."

"Good thought. And I'm glad you like it. I've been trying to stick to vegetarian proteins lately and I know you're a meat eater."

"Healthy." *And cheap. What the hell is going on with Mrs. Elliott's finances right now?* Now didn't seem to be the time to ask.

Stuart reached for the iced tea. "How's your mom?"

"Okay. Stubborn. It took some convincing to get her to agree to take some painkillers and lie down."

"Think she's actually sleeping?"

"She was asleep before I closed the bedroom door."

"You take good care of her." Stuart chuckled but Malcolm looked away.

"Someone's got to."

Stuart thought of his own family. It had been years since he'd spoken to any of them. *How many nieces and nephews do I have now?* His heart sank.

"Do you see your parents often?"

Stuart glanced over at Malcolm. Clearly, his mind had gone down a similar path as Stuart's.

"No. I haven't spoken to anyone in my family in more than a decade."

"Oh. I'm sorry." Malcolm cleared his throat. "Seeing you with my mom... You were good with her earlier. It made me curious. I didn't mean to pry."

"I know you didn't." Stuart lay back, pillowed his head on his hands and stared up at the branches overhead. "You want to hear the whole sordid tale?"

"Only if you want to tell it."

Stuart wet his lips. Malcolm meant that, he was sure of it. If he chose not to tell his story, Malcolm wouldn't push. But maybe if Stuart let himself be a little vulnerable with Malcolm, he'd reciprocate and open up more. Besides, Stuart trusted Malcolm.

"I grew up an hour outside of Salt Lake City. I'm the second oldest of six."

Malcolm whistled quietly under his breath but didn't respond otherwise.

"I was raised Mormon." Stuart cleared his throat. "When I say that, people get weird ideas that I grew up in some kind of cult. It can be cult-ish in a lot of ways, but as a kid, my world seemed normal. My dad owned the carpentry business. My mom stayed at home with us kids. She didn't homeschool us or anything—we went to the public schools—but she did everything else. Cooked, cleaned, ran us around to all our after-school activities. In most ways, it was a very normal middle-class childhood. We took vacations, went camping and hiking and had barbecues with the neighbors."

Stuart listened to the buzz of insects and the faint whine of a lawnmower engine in the distance. It reminded him of summer afternoons back in Utah when he'd been a kid. Taking a break from riding bikes or playing soccer with his brothers, he'd relax under a tree and stare up at the blue sky, watching the clouds change shape.

"My parents were decent people," he continued. "They loved me and my siblings. They wanted what was best for us. They believed following the church teachings would give us that. The Mormon faith emphasizes family. If you go against the church, you won't end up in the celestial kingdom with your family. That is a real, visceral threat to people whose entire faith is built on the idea of the celestial kingdom."

"I can imagine," Malcolm said softly. "Did you know anyone who was gay when you were growing up? Or was it all hidden?"

"I didn't know any gay couples personally. The community where I lived was insular. One of those small towns where the Mormon temple is right in the center and the whole place is laid out in an orderly grid. Everyone knows everyone else." He took a deep breath. "When there was anything on the news about gay people or gay rights, my mom's lips would get really tight and my dad would let out this irritated-sounding huff. At church, sometimes the sermons were about why homosexuality was wrong. Being Mormon's not compatible in any way with being gay. The emphasis on family and being together in the celestial kingdom ties into that. Mormons — along with plenty of other people — believe it's a choice and that you can choose to not be gay anymore. That's one reason rehabilitation centers and conversion therapy still exist." A spark of anger lit up inside Stuart.

"Did I know I was different than my siblings growing up? I think so, on some level anyway. It wasn't obvious. I know some gay men have these vivid memories of signs that pointed to crushes they had, but I don't. I wasn't a rebellious kid — I didn't get in trouble any more than my brothers — it was just this feeling that I was different somehow. I was out of step with everyone around me. Outwardly, the fact that I liked to cook set me apart from my siblings. It was considered women's work. My mom let me help her make meals as long as I didn't talk about it outside of the home. I loved it." Stuart turned his head and shot a faint smile at Malcolm who was staring intently at him.

"Contrary to the popular myths about Mormon cooking in Utah, it wasn't all mushroom soup casseroles and Jell-O salads. My mom did a lot of home canning and preservation. She made jam from strawberries and peaches. She'd pickle fresh cucumbers. She always had a garden in the backyard, so she'd pick tomatoes and make spaghetti sauce and soup and freeze it. She liked using herbs."

"Is that where you got your love of food from then?"

"Yes. In high school, I worked as a busboy and dishwasher in this little restaurant on the outskirts of town. I even badgered the head cook into letting me assist him and I learned some things about working in a kitchen."

He glanced over to see Malcolm lean back and brace himself on his hands. It made the muscles and tendons in his arms stand out. Stuart had to look away.

"Anyway, growing up, I dated girls. And it wasn't so hard. Sex before marriage is frowned upon so no one questioned it if I wasn't pushy about it. The girls I dated assumed I was a nice guy. Respectful. A devout Mormon. The harder I struggled inside knowing something was off, the more I tried to double down on being the perfect member of the church. After high school, I even went off and did my two years as a missionary."

"Where did you do that?"

"Greece."

"Huh. I didn't know missionaries were sent to Europe. I figured it was always South America or Africa."

"Nah, they go everywhere, even the U.S. I think Mitt Romney went to France." Stuart shrugged. "I don't know what that was like for him, but Greece was resistant to Mormon proselytizing. The Greek Orthodox Church in particular. I tried the best I could." He smiled faintly, remembering the fervor that had seized him. *The desperation.* If he could just make inroads there, it would have meant he belonged. "You wouldn't have recognized me then. No beard, no tattoos, suits all the time… I even had the name tag that said, '*Elder Morgan*'."

"I… No, I'm having a hard time imagining that."

Stuart grinned at Malcolm. "When I got there, I believed in what I was doing. Few people were interested in converting, but I learned Greek, discussed philosophy with the locals and tried new foods — you can't believe what the food there was like — and the experience changed me. Maybe not at first, but I began to understand the world in a different light. See how much more was out there. It planted those seeds for my future. Ironically, I think going on a mission was ultimately what turned me away from the church." The Greek men he'd looked at had played a part in that as well.

"How so?"

"The standards of behavior for missionaries are very rigid. They tried to keep us on the straight and narrow with strict schedules and we were forbidden from dating or having relationships. Still, I was exposed to the world more. When I came home, I tried to continue like I had been. I started dating a woman named Becky, I worked for my dad in his carpentry shop…I tried to be the man I was supposed to be." He laughed softly. "I got a side job as a cook in the restaurant where I'd worked before, though. My dad was pissed at me. I was the eldest son and he wanted me to take over his business someday. I told him I was cooking to make extra money and save up for a wedding, and my parents were happy when Becky and I got engaged, then married."

"Were you… I mean, I don't know how to ask this…"

Stuart glanced over at Malcolm when his words trailed off. "Was I attracted to my wife?"

Malcolm nodded.

"Attracted enough to have sex, yes. I cared about her. Loved her, even. Just maybe not in the way she wanted me to love her. There was always something missing. The sex wasn't passionate or exciting. It was…a bodily function. You'd expect Mormons to be prudish about sex. Oddly enough, they're not after marriage. Sex is strongly encouraged for couples, not only for procreation but for 'expressing love and strengthening emotional and spiritual bonds between husband and wife.' That's a direct quote, by the way.

"Sex didn't do that for Becky and me. I know I disappointed her, and I didn't live up to my duties as a husband." Stuart winced. He'd hated that. Hated the disappointed look in her eyes before she rolled over to go to sleep. "Day by day, it got worse. We'd been married for maybe six months when this guy came into the restaurant. It was an open kitchen and I caught a glimpse of him, heard him laugh at a comment the waitress made, and something in me…gave way. Like all the walls I'd put up about the truth about who I was were gone."

"Was he gay?"

"I have no idea. He came in for weeks every day for lunch. He was from out of town, there on some kind of business or other. I hardly spoke to him, but I couldn't stop thinking about him." Stuart held up his left hand. "That scar there—where my thumb and my wrist meet—I burned myself on a hot pan because I was so distracted by him while I was cooking." The man had taken off his suit jacket and rolled up his sleeves and Stuart had been so dizzy with lust that when the head cook had called his name, he'd jerked and bumped his hand into searing hot metal.

"Is that when you came out?"

Stuart's laugh was humorless. "No. I never planned to come out. I wrestled with it, sure it was just temptation, a test of my faith that I could overcome. I loved my wife. I couldn't be gay. Those seeds that had been sown in Greece had taken root. My head was full of doubts about the church and about my place in it and who I wanted to be.

"Sometimes, late at night, I'd give in and watch gay porn. When I did, I discovered things about myself that I...I knew went against every teaching in the Church of the Latter-Day Saints and would horrify my wife." He wet his lips. "So, I did them in secret. I made this locked box that held" — he looked over at Malcolm — "well, some things that I wasn't comfortable sharing with anyone."

Not even Malcolm. There didn't seem to be a judgmental bone in Malcolm's body, yet Stuart still couldn't bring himself to tell him about his secret. He couldn't bear to see Malcolm's expression change the way Becky's had.

"I used to tell her the box held gifts for her." It had been a stupid thing to do and he'd always wondered if some subconscious part of him had wanted her to find out. The lie had burned in his chest until he'd bought a few things and stashed them there, giving them to her periodically. It had assuaged some of his guilt. But not all of it. Especially not when she'd gush to her sisters about the necklace he'd given her. Or when they'd sigh about what a perfect husband she had. But Stuart saw the pain in her eyes. The loneliness that he was causing.

"I don't know if I just forgot to lock the box one day or if a part of me wanted to get caught. I felt so trapped. So miserable about lying to her. Becky wanted kids and wanted to get started, so she'd been talking about going off birth control and I..." He sighed. "Becky walked in on me and my secret was out. She kicked me out of the house and told me I wasn't allowed to come back until I admitted my sins and was healed."

Stuart closed his eyes. "That was it. I snapped. Permanently. I knew I couldn't do it. I couldn't go back and lie to my wife every day and have children with her. I couldn't make her happy and I sure as hell wasn't happy, so I went to the owner of the restaurant and he helped me. He let me sleep on his couch for a couple days. I had a few belongings I'd packed. I withdrew enough money from our checking account to get by, bought a motorcycle and drove out of Utah as fast as I could and straight to New York. I've only spoken to Becky via our lawyers since and my parents sent a letter telling me I was no longer welcome in the church or in their lives. I've been excommunicated and I haven't heard from my parents or my siblings since."

Stuart's voice was a little raw by the time he was done, but a weight had been lifted off his chest, too. He'd told very few people in his life that entire story. He'd received varying reactions over the years — shock, horror, sympathy. Malcolm said nothing. Instead, he laid a hand on Stuart's forearm. His palm was warm against Stuart's skin as they sat there silently in the backyard with the scent of sawdust and fresh-mown grass around them.

Chapter Seven

Malcolm jogged down the staircase toward Under and ignored his phone's buzz in his pocket. His brother had taken Malcolm's place at the Staten Island house and he'd messaged and called often. Malcolm sympathized, he truly did. Having to face their mom's dysfunction head-on was mentally draining because neither of the Elliott brothers knew how to call her out on the obvious problems. Like the empty refrigerator or the house repairs that went undone, not to mention the utility bills they paid, all while Kim acted like nothing was amiss and spent money she didn't have.

You could tell her to get a full-time job.

Malcolm's stomach twisted. Yes, he could do that. If he ever figured out how to call his mother out on her behavior. Which he hadn't. Despite the current state of his own finances. He hadn't planned for the porch repair or Kim's visits to the doctor and even with Jackson's help, the extra expenses combined with keeping himself housed and fed had drained his accounts to the lowest they'd ever been. Currently, he was too broke to buy himself groceries, which had worked out in a morbid kind of way because any time Malcom thought about it, he felt so sick he could hardly eat. So he'd spent the last couple of days nibbling saltines he'd found in a package at the back of his pantry and counting down the hours to his next paycheck.

Jesus.

Malcolm shook himself hard and pushed open the speakeasy's front door. He was not going to think about his mom tonight, or his brother, or the distinctly Dickensian vibe overtaking his own life. Malcom needed a break, damnit, and to catch up with his friends and focus on something other than money.

"You came back!" Kyle called from the bar as Malcolm shook hands with Jim. Then he was there, wrapping Malcolm up in a hug.

"What's this about?" Malcolm laughed. "I called Jim and let him know I was coming."

"I know. You were gone almost a week, though, and I started thinking you'd defected to the 'burbs."

"Please. Like that would ever happen." A sweeter kind of ache than usual took hold of Malcom's gut. Knowing he'd been missed felt nice. Malcolm groaned when Kyle leaned back enough to reach up and mess with his hair and struggled to get free. "Dude."

"You love it." Kyle smirked. "You deserve it for standing me up at yoga class."

"Believe me when I say that I missed class more than you know."

"Mmm. Looks like you've been working out anyway." Kyle eyed his friend up and down in a way that made Malcolm's shoulders tense. "You're starting to get skinny, dude."

"I've been running a lot in the last week, mostly to get out of the house," Malcolm said. "And if you ever tell my mom I said that, I'll deny it 'til I'm blue in the face."

"Your secret's safe with me. How's she doing?"

Kyle dragged Malcolm toward the bar and the two of them laughed when Malcolm nearly tripped. Clinging to one another, they kept him upright while they talked about Kim's recovery.

"I'm glad she's okay." Kyle headed back around the bar after Malcolm was seated. "I'll bet she'll be glad to ditch the crutches, too."

Malcolm nodded. "She should be up and around again by the end of this week if she keeps off the bad foot. Jack's there to help out, though I'm sure she'd fight him for the car keys. Which is funny because you'd think she'd welcome the opportunity to be chauffeured around."

"Maybe you're just a shitty driver." Kyle waggled his eyebrows, then bent and opened one of the refrigerators under the bar. "Anyway, you know I love seeing you, but I'm certain there's a reason you're here on a Wednesday night and still in your work duds, no less." He set a brown paper bag on the bar top.

"I came from the office, doofus. I also invited Stuart for a drink." Malcolm ignored his friend's inquisitive expression. "He got my mom out of a jam with the repairs to her porch and I really want to at least treat him to say thanks."

"Okay, babe."

Never had Malcolm been so grateful for Kyle's easygoing nature. Not that Malcolm was lying exactly, but he hadn't come anywhere close to the whole story. Outside of any kind of favor Stuart had done for

Malcolm's mom, Malcom wanted to see him again in the worst way and talk face-to-face for the first time in nearly a week.

He'd been floored by the story Stuart had told under the shade of the trees growing in his mom's yard, and not only because of what the man had endured. No, it was the trust Stuart had shown Malcolm. The extraordinary courage and strength and grace he'd displayed while speaking words of pain and shattered dreams, and of his journey to rebuild.

Malcolm often heard coming-out stories in his work at CEC, and of people's struggles for self-acceptance and love. Every one of his close friends had endured a coming out of their own, and while they ranged from traumatic to almost comically mundane, each had been life changing. None of those stories had struck a chord in Malcolm as deeply as Stuart's had, however. That fact alone scared Malcolm almost as much as it thrilled him, as did the knowledge that he wanted more contact with Stuart every day.

They'd spoken many times following the porch repairs, often in the evenings after Kim had gone to sleep. Nothing extraordinary had been said during those exchanges and there were no more dramatic reveals. They'd spent the time watching old episodes of *The X-Files* on Netflix together instead, and Malcolm had looked forward to every call. Those conversations had intensified the pull he felt toward Stuart. Lying in his childhood bedroom and listening to Stuart's deep, sometimes sleepy voice provide commentary on Mulder and Scully's adventures, Malcolm had felt less solitary and better connected to the city he'd left behind.

"So, what?" Kyle narrowed his eyes at Malcolm now. "You came in early to give me a pep talk and make sure everything we mix tonight is perfect?"

"Pfft, no. Everything you mix is perfect. I came in because I missed you and wanted to catch up."

Kyle smiled. "You're sweet. And, your timing couldn't be better because Jes is on his way in, too, and Stuart sent me the fundraiser menu along with the beer and wine King's plans to serve. We can go through the cocktail selection and make sure everyone's on the same page."

"Sounds great."

"Hopefully, your chef leaves his bike at home tonight, so he doesn't need to play designated driver." Kyle's eyes gleamed. "Or maybe you'd do the driving?"

"Oh, hell, no." Malcolm's stomach dipped in a giddy swoop. He enjoyed riding behind Stuart far more than he would have guessed. The idea of taking control of the huge machine was actively terrifying. "I'm not driving that beast, assuming Stuart would even let me touch it."

"C'mon, man. You're tall enough to handle that bike with some practice. And think about how hot you'd look doing it." Kyle raised his hands to handlebar level, then mimed twisting a motorcycle throttle, and Malcolm burst out laughing at his exaggerated leer.

"Whatever the hell is going on here, I approve," a familiar voice called. Gladness thrummed through Malcolm as he turned and met Jesse's grin. "Welcome back, Maleficent!"

Normally, Malcolm rolled his eyes at the silly play on names, but the genuine delight in Jesse's face stopped him.

"Hey, Big Money." He exchanged a quick hug instead and groaned when Jesse tousled his hair yet again. "What is it with you guys and messing with my hair?"

"We like you messy," Jesse replied with a wink. He looked very blue-eyed and blond in his light wool suit and Malcolm could tell his friend was in a good mood. "That's from Cam, too. He'd be here to say welcome back in person, but he's working late tonight."

Now Malcolm did roll his eyes, albeit with a big smile. "I was gone five days total. Your trips overseas usually last twice as long."

"And look at how much you all fucking miss me!" Jesse walked around the bar toward Kyle, the impish gleam in his eye shifting and a softer expression falling over his features. "Hey, gorgeous."

"Hey." Kyle's smile made his whole person glow. He stepped into Jesse's bear hug and they shared a lingering kiss that was by turns sweet and very, very hot.

Wait.

Goosebumps rose along Malcolm's arms. He didn't think that way about people and particularly not his friends. Over the years, he'd grown used to the easy affection the men in his life showed one another. Few of the speakeasy guys were as open as Jesse and Kyle, but each was out and proud in their own way and all the couples were as affectionate as they were honest about where they drew the lines between sex and love.

Carter and Riley were wholly committed to one another, just like Will and David, both pairs wired to be monogamous. Kyle and his boyfriend, Luka, considered their relationship more open, even though the times they engaged with other partners were so rare as to be exceptional. And last came Jesse and his partner, Cam, each as free-spirited as the day they had met. They reached outside of their partnership often, both individually and as a pair, but always came back to one another at the end of a figurative day.

They do what feels right.

Malcolm's heart squeezed as that truth filtered over him. The love that bound his friends wasn't a single emotion. It had shades and variations, and it twisted all around them with a grace both beautiful and powerful, like the designs inked into Stuart's skin. That love extended to Malcolm, too. While his place among the speakeasy crew had always been as a friend to all and lover to none, every one of those men cared about him. They made Malcolm feel like he fit, too, and that it was perfectly understandable that he didn't want more.

Except maybe Malcolm did want more and simply never noticed until now. Until Stuart.

The rattle of a cocktail shaker broke through the haze in Malcolm's head. Cheeks hot, he saw that Kyle was setting out trays of sushi rolls and sashimi while Jesse poured drinks.

Kyle gave Malcolm a smile. "Everything okay, babe?"

"Sure." The smell of nori and pickled ginger made Malcolm's mouth water and he had to clear his throat around the fib. "What's all this?"

"Dinner." Kyle reached for a stack of napkins. "I placed an order after Jim told me you were coming. Figured we'd go over the drinks menu while we eat and get Jes' take."

Jesse set a coupe glass down in front of Malcolm. "This is a Southside," he said of the milky white concoction he'd garnished with mint. "Also known as a gin daiquiri, minus all the fruit, slush and other junk people insist on dumping into a perfectly innocent cocktail."

"Spoken like a true booze nerd." Kyle accepted his own glass with a chuckle. "You've no doubt guessed that the Southside is on the fundraiser menu, along with the Old Fashioned, a Rosemary Paloma and the ever popular Cosmopolitan."

"Is it me or are Cosmos a bit out of character for you?" Jesse asked Kyle. "'Sex and the City' is so not your craft cocktail vibe."

"I wasn't a huge fan of the show, but a Cosmo now and then with homemade triple sec is all kinds of nice." Kyle sipped his drink. "The citrus will pair well with the seafood on the chef's menu, and the cranberry is a low-key shout-out specific to the New England lobster salad."

"I like that," Malcolm said. "Pretty sure Stuart will too, once you explain it to him."

An hour later, Stuart smiled down at the cocktail menu, his chef's brain picking out the flavor notes without even trying.

"I like where you're going with these. I'd drink any one of them too, fundraiser or not, because they all sound fantastic," he said and rubbed a hand over his beard. He seemed relaxed and almost cheerful tonight in jeans and a Judge Dredd T-shirt and Malcolm loved that look on him. "Not a good idea for me to mix all of them together if I want to make it home in one piece, however."

Malcolm's mood dipped a little at the idea Stuart would have to monitor himself yet again. "You rode your bike?"

"Actually, no. I took the subway so I wouldn't have to worry about a DUI. However, there's bourbon, tequila, vodka and gin on this menu and my body will not be happy if I drink them all. Gin in particular—it does a number on my head." Regret flickered across Stuart's face as he set the menu card down. "I'm so intrigued by these flavors."

"I'll make you a tasting flight," Kyle said. "That'll give you all of the flavor yet save you the headache."

Stuart nearly beamed. "Perfect, thanks." He glanced at Malcolm. "You want to go through them with me, or did you do that before I got here?"

"I'd be face down under the bar if I went through four drinks in an hour, and so would Kyle and Jes." Malcolm savored Stuart's laugh. "We each had a Southside, then switched to water. Jes also disappeared into the office and has yet to emerge."

"He'll be along in a bit," Kyle said. He moved up the bar, plucking bottles from the shelves. "He had some calls to make out to the West Coast, but I imagine he's ready to wrap up."

"Jes is looking forward to meeting you." Malcolm pitched his voice lower. Everything in him seemed attuned to Stuart, who was sitting close enough to Malcolm that their elbows brushed. Malcolm didn't mind a bit, particularly the way Stuart's woodsy cologne mixed with the scent of the leather jacket. "Jesse's parents are looking forward to the fundraiser, too. All of the Murtaghs have been CEC donors for years. Jesse's the one who suggested Carter check out their jobs board back when he was looking to make a career change."

"And Carter hired you."

Malcolm shook his head. "Carter's not my direct manager so, no, he didn't hire me. He let me know about the job opening so I could apply."

"Cool." A thoughtful expression crossed Stuart's face. "Does that ever get complicated?"

"How do you mean?"

"I know Carter's technically not your boss. He leads your department though, right? That makes him responsible for the fundraiser's success, which is your project and an event in which a lot of your friends are participating."

Stuart raised his right hand and rested his chin in his palm. "Your friend, the senator, is making a speech and your other friends and the staff of two separate establishments are providing the space, food and drink. Hell, I'm responsible for making sure everyone's belly gets filled and you and I are more friends than business contacts, too." He quirked a grin at Malcolm. "Guess you guys aren't big believers in not mixing business with pleasure, huh?"

Malcolm liked hearing that Stuart considered them friends. And even more that Stuart considered their interactions pleasure rather than business.

"You might not believe it, but outside of Car and me working together, this is the first time the crew has truly mixed business and pleasure," he said. "Not counting Kyle and Jesse, of course."

"Meaning what?"

As if on cue, Jesse reappeared, mobile phone still pressed to his ear. He stepped up close and patted Kyle's ass, and the way his hand lingered at the small of Kyle's back screamed intimacy. Malcolm watched Stuart's eyebrows rise.

"Ah. So, they're—"

"More than business partners," Malcolm replied. "A lot less so since Kyle met Luka, but what they have goes beyond regular friendship. I don't see that changing, either."

"Their boyfriends don't mind?"

"Not at all. Jesse and Cam's relationship is wide open. They'd also cringe at the word 'boyfriend.'"

Stuart chuckled and met Malcolm's gaze. "That definitely sounds complicated, Mal."

"I suppose it would to someone who doesn't know them. I don't always understand every nuance myself. Even so, to us, it's all very simple."

Malcolm smiled. *Funny*. A few weeks ago, he'd gone out of his way to avoid talking about the personal lives of his friends with Stuart. Now, he couldn't think why it'd seemed like a big deal at all. He liked Stuart's use of his nickname, too, and the way he said it sent a pleasant zing through Malcolm.

"Jesse and Kyle are the tip of the iceberg, by the way," he said. "I'll draw you a diagram someday of all the speakeasy connections, then open the floor for questions."

"A diagram?" Stuart's eyes went round. "What is this, a wife-swapping situation?"

"What? No!"

Stuart's expression turned droll. "Dude, I'm an ex-Mormon and I've studied the teachings of Jacob Smith. I know a-a-a-ll about how sister-wives work."

"Oh, God."

"I'd like to leave God out of this, if you don't mind."

The two of them were still cackling when Kyle and Jesse sauntered up, each bearing a tray upon which a variety of small glasses had been arranged.

"You two sound like chickens with a fresh pan of feed," Kyle said, a broad smile on his face as he set his tray down in front of Malcolm.

Stuart let out another laugh. "That's more accurate than it should be." His dark eyes shone as he glanced from the tray back up to Kyle. His expression shifted when his gaze landed on Jesse.

Jesse, in the meantime, set the tray in his hands down before Stuart and extended a hand. "Jesse Murtagh," he said. "Kyle's business partner and partner-in-crime."

Malcolm had time to notice that Jesse's smile wasn't nearly as bright as usual before Stuart's next words pulled the rug out from under him entirely.

"We've met, right? At The Cathedral?"

"Yep." Now Jesse shared a very different kind of smile with Stuart. The sly humor in it made dread pool in Malcolm's stomach. "I was there with my partner, Cam."

Stuart snapped his fingers. "The redhead, yeah! I remember you both now."

"Oh, get the fuck out," Kyle said with a laugh. He gently elbowed Jesse in the ribs. "Over eight million people in this city. Leave it to you to hire someone you picked up in a gay bar."

Jesse held his hands up as if in surrender. "Hey, I didn't hire anyone. That's on Carter and Maleficent here." His eyes twinkled as he met Malcolm's gaze and, somehow, that made Malcolm feel even worse.

"Holy shit." Stuart's face lit up. "Tell me there's history behind a nickname like that."

"It's too long to be a nickname," Malcolm muttered. "And there isn't any history. Just…Jesse being Jesse."

"That is both a monumental understatement and entirely true. Okay, drinks." Jesse rubbed his hands together and turned his attention onto the trays. "Kyle added a raspberry mule to your flight." He pointed at a glass holding a vibrant fuchsia mix. "He felt bad about not inviting rum to the party."

Kyle snickered. "The fruit and agave should pair well with your food, too, the duck and Brie in particular."

"I like that." Stuart sipped from the glass and flashed a smile at Kyle. "A lot, actually. These will also be great with the zucchini blossoms I'm serving. The acid from the lime and the bite of the ginger beer will balance the ricotta filling very well."

Jesse made a low noise of appreciation. "I'm going to need a preview of both the food and the drinks if you two keep talking like this."

"That may be something I can arrange," Stuart replied.

Malcolm plucked a glass at random from his tray. He barely tasted whatever potion passed between his lips. He didn't much register the conversation washing over him either, though he gathered it centered on how good both Stuart and Kyle were at their respective crafts. No, Malcolm was far too busy thinking about how Stuart knew Jesse and Cam. Through a pickup at a gay bar, no less, because that was how Malcolm's world worked. Hadn't he and Stuart just been talking about the connections among the guys' speakeasy crew? Of course, the one time Malcolm felt real interest in another person, not only would that person be a man, but they'd also know his two most uninhibited friends.

What did you expect? That Stuart would be like you?

Malcolm's insides froze at his own question. He already knew Stuart wasn't like him. Stuart was normal. The man had desires and fell in love and, when pushed hard enough, fought for the life he wanted to live, regardless of the consequences. Stuart was brave and strong and knew what he wanted, just like everyone else, and Malcolm…was a mess.

He didn't know anything about desire or love. He had no idea how to take control of his life. Outside of his job, most days it felt like he'd been set adrift in a boat that was slowly taking on water. But he hid that from his friends and family and lied to nearly all of them every single day. He wouldn't know attraction if it hit him over the head and he had zero concept of how to process the feelings he had about the man sitting beside him.

No, Stuart was nothing like Malcolm, regardless of how badly Malcolm wished otherwise.

"Carter and Malcolm already have that covered."

Malcolm's focus slid back with a jolt that jarred him enough that he almost spilled his drink. Quickly, he set the glass in his hand down and noticed only then that half of the cocktails on his tray were already empty and Kyle had moved off down the bar to attend to another customer.

"Sorry. I lost the thread there for a sec."

Stuart rolled his eyes, his expression teasing. "We were talking about Plan B if the weather goes bad on the night of the event and makes The Over Under impossible."

"Oh, sure. Car and I talked it over with Matt and Kyle," Malcolm said, words coming out of him as if on autopilot. "Under is larger than Lock & Key, which makes it the better choice. People get a kick out of the cloak-and-dagger routine, too, what with the blank doors and secret staircase and all that."

Jesse nodded. "Sex and intrigue always sell."

Malcolm frowned. That wasn't even close to what he'd meant. Before he could say so, Stuart hummed.

"You've got that covered," he said, appreciation plain in his gaze as he cast a look at the space around them. "This place is both beautiful and seductive without even trying. Which I suppose was your goal in the first place."

He tossed an easy grin at Jesse that Jesse instantly returned and Malcolm saw with absolute clarity that they were flirting. The interactions were friendly and subtle and unlike any behavior Stuart had ever shown around Malcolm. Not that Malcolm would have known what to do if Stuart had flirted with him. He didn't have a clue how to do any of this. Which was exactly the reason he had no business wasting Stuart's time, tonight or any night.

Malcolm pushed back his bar stool. "Be back in a minute," he said and got to his feet, his gaze on the floor as he headed toward the restrooms.

However, once he'd reached the doors, Malcolm walked past them and the elevator too, moving toward the fire exit that lay at the back of Under's space and the staircase that sat behind it. He had a hand on the door's push bar when Malcolm felt a touch at his elbow.

"You'll set off the alarm, babe," Jesse said, his voice quiet but firm.

"I know." Malcolm dropped his hands and blew a noisy breath out through his nose. "I wanted some air. I should have used the elevator. I don't know what I was thinking."

"I do." Gently, Jesse guided Malcolm around so they faced one another. "You're thinking something went down between your friend and Cam and me. And you're wrong," he continued, despite Malcolm's headshake, his expression so serious it was almost somber. "Yes, Cam and I met Stuart at a bar and yes, we'd have welcomed the chance to play with him, Cam in particular. Stuart said he wasn't into groups, though, because he'd had an experience go bad with another couple. He told us that as soon as he realized Cam and I were there together."

"Oh." Malcolm knew in his bones that Jesse's candor was one hundred percent real because Jesse didn't lie to anyone. And he felt inexplicably lighter, as if bags of sand that had been trailing behind him had been cut loose. "Okay. I didn't know what to think, I guess. And you didn't have to tell me that, either."

"Yes, I did. I don't want you making any assumptions about the chef out there." The corners of Jesse's mouth twitched upward and humor made his blue eyes gleam. "You know what happens when you assume, don't you, Mal?"

"Yeah, yeah." A low laugh worked its way up into Malcolm's chest, but he refused to say, 'I make an ass out of you and me.'

"You shouldn't make assumptions about Cam, either, because he's a fucking delight," Jesse said. "I understand why you would about me, of course, considering my well-earned reputation as New York's sluttiest playboy."

His wry smile sent a trickle of unease through Malcolm. True, he didn't understand Jesse or Cam's choices. Their attitudes toward monogamy puzzled him and a part of Malcolm wondered how they managed to stay together when both of them so clearly enjoyed finding partners outside of their relationship. Regardless, what Jesse and Cam had together worked. Malcolm loved them both too, and he was as proud as he was happy to count them as friends.

"I don't think those things about you."

"That's because you're a nice man, Malcolm Elliott." Jesse's smile grew wider. "To be clear, I didn't fuck around with your boy."

Malcolm's whole face flamed. "Stuart's not my...boy. We're friends."

Jesse cocked his head and said nothing for a beat. "Okay. I didn't fuck around with your friend, then. I wouldn't even think about it, either, knowing you guys have gotten close. Unless you were both cool with it and, in that case, tally-fucking-ho."

"Understood." Malcolm laughed again. Jesse caring enough to explain the connection to Stuart made his heart ache in a nice way, too. "Thanks, babe. You're a good friend."

"I know this." Jesse reached up and gently smoothed Malcolm's hair back instead of messing it up, then tipped his head back in the direction of the bar. "We should get out there before Stuart starts making assumptions of his own."

Sure enough, Stuart was glowering by the time Malcolm had seated himself again. He had fresh drinks, too, in the form of a regular-sized Paloma for Malcolm and a Moscow Mule for himself, this time served in the traditional copper cup.

"I remembered you like tequila," he said, his gaze flicking to Jesse, who had moved down the bar and stood beside Kyle, the two chatting while they mixed cocktails. "Everything okay?"

"Everything's good," Malcolm replied. "Just hashing out a few things." He ran his fingers over his mouth and the pull inside him pulsed. "Jes told me more about how the two of you met."

Stuart's frown deepened. "Then you know we didn't hook up. I would have told you that if you'd asked me."

"I didn't know how to ask." Malcolm worried his bottom lip between his teeth. "I've never been in a situation like this before."

"What kind of situation is this, exactly?"

"The kind with connections among my old friends and new."

"Except there aren't connections." Everything about Stuart softened, from his expression to his posture to his voice. "I didn't even remember meeting them until Jesse introduced himself tonight."

"I know."

"What's confusing about that? Better yet, what difference would it make if I did have connections with your friends?" Stuart licked his lips, a deep crease forming between his eyebrows as he and Malcolm stared at each other. "Why would it matter to you if Jesse and Cam and I had hooked up?"

"Because then you might compare me to them. To Jes and Cam. To other people." Stuart's soft laugh made the pull in Malcolm ache.

"I wouldn't do that. You're not like other people, Mal."

"I know."

Malcolm turned his attention to his highball glass and he picked it up, eyes burning. God, he needed to get away from this disaster of an evening. However, he realized a second later that Stuart was still talking, and every intention Malcom had of leaving went up in smoke as he listened.

"I like that you're not like everyone else," Stuart said. "That you're...quiet. Reserved, maybe. Also interested in everything. Willing to try new things, too, even when they freak you out."

Malcolm heard the smile in Stuart's voice. "The first time I asked you to get on my bike, I thought for sure you'd turn me down. But you did it. Took the helmet and climbed on the back, even though I could tell you were scared. That was impressive. You had faith I'd get you home in one piece, and we hardly even knew each other."

"I was scared shitless." Malcolm set his glass down, and Stuart's soft laughter warmed him from head to toe. "I came so close to hurling all over the both of us multiple times."

"Oh, God." Stuart's eyes shone with sympathy when Malcolm met his gaze. "Why did you say yes?"

"I didn't want to disappoint you. I just didn't understand that at the time."

Stuart said nothing for a long moment. "You understand it now?"

"I've started to." Malcolm breathed deep and held it. Now or never, the voice in his head whispered, and this time when he spoke, the words flowed out of him as easily as that breath. "I'm interested in you, Stuart, and I have literally no idea how to handle it."

Stuart nodded. He opened his mouth as if to speak, then seemed to think better. He cast a glance toward Kyle and Jesse. "You wanna move to one of the tables?" He showed Malcolm a crooked smile. "Your friends are cool, but I'd rather have this conversation without having to worry about how they'll kick my ass if I say the wrong thing."

"You never say the wrong thing." Malcolm's laugh made Stuart smile wider, though he still looked uncertain. "Kyle and Jes aren't like that, either. But sure, let's grab a couch."

"Is it because I'm a man?" Stuart asked after they'd moved to the seating area located furthest from the bar.

Malcolm didn't need Stuart to clarify his question — he wanted to know why Malcolm had said he didn't know how to handle his interest. Malcolm wasn't sure he had an answer, but he'd try. He owed Stuart that much after the conversation on Staten Island.

"I've only ever been interested in one other man. It was never the same as what I'm feeling for you. Nothing's ever been like this." He sipped his drink and swallowed. "Generally, I don't feel this way about other people."

"Can I ask why?"

"It's the way I'm wired, I think. I'm gray ace and that has an effect on the way I look at other people."

Stuart blinked a couple of times before Malcolm saw the penny drop. "Ace as in asexual?"

"Ace as in asexual, yes, but gray as in the gray area between asexual and sexual. It's who I am. Not one or the other. Somewhere in that spectrum of gray."

It hurt seeing both confusion and pity flicker in Stuart's eyes. *Damn.* This was why Malcolm didn't tell people about this part of himself. To his credit, Stuart merely nodded.

"This is going to sound stupid," he said, "but I don't know what that means, even after your explanation. I... Well, I don't understand asexuality."

Malcolm swallowed down that little thorn. "A lot of people don't. Knowing it's part of who I am is somewhat new for me too, and I'm still learning about what it means to be on that spectrum. I know I'm not entirely asexual. I've had girlfriends and I liked being with them, so it's possible I'm demisexual."

"And what is that?" Stuart ran a hand over his beard, his expression so intent Malcolm had to smile.

"It's when a person only feels attraction after developing a close bond with someone," Malcolm said. "I, um, don't mind sex when I have it and I enjoyed it with my girlfriends. Outside of those relationships, I've never thought about it much."

"Really?"

"Really. Sometimes, I'll meet a person who makes me feel wound up, if you know what I mean. It's a rare thing, though, because I don't typically feel attraction for people." Malcolm licked his lips. "I'm sure this won't make sense to you, but I'd rather hang out with my friends than hook up with a stranger. I don't even know how I'd hook up, assuming I'd want to in the first place."

"It sounds like you don't have sex much, then." The red that flooded Stuart's cheeks made Malcolm smile instead of bristle, particularly when Stuart clapped a hand to his forehead. "Damn, I'm sorry. That was rude as fuck. I don't mean to sound like such a pig."

"Stop it." Without thinking, Malcolm reached up and tugged Stuart's hand from his face and the sensation of warm skin under his fingertips sent a pleasing tingle up his arm. Malcolm's whole body hummed. "You don't sound like a pig. You sound like someone who is trying to understand."

"I really am." Stuart wrapped his hand around Malcolm's and the humming inside Malcolm strengthened. "Look, I'm interested in you, too. More to the point, I like you. As in I'd like to, you know, see if there's something there between us. I'm attracted to you, and the last thing I'd want to do is make you feel pressured or skeeved out." His expression grew earnest so that he looked almost like a young boy instead of the churlish badass Malcolm had come to know.

"I don't feel either of those things," Malcolm said. "Sex doesn't repulse me. I just don't think about it. As in, it doesn't occur to me to think about it. For what it's worth, I like you, too, so trust me when I say I wouldn't be here unless I wanted to be."

"I'm glad to hear it." Stuart glanced down to where their joined hands rested on the couch cushion. "This is okay?"

"Totally okay." Malcolm wound his fingers with Stuart's and nearly shivered as the hum spread. It moved under Malcolm's skin, making him feel loose and light, and like he'd had several drinks though his thoughts were clearer than ever. "I like this."

Stuart wet his lips with his tongue so they shone in the low light, and he smiled. "Good. I like it, too. You'll tell me if you change your mind?"

"I will." Malcolm had to smile, too. "Don't think that'll happen, though. That's how I know this is different."

"Because I'm a guy?"

"No. Because you're you, I think." Malcom frowned. "I told you that I was interested in a man before. So maybe it doesn't matter what gender a person is. Maybe what matters is who they are. And specifically, who they are to me. Is that weird for you?" he asked, then immediately wanted to crawl under the table. "I mean, I'm sure everything about this is weird, given I'm not like other guys you'd meet."

"Mal—"

"I meant is it weird to be interested in a guy who's not explicitly gay? Because I know you're not into women anymore, and outside of being gray ace, I have no idea where my sexuality falls."

"Whoa, slow down." Stuart rubbed his thumb over Malcolm's knuckles and the way he pitched his voice low soothed Malcolm in a way he couldn't describe. "I'm not sure it'd be truthful for me to say I'm explicitly gay. I definitely prefer men, but I was married to a woman, and at the time, I didn't mind it. So, maybe that makes me closer to bi. I've been with bisexual men since coming out, too, and it never made a difference to me."

Stuart pursed his lips. "I haven't known anyone who told me they were ace. I don't know how to be with someone like that. As in dating, if you wanted something like that."

"Would you want to?" Malcolm asked, his voice hushed. "Date someone like me, I mean?"

"Yes, I would. Frankly, I've been wondering if we weren't already doing that." Stuart frowned. "What's with the face? You look like your brain is about to catch fire."

"That might be accurate." Malcom huffed out a laugh. "Given what I've told you, I'm having trouble imagining you'd want to go out with me."

"Why, because you're not into sex?"

"Well, yeah. I'm not, you know, like guys you've been with."

"I think we covered that already." While Stuart's voice held a teasing note, his expression was kind and his touch steady. He shifted closer and the scent of wood and leather filled Malcolm's nose. "Yes, I've had sex with a lot of guys and enjoyed it. I didn't like even one of those guys as much as I've come to like you in the short time we've known each other. It's fine if you're not sure about me yet, too, because I'll still be your friend."

"Okay." Malcolm smiled. "I'm sure about you though. Sure we're friends, anyway. I've never told anyone I'm on the ace spectrum before. Carter's the only other person who knows."

Stuart's eyes widened. "No shit?"

"No shit. And I'm sure I'd like more with you. Dating, I mean. I'm just not sure where to go from here."

"That makes two of us," Stuart said. "A fact I'm surprisingly okay with. That works, right? Ain't no rules that say we can't make it up as we go."

Malcolm let out an exaggerated sigh. "Well, that's just typical."

He relished the laugh his teasing got and the way Stuart looked more relaxed than he had all night. What's more, Stuart didn't let go of Malcolm's hand and Malcolm liked that fine.

Chapter Eight

'I'm gray ace.'

The words echoed in Stuart's ears as he diced red onions. It was the morning of the CEC event. His staff had the prep work under control and had seemed confused when he'd said he was going to help.

Stuart doing prep cook work was completely unnecessary, but mindless cooking tasks had always helped clear his head. He found it meditative. Right now, his brain could use all the help it could get.

Ever since his conversation with Malcolm the other night, his mind had been whirling with the news Malcolm had given him. No question about it, he was thrilled Malcolm was interested in dating him. Despite Stuart's bold words stating that they could make things up as they went along, he felt anything but bold right now.

He wanted to date Malcolm. He simply had no idea how to.

Stuart had gone home that night and pored for hours through online articles and websites about gray asexuality and demisexuality. Unfortunately, they had left him more confused than ever. The only thing that was clear from his research was that the experience of being gray ace varied wildly from person to person.

Which of course made sense, but it would have been nice to have something more concrete to work with. How was he supposed to know what to do and say so he didn't fuck it up?

Thankfully, Malcolm hadn't seemed offended when he'd said, '*It sounds like you don't have sex much,*' but Stuart had regretted the words as soon as they'd left his mouth. What had he been thinking? Malcolm had been telling him that it wasn't all about sex to him and what had Stuart done? Made it all about sex.

Stuart couldn't deny he was relieved that Malcolm didn't find sex repulsive. Because Stuart wasn't sure he could date someone who did. And that made him feel like a pig despite Malcolm's reassurances that he wasn't one.

"What did that onion ever do to you?"

Stuart turned to see Marisol staring at him with an amused expression. He glanced down at the cutting board to see that the onion had gone way past a fine dice and even past minced. It was practically a paste. "Shit."

Although muscle memory had kept his fingers out from under the blade, he admitted he shouldn't be working with knives while he was thinking about this situation with Malcolm. With a sigh, he scraped the mangled onion into the bin, then placed his knife and board near the sink to be washed.

"You need to talk?" Marisol said with a pointed glance. Dressed in street clothes and with her hair down, she looked less serious and businesslike than when she was on the clock. Her expression spelled out how serious she was right now.

Stuart sighed. "If you've got the time."

"Get your ass to my office and we'll straighten whatever this is out." She turned and left the kitchen without another word, which was just as well. There was no arguing with Marisol when she started ordering him around.

Stuart glanced at the man across the line from him. "James?"

The *garde manger* chef glanced up from his own prep work.

"Someone's going to need to dice more red onion because I decimated mine. I'll be in Marisol's office if you need anything, but I'll be ready to leave in an hour, like we discussed earlier."

"Yes, Chef."

Marisol was seated at her desk when he walked through her door and shut it behind him. She had two glasses of rye whiskey set out. This wasn't the first heart-to-heart over a drink they'd shared throughout the years, though they didn't typically take place at this hour of the day.

"What's up with the onion paste?" she asked after they'd clinked glasses.

Stuart chuckled into his drink. Marisol was a whiz with a knife, but she wasn't one to mince words. "I've got a lot on my mind."

"I'd worked that much out. Guy trouble?"

"Yes?"

"You don't sound too sure about that. Is it that you're not sure if he's a guy or you're not sure if he's trouble?"

"Malcolm is definitely a guy."

She raised an eyebrow. "Malcolm. He's the guy from CEC you've been dealing with, right?"

"Yeah. We've been... Well, we've been getting to know each other outside of planning for the event."

"And by getting to know each other you mean you've been having copious amounts of sex?"

"Ah, no. The confusion comes in there."

"Stuart." She leveled him with a look. "Am I going to have to keep dragging answers out of you or are you going to tell me what's transpired between you two?"

Stuart didn't know why he was having such difficulty getting it all out. Marisol knew the dark, ugly side of his past with Becky—she was the only person he'd ever told about his lingerie kink outside of a few men he'd dated—and Stuart was damn sure he could trust her. So, he took a deep breath and let it all spill out. The dates that he wasn't sure were dates. The trip out to Staten Island to help rebuild Kim's steps. Telling Malcolm about his past. Malcolm telling him about his sexuality.

Marisol sat back with a frown when he was done. Marisol's wife was transgender, and over the years, Stuart and Marisol had discussed how complex sexual and gender identities could be and the various complications they could add to relationships. At least to his knowledge, neither Marisol nor Stuart had been involved with someone who was ace or demisexual before.

"Okay. Well, does it change how you feel about him?" she asked.

"No! Not at all. Actually, it helps me understand him a lot better. I'm a sexual guy though. I've had way more sexual encounters in my life than long-term relationships, and now I feel like I have no idea what I could offer Malcolm. If Malcolm's confused about how he feels about sex, the natural solution would be for me to help guide him, right? But how? How can I guide Malcolm if I have no idea how to do it? I'm completely out of my league."

She hummed. "I can see why that might be overwhelming."

"The last time I had a relationship that didn't begin with sex was with Becky!" he continued. "Ever since, I've used sex as a way to connect to people. With Malcolm, it would be the other way around. And I'm totally floundering, trying to figure out how to move forward. I also worry that I won't get it right. I want to be able to give him what he needs and go slow and be patient as we figure this out, but I'm afraid I'm going to fuck it all up," he admitted. He took another sip of his drink, enjoying the smooth, dark honey notes in it. Focusing on the flavors kept his panic from rising any higher.

Marisol snorted. "You probably are."

He gave her a sour look. "Thanks for the vote of confidence."

"I'm just saying there are no guarantees in dating," she said with a shrug. "No one ever gets it right all of the time."

"This feels bigger than usual."

"Because you've never dated someone who is on the ace spectrum before or because Malcolm matters more to you than anyone else has before?"

Stuart froze with his glass halfway to his lips as her words hit home. "Both? I think?"

She smiled at him. "Maybe you'd better think hard about that second part for a while. It seems to me that's what has your head spinning."

"You're probably right about that."

"Just...don't chop any onions while you're thinking, okay? I can't have a fingerless sous chef. That would be bad for business."

He smiled. Marisol wasn't the warm fuzzy type. From her, that was practically a declaration of her affection. A listening ear, some choice words of advice and a drink topped off with a dollop of tough love were her flavor of friendship. Stuart valued it all.

"Thanks for the drink and the talk," he said as he stood.

"Any time." She grinned up at him. "Now, go knock the donors' socks off at this event. Wow 'em with the old Stuart Morgan charm and bring them into my restaurant after they write fat checks to CEC."

Stuart laughed. "Yes, Chef."

* * * *

"Watch the serving trays like a hawk all night," Stuart instructed the servers. "Don't wait until one is two-thirds empty to refill it. I want them full at all times. We're going for abundance here. The booze will be flowing and the food should be equally generous. Anything leftover will be going straight to a food pantry, so we went a little heavy on ordering and we don't have to worry about anything going to waste. Understood?"

"Yes, Chef," everyone chorused.

"I know there are some new faces here, so, King's people, be mindful of the staff from Lock & Key and vice versa. We need you working together. If you have a question about anything, don't hesitate to ask James or me. James will run the line tonight so he's your point of contact down here. I'll be at the event talking up the food and, with luck, helping people decide to donate generously, so I'm your point of contact up there." He pointed upward, indicating the rooftop. "The hallways that lead to the staff elevator are tight, so be mindful as you pass each other, especially when you're carrying full trays. I don't want any collisions. If you're watching the trays and reacting early, you won't need to rush, okay?"

"Yes, Chef."

"Does anyone have any questions?"

Everyone shook their head and he heard a few "No, Chefs."

"All right." He smiled at the people in front of him. "Now, I hope you're all excited about tonight. This is going to be a great event."

"Yes, Chef!"

The servers scattered to relax for a few minutes before the event got underway. Stuart looked around and saw Malcolm leaning in the doorway, watching him with a soft smile. Stuart walked over to him, drinking in the sight of Malcolm in a tux. Malcolm had been dressed casually and occupied with a florist when Stuart and his staff arrived. He'd checked in to make sure Stuart had everything he needed, and he must have changed at some point since then.

"Wow," Stuart said quietly. "You look..." He reached out and squeezed Malcolm's upper arm. "Just wow." He wanted to touch Malcolm a whole lot more, but he didn't want to come on too strong. *Let Malcolm lead when it comes to physical affection,* he reminded himself.

Malcolm's smile was bashful and pleased. "Wow yourself. I like seeing you like this."

Stuart glanced down. "Like this? Didn't you see me in my uniform when we met at the restaurant?"

"I meant in charge," Malcolm said. He looked down and swallowed. "It was interesting seeing you in your element, taking charge of the staff, all that."

"Yeah?" Stuart smiled. So Malcolm liked it when he got bossy? Stuart was totally okay with that. It offered up a lot of interesting possibilities when they did decide to explore things in the bedroom. "Good to know."

Several hours later, Stuart surveyed the crowd with a pleased look. The fundraiser was in full swing and going beautifully. The weather had cooperated and the unseasonably oppressive heat of the past few weeks had mellowed to give them a pleasant early summer evening.

The French bistro feel of the black-and-white tiled floor, wrought-iron chairs and glass-topped tables were as beautiful as the evening Stuart had first seen The Over Under. The glow of the lamps and backlit bar had been augmented by strings of lights and candles and it all shone rich and warm against the dark night. The rooftop felt both spacious and cozy for mingling, exactly what they'd all been aiming for.

Malcolm and Stuart had agreed on a mix of buffet and passed hors d'oeuvres. While the word "buffet" conjured up images of bland, watery food in chafing dishes, this was as far from kept lukewarm and boring as possible. It was downright spectacular. Stuart's chest filled with pride as he looked over his contribution to the evening.

A banquet table held cheese, charcuterie, olives, mustards, breads and crackers, along with grapes, Marcona almonds and membrillo — a Spanish quince paste—that offered just the right amount of sweetness to offset the saltiness of the cheeses and cured meats. People could help themselves and snack as they perused the tables set up for the silent auction.

Black-clothed servers strolled the area, offering bites of food and, of course, Kyle's incredible cocktails flowed freely and complemented every bite. Outside of King's, it was rare Stuart had the opportunity to work with a bartender who was every bit as meticulous and committed to quality as he, and he welcomed this collaboration. Stuart suspected this could be the first of many between Kyle and himself, not to mention the CEC.

"I didn't think I liked oysters," a handsome blond man in a well-fitting tux said. He laid a hand on Stuart's arm. "But you've made a convert out of me. Who would have thought to grill them?"

A chef? Stuart thought. He put on a pleasant smile. "I think one of the best parts about my job is introducing people to new things."

The man traced his fingers lightly across Stuart's arm. "Are there other things outside of the kitchen you like to explore?"

"Yes," Stuart said. His gaze traveled to Malcolm, who stood twenty feet away, talking to an older couple. "These days, the exploring I do outside the kitchen is with the man I'm seeing."

"Pity." The man's fingers slid away from Stuart's arm, though he didn't look upset.

While Malcolm and Stuart hadn't set out any explicit rules yet about seeing other people, Malcolm's reaction to what he'd thought was Stuart's involvement with Jesse Murtagh and his partner had left no doubt as to where Malcolm stood on the idea of open relationships.

Stuart agreed. He had tried group sex a few times, and it had done little for him. He preferred to focus on one person at a time, and he didn't have any desire to share someone he cared for with anyone else. He cared about Malcolm already, and he had a feeling that if he and Malcolm could figure out how to navigate the physical side of their relationship, this was going to be major for both of them.

Stuart didn't want to fuck that up, much less with someone he'd barely exchanged a dozen sentences with.

The gentle clinking of flatware on a glass turned everyone's attention to the small stage area set up where Carter Hamilton stood in front of a microphone.

"Thank you all for coming tonight," he said. "We're about to begin the speech portion of the evening so I hope you've fortified yourself with one of the delicious drinks we have available."

The crowd tittered. Carter seemed wholly at ease in front of them. He wore his tuxedo like a second skin, and Stuart could see his partner, Riley, at the edge of the crowd. Even from a distance, his affection for his fiancé was palpable. Stuart had rarely seen couples with a connection like that, and it gave him hope that someday he'd find it for himself.

Once again, his gaze landed on Malcolm.

Maybe he had met someone with whom he'd be able to create that kind of relationship. Carter and Riley had been through some extraordinary challenges to be together. Surely, Stuart and Malcolm could manage to navigate the unknown territory of Malcolm being gray ace.

As if he'd sensed Stuart's gaze, Malcolm turned his head. He looked seriously at Stuart for a few seconds before a bright smile bloomed across his face. Stuart's heart stuttered in his chest, and he thought then and there that no matter how long it took, or how difficult things might get, he and Malcolm would make this work.

Because he wanted to see a whole lot more of that smile in his future.

After a moment, Malcolm looked away and Stuart turned his attention to Carter again.

"I would be remiss if I didn't acknowledge some of the wonderful people who partnered with us to make tonight a success. First, our thanks to Jesse Murtagh, Kyle McKee and Matt O'Hearn for the use of this incredible space. Kyle is also the genius behind those delicious drinks you're enjoying."

Jesse looked like he was drinking in the accolades as everyone clapped while Kyle and Matt simply waved.

"Stuart Morgan of King's in Tribeca provided this marvelous food and we feel very lucky he was able to step in on short notice to help us out."

Stuart raised a hand and acknowledged the applause with a smile.

"And last, but not at all least, we have Malcolm Elliott, our Social Organizer here at CEC. Without him, events like tonight wouldn't happen and I think we can all agree that would be a terrible shame. So please, a big round of applause for Malcolm."

Malcolm ducked his head a little but waved, too. Stuart applauded louder than anyone and if he hadn't known it would embarrass Malcolm, he would have put his fingers in his mouth and whistled. After the applause had died down, Carter continued.

"May seventeenth is International Day Against Homophobia, Transphobia and Biphobia to raise awareness of anti-LGBT violence and repression worldwide. While this alone would be enough of a reason to hold this event now, as many of you know, advocating for the LGBTQIA workforce in corporate environments is a very personal cause for me as well. For many people in our community, coming out can have drastic repercussions for our careers.

"CEC's goal is to ensure that all people – regardless of gender identity or sexual orientation – have equitable treatment in the workforce!"

The crowd cheered and Carter waited for the noise to die down before he continued.

"Following last year's historic victory for marriage equality, corporate America is making strides in equality for the LGBTQIA community. Workplace discrimination protections are becoming more commonplace in the business world, and unfortunately, the federal and many state governments lag behind in addressing discrimination against LGBTQIA workers.

"The Corporate Equality Index was launched in 2002 to assess LGBTQIA-inclusive policies and practices at Fortune 500 companies and I'm pleased to announce that, in recent years, record numbers of businesses have earned top scores. Companies looking to recruit and retain top employees and maintain and grow their market share has resulted in the improved lives of millions of LGBTQIA Americans.

"In its inaugural year, only thirteen businesses earned a one hundred percent score. In 2013, a record two-hundred-plus businesses achieved the top rating and the distinction of being the 'Best Places to Work for LGBTQIA Equality.'"

Another, even louder, cheer rose from the crowd.

"We're here today because we're committed to making sure that every last company reaches that top rating, and we need your help to do it." Carter grinned and gestured to the handsome man at his side. "I'd like to turn the floor over to New York State Senator David Mori. Please give him a warm welcome."

Carter and David shook hands before the senator took Carter's place at the microphone.

"Thank you for joining us this evening," David said. "As Carter said, I am a New York State Senator and Japanese-American. What some of you may not know is that I'm a Republican."

The crowd went very quiet and Stuart had to stifle a laugh. Although the interactions he'd had with David Mori had been very positive, Stuart was still trying to wrap his brain around a gay Republican senator.

Stuart liked the man. He just didn't understand his position.

David raised a hand. "I know, I know, that doesn't endear me to a lot of people in the LGBTQIA community. I'm working to change that. I'm committed to reaching across the aisle and working with senators of all political affiliations to enact change. Unfortunately, in the political world, that can mean progress is slow. While I and others work to bring about those desperately needed changes to laws, we need you to help organizations like Corporate Equality Campaign raise funds to support their portion of the fight.

"By purchasing a ticket to this event tonight, you've already taken the first step. We have two other ways you can contribute as well. A generous donation to CEC is one. Another is to enter our silent auction. Numerous companies have made donations to tonight's auction to help ensure its success and now it's your turn to step in."

Stuart felt a touch on his elbow and turned to find one of the servers from King's at his side. "What is it, Nicole?" he asked softly.

"We've got a problem. James asked for you to come down."

Stuart nodded. If James didn't want to handle a problem on his own, that meant it was big.

Maybe one of the breakers had blown in the middle of the food prep. It wouldn't have been the first time that had happened. It could be something as innocuous as someone knocking over a tray of prepared food or prepped ingredients. Unless they were forced to change what was being served because of the loss, James could handle that.

"What is it?" Stuart asked her once they'd reached the hallway. "Breakers?"

"Not this time." Nicole had been serving with him the last time they'd had power issues. "One of the Lock & Key people bumped into the big glass tiered tray we'd set up for the dessert display. It's in about ten million pieces on the kitchen floor right now."

Stuart groaned. The tiered stand was the centerpiece of their dessert offerings. "Fuck."

"Desserts are nearly assembled, but we have nothing to display them on."

Stuart glanced at his watch. There wasn't time to go out and get something else. He'd have to see what Lock & Key had on hand. The pub wasn't an upscale place so he wasn't sure they'd have anything that would be cohesive with the style of the event. If that was the case, he'd improvise and make it work somehow. This certainly wasn't the first disaster Stuart had overcome.

It wasn't until he and Nicole had reached the kitchen that an idea popped into Stuart's head. Under. Its vibe jibed more closely with the party. And while they didn't serve food, he knew Kyle was a huge proponent of presentation and might have something they could use without the guests being any the wiser.

Stuart turned to Nicole. "Do you know who Kyle McKee is?" She shook her head. "Tall guy, black hair, very pale. He's in a tux since he's not an official bartender tonight. I need you to go upstairs and find him. If you aren't sure who he is or can't find him, check with one of the bartenders. Tell Kyle I need him to come down here as soon as possible."

"Yes, Chef," Nicole said. She turned and made a beeline toward the elevator again while Stuart headed into the kitchen.

The moment he stepped inside, he zeroed in on the culprit, a skinny young guy named Greg. Based on the tortured look on his face as he swept up glass, he would have rather stuck his head in the dishwater. Greg glanced up and froze when Stuart approached him.

"I am so sorry, Chef," he babbled. "I didn't realize it was behind me and I turned too fast and—I'm gonna pay for it, I swear. You can take it out of my wages for tonight and—"

Stuart gripped Greg's shoulders to quiet him and noticed then that the poor kid looked terrified. Realizing he'd been glowering, he tried to relax his expression. When the boss for the night was a big, bearded, tattooed guy, it was probably intimidating as hell seeing him look angry.

Greg had no idea what the display cost—far more than he'd earned tonight, that was for sure—but Stuart wasn't about to charge him for it. Accidents happened in kitchens. If everyone still had all their digits and no one had to be rushed to a hospital, he'd count that as a win.

He kept his tone soft. "Greg, I don't care right now. I really don't. My priority is finding a way to display the desserts. Just get the glass cleaned up, please." Stuart stepped back. "We don't need any more accidents tonight."

He turned to James. "What are our options?"

"I checked around—nothing they've got down here will look right," James said with a frown. "We could maybe bring some of the wooden cheese boards down and get them washed."

"I don't love it, but they'll have to do if there's nothing else." Stuart jerked his thumb at one of King's servers. "Johanna, you go take care of that. Nicole is finding Kyle—the owner of the speakeasy downstairs—to see if he's got something."

"I'm here," Kyle said from behind Stuart. "You need serving trays?"

Stuart faced him. "Yes, for the desserts. They can't look out of place with our other food displays."

Kyle hummed. "I've got a couple of slate boards. Would that work?"

"Sounds like it might."

"Why don't you come downstairs with me? I don't have a lot of options, but if you see anything else you'd prefer, grab it."

"Perfect. Thank you," Stuart said, already on the move. "Let's see what you've got."

* * * *

Stuart glanced at his watch as he slipped back into the crowd to mingle. Kyle's slate boards had worked nicely with the rest of the displays and Nicole and Johanna were setting out the desserts. *Right in the nick of time, too.*

Squaring his shoulders, Stuart took another breath, this time slower and deeper. He'd done it. There was always a surge of adrenaline after a near disaster and it would take him a few minutes to come down.

The party had continued without any other issues. A small four-person band had begun performing while he'd been gone and while Stuart didn't recognize the song playing, its beat made him want to move. He saw dozens of people on the dance floor and he wondered idly if Malcolm enjoyed dancing.

He'd have to find out. The thought put a smile on his face as he got swept up in conversation again.

As the evening continued, the drinks flowed, the food was gobbled up and donation after donation was placed. Several times, Stuart caught Malcolm's glance across the room. On every occasion, Malcolm smiled and Stuart knew no matter what they had to get through to figure out how to be together, it would be worth it.

* * * *

After the last of the partygoers left The Over Under, the staff began to clear away the remnants of the party. The speakeasy crew hung back, of course, as well as the teams of organizers from the CEC, and everyone looked tired but pleased. Stuart watched Carter lean on Riley, and he caught a glimpse of the senator kissing his boyfriend, Will. They were an interesting group, that was for damn sure. Rich, yes. Certainly not the idle rich, however. These men worked hard to spread good in the world.

Then Malcolm rounded the bar, his face glowing as Stuart crossed the space to meet him.

"That couldn't have gone any better," Malcolm said when they were face-to-face. "The donations went far beyond what we'd hoped for and everyone raved about the party. They loved the venue, they loved the drinks and they really loved your food."

"Yep. We nailed it!" Stuart swept Malcolm up into a tight hug, pulling him up off his feet for a moment before lowering him to the ground again. It wasn't until their bodies were pressed together full-length that Stuart froze, realizing he'd crossed a boundary he shouldn't.

"I'm sorry," he croaked. "I was going to leave all physical contact up to you and…" He dropped his arms but Malcolm didn't. His grip remained tight around Stuart's body.

"You don't have to apologize." Malcolm's voice sounded rough. Stuart tipped his head back to look at him. "You don't have to stop touching me, either. I like this."

"You sure?" Stuart asked.

Malcolm nodded once. His eyes were still shining blue and filled with trust. Stuart carefully wrapped his arms around Malcolm again, snug, yet easy enough for Malcolm to shake off if he wanted. The air between them was charged with tension and Malcolm's gaze filled with something Stuart hadn't seen before.

"Do you wanna—" Malcolm cleared his throat. "Could we go back to your place tonight? If you don't have other plans, I mean."

Stuart blinked at him.

"I, um, would like to spend time with you tonight. Alone." Malcolm licked his lips. "Not for sex. Obviously. But maybe—"

Stuart held a finger in front of Malcolm's lips. "I'm happy with whatever you want to do. We'll go back to my place and if all we do is hold hands, it'll be perfect, okay?"

The grin that lit Malcolm's face was even brighter than the one he'd worn a few minutes before.

And that made Stuart happier than he'd been in a long time.

Chapter Nine

Clad in a borrowed leather jacket, Malcolm felt buzzed by the time he climbed on the back of Stuart's bike. This time, he couldn't blame Kyle's drinks. He'd sampled a couple of cocktails as the party had progressed, of course, just like he'd tasted the food, and every single thing had been delicious. He'd wanted to keep a clear head, though, and not only because he'd been working. He simply hadn't wanted to miss a minute of watching the magic of everyone's hard work come together.

Matt from Lock & Key with Stuart and Kyle, all three operating with cool precision and none of their usual bluster. The donors talking and laughing under the evening sky. Jesse and David in their element, surrounded by admirers. The satisfaction in Carter's expression. And Stuart, who repeatedly caught Malcolm's eye across the crowded rooftop and flashed a grin that made the rest of the world blur out of focus.

Not that Stuart needed to do anything special to get Malcolm's attention. He almost shone under Malcolm's gaze, his colors more vibrant than anyone else's and his motions broader, even when he was standing still. Stuart's voice sounded clearer to Malcolm's ears, too, as if he were speaking more loudly when, really, he wasn't. The pull Malcolm felt toward him had become impossible to ignore. Malcolm couldn't get enough of it, either.

The buzz prickled his skin as Stuart laid a hand on his shoulder.

"You good?" Stuart asked, his voice muffled by the motorcycle helmet. His dark eyes danced when Malcolm glanced his way, and the corners crinkled at Malcolm's thumbs-up.

"Yep."

Together, they moved the helmet visors into place and Malcolm didn't hesitate to reach for Stuart once he'd settled behind the handlebars. Some impulse made Malcolm slide his arms around Stuart's waist instead of his chest this time, and he could tell right away that Stuart liked that. He patted Malcolm's hands where they linked over Stuart's belly, the touch lingering before he hit the ignition.

Malcolm actually enjoyed riding with Stuart. He liked the deep thrum of the motor's engine and the gloss the city lights took on through the helmet's visor. The smell and feel of Stuart's leathers. The solid warmth of his body and his total command of the big machine. Malcolm felt safe on the back of the Suzuki, a feeling he wouldn't have guessed at in a million years.

He tuned out a little as Stuart steered them onto 9A, and the stress of the evening caught up with him as they sped along the Hudson River. Fundraising events were always tiring, even when everything went off as beautifully as they had tonight. Malcolm had struggled to focus when Carter had gathered everyone and thanked the teams for their hard work and the closeout activities had passed in a blur, Malcolm performing the duties on his checklist by rote.

Several times, Carter had seemed about to speak. He always made time after events for Malcolm, but he'd been oddly quiet tonight, as if he'd sensed Malcolm wasn't in the mood to chat beyond the tasks at hand. The rest of the speakeasy crew must have noticed, too, because not one of them blinked after Malcolm had turned down their offer for post-party cocktails and instead simply bade him goodnight.

Maybe because they saw you hugging Stuart like a stuffed animal you won at the fair.

Malcolm closed his eyes. *Right.* He'd done that. Hugged the chef he'd hired, in front of all his friends. Laughed when Stuart had managed to pick him up. At the time, Malcolm hadn't thought a thing about the hug, either. He couldn't think straight when Stuart touched him, the sensations so strong and pure he literally forgot how unusual those touches might look to anyone else.

No wonder Carter and the others had let him go without a fuss.

He scooted closer to Stuart on the seat, seeking warmth, and the tension of being switched 'on' for so many hours gradually faded, leaving his eyelids heavy. His teams had been on the go all day, tending to a hundred little details that went unseen by everyone else, and Malcolm had been so eager to get Stuart alone tonight, he hadn't given either of them even a minute to unwind.

We should have stayed and fueled up. 'Cause if I'm this tired, isn't Stuart, too?

A tap on Malcom's knee broke through his haze of drifting thoughts. He blinked once, then again when he saw a sign for the Lincoln Tunnel, aware that meant they were already at Midtown but...how could that be? He'd have noticed traveling over five miles, right? Then again, he hadn't noticed setting his head against Stuart's shoulder or pressing so close his entire torso had molded to Stuart's back.

Stuart tapped Malcolm's knee again, the motion more insistent, and Malcolm could practically feel his concern. He straightened up, careful to keep his motions fluid and easy as Stuart had instructed, then squeezed Stuart's waist gently. Stuart moved his hand to Malcolm's and he patted, asking without words how Malcolm was doing.

Okay, Malcolm told him with a thumbs-up. *Except for the part where I might have dozed off on the back of a death machine going forty miles an hour.*

Part of Malcolm cringed. Another, larger, part of him didn't care. It maybe even liked the idea of curling up for a nap while the road dropped away because Stuart was driving and Malcolm felt safe perched behind him.

His head grew muzzy again over the next couple of miles. He forced himself to stay upright instead of drooping forward. When he caught sight of a sign for Canal Street and Stuart guided them off the highway, he knew he'd drifted once more. Traffic signals made the last leg of the journey more stop and go, which also made it easier for Malcolm to stay alert, helped along by Stuart's hand on his each time the bike came to a stop.

"When's the last time you ate?" Stuart asked even before he'd pulled his helmet off. They'd lucked out with a parking space not far from his apartment, and he held up a hand when Malcolm moved to climb off the bike. "Sit there for a sec and get your head together while I lock up the bike."

Malcolm slid his helmet up and off. "I'm just tired."

"Uh-huh, and avoiding answering my question, too. When was the last time you ate, Malcolm?"

"Breakfast," Malcolm replied. "Carter picked up bagels and lox before we met up this morning. We got busy getting everything uptown and set up, and we didn't have time for anything except snacks after that. I ate a lobster roll and some of your ceviche during the party, though. Oh, zucchini blossoms, too. You should make those for every party you work."

That put a grin on Stuart's face. He paused in the act of weaving one of the heavy chains he carried through the bike's front wheel. "You liked?"

"They were phenomenal." Malcolm smiled. "Unfortunately, I didn't get to the oysters."

Stuart tsked. "Too bad," he said. He walked around to the back wheel with the second chain. "Good thing the chef always sets aside portions as a treat."

"Look how smart you are." Malcolm liked the way smug looked on Stuart's strong features. "Now, can I stand up or are we still acting like I'm some Victorian damsel about to swoon?"

"Sure, you can stand. There's not enough room under the bike cover for you anyway. C'mon upstairs and have a bite, and we can talk about where you're gonna crash tonight."

Malcolm held on to their bags and the sack of food Stuart produced from one of the panniers, and they chatted as he drew the bike's black cover tight. Stuart kept up the mother-hen routine once they were inside his apartment, his fussing made all the more amusing when he peeled off his jacket and put on an ancient-looking AC/DC T-shirt so that his inked sleeves were on full display. He allowed Malcolm to open a bottle of wine and pour out two glasses, then shooed him out of the kitchen so he could work on the food.

Though no longer sleepy, Malcolm was weary and he retreated without argument with his drink to the side of the room that held Stuart's bed. Setting the glass on the nightstand, he'd raised his hands to his jacket's collar when his phone buzzed, and the message he found from Carter on the screen made him smile.

Everything about our success tonight comes down to you. Thank you, Mal.

You're welcome, he replied. *Thanks for making this a job I love.*

Malcolm's heart panged. He did love his job. Working for Corporate Equality Campaign made him feel fulfilled in ways he hadn't when he'd been employed in the private sector. Carter's unwavering support was a bonus, too. Especially tonight, when so many of the people they loved had been there to share in Malcolm's success. He should have stayed for at least one drink. Long enough to give Carter the chance to say thank you in person, at least. Maybe to field a question or two about Stuart because the guys had to be curious about what was going on, even if none of them had made a peep.

Things were going to get interesting the next time Malcolm saw the crew, that was for sure. He'd lit out of The Over Under without even bothering to change his clothes. And that realization sent a creaky-sounding laugh through him as he pulled off his jacket.

"What's funny?" Stuart asked.

"Just fully realizing what kind of picture you and I must have made on the way back here tonight." Malcolm snickered again. "I'm in a tuxedo and a biker jacket, for crying out loud, bow tie and all. Plus you in your leathers, and the both of us on that beast of a bike? We probably looked like extras in an action movie."

Stuart belted out a laugh. "We might have if you hadn't fucking dozed off. I still can't believe that happened!"

"I can't either." Malcolm ran a hand over his head, realizing only then that it was mussed from wearing the helmet. *Jeez.* "I don't know what to say."

"Well, you're tired and I get that. I've heard of passengers falling asleep, but it's never happened when I've been driving before tonight." Stuart carried his wine and a platter heaped with food to the bed, then set the glass on the nightstand. "I thought you were just chilling at first, and then you went sort of heavy against my back—I knew something was off."

"I'm sorry."

"I'm sorry, too." He sat across from Malcolm, lips pursed, and placed the platter on the bed between them. "I should have known better than to let you climb on before we ate. Not sure I trust you to make it home in a Lyft without passing out." He didn't smile when Malcolm barked out a laugh.

"I'm not sure I trust myself, either."

"So stay. For a while or the night, whatever you need." Stuart shrugged and picked up a profiterole, then held it to Malcolm's lips. "Eat." His eyes didn't leave Malcolm's until the food was in Malcolm's mouth.

The air between them crackled with unspoken words, though the silence wasn't heavy. As Malcolm chewed, Stuart wiped his hands on a napkin, then busied himself with Malcolm's tie, his fingers nimble. He set the tie on the mattress by the platter and unbuttoned Malcolm's collar, then scooped up an oyster after Malcolm had swallowed.

"Ideally, these would be warm," he said, voice low, "and served with one of Kyle's cocktails. I think we're both hungry enough not to care either way."

Malcolm battled back a groan as the taste of sea and butter and charred herbs exploded over his tongue. "Tastes amazing," he mumbled, too close to blissed-out to care about talking with his mouth full. He didn't hesitate to pluck a piece of bruschetta from the platter and hold it up for Stuart, and the gleam in Stuart's eyes as he took the bread with his teeth made Malcolm shiver.

They fed each other bite by bite, stopping often for wine and to talk about what they were tasting or just hold hands. The more they touched, the stronger the energy between them buzzed, settling warm and low in Malcolm's belly. He felt dizzy with it by the time they stood to clean up their feast. His nerves kicked up when Stuart mentioned wanting a shower, though, and Malcolm retreated to the bathroom with his garment bag.

Eyes on his reflection in the mirror, he listened to the muffled hiss of the shower. What the heck was he doing? Better yet, why was he hiding?

Stuart had said he didn't expect anything physical tonight and Malcolm knew he'd meant it. Except…now

Malcolm wanted to do more than hold hands. He was ready for that. But what exactly? Malcolm was out of practice dating in the first place, much less dating a man, so how would he know if anything he did was right?

Those fretful thoughts raced around his head as he changed into the T-shirt and joggers he'd worn prior to the party. Leaving now would be so easy. Stuart wouldn't stop him, not if Malcolm made an excuse that he was too tired for more talking. They could touch base tomorrow and maybe make plans for another hike, provided Stuart had time for Malcolm now that the fundraiser was over.

Ugh.

Malcolm stopped himself in the act of reaching for his running shoes. He hated feeling uncertain. He hated hiding even more and he really was so tired. He and Stuart deserved some much-needed rest and that meant Malcolm had to make a choice—did he stay or did he go?

The sound of the shower cut off.

Everything in Malcolm told him to stay. He owed Stuart more than a brush-off. He owed it to himself to stop looking for answers here in this tiny bathroom, too, because they weren't coming, no matter how hard Malcolm stared at himself in the mirror. So he hung the garment bag on a hook, counted backward from thirty, then opened the bathroom door.

He could smell the woody notes of Stuart's shower gel clear across the room, and the gladness in his expression eased Malcolm's nerves at once. Stuart's hair was damp and surprisingly curly, and he wore a pair of black-framed eyeglasses Malcolm hadn't seen before. Stuart had also donned a threadbare white tank with a pair of gray jersey shorts, both of which looked wonderfully soft. They showcased his tattoos, too, and for the first time, Malcolm understood that trails of ink snaked around the muscles of Stuart's right thigh and covered his left leg from ankle to knee.

"Oh," Malcolm said, his voice barely a breath. "I had no idea."

Stuart glanced down at himself. "Not sure I mentioned the…southern ink when we were hiking in Jersey." Despite his chuckle, a flush colored the tips of his ears. That rosy glow made Malcolm's insides wobble, as did the sight of Stuart's bare toes.

The tough guy chef was feeling exposed. Maybe uncertain, too, as Malcolm had only moments before. Knowing that made Malcolm brave. He crossed the room and took hold of Stuart's hand.

"No, you didn't tell me. You did say that you don't mind people touching your ink."

Stuart lips curved in a smile. "I certainly don't mind if you do."

Malcolm was glad to take the hint. He started at Stuart's wrists, tracing the designs with care before he ran his fingers up those muscled forearms, stroking the inky shades like he'd wanted to the first time he'd seen them. Stuart's olive-toned skin was as warm and smooth as Malcolm had imagined, and as usual, he smelled delicious. His skin was infinitely softer over those hard planes of muscle than Malcolm would have guessed. He slid his palms over Stuart's upper arms and shoulders. Now that he was touching, he didn't want to stop.

"This is okay, right?" he asked, eyes flicking to meet Stuart's.

"Yeah." Stuart's voice sounded gravelly. "I like the way your hands feel on me. Want me to take off my shirt?"

Malcolm could only nod. He helped Stuart pull off the tank and Stuart sighed when Malcolm's palms met his pecs. That soft sound sent a shockwave of awareness through Malcolm's whole person.

"I like this, too," he whispered, and hot damn, he did like it. Malcolm watched in wonder as Stuart's chest hitched under his hand.

They stood like that for God knew how long — Malcolm petting and exploring, Stuart's quiet breaths hushed between them. Slowly, Malcolm circled him, breathing Stuart in, lavishing attention on the beautiful designs that adorned his back, the muscles sometimes jumping under Malcolm's fingertips. He bit back a gasp as a shiver ran through Stuart's frame, and when he stepped back around to see Stuart's face, the intensity he glimpsed in those eyes made his mouth go dry.

Holy shit.

"What's wrong?" he whispered.

"Nothing at all." Stuart swallowed. "I'd like to sit down."

"Of course."

Stuart stepped away long enough to turn off the overhead lights, then was at Malcolm's side again, both of them moving toward the bed in the glow of a single nightstand lamp. They sat, but as soon as his ass hit the mattress, a craving for contact stronger than any Malcolm had ever known came over him. He shifted backward on the bed, lifting his feet as he moved, his eyes on Stuart to gauge his reaction.

Stuart had been so careful with Malcolm. He'd followed Malcolm's lead to the letter and asked for permission before he touched, either with words or his glance. Stuart didn't ask for permission this time, though. He crawled into the bed with an impish grin that made Malcolm smile back.

That was also the moment he noticed the bulge in Stuart's shorts.

Is that because of me?

Heart in his throat, he watched Stuart stretch out beside him, hands at Malcolm's waist. The longer Malcolm stared, the more he noticed, even in the low light. The flush on Stuart's cheeks, neck, and chest. His dilated pupils behind the glass lenses, so wide they made his brown eyes shine almost black. The goosebumps on his chest, practically begging to be touched.

Stuart uttered a quiet moan when Malcolm did just that and *oh, my God. That sound!*

"Sorry," Stuart murmured. "Don't mean to make you feel weird."

Malcolm couldn't get over Stuart's voice right now — deeper and lower than usual, and nearly breathless. "You're not. I like this. I'd tell you if I didn't."

"Good." Stuart's eyelids fluttered shut. "I should tell you, then, that you're kind of driving me out of my mind."

A sense of power flooded through Malcolm. He had done this. *Made this big man shiver and groan. Made him hard.*

"Do you want me to stop?"

"I hate to say it but...I think that might be a good idea." Stuart peeled an eyelid open. "I might embarrass myself otherwise." He aimed a sleepy smile at

Malcolm. "Okay if I touch you, instead? It's okay if you want to say no. I'd love to make you feel good, too."

Malcolm bit his lip. "I'd like that."

Stuart plucked off his glasses and shifted so he could lay them on the nightstand. "Don't hesitate to say stop if you need to, okay?"

"Okay." Malcolm closed his eyes. "I didn't know you wore glasses."

"I don't usually," Stuart replied. He eased his arms around Malcolm so their chests met. "I only need them when I'm beyond tired, like tonight."

With the perfect mix of firm and gentle, he rubbed circles into Malcolm's muscles through his T-shirt, pushing heat into Malcolm's skin. The buzz in Malcolm mellowed with each movement, going deeper, like the Suzuki's engine when it idled.

Mmm. Nice.

Malcolm sank into the mattress. "I think you wanted an excuse to cuddle," he said without really thinking, then smiled as a rumbling laugh rolled through Stuart's chest.

"Hah, maybe I do."

Maybe Malcolm had also wanted that excuse with this big, sleepy bear, a side of Stuart he hadn't expected. He'd come to understand Stuart was far more complex than one might think at first glance. Tattooed biker. Perfectionist chef. Carpenter and ex-Mormon. Emancipated gay man. They were all sides of Stuart that Malcolm had come to know. And as he laid his head against Stuart's shoulder for the second time that night, Malcolm looked forward to understanding the sides of this intriguing man that he had yet to see.

* * * *

The sky outside Stuart's windows was still dark when Malcolm woke. He studied the man beside him in the lamplight, waiting for his brain to freak out. Waking up beside a man in bed was out of the ordinary in Malcolm's experience, after all. He'd bunked in the same bed with his brother often in the past and sometimes with Kyle during trips out to Long Island with the speakeasy guys. Sharing a bed with Stuart was nothing like bunking with a brother or friend, however. Especially seeing as Malcolm had a hand splayed over the man's bare chest.

Even so, his freak-out didn't come.

Stuart lay on his side facing Malcolm, one arm under his pillow and the other looped around Malcolm's waist. There was enough light to illuminate his strong features, all heavy eyebrows and bold lines. Nothing about Stuart's face was delicate. Sleep made him softer and erased the crease between his eyebrows that was so quick to form. His thick lashes fanned out over the delicate skin under his eyes, and his lips were slightly parted beneath his lush mustache and beard.

Awareness hummed inside Malcolm. Stuart's mouth was full and red, far more so than Malcolm had ever noticed before. His lips looked beautifully soft. *Tender. Kissable.* Malcolm was drawn to touch them. The hum inside him increased in strength.

Movements slow and careful, Malcolm raised his hand from Stuart's chest and laid it against the side of his neck. He bit his lip as Stuart's next breath thrummed beneath his fingertips, then stretched forward and brushed the softest of kisses against Stuart's mouth.

Oh, wow.

That brief touch went all through Malcolm. Delight spread under his skin and everything around him seemed to melt away. He pressed another kiss to Stuart's lips, this one firmer, and a hum escaped him before he could stop it.

Malcolm had kissed people before. Most times he'd wanted to stop, but kissing Stuart was unlike anything he'd ever experienced. These kisses Malcolm felt right down to the soles of his feet. The whisper of beard against his own face, the soft exhalation of air on his lips, the way Stuart's lashes trembled as he dreamed — it was all so, so good. Malcolm wanted more. And he kissed Stuart gently again and again, his skin prickling as Stuart stirred.

"Mmm."

Malcolm had to close his eyes at that sleepy sound. Then Stuart cupped Malcolm's jaw with one hand and Malcolm thought for sure his bones turned to water. He couldn't stop his groan.

"Mal." Wonder was plain in Stuart's whisper. Outside of the hand on Malcolm's jaw, he didn't move. Malcolm still recognized the tension in Stuart's body and heard the question he didn't voice.

"I'm okay," Malcolm murmured, then swallowed a gasp as Stuart rolled just enough that his weight pressed Malcolm into the mattress.

God.

Yeah. Malcolm really hadn't known anything like this. Had never been held by someone as strong — maybe stronger — as himself. Or been kissed the way Stuart kissed him, deep and slow, almost drugging, so Malcolm's head spun. All he could do was grab Stuart's shoulders, his fingers tingling at the heat in that soft, inked skin, and hold on, his heart thundering in his ears as the kisses went on and on.

Malcolm felt alive. Like every nerve ending inside him was heightened and firing all at once. Even a simple action like Stuart raking his fingers through Malcolm's hair sent sparkles of sensation through him. He sighed as Stuart's chest pressed against his own, that weight practically melting him on the spot.

Malcolm's heart squeezed. He'd never felt so safe with anyone. Like he could really let go, secure in the knowledge that he'd be okay. He knew Stuart wouldn't push or go too far. Even now, Stuart started backing off, before Malcolm needed to ask to slow things down. Their kisses changed, becoming languorous and sleepy, more like nuzzles as Malcolm and Stuart rearranged themselves against the pillows.

"You're full of surprises tonight," Stuart said at last, his lips at Malcolm's temple and a smile in his voice.

Malcolm wanted to look up at him, but he simply could not get his eyelids to function. He settled for running a hand over Stuart's chest instead. "I'm jus' as surprised as anyone," he said, words slurred.

"And that's good?"

"Yeah, it is. 'M glad about that."

"Me too." Stuart dropped another kiss against Malcolm's hair. "Feel free to surprise me anytime you want, okay?"

Malcolm smiled to himself. He could manage that. He looked forward to the challenge, too, more so than anything in recent memory.

Chapter Ten

Stuart's head was still buzzing from the feel of Malcolm's lips against his as he walked into King's the following morning. He didn't know what had shifted for Malcolm at the fundraiser. It was clear something had. Some wall between them had come down and a whole new side of Malcolm was venturing out. Stuart felt like they were both tumbling into something deep and wonderful. He'd never had a relationship that fostered so much raw, honest communication. What he was building now with Malcolm was new and wonderful and it fed a part of him he hadn't known hungered for more.

Falling asleep together in his bed and waking up to Malcolm's kisses had started Stuart's day off right. It had been difficult saying goodbye this morning on the sidewalk in front of his building and Stuart knew he'd float through his day as he counted down the time until he'd see Malcolm again.

For now, it was time to try to focus on his duties as chef.

The kitchen he surveyed was quiet. Everything was neat and tidy, from the gleaming steel pots and pans to the columns of pristine white dishes stacked and ready for the day.

Stuart dropped his messenger bag in the office, changed into his uniform, then prepared an espresso and drank it as he checked to be sure there were no callouts for the day. Finding none, he reviewed his list of orders to place, people to call, emails to send, menus to create… It was endless. After he'd checked the most urgent off his list, he went back into the kitchen.

"Morning, Seth, Vera," Stuart said to the baker and the morning prep cook, and Ronnie and Emilio, the dishwashers who had just arrived. The kitchen had begun to hum as the ovens, fryers, flat tops and hoods were fired up.

As Stuart went through his usual routine of inspecting the storage fridges and their contents, he thought again of Malcolm. His skin still tingled with the memory of Malcolm's touch and an echo of the ache that had settled low in his groin as he'd fallen asleep. The slow pace was both wonderful and excruciating. He'd wanted so much more. To strip Malcolm's clothes off and taste his skin, to wrap his lips around Malcolm's cock and to slide inside him. He definitely missed sex and he'd been masturbating more. It didn't diminish his enjoyment in the slow exploration, however.

The denial had added another level to his pleasure, and it felt good to go at Malcolm's pace. Making Malcolm feel safe and relaxed was at least as pleasurable as anything else they could have done, though Stuart did look forward to everything they had yet to explore. What they had yet to explore together dizzied him. While Malcolm had been intimate with women before, he hadn't with a man, and the idea of introducing Malcolm to everything for the first time made Stuart's blood heat.

Of course, that was assuming Malcolm wanted to explore all those things. If he didn't... Well, they'd have to cross that bridge when they got to it. If Malcolm didn't want to have sex, would they be able to sustain the relationship? Stuart wanted to, although he also had no idea if he could go without sex long-term. Be patient? Absolutely. Abstain completely except for masturbation? Well, that remained to be seen. In the meantime, he'd let Malcolm set the pace and remain open-minded.

When the door to the cooler opened, Stuart turned and came face-to-face with a concerned-looking Vera.

"Everything okay, Chef? You've been in here a while."

"Yes." Stuart smiled. "Everything's great."

She gave him a puzzled smile in return, retrieved some shallots, then left. Stuart forced himself to continue his careful inventory, making sure each item was where it was supposed to be, matched with the delivery inventory and stored in accordance with the health department codes.

Deliveries had arrived and bags of flour and slabs of meat were lined up near the service entrance. The scent of fresh vegetables with dirt still clinging to them filled the air and he opened a crate stuffed with Spanish cheeses, Greek olives and Indian peppercorns. Stuart also double-checked the work of the cooks who'd closed the night before and made sure everything was in readiness for the day ahead, then checked the equipment and made sure the entire kitchen was spotless.

After, he went to the office with Hugh, the P.M. sous chef, and caught up on some of the drama in the service industry.

"You haven't come out with us for drinks after work lately," Hugh said. He'd just finished telling Stuart about sexual harassment allegations against Jake Mann, a well-known executive chef at a restaurant on the other side of Midtown. *Horrifying stuff.* Stuart was doubly grateful to be working for someone like Marisol. Not just because she was a fellow queer person but because she was one of the most ethical people Stuart had ever worked for, inside the restaurant business and otherwise. "If you'd come out with us more, you'd be up to date on all of this."

Stuart shrugged. "I'm seeing someone. I've been spending all my free time with him."

"Oh, well then." Hugh grinned and winked. "That's allowed, I suppose. We should probably discuss where we're at for dinner prep."

Their focus turned to the day ahead and they walked back to the kitchen. Stocks were simmering, garlic was peeled, herbs were snipped, shrimp had been peeled and deveined, along with a host of other tasks, so everything was under control. Gustavo, the *rôtisseur*, who was in charge of preparing meat, would be in soon and the kitchen was already buzzing with activity.

Marisol's arrival twenty minutes later made spines straighten and everyone snap to attention. She made her usual rounds in the kitchen, greeting the crew and checking their work, before she crooked a finger at Stuart.

"Come talk to me about the fundraiser last night."

Stuart followed her into her office. "It went incredibly well," he said. "Minus a disaster with the dessert display stand."

She winced when he described the shattered glass. "Any injuries?"

"No."

"Who broke it?"

"One of the servers from Lock & Key."

She nodded. "Makes sense. They wouldn't have the experience with events like that."

"He offered to pay. I told him no."

"Good. No reason to make the poor kid go broke trying to cover the cost. I'd bet he's learned his lesson."

"Exactly," Stuart said. "We made it work with some slate boards and no one noticed the last-minute swap."

He ran through the overview of the rest of the night and Marisol looked pleased when he was done.

"Well, sounds like an unequivocal success to me," she said. She'd braided her long dark hair while they spoke and now she neatly pinned it up and out of the way.

"It was," he agreed. "I'm confident CEC will want to partner with us again on events."

"Are you interested in future collaborations?"

"Yes," Stuart said without hesitating. "Assuming they want me. CEC was a dream to work with. When the worst issue we had was an inexperienced server breaking a serving piece, that is as good as it gets." Marisol nodded. "And I'm all for working with Kyle McKee from Under, again. There aren't many bartenders who put as much care into crafting their cocktails as I do my food."

"Excellent. I like building connections like that."

"So do I."

Marisol snorted. "I know all about you and your connections. How are things going with the CEC guy you were spending time with? Malcolm, right?"

"Yes. Malcolm and I had a bit of a breakthrough," Stuart admitted, a smile stealing across his face before he could stop it. "We're dating. And...beginning to explore what that means for him."

"I take it that it's going well?"

"It is. It really is."

Marisol snickered. "This guy has gotten under your skin, hasn't he?"

"I guess he has," Stuart said. "He's not like anyone I've ever met before."

"Good," she said. "I told you you'd figure it out."

Sometimes, Stuart hated when his boss was right. In this case, he was grateful.

"So, Hugh told me about the sexual harassment allegations at Jake Mann's place," he said, moving the conversation away from his personal life.

"He's an asshole," Marisol said. Her mouth turned down in a hard, tight line. "Always has been and we all knew it. I'm sorry he's been able to get away with it for so long. Hopefully, things are improving."

"I'm grateful to work for you, you know?" Stuart said. "As a guy, I'm rarely going to have to deal with that sort of thing. Plus, I'm big and scary enough that few people would try. I could have had to deal with a lot of shit about my sexuality, though, and I just wanted you to know I appreciate the culture you've created here."

"And I'm grateful to you for all of the hard work you do to make this place a success," she said with a small, rare smile.

Stuart straightened in his chair as he watched her shift into work mode. "Now, let's discuss tonight."

* * * *

"Service!" Stuart called, and Mike, the back waiter, appeared to whisk the plate of pork loin off to the customer who had ordered it. Everyone in the kitchen let out an audible sigh of relief after he'd disappeared through the swinging doors. Stuart stretched, feeling the burn between his shoulder blades from having been hunched over the pass, plating almost a hundred and fifty dishes tonight.

It had been surprisingly busy for a Sunday evening. They'd had more walk-in customers than usual, so the kitchen had been working at full tilt over the past few hours. Not as bad as a Friday or Saturday night, yet still busy. Now that the final order of the evening was off to the front of the house, Stuart could wrap up his day and head home.

"Start breaking down," he called out to the cooks. They would send their smallwares—pots and pans, cutting boards and the like—to the dishwasher. They'd log and label the leftover ingredients and store them overnight. Hugh would do his closing sous chef duties and oversee all of it, but Stuart was done for the night.

He changed out of his uniform and back into street clothes. On his way out of the restaurant, he waved to the people pulling up the carpet runners and emptying the trash and thanked them for their hard work.

It was cooler in the alley, though not much. The heat of the summer day hadn't dissipated yet and Stuart was looking forward to the cool wind that would blow across him on his drive home. He was tired from the long day and eager to take a shower.

The ride home brought him to life again, and after the shower, he felt almost human. He thought of Malcolm as he rubbed a towel across his body, soaking up the water droplets that still clung to his skin. Rather than change into his usual shorts and tank, he hung the towel over the curtain rod and walked across the room, nude.

Memories of the night before washed over him. Malcolm's gaze as he'd looked Stuart over. His fingertips, then his palms, on Stuart's skin. Exploring his ink and mapping out his body. Stuart's cock grew thick as his body buzzed with memories of being touched so slowly and thoroughly.

The siren song of the lingerie in his dresser called to Stuart, and unable to resist the lure any longer, he crossed the room and knelt down. He didn't indulge his kink often — it usually made him feel more alone — but he'd been feeling so good since he'd begun dating Malcolm that his need had grown to levels he couldn't resist. Sliding open the bottom drawer, Stuart sifted his fingers through the soft fabrics, enjoying the tactile pleasures of slippery satin and frothy lace on his work-roughened hands.

Stuart felt almost hypnotized as he drew out a pair of black panties. He slipped them over his feet and stood, drawing them up his legs, the whisper-light touch of the fabric making his skin tingle. He settled the wide, ribbed band around his hips and cupped his balls and cock to arrange them under the satin triangle of fabric in the front.

Walking slowly over to the mirror that hung on the back of the closet door, Stuart stared at himself in the lingerie. He turned to look at the view from the back and his cock throbbed at the sight of the fine lace curving across his ass.

Unlike some men, Stuart didn't feel feminine when he put panties on. The breadth of his shoulders and the heavy, dark hair of his body were too masculine to hide, and he'd never had any desire to downplay them. In fact, the contrast of the rough hair and vivid tattoos against the delicate fabrics excited him, and he wondered if Malcolm would like that, too. Given his prior experiences, it seemed unlikely, and yet Stuart couldn't stop imagining it. He settled on the bed, lying down on his back before he began to touch himself. He dragged a hand over the hard length beneath the silky-soft fabric and hummed.

Stuart stroked his cock through the panties and pictured Malcolm watching him. No, even better, Malcolm touching him. Stuart closed his eyes, imagining Malcolm's long, slender fingers trailing across the smooth, slippery fabric, gently rubbing the head of Stuart's cock with his thumb and making a little wetness seep through. The texture alone aroused him and the idea of Malcolm taking part sent his desire into overdrive. It sent a shudder through Stuart, all the way to his toes, and he reached beneath the fabric and wrapped his fist around his shaft, enjoying the slide of the fabric against his knuckles and the feel of his skin against his palm.

His breathing grew strained as he pictured Malcolm nuzzling his inner thigh and rubbing his cheek across the satiny fabric. He imagined the care with which Malcolm would explore him. Stuart raised his palm and licked it, then took himself in hand, stroking faster and wishing it was Malcolm's hand and lips on his cock. How would his eyes look as he gazed up at Stuart and took Stuart into his mouth?

Stuart's orgasm built fast and insistent and he let out a tortured groan when cum arced up, spattering onto his chest and down his stomach before the last few shots dribbled onto the black fabric of the panties. His chest heaved as the images dissipated like smoke and doubt immediately crept in, overtaking the pleasure.

Stuart desperately wanted Malcolm to know about his love of lingerie and how much it turned Stuart on to wear them. But what if he reacted poorly?

Malcolm was so new at all of this. Unused to exploring his sexuality. How could Stuart ask him to not only step outside his comfort zone but leap into unknown waters? Especially because Malcolm didn't even know where his own comfort zone lay. Men with years of experience had balked at Stuart's predilections and called him a freak. How could he expect Malcolm to understand?

Stuart stood, the fear and worry crowding out all the contentment the orgasm had brought him. His stomach clenched as he slid the scrap of fabric off his body. He gripped the underwear tightly in his fist and walked to the sink to wash them.

He'd spent the years since he'd moved from Utah knowing that building the kind of relationship he wanted would mean full and complete honesty about his kink. If Stuart wanted that kind of life with Malcolm, Malcolm needed to know the truth. But how?

Malcolm was too kind to hurl insults at Stuart and call him names. That didn't mean he'd ever accept Stuart's kink, however. Or that he'd feel comfortable being involved. Or even want to be with Stuart at all once he learned the truth.

What if knowing changed the way Malcolm thought of him? What if—like so many guys before—Stuart's kink repulsed him? There was no coming back from that. If Malcolm couldn't accept Stuart's secret, there was no way to un-ring that bell. It might drive Malcolm away from Stuart in fear and disgust.

Hands shaking, Stuart twisted the underwear to wring the water out and draped them over the shower curtain rod to dry. He dressed in his usual sleepwear of shorts and a tank, then crawled back in his bed, exhaustion from a long, tiring day creeping over him. The mental turmoil after his orgasm hadn't helped, either. This was why he so rarely dressed in lingerie and got himself off—afterward, loneliness overcame him. Even more so when he was dating someone and the guilt over keeping secrets weighed heavy on him.

Malcolm was very different from most of the men Stuart had dated but the depth of Stuart's feelings for Malcolm gave the worry extra gravity.

Stuart reached to turn out the light and noticed his phone had a new text message notification from Malcolm.

I'm heading to bed soon. Hope you had a good night.

Stuart checked the time. It had arrived twenty minutes ago. Malcolm might already be asleep, but he'd see the reply in the morning.

Long, crazy day. Anything was going to be downhill after this morning. Sleep well.

To his surprise, Malcolm answered. *It was a nice way to fall asleep last night for me too.*

Stuart smiled. *I agree. Maybe we should do that again.*

Yes please.

They texted back and forth for a few more minutes until Stuart's eyelids grew heavy and he said goodnight. Drifting off, his thoughts stayed with Malcolm. While Stuart didn't believe in God anymore, he said a little prayer out into the dark that, somehow, Malcolm would understand and accept him.

Chapter Eleven

"Morning, Carter."

"Good morning." Carter glanced up to where Malcolm stood in his office door and smiled. "There are baked goods in the kitchen—make sure you grab something if you're hungry."

"All set." Malcolm held up a cinnamon scone and grinned. He'd run out of oatmeal and yogurt a few days before and had wanted to cheer when he'd spotted a bakery box and platter of cheese this morning. "Still a good time to meet?"

"Yep, c'mon in." Carter gestured to the guest chairs on the other side of his desk. "Tara should be here in a minute."

"Cool." Malcom stepped into the tiny space and took the chair farthest from the door, nerves fluttering in his chest. Carter hadn't broached the topic of Stuart and The Hug yet, but Malcolm didn't know how to start, especially with only minutes to spare before they had company. "Thanks for this," he said instead and nodded at the pastry in his hand. "I can't remember the last time I had a scone and it's delicious."

"You're welcome. I bought it from that bakery you like on 33rd and Madison."

"Born and Bread? Nice." Malcolm regarded his snack with new pleasure. "They're closer to my place than yours, though."

"Ri wanted to try somewhere new." Carter shifted his attention to the tablet before him on the desk. "We had my mother over for brunch on Sunday."

Malcolm stared at his friend, who didn't look up. Carter's relationship with his parents had been a royal mess for several years. He hadn't said anything about his mother visiting while he and Malcolm had been working on Saturday, either.

"You had Eleanor over? That sounds...momentous?"

Carter hummed. "Certainly felt like it. We overcompensated with enough to feed an army instead of three. There's quiche and pasta salad that I'll put out later."

Watching Carter press his lips thin, Malcolm suspected he'd eaten little of that food. The stress Carter experienced even speaking to his parents played havoc with his anxiety disorder and the dark shadows under his eyes spoke to a sleepless night. Before Malcolm could ask for details, his manager, Tara, stepped into the room and shifted everyone's gears into work mode.

Malcolm sipped his coffee. He'd wait Carter out. Maybe talk about Eleanor Hamilton instead of what he and Stuart had gotten up to over the weekend. Though, come to think of it, Malcolm didn't want to hold back talking about Stuart, to Carter or anyone. That had him hiding a smile behind his cup.

"Congrats again on a great night, guys, and beating another fundraising goal," Tara said as they wrapped up over an hour later. "I know nitpicking through paperwork is a pain in the ass, but you hired me to do exactly that."

"You're fabulous at it." Carter shared a long-distance high five with her. "And now we're ready to shift into high gear for the fall fundraiser!" He grinned when Malcolm mimed choking him. "Until then, let's enjoy a well-deserved break."

"You're not getting much of a break, what with jumping right from the fundraiser into planning your own wedding," Malcolm said after Tara had headed out. "I can't believe it's only a few weeks off now."

"I can't believe it either." Carter gave him a big smile. "Riley's got everything covered. This wedding is small and casual, which is nice because we had our fill of giant wedding shenanigans the first time around. It's funny—Ri's taken way more pleasure than I ever expected in planning. All I've had to do is coordinate the wedding date with an officiant from the Southampton Court and vote on the choices Ri gives me."

"Which you love."

"I can't express to you how much, both as a lazy person and a man who wants his partner happy."

Malcolm grinned. "Ri is happy. He's getting a wedding he really wants this time."

"That makes two of us." Carter pulled off his glasses and set them on the desk. "I called him 'Bridezilla' last night, though, after he spent twenty minutes talking flower crowns and cupcake trees with the kids."

"Oh, damn. How'd he take it?"

"He threw the taco he was eating at me and messed up my shirt."

Malcolm laughed. After having watched Carter struggle in the aftermath of his first marriage going bust, he loved seeing his friends settled.

"Doing the wedding our way was a hot topic during brunch yesterday," Carter said. "My mother was very keen to discuss it, much to my surprise. I had no idea she even knew Ri and I were engaged."

Malcolm grimaced. "Who told her? The kids?"

"Mmmhmm. Which is wonderful, of course. I'm glad they're happy their dads are getting hitched. I didn't consider how their grandparents would react, however, or even that I should have let them know." A troubled expression crossed Carter's face. "I absolutely did not expect my mother would want to attend."

"Your mom wants to come to your wedding?" Malcom's jaw sagged. "To Riley?"

"I know, right?"

Carter's humorless laugh hurt to hear. The Hamiltons had disowned him after he'd come out as bi and, for a long time, his only contact with Brad and Eleanor had been through his children, Sadie and Dylan, and ex-wife, Kate. After Eleanor had reached out to Carter last year, they'd rebuilt a fragile kind of truce and now she was almost friendly toward both her son and Riley. Never in a million years would Malcolm have guessed she'd show interest in their wedding, however. He didn't need to ask whether Carter had heard from his father, either, because the stress lines around Carter's eyes told their own story.

Malcolm suppressed a sigh. So much time and emotion wasted, all because Carter had fallen in love with a man.

Malcolm's parents would never treat him so badly. They supported him always, even when they didn't understand his choices. And while Kim complicated Malcolm's life in a dozen different ways, she loved him. Malcolm didn't doubt for a moment that she and his dad wanted the best for their sons. That only increased Malcolm's desire to tell people about Stuart and how special he'd become to Malcolm.

"Mothers are mysterious creatures," he said. "So is your mom coming to the wedding? I'm happy to keep an eye on her if that would help."

A twinkle entered Carter's gaze. "What, like be her date?"

"Sure." Malcolm shrugged. "Minder-slash-date, if you want to call me that. I'd make sure she behaved and had a good time. Nothing too crazy," he added, "though I'd have to fight Jesse on that."

This time, Carter's laughter was genuine. "Shit, I'm sure you're right. The way he looks at her when they meet unnerves me. I can feel how much he wants to lay into her about her behavior."

"We all want to. The only reason no one says anything is because it would make you feel bad."

Carter sighed. "I know. I love you guys for that, too. No need to worry about the wedding because my mother will not be attending. Riley was kind yet very firm about telling her no."

The sad note in Carter's voice made Malcolm want to hug him. "How'd she take it?"

"Better than I expected. I think she gets it now. That there's no coming back from what happened and everything we do going forward is on Riley's and my terms." Carter flapped a hand in the air. "Anyway, even if she did come to the wedding, I wouldn't ask you to be her date. You don't need to do anything that day except have a good time and chill out as much as possible."

"I can do that." Malcolm licked his lips. He knew an opening when he heard one and bless Carter for giving it to him with such grace. Still, his pulse sped up as he spoke. "I might bring an actual date, too, so that works out."

Carter gave him a soft smile. "Might?"

"I haven't asked yet. I'm going to, though." Malcolm smiled back. "Ask, I mean. This week, if we can meet up after work."

"I'm glad to hear it, Mal. We'll make room for anyone you bring—you know that, right?"

"I do. And thanks for saying so. It's Stuart." Fire raced across Malcolm's cheeks and his heart practically expanded with every word he spoke. "We've been dating for a couple of weeks. You probably guessed that."

"I'd never assume anything you didn't tell me," Carter said. "I was hopeful."

"Really?"

"Yes. You look happy when you're around Stuart or even just talking about him. Like you're lit up from the inside." Carter shrugged. "It's nice to see."

That had to mean other people had noticed Malcolm's behavior, too. *Ugh.* Now his face was really hot.

"Did you guys talk about us after Stuart and I left on Saturday?"

"A little," Carter admitted. "Not sure you can blame us after the way you were acting. We talked more about whether Stuart is a good guy than anything else." He offered a wry smile when Malcolm frowned. "He's someone we don't know very well, who may or may not have been involved with our friend, babe. The crew wants to be sure he'd treat you well."

Malcolm had to hand it to his friends — not even he could argue with that. "You and Riley know Stuart," he said.

"We do, yes, and we made sure everyone knew we'd vouch for the man as much as we could." Carter sipped his water. "You didn't talk to Kyle about this after yoga class?"

"I skipped yoga yesterday. I didn't actually leave Stuart's until almost ten."

Carter gave a single slow nod. "I see."

"Nothing happened. Or...almost nothing. Some kissing."

"You don't have to explain — "

"I want to, though. Because I liked it. More to the point, I like Stuart. The whole thing kind of snuck up on me," Malcolm said, then knit his eyebrows together. "That's not true. I noticed him right from the start — he stood out to me during the first meeting at King's. Like he was brighter than everyone else. The more time we spent around each other, the more I wanted to know him."

"Like a crush?" Carter said.

"Exactly." Malcolm seized the suggestion. "That word is sort of juvenile, but yes, it was an infatuation that changed into something else because I did get to know him. We went out as friends a few times. He helped my mom and me when her sun porch fell apart, too."

"I remember." Carter cocked his head. "That was around the time I started to think maybe Stuart was interested in you."

"Really?" Malcolm fell silent for a beat. Had Stuart been interested in Malcolm all along and kept it to himself? Of course, Malcolm hadn't noticed. "What I felt for him changed after the thing with the porch," Malcolm said, his voice quieter. "By the time I came back from helping out my mom on Staten Island, I knew I liked him. And I like him even more now."

"I can tell." Carter's tone held a tease, but the crinkles around his eyes as he smiled were happy. "What do you think this means for you?"

"I'm not sure, though I guess I'm bi. I just know I like him, and that Stuart likes me, too." Malcolm cast his gaze down. The words made him so light he wanted to grab on to the chair to keep himself from floating away. "We decided we'd try dating and it's good, you know? Right."

He makes me happy. Like I can do anything.

Malcolm met Carter's gaze again. "Maybe it should feel strange dating a man, but it doesn't."

Carter clasped his hands together on the desk. "Why would it feel weird?"

"Because I've never done this before? I've only ever been with girls, Car — I've never dated a guy." Malcolm sat forward in his chair. "Not that it matters when Stuart and I are together because whatever we do, the pieces fall into place."

"I think I sense a 'but' in your voice, however, and I have a feeling I know why."

Malcolm nodded. He saw understanding in Carter's eyes. He'd been in Malcolm's position himself once, an adult man trying to figure out a wholly new part of his identity and how it fit into the world around him.

"I really don't know what I'm doing," Malcolm said. "I can't help worrying about that sometimes. With me being the way I am and Stuart being…not. What if I'm not giving him what he needs? Or if I'm going too slow?

"He knows about me." Malcolm gulped. God, he wished now he'd asked Carter to go for a walk so they had some privacy. The glass walls in this tiny office didn't even go all the way to the ceiling and Malcolm's voice sounded very loud in his own ears. "I told Stuart I'm gray ace and we talked about what that means for both of us."

"Holy shit." Carter rose from his seat and came around the desk so he could close his office door. "That's huge." He settled into the chair beside Malcolm, his eyes wide. "I'd be lying if I said I hadn't wondered. At the risk of sounding like a pompous ass, I'm proud of you." He set his hand on Malcolm's shoulder. "Really, I mean it."

"I know you do." Malcolm raised his hand and squeezed Carter's. "I'm proud of me, too. It wasn't even hard once I made up my mind to do it. Stuart's that easy to talk to."

"Then keep talking," Carter said. "I'm not a fan of giving advice, but I'll say this a million times to anyone who will listen—communicate with your partner, boyfriend, wife, whatever, and listen to them when they speak. You can talk to me any time, of course, just like you can Kyle or Ri, and any other friend you have. Just make sure you're talking to Stuart, too."

He patted Malcolm's shoulder once more. "If he's the man I think he is, he'll be okay with figuring out how things work on your terms."

I hope so.

Malcolm's heart sank at the thought. He already liked Stuart far more than seemed wise. There was nothing he could do about it, either.

* * * *

In the end, Malcolm didn't have time to stress over how to properly date a man because Stuart asked him over for dinner and Malcolm wasted no time getting to Little Italy.

"Hey." Stuart grinned and waved Malcolm in. "Glad you're here. I made rice and there is way more than I can handle on my own."

Malcolm stepped inside and smiled down at Stuart's bare feet. He wore jeans and a beat-up Max's Kansas City T-shirt, and though Malcolm should have felt overdressed in his work clothes, Stuart's easy smile filled him with a cozy feeling instead. He inhaled the aromas of spices and meat while his mouth watered.

"Smells amazing in here. Do you always cook like this on your days off?"

"It depends." Stuart waited for Malcolm to hang his bag on the hook by the door, then set his hands on Malcom's shoulders. "Some days, I eat whatever's on hand—eggs, cheese, meats. Sometimes, I feel like waffles or spaghetti. Today, I wanted to try something new, so I made rice pilau with beef and potato. Nothing fancy. It should be just about done, so your timing is impeccable."

A week ago, Malcolm would have nodded and let the man go about his business. He couldn't let that happen now, not when a buzz of need surfaced in him and grew. Without a second thought, he stepped forward and slid his arms around Stuart's waist.

"Hi." Satisfaction washed over him. "Thanks for having me."

"Are you kidding?" Stuart wrapped Malcolm up in a hug, a gleam in his dark eyes. "You're welcome here any time. I don't extend invitations like that to just anyone, you know." Gaze steady, he pressed a kiss against Malcolm's lips.

There.

Malcolm closed his eyes. The soft scrape of beard on his mouth made him shiver and he leaned into the kiss. Tightening his hold, Stuart opened his mouth enough to give Malcolm a taste of something bright and citrusy. Malcolm chased after it, angling his head so he could deepen the kiss, and a low noise rumbled through Stuart's chest. Goosebumps rose along Malcolm's arms.

The buzz in his core intensified as Stuart moved a hand to the back of Malcolm's head. Malcolm splayed his hands over Stuart's lower back, digging in with his fingers, then went still as Stuart teased his tongue gently under the edge of Malcolm's upper lip. A sensation like falling swept through Malcolm, so strong he swore his whole body sighed.

What is happening to me?

Before Malcolm could start thinking too hard, Stuart had backed off, his movements easy as he slowly, slowly brought the kiss to an end.

"Fuck." He set his forehead against Malcolm's with a hum. "You're really good at that."

The pleasure in Stuart's deep voice pulled a laugh out of Malcom. He didn't open his eyes or turn Stuart loose because, while he wasn't really hiding, Malcolm needed a moment to center himself. Thankfully, Stuart didn't let go either and held on to Malcolm as they stood by the apartment door, breathing each other in.

"Is your rice okay?" Malcolm forced his eyes open and leaned back so he could see Stuart clearly, and his heart squeezed at the smile on Stuart's face.

"Just, I think. We'll be eating omelets again otherwise."

"You say that like it's a bad thing."

"I don't mean to. I'm in the mood for more than eggs, though." Stuart cocked his head and only let go after Malcolm unwound his arms from Stuart's waist. "I got this recipe from a coworker who says it's faithful to East African pilau. We'll see how true that is."

He stepped away and Malcolm crossed his arms over his chest to stop himself from following. Glancing around the apartment, he noticed a braided rug covering the formerly bare hardwood floor beside the bed. The complementary shades of brown and blue added a welcome splash of color to the drab space and Malcolm saw then it wasn't the only new addition. There were tiny potted succulent plants on the nightstand and a sphere made of cobalt blue glass hung in the window by the bed. A pair of beautiful wooden stools stood against the wall too, clearly handmade, and Malcolm quickly toed off his shoes and moved toward them.

"Are you re-decorating?" he asked.

"More like digging stuff out of storage," Stuart replied from the stove. Picking up a spoon, he lifted the lid of a Dutch oven and stirred its contents, a fragrant cloud of steam rising into the air. "I stashed some things at Marisol's when I moved in here and figured now was as good a time as any to put them to use. She gave me the plants — said I needed more green in my life."

"That was nice of her." Malcolm ran a hand over one of the stools, admiring its glossy seat and long legs, which sported graceful, unexpected curves. As if someone had picked a bundle of branches up from the ground and fashioned them into something functional. He caught Stuart's eye across the room. "Did you make these?"

"I did. There's supposed to be a cafe table, too, except I haven't gotten around to it yet." He shrugged one shoulder. "I got busy at King's and the project kind of stalled."

"They're beautiful." Malcolm gave the stool's seat a final pat. "Can't wait to see what they look like with the table when you find time to finish." He unbuttoned the right cuff of his shirt so he could roll up the sleeve. "You need me to do anything?"

"How about some drinks? There are bottles of IPA in the fridge that should balance well with the rice, or water if you don't want alcohol."

They chatted as they set up their meal and the contented feeling inside Malcolm filled him head to toe. Spending time with Stuart made him happy, more so than he'd been...maybe ever. And while Malcolm didn't know what that meant yet—or even how to handle it—he wanted it to last.

"How'd I do?" Stuart asked as they ate, amusement flickering across his face when Malcolm was forced to mumble around a mouthful of food.

"It's fabulous."

He really liked the pride in Stuart's smirk. The rice was wonderful, with chunks of tender beef and potato, all deliciously spicy and rich. They'd spread out their picnic on the floor this time and sat atop the braided rug with their backs against the bed. Malcolm basked in the vibe that wound around them. Stuart made him forget about the outside world, so much so he didn't even want to consider the idea of leaving for his own apartment.

Smiling, he picked up his beer and held it out. "Cheers to you and your kickass rice."

"Hah." Stuart clinked his bottle against Malcolm's. "Thanks for being my guinea pig."

"Like this is a hardship." Malcolm sipped his drink, then set it down. "I've never had African pilau before and I hope it always tastes this good."

"We'll have to go out and get something authentic so you can compare," Stuart said. "I've had excellent Ethiopian varieties here in Manhattan and Somali in Harlem. The best I've ever had can be found in a Kenyan barbecue joint out in Jersey. We should take a drive out the next weekend we're both free."

The food Malcolm had savored a moment before turned to sawdust in his mouth as he listened to Stuart describe the place he'd found in a Teaneck strip mall one day after a hike. Malcolm didn't have money to spare for a meal out, even in what sounded like a low-key joint. His finances were still in bad shape, despite all his scrimping, and he absolutely lived paycheck to paycheck, a state of being that caused him considerable anxiety. Malcolm couldn't afford things beyond rent and utilities, even with Jackson pitching in. Christ, Malcolm could hardly feed himself, and if his annual membership to the yoga studio hadn't been paid for already, he'd have been forced to give it up.

"You okay?" The crease between Stuart's eyebrows was back. "You went quiet all of a sudden."

Malcolm forced a smile. "I'm fine. Remembered something I wanted to ask you later, that's all. What were you saying?"

Stuart eyed Malcolm, his gaze was almost too sharp, and the frown didn't leave his face. "I asked if the beef was too much. You mentioned focusing more on plant proteins — "

"Beef is fine. I'll eat pretty much any meat when it comes down to it." Malcolm licked his lips. "I've been watching my budget and — "

"Not buying meat helps with that," Stuart finished. "Okay, got it." He nodded at the bowl in Malcolm's hand. "So if I made bone marrow with shaved bonito and teriyaki, you'd be game to try it?"

"What is bonito, exactly?"

"Dried, fermented fish that's shaved thin into paper-thin flakes. Totally delicious."

"O-o-okay." Malcom thought that over for a second. "I like everything you cook so I'm sure they'd be fantastic."

Stuart tipped his head back and belted out a laugh, and God, Malcolm's breath caught. Stuart was... beautiful, really, with his strong features and plush mouth and Malcolm so wanted to touch him again. He gripped his bowl tighter to stop himself from doing so but Malcolm's brain didn't get the message about holding back and he started talking without meaning to.

"Hey, do you want to go to a wedding with me?"

Stuart's eyes went wide. "A wedding?"

"Sorry, that kind of came out of nowhere. Let me start again," Malcolm said with a chuckle. "Carter and Riley are getting married in Southampton next month and I wondered if you'd be my date.

"It's fine if you think it's too much too soon," he hastened to add. "You know Car and Ri, though, and what they went through to be together. It would make me happy to have you there with me."

"Wow." Stuart set his bowl aside. "I haven't been to a wedding in a long time. Definitely never a same-sex wedding." His expression was solemn when he shifted his focus to Malcolm. "My father was fit to be tied when Becky and I divorced — he'd really rage if he knew I'd witnessed two men vow to love each other until death do they part."

"Shit." Malcolm's stomach fell. He hadn't meant to stir up Stuart's awful past. He grabbed hold of Stuart's hand and squeezed. "I'm sorry."

"Don't be." Stuart squeezed back. "My mind got away from me for a second. Do the grooms know you're bringing a date?"

"Carter does. I told him about us today." Malcolm knew he'd said exactly the right thing when Stuart's face lit up. "He's happy for me."

"I'm happy for you, too, Mal."

"I want to tell the other guys. The next party at Under is in a couple of weeks, and while I'll see Kyle before then, I figure that'd be a perfect time to talk to everyone else."

"I like that idea." Stuart knocked his shoulder gently against Malcolm's. "And I'll come with you. To Under and the wedding. Just tell me which days and I'll work with the staff at King's to make it happen."

Happiness bubbled up in Malcolm's chest. "Yeah?"

"Absolutely." He ran his thumb over Malcolm's. "I'd love to be your date. I know enough about your friends to guess they'll support you. I still want to be there for you when you come out to them if you're okay with that."

When you come out to them.

Those words reverberated through Malcolm as he and Stuart turned their attention to cleaning up the meal. He would be coming out by bringing Stuart with him to Under and the wedding, or even to Staten Island for dinner with his mom. The world would assume he and Stuart were in a gay relationship because that was a logical jump, though the truth was far more complicated.

Is it?

Malcolm frowned. What he and Stuart did or didn't do together in private was their business and no one else's. So if people assumed Malcolm was gay? He couldn't see why that mattered. Turns out he wasn't exactly straight, so if the world needed to label their relationship, that was fine. Malcolm knew what he wanted, and that was to be with Stuart. Even more amazing, Stuart seemed to want to be with him, too.

"There's coffee granita if you have room for dessert," Stuart said. He'd moved to the refrigerator, and though his words sounded careless, Malcolm saw tension in the line of his shoulders.

Maybe because you've been stewing in silence for the last ten minutes.

Malcolm moved to Stuart's side. He needed to get better at talking about the crap going through his head. At least when it came to this man. Anything else could wait.

"You told me you didn't get fancy on your days off," he said and slipped his hand into Stuart's again.

"Granita is basically slush you eat with a spoon." Stuart leaned his shoulder against the fridge, his features more relaxed. "You can't get less fancy than that."

"I could try. Got any canned cheese?"

"Gah, no."

"Don't be a snob," Malcolm said with a laugh. "Will the not-fancy slush keep for a while?"

"If it needs to." The corners of Stuart's lips curved upward. "Why?"

"Because I'd like to go back to kissing you if that would be okay."

Stuart pulled Malcolm close. "You never have to ask me that," he said, voice a low purr that got right under Malcolm's skin. "I only stopped before because I didn't want to push."

Malcolm rested his hands on either side of Stuart's neck. He sensed power in the body pressed to his, like the man was a coil about to spring. Closing his eyes, Malcolm rubbed his lips against Stuart's beard and sighed at the tiny shockwaves of bliss that simple motion brought.

"You'll know if I don't want something," he promised. While a part of him still wondered what he was getting into, all rational thought fled when Stuart slotted their mouths together.

Yes.

As before, Malcolm felt the kiss everywhere, this time the sensations even more heightened. His skin and lips tingled, and the first time Stuart slid his tongue against Malcolm's, Malcolm groaned. Heat slashed through him, warming him inside and out so every nerve hummed.

"Fuck," Stuart whispered.

They kissed some more as they crossed the room, and then Stuart was opening Malcolm's shirt, plucking at the buttons with a dexterity Malcolm couldn't fathom.

"This okay? I need to feel you," Stuart explained in between nips, and yeah, Malcolm wanted that, too. He needed to touch skin and tattoos and to breathe in wood and musk and Stuart.

Malcolm really couldn't stop kissing him, though, and got distracted halfway through pulling off Stuart's shirt. Happily, he let Stuart take over, and soon they were both stripped to their underwear.

"Gorgeous." Stuart's eyes glowed as he looked Malcolm up and down. He brought a hand to Malcolm's chest, smoothing the lean muscle and creamy, fair skin with his palm. "You should show this body off more, Mal."

The buzz inside Malcolm stole his voice. He sat on the bed at Stuart's urging and watched in a daze as Stuart straddled his lap. Grasping Stuart's hips with both hands, he pressed his face against the tight torso before him, slowly rubbing his cheeks, nose and mouth against Stuart's tattooed skin, eyes closed and elation rolling over him in waves.

"Feels so good," he murmured, sweat springing out on his skin. "God, you feel so good, Stuart."

"You do, too."

They groaned together as Stuart settled down against Malcolm's lap, his erection rigid against Malcolm's belly. Malcolm's head spun. He whimpered softly when Stuart rolled his hips and, eyes still clenched closed, tilted his head back, seeking a kiss with a desperation he'd never, ever known before. Stuart's mouth on his seared away the last of Malcolm's nerves.

"Show me what to do," he begged when they finally came up for air. Staring up at Stuart as he was, every part of him ached. "I want to make you feel good."

"You do." Stuart kissed Malcolm again, slower this time but with no less feeling. Malcolm's insides trembled.

God, how he wanted! So much more than he'd felt with the girls he'd dated, even Liz. Malcolm wanted to crawl inside this man. Feel him head to toe. Watch Stuart tremble and come undone. Hold him for as long as he was allowed.

Malcolm's hands shook as Stuart climbed off him. Standing beside the bed, he slid off his briefs, movements lithe, revealing the miles of skin that Malcolm craved. Stuart's cock stood erect and red against his abdomen, and Malcolm couldn't tear his eyes away.

This is really happening.

He shifted higher onto the mattress, his heart pounding in his throat, and Stuart pulled a small bottle from the nightstand drawer. Stuart slicked his hands, then stretched out beside Malcolm and kissed him until the need inside Malcom sharpened to a point it almost hurt.

Malcolm wrenched free with a grunt. "Show me," he whispered, voice hoarse. "Please," he began again and stopped when Stuart gave him the tenderest of smiles.

"Okay."

Linking his free hand with Malcolm's, Stuart guided him, spreading lube between their fingers with that easy motion. Together, they took Stuart in hand and Malcolm bit his lip at Stuart's sharp inhale.

"Slow at the beginning," Stuart said. "Slow and tight, so I can really feel it." His eyelids fell to half-mast as they pumped, and his chest hitched as Malcolm gripped him harder. "Uhhh...hell. Just like that."

Sliding his other arm under Stuart's shoulders, Malcolm pressed their mouths together and clenched his eyes tight when Stuart moaned against his lips.

Stuart brought his free arm around Malcolm's neck and their kisses grew sloppy because Malcolm needed that contact more than air. Stuart broke away with a gasp.

"Fuck, Mal."

The plea in his voice sent a shock of heat through Malcolm unlike anything he'd ever experienced. *I've got you,* he thought, and though he couldn't say the words out loud, he meant them, body and soul.

He and Stuart swapped lingering kisses, their strokes growing faster while Stuart's breaths echoed through the quiet room and he bucked and writhed. Stuart's hold on Malcolm turned to iron.

"Oh, fuck. Gonna come," he babbled, his whole body trembling. "You... 'M gonna come so hard."

"Let me see you," Malcolm murmured, his chest twisting when Stuart's glazed eyes locked with his.

Stuart's mouth fell open in a silent scream. He arched his back, thrusting his chest up, and a hot slick of cum spread over Malcolm's fist. Awestruck, Malcolm held Stuart as he came apart, cradling him tight until Stuart went mostly limp and his eyes fluttered closed.

"Mmm." Stuart nuzzled Malcolm's cheek with his nose and lips. "So good, baby."

Eyes burning, Malcolm pressed a kiss against the corner of Stuart's mouth. He wanted to smile at the mumbled endearment, but the moment felt too big and important, and everything about Malcolm was strung so tight he could barely breathe. He actually flinched when Stuart brushed a finger against the waistband of Malcolm's boxer briefs.

"Hey. That was amazing." Stuart kissed him, his touch so gentle, and his gaze shone bright when Malcolm peeled open his eyes. "I'd like to return the favor if you'll let me."

"I'm good," Malcolm promised. His skin pebbled as Stuart rubbed a sticky hand over his belly. "That was for you."

Stuart uttered a low chuckle. "Is this for me, too?"

Before Malcolm could ask what he meant, a big hand spread over his very erect cock and the touch sent a shudder up his spine.

"Holy shit." Malcolm huffed out a shaky laugh.

"You didn't notice?" The tender expression was back on Stuart's face. He rolled so he was half on top of Malcolm and that delicious weight turned Malcolm's bones liquid. Jesus, he loved Stuart's body over his, pressing him down.

"Oh, fuck."

"Mmm. You like that?" Stuart rubbed a thumb over Malcolm's lips and smiled when Malcolm moaned. "I kind of like it when you swear."

"I try not to usually." Malcolm shivered again. "Been more focused on you than anything else."

"Well, now it's my turn. I'm going to make you feel good."

Fire flooded Malcolm's veins. He rarely got hard without direct physical contact. Then again, everything with Stuart was different. A hundred times more powerful and intense, so that even when Malcolm's attention was on Stuart, something inside him reacted, too.

He grabbed on to Stuart's waist with a force he knew was bruising. "Stuart. I need…oh, need more. Please."

Stuart pressed their foreheads together. "Of course."

Malcolm managed to hang on to his sanity until they got his boxer briefs down around his thighs. When Stuart wrapped a hand around Malcolm's cock, he rocked his world on its axis.

He couldn't remember ever feeling so good.

Body jolting, he muffled a shout against Stuart's shoulder, his body screaming for relief he hadn't known he craved. Stuart held him close, crooning sweet nonsense as he stroked Malcolm off, while Malcolm moaned and gasped, too far gone to return the kisses being dropped on his face and neck.

"I've got you," Stuart said, his low words an echo of the silent pledge Malcolm had made only minutes before.

A lump rose in Malcolm's throat. He soared and fell, all at the same time, his brain and body pulsing, and he turned his face into Stuart's throat, craving closeness even more as he came so hard he could barely breathe.

He had no idea how much time had passed when he surfaced again. He found Stuart holding him, however, his grip firm in a way Malcolm needed. In the next second, he noticed his boxer briefs had been peeled away and his skin wiped clean, too, and that his and Stuart's legs were tangled together beneath the sheets. Cheeks warm, he made to move, then settled back quickly when Stuart shushed him.

"Where do you think you're going?"

"Don't know." Malcolm smiled against Stuart's shoulder. Funny that he'd feel even the least bit shy after what they'd just shared. "Didn't want to overstay my welcome."

Stuart ran a hand over Malcolm's hair. "Not sure that would be possible. I was planning to hang on to you until morning, if you don't mind, and there's still not-fancy coffee slush in the freezer for us to eat."

"You may be sorry you said that when I'm wide awake in the middle of the night." Affection swelled in Malcolm's chest as he listened to Stuart laugh.

"Fair enough. I'll make sure you're up in time tomorrow to get home and changed for work."

They lay quiet for a bit longer, Stuart petting Malcolm all the while, and when Stuart spoke again, his voice was much softer.

"How do you feel right now?"

Like I've been half-asleep my whole life and am just waking up.

Malcolm drew in a deep breath. "Better than I have in a long while," he said. "And like I'm starting to know a whole different side of myself I didn't know existed."

Stuart hummed against Malcolm's hair. "I think I know what you mean by that."

Chapter Twelve

"Man, I really worked up an appetite hiking in the Ramble today," Stuart said as he filled a water glass from the tap. He guzzled it down, then refilled it to sip more slowly.

"Me, too," Malcolm called out from the other room. "I'll get a change of clothes and throw together an overnight bag so we can head to your place and eat there. I promise I'll make it quick."

"Do you want to stop somewhere and pick up takeout on the way?" Stuart offered, hoping they wouldn't have to wait quite that long. After the hike, they'd eaten a small picnic Stuart had packed, then given bouldering a try on a nearby rock. Apparently, lunch hadn't been quite hearty enough to tide him over. His stomach was rumbling already.

"I'm watching my budget, remember?" Malcolm said.

"My treat. Nothing fancy. I was thinking of this place around the corner from me. Amazing Northern Italian stuff."

"I'd rather not, if that's okay." Malcolm's voice sounded strained even from two rooms away.

"No problem." Stuart knew Malcolm didn't like feeling indebted to him, although he'd hoped he'd relax about it now that they were dating rather than just hanging out as friends. *Oh well.* Stuart pulled open the refrigerator door and called over his shoulder. "Hey, how about I cook here? I'm seriously famished and I'm not sure I can wait another hour or so to" — Stuart furrowed his brow as his gaze landed on the puzzling sight in front of him — "eat."

Malcolm's fridge was empty. Like a box of baking soda and some condiments kind of empty. Not even a small block of cheese or eggs. The only time Stuart had ever seen a refrigerator with so little food in it was when someone didn't cook. At all. And Stuart damn well knew Malcolm could cook. They'd talked about it plenty of times and he'd eaten the delicious taco salad Malcolm had made at his mom's place. Something was off here. Very, very off.

"Sorry, that won't work. I haven't been to the store," Malcolm called back.

Various scenarios popped into Stuart's head as he closed the refrigerator. He opened a couple of cabinets, finding plates and glasses before finally spotting the food storage. Except there was almost nothing in it, either. He picked up a jar of peanut butter that was scraped so clean there was barely a teaspoon left. One can of beans on the shelf. Maybe a quarter cup of rice in a container. Stuart pulled open a few more cabinets, but no, there was no food in them outside of spices and condiments like soy sauce. Almost nothing that an actual meal could be made from. Stuart was still staring at a set of empty shelves in confusion and dawning worry as Malcolm walked up behind him.

"Are you moving?" Stuart asked as he closed the cabinet door. He'd let his food stores run low before moving to make life easier. This felt like more than that. Malcolm certainly hadn't mentioned he was leaving this place. Nor had Stuart seen boxes or other signs of packing in the rest of the apartment.

"Oh." Malcolm's laugh held a nervous edge. "No. Like I said, I uh, haven't made it to the store lately. I've been so busy and I've been spending a lot of time at your place. I haven't had time. You know how it is."

A trickle of unease ran through Stuart as he turned to face Malcolm.

"Mal," Stuart said slowly, not sure what the best approach was. His instincts told him something was very wrong and he wanted to handle it as gently as possible. Whatever Malcolm was going through, it worried Stuart. "This seems like there's more than you just being busy. I'm concerned." Malcolm had been looking a little thin and tired lately. Jesus, was he not eating at all when he was home? They'd spent no time here since they'd been dating and had never eaten here. It hadn't struck Stuart as odd at the time since Malcolm hadn't told his brother about their relationship yet but now Stuart wondered if there was more to it than that.

"It's nothing, Stuart. Really." Malcolm wouldn't look him in the eye. He stared over Stuart's shoulder, worrying his lower lip with his teeth.

"Hey, come on, talk to me. You can tell me anything that's going on with you. I don't want us to keep secrets from each other." Stuart winced internally. Okay, that was a little hypocritical. He still hadn't told Malcolm about his kink. One big issue at a time, though, and this was one they needed to deal with immediately. His interest in lacy underthings could wait.

"You're making a big deal out of nothing," Malcolm protested. "Let it go."

Stuart reached out and gently clasped Malcolm's face, forcing him to look him in the eye. "If you're dealing with a health problem, I want to help you. I'll do whatever I can. I just need to know. If food's the issue…"

An eating disorder wasn't unheard of in men. At all. In fact, Stuart had dated a guy who'd struggled with anorexia, which was why it was one of the first things that popped into Stuart's head. The more he considered it, the less that seemed to fit, however. Malcolm had seemed very open to eating anything Stuart offered him. He also hadn't shown any signs of him throwing food up after they ate, so it likely wasn't bulimia.

"Food's not the issue." Malcolm closed his eyes. There was so much pain on his face and Stuart wanted to wrap him in a hug, but he wasn't sure this was the time to push physical contact with Malcolm. However, he believed Malcolm was telling the truth.

Stuart scrambled to put all the pieces together. Malcolm had also been heavily leaning toward eating vegetarian lately and didn't want to eat out. In fact, he'd turned down doing a number of date ideas that Stuart had suggested. Even when they had nothing to do with food.

Oh. The pieces clicked into place. *Money.* It had to be money.

"Mal, are you having trouble with money right now?" Stuart asked softly, trying to keep his tone as non-judgmental as possible.

"Why won't you just drop this?" Malcolm's tone was defensive. This conversation had clearly made him uncomfortable, and while Stuart kept his own tone soothing, there was no way he was dropping this.

"Because I care about you. A lot. And I want to help. We've already told each other about some big things. My previous marriage and Mormon upbringing. Your sexuality. There's nothing we can't talk about. I want you to be honest with me so I can help. If I can help —"

"There's nothing you can do!" There was a stubborn set to Malcolm's jaw.

"But there is a problem?" Stuart prompted.

Malcolm sighed. "Yeah."

"And it has to do with money?"

He nodded once. Reluctantly.

Stuart hazarded a guess. "Does this tie into your mom's money troubles?"

"Yes." Malcolm's shoulders slumped and all the tension seemed to go out of him at once. "I've been in a bad spot since her injury."

Stuart put an arm around Malcolm and led him into the living room. Malcolm didn't protest. In fact, he was so docile he worried Stuart. He seemed almost robotic.

"Hey, come on," Stuart coaxed. He took a seat beside Malcolm and angled his body so he could look at Malcolm's face. "Talk to me. I promise you'll get no judgment from me about this. I've lived paycheck to paycheck before. Hell, I was broke when I was going to culinary school. I didn't go hungry because we ate what we made at the institute, but I was scraping by otherwise. I even went without heat for a couple of months one winter because I got behind on payments. I know what it's like to be short on funds. So what's going on with your mom?"

"She's terrible at managing money," Malcolm said softly. "After she and my dad got divorced, she didn't adjust to the change in income or bother to manage the household for one person and not two. Then she lost her job and never stopped spending money like she did before."

Stuart nodded.

"Jackson and I have been helping out. Filling up her gas tank, paying her utility bills, buying groceries..." He sighed. "Then she got injured when the steps gave out."

"Does she not have insurance?"

"No, she does. I put her on my insurance when she wasn't able to buy her own after the unemployment benefits ran out. That means I'm covering the deductible from the ED visits and follow-ups with her doctor."

Stuart grimaced. Insurance was a killer. Marisol offered health coverage to her employees. Not every restaurant owner was so generous. He'd lived for a lot of years without it and spent every day crossing his fingers nothing catastrophic would happen.

"Okay. I see why things are so tight for you," Stuart said. "Do you need a loan? I have some savings. I'd be more than happy to —"

"No." Malcolm shook his head. "No, I don't expect you to do that."

"It's not a matter of expecting it," Stuart argued. "I'm offering. I want to help."

"I can't. I really can't accept that."

Stuart sighed and nodded. "Okay. What about groceries? Will you at least let me buy you groceries for the next few weeks? Just to get you by until things improve. I can't stand the idea of you going hungry when I could do something about it."

"I can take care of myself." There was a stubborn set to Malcolm's jaw.

"I know that. Clearly, you're taking wonderful care of your mom, too. I could make things easier for you if you'd let me."

Malcolm shook his head again and Stuart knew he had to back off on this or risk Malcolm clamming up completely. "Okay. What about your brother? He lives here, right? Doesn't he contribute to groceries? Hasn't he noticed how tight things are for you?"

Malcolm shook his head. "Jackson's never here anymore. I don't think he's been at the apartment overnight in at least a month and he only drops by to get clothes or whatever else he needs. He doesn't cook or eat here so he wouldn't have noticed."

"Is he struggling as badly?"

"No. He works in the private sector, so he makes more than I do to begin with, and he shares expenses with his girlfriend. Plus, I'm the one who took on my mom's medical debt and the porch repair."

"Have you asked him to help out?"

"No."

"Why not?"

"My mom doesn't have anyone else to help her out. Taking care of her is my responsibility." Malcolm looked away.

No, it's your mother's responsibility – she's the parent, Stuart thought. He knew he couldn't say that aloud. He didn't want to alienate Malcolm right now and dealing with Kim Elliott's issues would be a long-term thing. Not that his heart didn't go out to Kim if she was struggling. It did. He also felt conflicted. While Stuart had many issues with the Mormon faith, he had been raised with the belief that he should look out for his neighbor and help them when they were in trouble. He still believed that. There was a point at which that struggling person could drag someone under, however. And it was clear that Malcolm was drowning.

"So, neither your mom nor your brother knows how much strain this is putting on you?"

"No. I haven't told them. I don't know how to talk to them about this. I know I should be able to, but I don't know what to say or how to say it. It feels like any way I word it will only make my mom feel worse and I know it'll make Jackson feel guilty. I know I need to. I just don't know how."

Stuart reached out and squeezed Malcolm's thigh. "I love that you're such a caring person. You shouldn't be expected to shoulder this burden all by yourself, though."

"It's not that they expect me to. I want to."

"And I hate the idea of you going hungry. I want to help," Stuart said softly. "Please. I care about you."

"I know you do." Malcolm clasped Stuart's hand in his own. "And I appreciate that. I'm not very good at relying on other people when I need help."

"I know." That much was very obvious.

"I guess I'm relieved that it's not a secret anymore."

"Yeah?" Stuart brushed his thumb across Malcolm's cheek with his free hand.

"I didn't like keeping things from you. It's good to talk about it to someone."

"Good." Stuart leaned in and pressed a lingering kiss to Malcolm's forehead. "You can always talk to me about anything, I promise."

Malcolm didn't respond verbally but he did put his arms around Stuart and pull him closer. Stuart held him tight. He reminded himself that this relationship had just begun. In Malcolm's position, he wouldn't have had an easy time accepting money from someone he was newly dating either.

All Stuart could do was be a listening ear and try not to add to Malcolm's stress — financial or emotional — while he wracked his brain for other ways he could help.

There had to be something he could do.

* * * *

After more prodding on Stuart's part, Malcolm relented and allowed him to pick up takeout on their way to Stuart's place. Malcolm seemed self-conscious as he ate the pasta, but he did polish off a healthy portion for dinner.

They had a quiet evening in. Malcolm seemed too emotionally wrung-out for anything sexual. Stuart had enjoyed the exploration they'd done lately, but this was not the time to push it. No matter how much he loved the feeling of Malcolm's fist wrapped around his cock or watching Malcolm's face as he got him off, that night, Stuart was content to hold him as they watched a movie. The soft rise and fall of Malcolm's breathing was a reminder that they were in this together. After they'd brushed their teeth and slid under the covers, Malcolm slept deeply while Stuart tossed and turned, his mind racing and his heart heavy with worry.

He made Malcolm an enormous omelet for breakfast the next morning and pushed the leftover Italian into his hands to take for lunch. While Malcolm looked vaguely annoyed, he accepted it without protest. As Stuart kissed him goodbye before they went their separate ways to work, an idea that had rattled around Stuart's brain all night re-emerged.

He debated letting Malcolm's friends know about the difficult situation Malcolm was in. The idea of going behind Malcolm's back wasn't something Stuart liked, but he knew Malcolm wouldn't reach out to them on his own. Stuart also knew the guys would be horrified to know that Malcolm was in such a bad position, especially when they could help.

Contemplating who he should approach, Stuart rode his bike to the restaurant and, once seated at the desk in the cramped office, sent a text to Kyle. Kyle seemed as approachable as any of the crew. Stuart and he had recently texted about the fundraising event so there was already a line of communication open.

Will you be at Under tonight after 10 p.m.? Stuart asked.

Sure. What's up?

Got a thing to run by you. It'll be easier to explain in person.

Come by any time. I'll be here until close tonight.

Stuart's day passed in a blur. King's was packed that night and one of the cooks' wives went into labor halfway through his shift, so Stuart had to fill in and prepare the remainder of the fish dishes while also juggling the plating. He was ready to crash by the time his shift ended. Unfortunately, the situation with Malcolm was too urgent for him to reschedule his meeting with Kyle. Stuart's worry had only increased since yesterday.

The ride to the speakeasy helped wake him up, and he greeted the staff at Lock & Key as he walked past them toward the back of the room. "Hey, guys."

"Hey, good to see you, Chef!"

"You, too."

"What are you doing here?"

"I'm meeting with Kyle," he explained as they waved him on.

Slipping through the plain door and into the hallway behind, Stuart ignored the phone, choosing instead to use the hidden catch in the blank door that Kyle had shown him. When the door opened, he jogged down the secret staircase.

Jim, the head of security, greeted him with a friendly smile. "Evening, Stuart. Good to see you again."

Stuart forced himself to smile back. "You, too."

He spotted Kyle behind the bar talking to a man sitting on one of the stools with his back to Stuart. The dark hair and lean but fit frame were familiar. He wondered what Riley Porter-Wright was doing here. Malcolm had told him that the guys now knew he and Malcolm were dating. It sent a glow through Stuart to know Malcolm had shared that with his friends. He wouldn't have done it if he weren't invested in being with Stuart. And nothing made him happier to think about.

Kyle looked up and smiled. "Hey. Glad you could make it."

Riley turned and smiled. "Nice to see you, Stuart."

Stuart greeted them both and took the stool next to Riley.

"You want me to head out?" Riley asked. "I stopped by to talk to Kyle about drinks for the wedding. We finished a while ago and have just been catching up."

"No, stay," Stuart said. "It's good you're here, actually." Riley had always seemed like a good guy and Stuart knew he cared about Malcolm a lot. "I need to talk to you guys about Malcolm."

Kyle and Riley both frowned.

"What do you mean?" Riley asked.

"The short version is Malcolm is in some financial trouble and he's having difficulty affording food," Stuart said, voice grim. Might as well cut to the chase immediately. "There are days he's going hungry because he's so strapped for money."

The exclamations of shock and worry were instantaneous. "What the hell is going on?" Kyle asked, leaning forward to brace his arms on the bar.

Riley's expression was perplexed. "Malcolm's the most careful person I know. How did this happen?"

"His mom's having money problems and they've gotten so bad they're impacting him, too," Stuart explained.

"I can't believe he didn't come to me," Kyle said, a deep furrow forming on his forehead. "To one of us at least."

"I know," Riley echoed. "I remember his mom having a minor injury when she fell through the steps, but I had no idea anything was that serious. What happened?"

Stuart went over everything Malcolm had told him and Kyle gave a heavy sigh.

"Damn it, I wish he'd told us about all of this," he said. "Or some of it at least. I had no idea."

"I had to drag it out of him. I also suggested Malcolm talk to you guys and he didn't want to. I think he's ashamed." Stuart paused. "Maybe ashamed isn't the right word exactly. He's very uncomfortable with the idea of telling you."

"Shit, he knows I was homeless and slept on couches for a while when I first moved to New York," Kyle said. "We've talked about it. I get why it might be harder for him to come to some of us – sorry, Ri – but let's face it, you, Carter, Will and Jesse have never had to worry about when your next paycheck is coming in. He should have known he could come to me, though."

Riley nodded.

Stuart knew he and the others Kyle had named came from families with money. He doubted they'd ever worried about paying rent or buying groceries, but there was no doubt they loved Malcolm and would have helped in a heartbeat. Still, Stuart understood what Kyle was saying. Of anyone, he was the friend who might best understand what Malcolm was going through.

Kyle sighed again. "I know Mal's a private person."

"At this point, I'm less concerned about why he didn't come to us than how we can help," Riley said.

"Exactly," Stuart chimed in. "That's why I came here tonight. I hoped maybe you guys could help me come up with some way to help him out in the short term. The only thing he'll let me do right now is cook for him whenever he's at my place."

"How often is he there?" Riley asked.

Stuart shrugged. "A few days a week at most. Not enough that I'm sure he gets three square meals a day every day of the week."

Riley shook his head. "That's not enough. Hmm. Maybe we can arrange for grocery deliveries?"

"You don't think he'll be pissed?"

"Oh, I'm sure he will be," Riley said. "But if we don't let him know who places the order, he'll be mad at all of us together rather than one person specifically."

Stuart smiled grimly. Riley had a point. "There's no way he'd refuse the deliveries, is there?"

"I don't think so." Kyle's answering look was equally stern. "I didn't think he'd keep something like this from us either, so who knows?"

"It's worth a try," Riley said.

"It is." Stuart dragged a hand through his hair. "He's going to be pissed at me for telling you guys."

"You did the right thing." Kyle ran his fingers over his mouth. "He needs help and none of us are okay with standing by and doing nothing while he struggles."

"I'd rather risk pissing him off than let him go hungry," Riley said.

They all nodded their agreement.

"The real problem is Malcolm's mom's finances," Stuart reminded them. "Without the added strain from her problems, he'd be making enough at CEC to be okay. So until she's in a better position financially, things aren't going to improve for him. Anything like a grocery delivery is a short-term patch and not really solving the problem."

"I know." Kyle frowned. "I'm not sure what to suggest, though."

"No, me, either."

"Let me think about it," Riley said. "There has to be some resource for her. Like a decent debt consolidation service if that's the issue or a financial planner."

"I'm not even sure she understands there's a problem," Stuart mused, "which I think is the problem. She's oblivious to the stress she's causing Malcolm and he's not willing to call her out on it."

"Okay. I'll work on him about that," Kyle replied. "Ri and I can update everyone else. With nine of us putting our heads together, we'll come up with ways to help."

"Thank you, guys," Stuart said gratefully. He'd made the right decision to come to them. Kyle was right. With that many people who cared working on the problem, they were sure to figure out a solution. There was no need for Malcolm to go it alone.

"No, thank you," Riley said. "I can't believe we didn't spot something amiss. Carter is going to be horrified when he finds out."

Stuart nodded. As Malcolm's coworker, he probably spent more time with Malcolm than anyone. If even Carter hadn't noticed, Malcolm really had gone all out to hide his situation.

"So we all know what to do, right?" Riley asked. "Kyle and I will talk to the other guys, arrange for groceries and figure out something that might help his mom."

"That sounds like a plan to me," Stuart said. "I'll focus on getting Malcolm fed for the next couple of days and being there for him if he wants to talk more."

He thanked Kyle and Riley again, shook their hands, then said goodnight.

As he got on his bike and drove home, worries began to creep in again. Stuart knew he'd done the right thing for Malcolm's sake, but he wasn't so sure it was the right thing for their relationship. Would Malcolm see this as a betrayal of his trust? They'd barely begun dating. What if it damaged what they'd been building together?

And what if the harm was irreparable?

Chapter Thirteen

The smells of furniture polish and cleanser hung in the air as Malcolm lugged a basket of freshly laundered linens and towels into his living room. He set it down on the couch and the motion made stacks of already folded clothes standing on the cushions waver and one topple over. Malcolm righted it with a smile. This is what he got for spending so much time out of his apartment in the last several weeks—a Saturday morning spent doing housework, including washing and folding what appeared to be every item of clothing, bedding and toweling he owned.

At least he enjoyed doing laundry. He planned to finish by midday, too, because Carter and Riley had invited him over for dinner. Carter had been withdrawn and stressed the last several days and Malcolm looked forward to spending time unwinding with his friend. Because Malcolm needed that time, too.

Stuart's discovery of Malcolm's empty refrigerator and pantry had been intense, to say the least. Stuart had wanted to talk about it even more when they'd seen each other since and help Malcolm plan ways to help his mom without exhausting his own resources. Stuart always cooked enough food for a crowd, too, even though it was only the two of them, then loaded Malcolm up with leftovers.

Normally, that kind of extra attention made Malcolm want to pull out his own hair but, for the most part, he felt only grateful. Trusting Stuart had lifted an enormous weight from Malcolm's shoulders. His guts still twisted with guilt whenever he considered what that meant, but he was glad Stuart had pulled the info out of him. God, if his mom knew her secret was out? Or that her problems were affecting her sons? Malcolm shook his head. Better not to go there at all and instead focus on Stuart. Malcolm had absolutely no problem going there.

'I care about you.'

Malcolm hauled in a deep breath. Stuart had told him that several times in the last week and a thrill went through Malcolm every time. Not that he even needed the words to be spoken because Malcolm swore he could feel how much Stuart cared in every touch and glance.

Cheeks warm, he reached for a towel at the top of the basket. He cared for Stuart, too, far more than he'd imagined possible in such a short time. What was more, Malcolm needed him. Needed Stuart's strength. His snarky humor and big heart, and his seemingly limitless patience. His…everything.

I wish he were here.

Malcolm dropped the towel he'd been folding back in the basket. Just thinking about Stuart made his heart squeeze and body heat, and his mind reeled a bit as his cock hardened. No one had ever affected him like this.

Made his nerves tighten with a yearning so intense his mouth went dry. Stuart's face flashed through Malcolm's mind, heightening the buzz in his groin, and slowly, he sank onto the couch and gave himself over to desire.

That was what he was feeling. This was more than making sure Stuart got what he needed when they had sex. Right now, Malcolm wanted to feel good, too. He craved Stuart with a hunger that would have shocked them both only a few weeks ago. Craved Stuart's kiss and touch and the way he made Malcolm want to beg for more, so that by the time Malcolm came, it felt like flying.

A shiver raced up Malcolm's spine. He palmed himself through his joggers, eyelids heavy, and his breath caught on a giddy laugh. "Jesus," he whispered.

He didn't do this. Didn't lose track of what he was doing because he was turned on. Didn't sit in his living room and think about getting off in the middle of the afternoon. Malcolm considered doing exactly that until the apartment's intercom rang.

He loosed a heartfelt groan. "You've got to be kidding me."

As if in reply, the intercom rang again, which got Malcolm quickly to his feet. He tugged the hem of his T-shirt over his groin as he crossed to the door and tried not to sound grumpy when he hit the Talk button.

"Hi, Henry."

"Hello, Mr. Elliott," the concierge replied, his voice tinny through the speaker. "Your grocery delivery is here in the lobby—okay if I send it on up?"

Malcolm frowned. "My... What kind of delivery?"

"Grocery, sir, from Diedrich's on 26th Street."

Well, that had to be a mistake. Malcolm didn't order groceries for delivery, nor did he shop at Diedrich's, even when his bank account was healthy. Diedrich's was the kind of gourmet market that Jesse and Will frequented instead of the big chain store on the next street. Asking Henry to sort out the problem wasn't fair, however, and Malcolm gave him the go ahead to send the delivery up. That turned out to be no help at all because Malcolm's name and address were indeed on the delivery slips and he still had no idea why. All he could do was look on while Tommy, a cheerful young guy in a Diedrich's uniform, unloaded what had to be two dozen canvas bags stuffed full of food from the plastic crates on his hand truck.

"Do I need to sign this?" Malcolm asked. He held the receipt up as Tommy restacked the empty crates.

"Nope—you're all set." Tommy shot him a grin. "Thanks for tipping ahead, too. Gratuities aren't expected at Diedrich's but I, for one, appreciate the gesture."

Malcolm blinked. "Uh, sure. You're welcome."

The words felt weird in his mouth, like he'd been to the dentist and his lips were still numb, and the apartment seemed far too quiet after Tommy had gone. Malcolm walked back to the kitchen, his gaze on the bags while disquiet gathered inside him. What the hell was going on? How had Diedrich's gotten his name on a—

Oh, hell.

Glancing back to the slips of paper in his hand, Malcolm really looked this time and his heart sank when he saw that nothing listed included a price. Even the total was missing and a handwritten *PAID* had been scrawled in its place. Malcolm slipped the receipts in his pocket and moved to the bags, feeling more and more anxious as he unpacked them.

Stuart, what did you do?

His mind boggled at the sheer amount of food. Dry goods and fresh produce. Meats, cheese, eggs. Three varieties of bread. Boxes, jars and bags — enough to feed a family. Or restock one person's empty kitchen from the ground up. And Malcolm had never felt less hungry.

He went still as he dug a package of cookies out of the final bag. They were a hard-to-find brand that David Mori had introduced him to, and not many people outside of the speakeasy crew knew how much Malcolm liked the little shortbread sandwiches with mango crème. He knew for sure he'd never eaten them around Stuart...which could only mean Stuart hadn't set up this grocery delivery on his own.

That knowledge made Malcolm's eyes burn.

* * * *

"Malcolm? What the fuck?" Thunder filled Stuart's brow as he jogged up, a reaction Malcolm now easily recognized as worry. "Is something wrong? How long have you been out here?"

"Not long," Malcolm lied. He unfolded himself from his seat on the stoop outside of Stuart's building and stood.

In truth, he'd been waiting over an hour. Stuart didn't need to know that, though. It would only distract them and delay the real reason Malcolm was in Little Italy at twelve-fifteen in the morning. *To talk.* Because yeah, something was wrong. Malcolm's insides were strung tight and his head was pounding, and not even the sight of Stuart in his leathers, dark eyes flashing, made him feel anything less than crap.

"A huge order of groceries showed up at my apartment today," he said, voice flat over Stuart's muttering that Malcolm could have been mugged. Stuart's eyes went wide. "Groceries I didn't order," Malcolm added, "and there was no indication of who had on the receipts."

Stuart stood frozen, just for a second, before he gently took hold of Malcolm's arm. "Let's talk inside."

"I don't want to go inside." Malcolm shrugged him off, then made himself step back despite the surprise streaking across Stuart's face. "I want you to explain to me why you told my friends about what's been going on with my finances after I asked you not to. Because I know you did."

"Mal—"

"Did you think I wouldn't find out?"

"I knew you would, obviously." Stuart sighed. "I wanted to tell you before then. I guess I got the timing on the grocery order wrong."

Malcolm licked his lips. "That's what concerns you? That you messed up the timing?"

"Well, it hasn't made this any easier." Stuart frowned at Malcolm's groan. "What?"

"Man, I don't even know where to start. I had to go to Carter for answers. And fuck…it's been a long time since I saw him that upset." Malcolm didn't even want to think about the emotions he'd glimpsed in his friend's eyes as they'd talked. "I knew he'd tell me if I asked him straight out what the hell was going on, and according to him, you told Kyle and Riley about my money problems and asked them to get the whole crew involved."

"That's not…entirely accurate."

"Seriously?" Malcolm's heart hurt as he stared Stuart down. "I talked to Riley, too. I know he was there at Under when you spilled the whole story."

"Okay, yes." Stuart blew out a breath. "I told him and Kyle about what you've been going through, and they proposed the whole crew get on board and help. We want to help, Mal. Because you going hungry?" Mouth tight, he shook his head. "I can't let you do that to yourself."

Malcolm's jaw sagged. "Let me?"

"I didn't mean it that way —"

"I'm not a project that needs managing, Stuart. I can take care of myself!"

"I understand that, but you need help this time!" Stuart raked a hand through his thick hair. "Jesus, Malcolm, I feed people for a living. I can't stand by while you starve yourself!"

Heat crawled up Malcolm's neck. Damnit, he couldn't remember the last time he'd been so angry. "That gives you the right to go behind my back?"

"I get that I shouldn't have done that and I was going to tell you, I swear. I just…" Stuart grimaced. "I couldn't figure out how. I knew you'd be mad and a part of me didn't want to deal with that. Fuck, I wish you had asked me instead of going to Carter."

"I asked him because I wasn't sure you'd be straight with me." Though Stuart's wounded expression hurt to see, Malcolm simply shrugged. "You've been lying to my face for days."

"I didn't lie!"

"Oh, Stuart, come on. Yes, you did. You promised not to tell anyone about my money problems, even after you already had."

"Can you blame me?" Stuart shot back. He set his hands on his hips with a muffled curse. "I was worried about you! You wouldn't let me help, wouldn't talk to your friends. You sure as shit wouldn't tell your mom that you are going broke supporting her while she pretends that nothing is wrong."

"Don't." The ache in Malcolm's throat made it hard to speak. "Don't you bring her into this."

Stuart's eyes went wide. "How can I not? Your mom is the reason we're even talking about this right now!"

"No. This isn't about Mom. This is about me trusting you with something important and you not giving two shits about that."

Stuart's face fell at the waver in Malcolm's voice. "That's not what I... Fuck." He grabbed Malcolm's hand between his. "I just wanted to help. You have to believe me when I say that."

"I do. And you were helping. By being there for me and listening." Malcolm gave a hard laugh. "You were great about everything. You didn't judge my mom's bad choices or mine, or preach at me to man up and tell her no. For the first time in a while, it was like I wasn't drowning, you know? Like I could count on you to be there for me, even with all my problems." He shook his head slowly. "Now, I don't know if any of that was real or if you were just humoring me."

"Oh, God. Of course, it was real. All of it." Stuart's throat worked and he took another step closer. "I know you're angry and I know I overstepped, and that's on me. But I saw a problem that I knew I could make better and I...I acted. I never meant to hurt you. Do you understand?"

Malcolm didn't answer. A part of him got it. Under Stuart's blithe 'I don't give a fuck' attitude, he harbored a mile-wide protective streak for the people he was close to. Malcolm had been on the receiving end of it a couple of times already. Generally, that caring nature centered him, gave Malcolm an anchor when he needed it. Tonight, though, he just felt exposed and out of control.

Anger fading, Malcolm rubbed a hand over his face, heartsore and stripped bare and once again overwhelmed with a sense that his ship was slowly going under.

"I know you were trying to help," he said, voice quiet. "I'm grateful to you and the guys for wanting to be there for me, too. That doesn't change the fact that I told you about my mom's situation in confidence and it's like that didn't even matter to you. Is this how things are going to work? You deciding how you want things to go while I try to catch up?" He squeezed Stuart's fingers, determined to be heard.

"I'm having dinner with my mom and Jack tomorrow and now I have to sit there and look her in the eye, knowing that a whole bunch of people she's never even met are aware of her situation and how much it affects her sons. She'd hate that."

Malcolm drew in a deep breath. "I know you don't understand why I feel responsible for helping her, but I do. My mom doesn't have any other family besides Jack and me. She has no idea what we've been going through. Hell, not even my dad knows what's been going on with the three of us. He thinks my mom is still living off her severance." Malcolm's throat was so thick it was a wonder he could speak at all. "I know how fucked up that sounds. I am fucked up. I don't know how to turn off wanting to help the people I care about, even when I should."

"I don't think you're fucked up, Malcolm. I am worried about you, though." Stuart clenched his eyes closed for several seconds. They were pained when he opened them again. "And I am sorry that I hurt you."

Malcolm gave a stiff nod. "You should have told me that you were going to talk to Kyle."

"I thought you'd ask me not to."

"Maybe I would have, but at least we'd have been working on it together. You didn't even give me a chance. You just decided that what you wanted was more important and went ahead like my opinion didn't matter at all."

Stuart blew a noisy breath through his nose. "I didn't think about it that way. Of course, your opinion matters to me. And I really, really hate that I've made you doubt how much I want to be there for you." Lifting Malcolm's hand, he pressed the palm flat against his own chest. "I'm here, however you need me. Even if only to listen because you need to talk. Okay?"

Malcolm wanted to agree. Agreeing would be easy and feel good, and it would wipe the stress from Stuart's face. Malcolm's head would still hurt, though. He'd still be angry and dejected and so fucking done with this day. He could tell from Stuart's expression that he wasn't done talking, either, and goddamn it, Malcolm needed to not fucking talk for a change. He needed time to recharge and get his head back on straight, and definitely not think at all about how his closest friends knew that his life was really screwed up right now.

Some of Malcolm's feelings must have shown on his face because Stuart looked more worried than ever as he gestured back to his door.

"Come inside with me," he said, even as Malcolm slowly shook his head.

"I'm gonna go."

"Oh, Mal." Stuart squeezed Malcolm's fingers. "Are you sure? You know you can stay for as long as you need—"

"I know," Malcolm murmured. "But I need to figure out what to do next. What to say to my mom and Jack about...everything. I can't do that here."

Stuart pressed his lips into a thin line for several seconds. "Okay," he said at last. "Let's get you a Lyft."

* * * *

"Mom?" Malcolm walked into his mother's kitchen, inhaling the scent of roasting chicken and aware of voices and movement on the sun porch through the open door. At least he didn't need to figure out what they were going to eat tonight. He hung his bag on the back of one of the kitchen chairs and set the box of mango crème cookies on the table. "Smells great in here. Is that Dad's car in the driveway?"

"You know it is."

Malcolm stopped short as his father's second wife, Genifer, stepped through the sun-porch door, looking sun-kissed and pretty in jeans and a white blouse.

"Holy crap, Gen! Hi!"

"Now that's the kind of greeting a gal likes to hear." Genifer reached up to give him a hug. "How are you, handsome?"

"I'm a little confused, but otherwise fine," he said with a laugh. "Are you sure we're in the right house?"

"Hah, Jack said something similar when he got here—he did a literal double-take when he saw me."

She stepped back and patted Malcolm's arm with a fond smile. "Your mom and I have been talking recently. Had lunch a couple of times and grabbed some coffee this week."

"Get out. Really?"

Genifer held her hand up like she was making a pledge. "All true. She and your dad and I want to be friends. Be a proper family, really, which is surprisingly nice. Especially if your dad and I get lucky with a baby someday."

"Nice for you and me both." Malcolm glanced toward the door where he could just see his mom and smiled. "I'm really glad to hear that."

Genifer had cocked her head when Malcolm looked back her way. "Are you all right?" she asked. "I don't mean to sound like a jerk, but you look completely wiped."

Malcolm made his right shoulder move in a half shrug. He looked like crap and knew it. His head still ached and he'd had trouble sleeping last night, unable to stop thinking about Stuart and their argument. Stuart had waited while Malcolm used his phone to order a Lyft, and while they'd held hands the whole time, he'd been oddly quiet. A somber expression had fallen over his features by the time the car pulled up, and his touch had lingered as he'd walked Malcolm to the car. Something unreadable in Stuart's eyes followed Malcolm even now.

What a mess.

"I'm fine," Malcolm said. "Just didn't sleep well."

Genifer hummed and gave him another pat. "Let's get you fed and watered. I was coming in to grab a second pitcher of Sangria from the fridge and mix up another, so why don't you go on out?"

Malcolm eyed her askance. "How much Sangria are you people planning to drink?"

"No judging." Genifer smiled, her brown eyes bright. "One pitcher only goes so far among five people. It's your dad's recipe, actually, and we brought a bunch of antipasti from the city, too, to help your mom with the cooking."

The next half hour was a blur of hugs and hellos while Malcolm caught up with everyone and hid his amazement at how at ease Genifer and his mom appeared with each other. Kim was acting like her typical self and fussing over Malcolm like always. She chided him for wearing a hoodie and for working too hard, then asked after his friends, but an air of real contentment hung about her. Malcolm knew that was in no small part due to having her whole family gathered together again, Genifer included, a thing Malcolm would not have predicted.

Seeing his mother so comfortable made him smile even as his throat grew tight. Stuart was right. Malcolm couldn't keep shielding Kim from the world — he was only hurting them both in the long run. They needed a plan that would work for everyone, today and into the future.

"Is it the wine?" he asked his brother, voice low, while Kim was chatting with Genifer and Stephen.

Jackson chuckled quietly. "I'm not sure. She didn't tell me they'd be here either, but she really seems okay with everything." He poked at the fruit in his glass. "I won't lie and say I'm not waiting for the other shoe to drop."

"Oh, good." Malcolm took a slug of his drink. "I don't need any more surprises in my life right now."

"What does that mean?" Jackson frowned. "Everything okay?"

"More or less, I think. We should talk later," he said, just as the timer in the kitchen rang and Kim got to her feet and started doling out tasks to everyone.

Malcolm found himself at the counter, carving one chicken while his dad carved the second, and Kim, Genifer and Jackson put together a massive platter of flat breads, cured meats, cheeses and various pickled vegetables.

"These olives are amazing," Kim said to Genifer. "I'm so glad you brought both black and green, even though none of the Elliott men will eat them."

"Olives taste like soap," Malcolm and Jackson said in unison while their father made a face.

"You can't have charcuterie without them!" Kim protested over Genifer's chuckling, and Malcolm rolled his eyes.

"Charcuterie are meats, Mom." He glanced over his shoulder at the tray on the table. "The rest of the things on that platter are antipasti, including the meat and things that taste like soap."

Kim waved him off with a laugh. "They taste delicious, you weirdo! And since when do you know so much about food, hm? Getting tips from your friend the chef?"

"I suppose I have." Face warm, Malcolm turned back to his carving, his family's chatter rolling over him.

"I didn't know you were still hanging with the chef, dude."

"I met him," Kim said to Jackson. "Stuart helped your brother fix the steps on the porch and do a few things around the house. He looks gruff and tough, but he was actually lovely. And much more of a gentleman than the guy I was dating."

Malcolm winced. His mother had ended things with Scott from Maine shortly after the ankle injury. His lackadaisical attitude toward her wellbeing hadn't done him any favors.

"You should have invited Stuart for dinner, honey," Kim called over to Malcolm now. "And, Jack, why didn't you bring Marissa?"

"You know Marissa works on Sunday," Jackson replied.

"An occupational hazard when it comes to retail," Stephen said. "Any chance she's given thought to making a career change?"

Genifer tutted. "Honey."

"The woman speaks fluent Arabic, Berber and French, Gen, in addition to perfect English." Stephen set his carving knife down. "You know we all support Marissa no matter what she wants to do for a living. She would make a hell of an interpreter or translator, however, and I've been telling her that for years!"

"It happens that Marissa agrees with you," Jackson said. He was grinning when Malcolm and his dad glanced back at him. "She starts at NYU to get her certification this fall and she's taking some classes this summer to prepare."

Malcolm smiled at his brother over the others' congratulations. "That's great, Jack."

"Hopefully, you'll think so after we both move back into the apartment in K-Town with you." Jackson grimaced. "With Marissa back at school, we'll be down one salary so…"

"I get it, believe me." Malcolm didn't need to pretend he was okay with the idea of having extra roommates again. He'd need to explain a few other things before Jackson and Marissa moved back in, of course. Like why he might get random grocery deliveries and why the chef Malcolm had mentioned a few times could be around more than Jackson might expect.

No time like the present, I guess, with everyone here.

But what if...

...what? His family reacted badly to the idea that Malcolm wanted to be with a man? Refused to accept it? Kicked him out of their lives?

Malcolm swallowed. His family wasn't like that. He knew it deep in his bones. They'd be okay with whomever he wanted in his life. Jackson wouldn't give a damn. Marissa had dated both men and women before they'd met. And Malcolm's parents had always maintained that they loved him and Jackson for who they were, inside and out, and that it didn't matter whom they loved so long as they were happy, and the person treated them well. They'd be okay if Malcolm told them he was falling in love with a man.

Which was exactly what was happening.

Malcolm carried the tray of chicken back out to the porch. The world had gone fuzzy around him. He was falling, no doubt about it. Up until yesterday, he'd never been happier with anyone he'd dated. Even now, still half-angry at Stuart and raw from their argument, Malcolm wanted him. Wished he were here on the porch with Malcolm and the Elliotts, chatting about how well the wine complemented the prosciutto and maybe fighting his mom and Genifer to see who could eat the most olives.

Without even knowing it, Malcolm had passed 'like' a long time ago with Stuart and started heading toward something bigger. *Much bigger.* He swallowed a giddy chuckle. Fuck, he was in deep. He wanted the people in his life to know it, too, at least a little.

"What do you think, Mal?" Stephen raised an eyebrow when Malcolm blinked at him. "Did you even hear me?"

"Sorry, no, I didn't. I was trying to figure out how to tell you guys that Stuart and I have been seeing each other," he said. "Then I figured it made sense to just say it out loud and not make things complicated. Stuart and I are dating."

The porch went silent and now it was Stephen's turn to blink. "Stuart...the chef your mother was talking about?" He glanced at Kim, whose eyes had gone wide. "The guy who fixed the porch, right?"

"Right." Malcom met the blank expressions of his family. "We started out as friends and it changed."

"It changed, huh?" his mom asked. Kim had begun to smile, and the sight made Malcolm's heart pound with a fierce happiness that almost made him dizzy. "Into something romantic?"

He felt sure his face had gone up in flames, and he wanted to roll his eyes at Genifer's gentle laughter. "Yes, into something romantic. That's kind of the point of dating, isn't it?"

"I knew it." Kim's smile shifted, and ugh, Malcolm saw where from a mile away. "I definitely saw something between the two of you that day!"

"We were still friends at that point, Mom, but hey, maybe you did. I like him a lot."

A big grin transformed Jackson's face, too. "Good for you, bro. Marissa and I would have tried to hook you up with guys too, if we'd known you were bi."

"I didn't really know it myself." Malcolm pushed the chicken on his plate around with his fork, excruciatingly aware of his father's eyes on him. "It's new to me, too."

"That had to have been confusing for you," Genifer said, her voice even more gentle than usual.

"It was." Malcolm tipped his head from side to side. "Still is on occasion. It's getting easier, though. I'm figuring it out. With Stuart, of course."

"Good." Stephen drew his brows together, and the expression on his face was as kind as Malcolm had ever seen. "This man, Stuart. He treats you right, son?"

Malcolm stared at his father. The sharp words he'd exchanged with Stuart the night before echoed in his head, but his heart beat louder and drowned them out in the sweetest way possible. Sure, he and Stuart had some work to do. Malcolm knew they could get through it.

"Yeah, Dad," he said with a smile. "He does."

* * * *

"So you're into guys, huh?"

Malcolm smiled down at his beer. After dinner—and way more talking about his personal life than he'd generally endure—Malcolm and his brother had hitched a ride back to Koreatown with their dad and Genifer where they'd bought a six-pack from the corner bodega and headed up to the apartment.

"Like I told you guys back at Mom's, I'm into Stuart." Malcolm met his brother's gaze. "Probably guys in general. Definitely him."

A crease appeared across Jackson's brow. "He's really the first man you've ever been with? You didn't specify earlier."

"He is." Malcolm licked his lips. "I wasn't hiding being bi from you guys or anything like that. I honestly didn't know it was in me. I'm still not even sure I am bi or if I'm something else. I've been...curious, I guess, about another man in the past and never felt the need to act on it. Never even considered it, honestly. This thing with Stuart surprised me. Him too, I think."

Jackson hummed. "Marissa says sexuality is fluid in some people."

"That's what a lot of current research indicates, yes. Sexual identity can shift over time, moving from exclusively heterosexual to bisexual, then from bisexual to exclusively gay or even back to straight. Or not." Malcolm shrugged. "Some people who shift from straight to bi continue to identify as bi or pan."

"Sometimes, I forget that knowing stuff like this is part of your job." Jackson clasped Malcolm's shoulder with his hand. "Maybe that's why you seem a lot less freaked out than I'd have expected in anyone else—you already have knowledge that an average person might not. Then again, you're you, so of course you're chill."

"Only on the outside. I have a lot of resources and opportunities to educate myself about sexual identity. I don't have all the answers, though. I definitely freak out sometimes and question myself." Malcolm winced. "I sort of knew what I was doing when it came to women, you know? Dating a man is different. And I'm not even talking about sex."

"Well, good. By the way, I really don't want to talk about my brother having sex with anyone, male or female, thank you very much." Jackson waited for Malcolm to stop laughing before he spoke again.

"You like this guy, Mal?"

"Stuart."

"Okay, Stuart. You like him, right? I'm not talking about sex, either, by the way."

"I do." Malcolm hauled in a deep breath. "He means a lot to me."

"I can tell."

"Yeah?"

"Mm-hm." Jackson gestured with the bottle. "I can see it in your face. You used to get a similar kind of look when you were around Liz. This is different, though."

"I know it is." Malcolm stared at his brother. "I'm different. What I feel for him is nothing like what I had with Liz or anyone else. This isn't just a crush or something casual."

Jackson's face softened. "That's great. Really. I can't tell you how glad I am to hear you say that. Except…"

"Except what?" Malcolm worried his bottom lip with his teeth when his brother frowned.

"You haven't seemed one hundred percent happy today, either. I can see that in your face too, like you're bummed out or stressed, and I gotta say it worries me." Jackson set his bottle down. "Is it Stuart or has something else got you down?"

"More like Stuart and something else," Malcolm said with a sigh. "This is why I mentioned wanting to talk back at the house. Because we need to make some changes, Jack. You, me and Mom."

The brothers talked for over an hour, weeding through everything that had happened in the last several months. Malcolm spoke candidly about how quickly things had snowballed following Kim's accident and about how hard he'd taken the discovery that Stuart had gone to the speakeasy guys behind his back. Jackson went pale when he finally understood the extent of Malcolm's struggles, and his voice came out gruff when he spoke.

"You should have told me. I'd have helped more, Mal. Tell me you know that."

Malcolm nodded. "I do. I was being stubborn about it. Stupid, really." He shook his head. "I'm not even sure why. Stuart said it last night. I have all these people in my life who would have helped or even listened and, for the life of me, I couldn't make myself tell them. Fuck, I blew off yoga today so I wouldn't have to talk to Kyle about it." Malcolm looked his brother in the eye. "I'm starting to think I'm just as bad as Mom when it comes to denial."

"You didn't want to hurt her. Or me. And I get that." Jackson swallowed hard. "You're not the only one who's been pretending there's nothing wrong. I haven't been entirely up front with Marissa about how much money we give Mom every month, either. She knows we're doing it," he added quickly when Malcolm's eyes got big. "Just not how much. You've been giving more, too...shit. I can't believe I had no idea. I thought you were working out too much, not going hungry!"

"That doesn't matter now. What does is knowing we can't keep this up. We have to talk to Mom. I mean really talk to her and not hold back. She needs to go back to work full-time. Change her habits. She has to help and stop pretending everything is fine when we know it's not."

"You're right." Jackson rubbed his fingers over his mouth. "I know we've been trying to avoid getting Dad involved but he needs to know, too."

"Fu-u-uck." Malcolm groaned. "Mom's going to be pissed. We have to make sure we tell them together, okay? Mom will be so hurt if she finds out we told Dad first." Malcolm could imagine only too well how crushed his mother would feel.

Sympathy flashed over Jackson's face. "I see your point and I'll handle it."

"What? No, that's not what I—"

"I know you didn't. But you've been carrying so much by yourself for too long." Jackson pinned Malcolm with a near glare. "Let me do this, okay? Not for Mom—for you. And, seriously, man, take your own observation to heart and let people in so they can help."

The lump in Malcolm's throat kept him from answering, but he managed a smile as he nodded at his brother. He accepted a hug, too, and chuckled when Jackson seemed reluctant to let Malcolm go.

"I'm okay, Jack," Malcolm said as he walked Jackson to the door. "Still pretty broke but things are turning around some." He sighed. "It helps that I don't have to worry about food so much."

Jackson winced. "I know you're mad at your friends for doing that, but I feel like I owe them a thank-you. Stuart especially. How long would you have gone playing martyr if he hadn't spoken up?"

"I wasn't being a martyr. Not intentionally, anyway." Malcolm scrunched up his nose. "I'm not sure how long I'd have let it go on. You and Marissa moving back in would have changed some things, obviously. Stuart going to the guys was a serious kick in the ass, however."

"A kick you resent," Jackson prompted. He leaned against the front door, gaze sharp as he looked Malcolm over.

Malcolm folded his arms over his chest. "I don't like it, no. Or that he seemed willing to lie about it. That crosses lines for me. At the same time, I understand why Stuart felt he had to and why the guys stepped up to help, too. I definitely know now that they did it because they care. Stuart especially."

"If the situation were reversed, would you have crossed the line, even if he'd asked you not to?"

"I'm not sure." Malcolm frowned. "I want to think I'd have respect for my partner's wishes. I know I'd bend over backward to help in any way I could."

"I figured as much. That attitude's kind of what got us into the situation with Mom to begin with, though," Jackson said with a smile. "So maybe we need to practice taking care of ourselves the way we do other people. That goes double for you."

Jackson's words bounced around Malcolm's head long after his brother had headed home. As healthy as they sounded, Malcolm wasn't sure either of them would have been able to follow them when it came to their mom's situation. They'd always step up to help her, even if that meant making sacrifices here and there.

At least now they could hope those sacrifices would taper off with time. Yes, Kim's problems were still out there, and yes, they had a mountain of work to do to fix them. Malcolm needed to work on himself, too. Knowing he wasn't alone to do that work felt wonderful to Malcolm.

He had Stuart to thank for that. Stuart had cared more about Malcolm's wellbeing than his own, and his own small sacrifice had changed Malcolm's life for the better yet again.

Chapter Fourteen

Stuart had to take a deep breath before he knocked on Malcolm's apartment door. He rocked back and forth on his heels as he waited for an answer. Malcolm had invited him so Stuart knew he was welcome, yet a small part of him was terrified that Malcolm would slam the door shut in his face.

When the door swung open and Malcolm offered him a tentative smile, some of the tension in Stuart eased.

"Hi," Malcolm said as he stepped back and made room for Stuart. It was too soon for him to have put any weight back on, but he looked far less tense and stressed than the last time Stuart had seen him.

"Hey." Stuart walked into the apartment feeling a hell of a lot more hesitant than he had the last time he'd been there. He wanted to believe tonight would go well, yet apprehension lurked under his skin. He didn't like this awkwardness with Malcolm at all and it was strange not to pull him in for a kiss.

"How was your day off?" Malcolm asked.

"It was good. I got caught up on laundry and some other chores I'd been neglecting." Stuart stuffed his hands into his pockets to keep himself from reaching out to touch Malcolm.

They'd messaged sporadically throughout the week, the words tentative and halting. While Malcolm hadn't seemed angry, he'd clearly wanted space. Stuart knew as much from their conversation earlier in the week and their message threads. So he'd been surprised when Malcolm had reached out last night and asked Stuart if he would come over after Malcolm finished work.

A wave of apprehension washed over Stuart. What if this was it? What if Malcolm had asked him to come over only so he could tell Stuart he didn't want to see him anymore? His eyes stung.

"Come on in," Malcolm offered and Stuart nodded, stooping down to unlace his boots and work them off. He left them in the entryway beside Malcolm's shoes.

Following Malcolm into the kitchen, Stuart rubbed his chest through his thin gray T-shirt. He'd spent all week fearing the worst. Wondering if he'd fucked up so badly there was no coming back from it.

Only after he'd stepped into the kitchen did he notice the scent in the air.

"Is that roasted chicken?" Belatedly, he wondered if maybe it was a bad choice to bring up anything food-related when that was clearly a hot-button issue between them right now. Malcolm merely smiled.

"It is. The grocery deliveries have been very generous and I'm trying to work my way through a lot of food before anything spoils. Most of the meat's gone in the freezer but I wanted to roast the chicken for you. I haven't really been able to reciprocate much when it comes to cooking or eating out so—" Malcolm cleared his throat. "Not that what I'd make could compare to what you can cook."

Stuart gently pressed a finger to Malcolm's lips and Malcolm stilled under him. "It smells delicious. I'm looking forward to having it for dinner."

Malcolm nodded, and reluctantly, Stuart dropped his hand. He wanted to keep touching Malcolm, but he didn't want to push his luck.

"Is there anything I can help with?"

"I'm going to throw some quartered potatoes in the oven and steam some asparagus. Everything is already prepped." Malcolm's gaze slid to the clock on the range. "It should go in shortly."

Some of Stuart's fear ebbed. Malcolm wouldn't have made him dinner if he intended to break up with him. He hoped.

"You clearly have it all under control," he said aloud. "If you'd like, I could whip up a dessert. Maybe a fruit crisp or a chocolate lava cake, depending on what ingredients you have?"

Malcolm's smile was wry. "I'm sure I have ingredients for anything."

Stuart's smile probably looked more like a grimace. "Which would you prefer then?" If Malcolm could joke about it, that was probably a good sign. Right?

"The fruit crisp. There's a ton of strawberries and I haven't been able to eat them fast enough."

"Perfect. Have any basil? Strawberry basil sounds nice."

"I do, yeah." Malcolm rummaged in the refrigerator. It was filled with food and more of Stuart's tension eased. As much as he'd hated upsetting Malcolm—he really should have handled the food situation better—

he was fucking relieved to know that Malcolm was eating now.

"How's your week been?" he asked.

"All right." Malcolm gave him a small, lopsided smile as he straightened. "I've had a lot to take in."

"I know." Stuart frowned. "I'm sorry for the way I handled things. I hope you know that. I'm relieved you have food, but I know I went about it the wrong way."

Malcolm opened his mouth to respond when the beep of a timer interrupted their conversation. "Can we talk about this after dinner?" he asked as he turned it off.

"Of course. Point me toward your cutting boards and baking dishes and I'll get this crisp prepped so it's ready to go in when the chicken comes out."

The familiar rhythm of coring and slicing strawberries and julienning basil leaves soothed Stuart. Once Malcolm slid the pan of potatoes into the oven, he offered Stuart a drink.

"I shouldn't be surprised that my friends think booze is an essential part of a food delivery but..." Malcolm held up a bottle of white wine and shrugged.

Stuart laughed. "It fits."

"Was that a yes?" Malcolm asked in a teasing tone.

"Please."

After accepting a glass, Stuart began to assemble a crumble topping for the dessert. Malcolm leaned against the counter and watched him work.

"Tell me about your week," Malcolm said.

"I've been busy." Stuart worked butter into the mixture of oats, flour, brown sugar, cinnamon and salt. "The *poissonier* — fish cook — has been out all week. His wife went into labor early and she and the baby are still in the hospital. It looks like they're going to be okay, but it's been rough for all of them. With him out, I've been doing double duty, so I'm wiped."

"That sounds tiring."

"For sure." Stuart had been grateful for the distraction, however. The less time he'd had to think about how he'd hurt Malcolm and could potentially lose him, the better.

"Does your coworker get parental leave?" Malcolm asked. "Kyle said the restaurant industry doesn't always offer much in the way of benefits."

"He only has parental leave because he works for Marisol and she runs her restaurant quite differently. In most restaurants, he could take unpaid leave if he had enough money to do it but that would be the only option."

"That's awful."

"It is. That's why I'm damn grateful to work for her." Stuart sprinkled the crumble over the strawberry mixture. "She treats her employees like humans instead of a means to profit. Don't get me wrong—I know as well as anyone that profit margins can be slim in the restaurant business. Still, I appreciate that Marisol is looking out for us. She and a few other restaurant owners here in the city are working hard to change the industry. It would be nice to see a better quality of life become standard in food service."

"I can't imagine that'll happen overnight."

"No, it won't," Stuart agreed. "It'll be a slow process. If those restaurants have lower employee turnover rates and become sought after places to be hired, it could create some real waves. Who knows what Marisol and her friends' efforts could turn into in ten, fifteen years?"

They were quickly absorbed again in dinner preparation. Malcolm's chicken came out of the oven, the potatoes were turned and asparagus steamed. Stuart's crisp went in as soon as the potatoes were finished.

They made small talk as they ate dinner, and when their plates were empty and their bellies full, Stuart gave Malcolm an appreciative smile.

"Thank you. That was delicious."

"You're welcome. Thank you for, uh, making sure I had food to prepare." Malcolm's answering smile was awkward and Stuart's mood immediately turned serious.

"I'm sorry I went about it so badly," he said. "I really am, Malcolm. I could have found a different way to make sure you were fed. I should have found a different way. I've spent the week feeling terrified I'd lost you."

"You're not going to lose me." Malcolm reached out and took Stuart's hand. "I know you had good intentions. I'm not mad, I swear. I just needed some time to think about it all. Get my head back together."

"I understand." Stuart squeezed back.

"I, uh, did something kind of big." Malcolm bit his lip. "I outed myself to my family last weekend."

Stuart set down his glass of wine, glad he hadn't taken a sip at the wrong moment or it would have ended up in his lungs. "What?"

"Jack and I had dinner with my mom, my dad and his wife, Gen."

From what Stuart understood, getting all of them together was somewhat of a miracle but that wasn't his most pressing concern. "And you told them..."

"That we're dating."

Another thread of fear in Stuart's heart disintegrated. If Malcolm had told his family, that meant he was serious about it. About them. Their argument had been just that, an argument. A small blip on the radar of their entire relationship. They could work through this. His mind whirled at the possibility.

"How did everyone take the news?"

Malcolm smiled. "They were great. My mom was thrilled and said she saw it coming when you came to fix her steps."

Stuart chuckled. He wasn't surprised. Kim had been trying to get them together. And if Malcolm hadn't known he was interested at the time, Stuart had been. "And everyone else?"

"My dad seemed perplexed. To him, it came out of nowhere. He was still very supportive. Jack's happy for me — said he and his girlfriend would have fixed me up with guys, too, if they'd known. We talked more about it after we got back here. It really was good." Malcolm toyed with his empty wine glass where it rested on the table. "I told him about my money issues, too."

Stuart's lips parted in surprise, but he let Malcolm continue.

"Jack and Marissa are moving in here together, actually. She's going back to school, so their income is changing. We talked about ways to help Mom. He's going to handle telling our dad. He doesn't like that I've been carrying this stress while he had no idea what was going on."

"That's great." Stuart felt a little stunned.

Malcolm looked down. "He also suggested I need to practice taking care of myself the way I do other people."

"That seems like solid advice to me," Stuart said softly.

"It is."

"Could you let me take care of you, too?"

Malcolm opened his mouth, then hesitated, so Stuart continued.

"I shouldn't have lied or discussed your personal issues with your friends. Trust is important in any relationship and I think it's probably even more important between us. If you need to feel a bond with someone to develop deeper feelings, I have to make sure you know you can trust me."

Malcolm nodded. "I agree."

"While I had the best of intentions, the way I acted was a mistake. It's one I don't intend to repeat. Going forward, can you trust me enough to take care of you?"

"I'll try." Despite Malcolm's hesitant tone, there was no hiding the sincerity in his gaze.

"Tonight was great. I enjoyed the dinner and I appreciate your desire to reciprocate. Not everything has to be exactly fifty-fifty, you know?"

Malcolm sighed. "That's hard for me. I do know that, though."

Stuart reached out and stroked Malcolm's hair. "You've let Carter help you out in the past. He loaned you his car and you've mentioned that he brings you lunch. Why was it different with me? Why couldn't you let me do things to help you?"

"I—I don't know why it felt different actually. That doesn't make sense, does it?"

"I understand that you want to keep things equitable between us—I do, too. But I'm not sitting around tallying up the things I do for you and that you do for me. I don't see it that way. If you're struggling now, I want to help. Someday, I might need your help and you'll have the opportunity to do that for me. On a daily basis, I'm happy when I can make your life easier and I love when you do that for me," Stuart said softly. "It's no reflection on how capable I think you are. If anything, you're so self-sufficient you push people away."

Surprise and half a dozen other emotions flashed across Malcolm's face before he slowly nodded. "You're right. I've never trusted someone at this level before. I didn't mean to make you feel like I didn't trust you. I've never had anyone to rely on this way, so I'm not used to it."

"I know that," Stuart said. "And I haven't had many relationships that have made it this far, either. I'm still figuring it out. I want to help you in any way I can because I care so much for you." Stuart brushed his thumb across Malcolm's cheek. "I'm sorry I made you question if you can trust me. I never meant for that to happen."

"I know." Malcolm leaned into his touch. "I do trust you."

"May I?" Stuart gently cupped the back of Malcolm's head and he nodded.

With a relieved sigh, Stuart leaned in and brushed his lips across Malcolm's. It sent a sharp pang through him as he wondered how he would have felt if Malcolm hadn't been able to forgive him. He would have been devastated, and it would have been the first time he'd ever felt that in a relationship. When his marriage to Becky had imploded, he'd felt guilt and devastation at the loss of his family and his entire life. He'd missed her as a person but not as a partner. His secrets had kept him from ever getting as close to her as he'd wanted.

Things were already becoming much deeper with Malcolm. Drawing back, Stuart rested his forehead against Malcolm's. "I was really scared I was going to lose you there for a while."

"I'm sorry." Malcolm pulled away far enough to look Stuart in the eye, their hands still clasped together tightly. "I didn't know you'd think that I wanted to end things. I just needed a chance to cool off and think more rationally."

"I understand."

"Why did you think that?" Malcolm asked. "What made you jump to that conclusion?"

Stuart grimaced. "I guess because my previous relationships haven't stuck. My marriage to Becky was doomed from the start because I was lying to everyone about who I was and what I wanted from my life. And the men I've dated since then weren't the kind of guys who didn't stick around when things got tough. They cut their losses and ran. And, well, I was okay with that. I never cared enough about them to fight for the relationship, either. When a major problem cropped up, we'd go our separate ways and it never mattered. But it does now." He squeezed Malcolm's hands more tightly. "I don't want to lose you."

"I don't want to lose you, either, Stuart. And I promise, even if I need space again in the future, it won't mean I'm giving up on us."

"I'll remember that." Stuart hesitated. "You do still want me to come to the wedding with you, right?"

Surprise flickered across Malcolm's face. "Yeah, of course. If you still want to be there."

"Absolutely."

"Good." Malcolm's smile was brilliant as he stood, drawing Stuart to his feet. "Come on, help me clean the table."

The mood was lighter as they picked up the plates and loaded the dishwasher. The dessert was taken out of the oven and filled the air with its rich, fruity scent while they worked. Stuart kept bumping elbows and finding excuses to casually touch Malcolm, mentally reassuring himself that he hadn't lost him.

When the kitchen was tidy, they retreated to the living room with bowls of the crisp topped with vanilla ice cream. Malcolm's friends had gone all out trying to make sure he had everything he needed, and Stuart was grateful for their generosity.

"This is delicious," Malcolm said after he took his first bite of dessert. His eyes were bright. "I've never had strawberry and basil together in anything except cocktails."

"It makes a good jam, too," Stuart said. "Or a sauce for chicken or pork. Great combo in spring salads, especially with goat cheese."

"Carter would like that, I think. I'll have to mention it to him."

"That reminds me. How's Carter dealing with everything that happened to you? I've been meaning to ask."

Malcolm frowned and poked at the ice cream in his bowl with his spoon. "He was upset I hadn't come to him about it."

"I'm sure."

"He looked absolutely gutted when we talked." A remorseful expression crossed Malcolm's face. "I felt awful. He couldn't believe he hadn't put the pieces together. I know he blames himself."

"He cares about you."

"I know. He wasn't exactly thrilled I'd kept my problems a secret from him. I know you're aware he's dealing with an anxiety disorder and lying and sneaking around can act as triggers for him. He's still stressed out even now."

Stuart winced and set his bowl aside. "That's on me. I'll have to apologize to him. I didn't mean to put any of your friends in an uncomfortable position. I was just worried about you."

"I know you were." Malcolm hesitated. "I'm grateful. I'm not happy about the way it all happened but it is a huge relief to get it all out in the open and let go of the burden of carrying it around by myself."

"I'm glad."

"And if Jackson and my dad and I can figure out a way to help my mom get back on her feet, that'll be good."

"You'll let me know if there's anything I can do to help?" Stuart asked softly.

"I will."

Malcolm placed his bowl on the coffee table, then leaned in to kiss him. Stuart kissed him back, relieved by the contact. It reassured him, soothing the raw edges of worry that had formed after the argument and during their time apart. The kiss was sweet and tender—almost tentative—and so perfect it made Stuart's chest ache. He could do this for hours, just kiss Malcolm and relearn the taste and feel of him.

Stuart shifted backward and Malcolm stretched out over his body until they were both horizontal. Malcolm threw his leg over Stuart's, and Stuart wrapped his arms around him, pulling him closer. Now that he had Malcolm close again, he had no desire to let him go. He wanted to gorge himself on the feel of Malcolm's lips against his and their bodies wrapped snugly together.

His chest was tight with feelings he couldn't express, so he let his hands and mouth do the talking as he leisurely explored Malcolm's neck and face, teasing his tongue against Malcolm's and tracing his fingertip along the shell of Malcolm's ear until he shivered. Stuart worked a hand up under Malcolm's shirt, enjoying the feel of Malcolm's skin against his palm.

Malcolm slid his palm over Stuart's stomach, then hesitated a few inches from his cock. "Could I do something for you?" he asked, voice soft and somewhat tentative.

Stuart gently captured Malcolm's hand and pulled it away. A puzzled frown crossed Malcolm's face as he looked down at Stuart, so he kissed Malcolm's palm and smiled at him. "I appreciate the offer, but honestly, my head isn't in it right now. I'd just like to hold you if that's all right?"

"That's great."

Malcolm settled against Stuart's body again, this time with his head on Stuart's chest. Stuart smiled and pressed a kiss to the top of Malcolm's head. He'd missed this so much. They lay like that as Malcolm's breathing evened out and eventually slowed as he drifted off. Stuart's eyelids were heavy too and he closed them, letting Malcolm's warmth and nearness lull him to sleep.

He awoke when Malcolm stirred and a glimpse at the clock showed they'd napped for more than an hour.

"I didn't mean to fall asleep on you," Malcolm said thickly as he sat up.

"It's okay. The nap was nice. I haven't been sleeping well," Stuart admitted. He sat up, too, shaking his hand. His arm had gone numb from the way they'd been lying.

"No, me, either." Malcolm reached out and grabbed his wrist. "Did your hand fall asleep?"

"Mmhmm." He could feel the prickly pins-and-needles sensation as the blood started to flow again. "I hate that feeling."

Malcolm rubbed Stuart's hand between his own, massaging it to speed up the process.

Stuart looked at Malcolm, taking in the crease on his cheek from where it had been pressed against the fabric of Stuart's shirt and the flattened section on the side of his head where his hair stood up funny. A lump rose in Stuart's throat. He hated to think how close he'd come to losing Malcolm.

I'll do better in the future, he thought. *I have to.* Because he couldn't bear Malcolm not being in his life. He was only now beginning to realize that he was falling hard and fast for Malcolm. He'd cared deeply for Becky as a friend, but he'd never loved her the way he should. The way he could with Malcolm if they kept going. This past week had been terrible, and he never wanted to go through that again. Which meant that he needed to tell Malcolm his own secret. *Soon.*

As if aware of his scrutiny, Malcolm glanced up and gave him a smile. Though brief, it filled Stuart with so much warmth he wondered if he were outwardly flushing. Malcolm leaned in and brushed his lips across Stuart's lightly, as if reminding him he wasn't going anywhere.

"Do you want to stay the night?" Malcolm asked as he drew back.

"I'd love to."

"Good. I'd love that, too." Malcolm leaned in for another kiss and Stuart hugged him close, humming against his mouth with the pleasure of being with him again.

Chapter Fifteen

The echo of childish voices pulled Malcolm from sleep. Despite the early hour, he smiled, then stifled a chuckle when Stuart stirred beside him.

"What the hell is that?" Stuart grumbled, his voice still thick with sleep.

"I think you mean 'who' and not 'what,'" Malcolm replied. He rolled so he could face Stuart, who used the arm he'd slung over Malcolm's waist to pull him closer. "In this case, the 'who' are Sadie and Dylan, Carter's kids."

"Mmm, right. Didn't know they'd be up early." Stuart peeled one eye open. They'd arrived at the beach house in Southampton after ten the night before, just ahead of Kyle and Luka. That'd given the adults time to relax and catch up a bit while the younger Hamiltons were already in bed. Stuart had yet to meet them.

He checked his watch now and groaned. "Ugh, it's not even seven. Don't kids sleep in on the weekends?"

"Depends on the kids, I think. Sadie and Dylan don't do that much. Plus, I'm sure they're excited about the wedding and that probably has them on the move even earlier than usual."

"Makes sense." Stuart closed his eyes again. "We don't need to be down there right now, do we?"

"Not unless you want in on the first wave of breakfast."

"First wave?"

"Breakfast comes in waves around here when there're a lot of us. There'll probably be three waves before the morning is done."

"I see. You people and your odd customs." Stuart set his chin on Malcolm's shoulder. "I'm good for now — got everything I need right here. I can wait for breakfast. And chatter. Too damned early."

Malcolm ran a hand over Stuart's thick hair. Between the occasional favor of an after-school pick-up and weekend socializing, he saw the Hamilton children with some regularity. Dylan had been a toddler and Sadie not much older the first time Malcolm had met them, and he'd grown to know them well over the years. He liked them. He liked kids in general, actually, yet realized now that he had no idea how Stuart felt about them. Not that Malcolm needed to examine why he wanted to know.

"You're really okay with this?" he asked instead. "I know we talked about how there'd be lots of people here this weekend, but we didn't go into it much."

"I'm fine. Your friends equal an acceptable form of people. Kids can be fun," Stuart said, then burrowed in closer, his voice drowsy again. "Always figured I'd have a couple at some point."

Malcolm nodded, though he knew Stuart couldn't see the motion. "Even after Becky?"

"The future got kind of murky after Utah, y'know? Had to find my way. Put stuff like family on hold. 'Cause it wasn't the right time."

"Sure. Makes sense."

"'S not like I forgot." A longish pause followed Stuart's words and Malcolm could tell he was fighting sleep. "Jus' need to figure myself out first."

Malcolm closed his eyes. This man had already figured out more about himself in a few years than most people did in a lifetime. He held Stuart close, the sounds of the house waking up around them fading as he savored the heat of the body against his. Satisfaction built inside Malcolm as Stuart's breathing evened out and he slipped back under.

They'd spent many nights together in the last two weeks doing exactly this—holding each other and sometimes kissing, often for hours, even after their bodies made it clear they would have welcomed more. Malcolm hadn't wanted anything beyond those simple and uncomplicated touches. He'd needed to reconnect with Stuart and work past the doubts that had sprung up in his mind in the wake of their argument. To Malcolm's quiet delight, Stuart had been on the same page.

He'd eased off trying to insert himself into Malcolm's money issues. He'd given Malcolm space to work on talking to the speakeasy guys about those problems, too, while still providing a friendly ear and honest words when Malcolm wanted them.

Malcolm quickly understood that he wasn't the only one who craved reconnection. The searching quality he glimpsed in Stuart's gaze these days said as much. A dark cloud hung over him when he'd been present for a second grocery delivery at Malcolm's and the tension that rose between them had lingered for hours. For whatever reason, Malcolm's withdrawal had shaken Stuart, and it seemed he needed time — and Malcolm's reassurance — to work through those feelings. That only made Malcolm more determined to work on improving the way he communicated as they moved forward.

* * * *

Dylan ran his fingers over the designs etched into the skin of Stuart's forearm, an eight-year-old's admiration clear in his voice and the way his blue eyes shone. "These are badass."

"Um, thanks." Stuart grinned and used his other hand to fork up some eggs while Malcolm and Carter pretended not to laugh. "Glad you like them."

Riley aimed a look across the table at Dylan. "Language, Dyl."

"Badass isn't a swear, is it?" Dylan raised an eyebrow. "Besides, Stuart's tattoos are cool. And his beard is the biggest I've ever seen in person."

The Hamilton-Porter-Wrights had gathered in the kitchen after Malcolm and Stuart had finally come downstairs, and Dylan and Sadie had immediately wanted to get to know the tattooed newcomer in their midst. Kyle and his boyfriend, Luka, turned up soon after and volunteered to fix breakfast, which included a tantalizing cold brew coffee for the adults spiked with homemade hazelnut liqueur and coffee milk coolers for Sadie, Dylan and Carter.

"Mmm, I dunno." Sadie fixed an appraising stare on Stuart that made him smile again. He seemed to enjoy the attention of the Hamilton children. "I think Kyle's beard was bigger last year," she said at last.

Kyle belted out a laugh. "It was pretty epic until Jesse taught me how to trim it."

"Remember we talked about decorating it for Christmas?" Sadie threw a playful grin his way. She'd be turning eleven in the fall and appeared suddenly very grown up and even more like Carter than Malcolm had thought possible.

"I absolutely remember," Kyle said. "Almost makes me wish I hadn't shaved it off."

"Why did you shave?" Stuart asked.

"I grew a beard because I had stitches in my face at the time. Despite its epicness, it wasn't really me. I did grow to appreciate it. Oops, I punned." Kyle ran his fingers over his chin and winked at Luka, who smiled in return. "I could always grow another one."

"We all know it wouldn't take you long—you've got a five-o'clock shadow by noon," Luka quipped. He set a hand on the nape of Kyle's neck. "Up to you, babe. You said Lady Sadie here wanted to dye it fun colors, right? That might give Stuart here a run for his money." Luka nodded at Stuart, who was watching them both with interest. "Kyle's beard really was epic. Almost as much as yours. Both are way more impressive than, say, Jesse's."

"I heard that."

"Which is why I said it." Luka's eyes twinkled as Jesse strode into the kitchen, a smile on his face.

"No fair talking smack about me," Jesse said, "or the gloriousness that is my beard before I've had even one cup of coffee."

Malcolm rolled his eyes. "Lack of caffeine hasn't slowed down your mouth." He smiled as Jesse swiped a hand over Malcolm's hair on his way to the stove. "Where's your better half?"

"Still sleeping." Jesse wrapped his arms around Sadie, who'd gotten up to give him a hug. "Cam had a nasty cold last week and he's still wiped. Poor guy needs some extra sleep." He straightened and stared at the remnants of food on the plates that sat on the table. "Is there really nothing left to eat?"

"There's a whole platter of pancakes and sausage warming in the oven, you big baby." Kyle waved Jesse off. "You're out of luck if you want eggs, though, 'cause I'm pretty sure Luka and I cooked whatever was left a little while ago."

"Well, heck." Jesse made a face. "Didn't you say you'd make cookies this weekend, Mal?"

"There're more eggs in the fridge out in the garage and extras for Malcolm's cookies," Dylan piped in. He crossed the kitchen and grabbed one of Jesse's hands, then inclined his blond head toward the door at the far end of the room. "I'll show ya. The dads always buy more when you're invited 'cause they say you never met an egg you didn't like."

A chorus of laughter rang out, Jesse's louder than anyone's.

"I'd be offended by that if it wasn't so painfully accurate." He shot a mock glare at Carter and Riley before he allowed Dylan to lead him away.

"What's all this about cookies?" Stuart asked Malcolm, who merely smiled.

"I like to bake," he said. "Cookies especially and I've got a ton of recipes." He glanced back to Sadie when she called for Carter's attention.

"Isn't Jesse always invited, Dad?" she asked.

"Yes, he is. And it's not like he'd listen if I said otherwise, honey." Carter shared a smile with his daughter, then gathered up some of the empty plates.

"Jesse is one of my favorite people — just like everyone else in this big family — and I love him to pieces. And we'll have even more people around when Will and David get here."

Sadie nodded. "What about Aunt Audrey and Uncle Max?"

"They'll be here, too." Carter set the dishes in the sink. "They're going to hook up with your Uncle Dan and Aunt Mel and rideshare with the kids."

Malcolm caught Stuart's mystified expression. "Audrey is Carter's sister," he said quietly as the others at the table rose. "Dan and Mel are old college roommates of his and Riley's. They and their three kids flew in from Chicago earlier this week."

"Ah." Stuart set his fork down. "Guess I didn't realize there'd be more than speakeasy people here. Which sounds silly now that I think about it."

"Outside of the aunt and uncle types, you're not far off. Oh, my coworker Astrid will be here with a date. She's another speakeasy person. Carter's ex and her partner, too." Malcolm smiled at Stuart's disbelieving chuckle. "I think that's everyone. Twenty-three's not a lot for a wedding, right?"

"Definitely not. Except I might need a cheat sheet where names are concerned, so don't wander off."

"I didn't plan to." Malcolm studied Stuart's face. "Something bothering you?"

"No. Why?"

"You look like you want to ask a question but haven't figured out how."

"Oh." Stuart rubbed his thumb over his forehead. "You're getting good at reading me, you know. I'm not sure yet if that's a good thing or bad." He gave Malcolm a wry smile.

"Good, I hope." Malcolm glanced up as Jesse and Dylan re-entered the kitchen with a double carton of eggs, then inclined his head toward Stuart's glass of coffee. "C'mon — let's take these outside."

"I really don't understand how all of this works," Stuart said once they'd stepped onto the deck connected to the kitchen. Leo, the family's old border collie, immediately got up from his spot in the sun and crossed the deck to Malcolm. "You told me about Carter dating both Jesse and Kyle, and that Riley and Will used to be an item."

"That's right." Malcolm settled onto a chaise. He scrubbed Leo's scruff with his fingers and smiled when the dog settled down by his feet. "Good boy."

Stuart sat beside Malcolm. "Then there's the other hookups with Kyle and Jesse and their boyfriends — "

"Well, there're a few more than that," Malcolm said. "I wasn't joking when I said I made a diagram showing the pairings-slash-groupings."

"Yet they're all friends? Along with Carter's ex-wife, who is coming to his wedding where he'll marry the man he left her for?"

"Carter didn't leave Kate for anyone. But yes, they all make it work."

"How?" Stuart stared through the glass doors into the kitchen where Jesse and now Cam were chatting with Riley and the Hamilton kids. "I can't imagine having stayed friends with Becky after we split, and we didn't have half the emotional baggage your friends do."

"Well, there were only two of you. Fewer people, less baggage." Malcolm waited for Stuart's grin.

"You're an ass."

"I know. I can't explain the hows of why this works. I'm not even sure I understand it myself." Malcolm turned his focus toward the beach nearby where a bamboo gazebo stood at the end of a short aisle drawn in the sand with white stones. A small army of white folding chairs stood on either side of the aisle, and both they and the gazebo were decorated with garlands of pink and white flowers.

"Carter and his ex have kids to keep them connected. The rest of us... There's more than friendship going on here." Malcolm glanced back down at the dog. "Carter wasn't speaking figuratively when he called us all a family because that's what we are. Maybe that sounds strange to someone who hasn't watched it grow over the years but it's true.

"Some of these guys — Carter, Riley, Will — lost a lot of people in their lives when they came out. The only McKee that Kyle has left to count on is his brother." He shrugged, though he could tell his words had registered with Stuart in the way he'd gone still. "I think those losses have made them fight hard to hang on to the people they love, which inspires the rest of us to do the same."

Stuart pursed his lips. "I get you. And yes, it is strange looking at it from where I stand. Maybe that has to do with the fact that lots of your friends have had sex with each other and some still do." He grinned when Malcolm clapped a hand over a laugh. "I told you, I know a thing or two about wife swapping. It's nice knowing you guys all have each other's backs. Great, actually. I miss that about being Elder Morgan. A sense of belonging to something bigger." Stuart's expression softened. "I get a little with Marisol and the crew at King's, but it's not quite the same."

Malcolm hid a smile. He'd seen the way his friends looked at Stuart. Seen the grins they'd exchanged any time he held Malcolm's hand or they showed each other affection. Stuart had gone to the speakeasy guys when Malcolm had needed help, an act that really made them want to know him. Which meant Stuart was going to be pulled into the speakeasy crew by hook or by crook and he had no idea.

* * * *

"Malcolm? Dad says he needs your help."

Malcolm turned in his seat at Sadie's voice. After spending the morning making last-minute preparations, Carter had sequestered himself on the second floor of the house. The other guests began to arrive at noon and a party formed on the deck with lots of snacks and agua fresca, as well as a myriad of mixed cocktails courtesy of Kyle and Jesse. Sadie looked calm to Malcolm, but her words set alarm bells off in his head. Nothing could go wrong today—Malcolm would see to that himself if he had to. The looks Jesse and Kyle were sending him said they would absolutely be his back-up, too.

"Anything wrong?" he asked Sadie.

"Nah." Sadie's rose-pink sundress set off her dark hair and tinted her hazel eyes green. She leaned in and dropped her voice to a near whisper. "He's having trouble with his tie. Ri-Dad always helps him but they're not looking at each other before the wedding." She paused then and frowned. "Which doesn't make sense because we all ate breakfast together. Twice."

Malcolm bit back a snort at her words. "Some people follow that tradition before they get married, meaning they don't see each other until they're ready to say vows. Usually, they don't see each other for a whole day."

"Well, that's silly. What if you have trouble with your tie and your boyfriend's on the other side of the house?" Sadie shrugged. "Anyway, Dad says you're the best one to help."

The tension forming in Malcolm's chest eased. Hopefully, Carter wasn't covering a problem more urgent than a stubborn necktie. "Got it. I'm good with knots, even though your dad and I don't wear ties much these days."

Stuart leaned past Malcolm and looked between him and Sadie. Which gave Malcolm another opportunity to admire the sight of Stuart in a natty pale-blue suit. Beyond his chef's whites, Stuart didn't go formal very often. He cleaned up exceedingly well, however, even if that meant his ink had gone into temporary hiding.

"Everything okay, guys?" he asked.

"Yep." Malcolm winked at him. "Be back in a minute. One of the grooms needs a hand with a wardrobe malfunction."

He and Sadie passed Cam on the way upstairs, and Malcolm stifled a laugh as he caught sight of a crown of pink and white roses resting on Cam's fiery hair. Like the rest of the men in the house, Cam wore a casual summer suit, but Malcolm knew without a doubt that crown belonged on someone else's head.

"You'd better not let Riley catch you wearing that," he said, and this time, he did laugh at the way Cam's face fell. "Sadie needs it for the ceremony, dude."

"Yes, of course." Cam pouted. "I was just keeping it from getting crushed. And the colors look really nice against my hair. Against yours too, pumpkin," he added when Sadie set her hands on her hips.

"I have an extra one in my room you can wear instead," she said. "It's more white flowers than pink because the florist guy said it was a backup. You should wait until after the dads are married to wear it, though."

Malcolm left them to their negotiations and continued on to the master suite where he found Carter before the full-length mirror dressed in a beautiful silver-gray suit, both hands on his tie and his face screwed up in a mask of concentration.

"Oh, thank God." He practically beamed as Malcolm slipped past the door. "I hate to ask, but help? I'm all thumbs today, and every time I've tried with this thing, I end up looking like an absolute idiot."

"Of course. And, seriously, you look great." Malcolm crossed the room and carefully straightened the silk necktie around Carter's neck so the broader end hung lower against his pale-pink shirt. "I still can't do it unless I pretend I'm doing the tying, so hang on a second."

They both laughed as he turned Carter toward the mirror, then rose up on his toes enough to see over Carter's shoulder. The last of Malcolm's worry faded as he worked with the dark gray tie. Carter looked happy and relaxed, his eyes clear and his body language easy.

"It's been a while since you had to do this for me," he said to Malcolm.

A dozen memories rushed into Malcolm's head of helping Carter with his jacket or tie during their time together at Hamilton Advertising. Years that now seemed a lifetime away when they'd had a different kind of working relationship and lives that were unrecognizable compared to those they lived today. That time had changed the path of Malcolm's life, though he hadn't known it at the time.

"Lucky for both of us I can still tie a wicked Windsor," he said. Malcolm wound the broad end of the tie around in a final pass, then looped it up and over to complete the knot. "I offered to help Stuart with his tie earlier, but it turns out he is great at a Kelvin."

"He really is badass." Carter followed Malcolm's fingers with his eyes as he smoothed the silk. "You know, if we were Jesse and anyone else on the crew, we'd move on to talking shibari right now."

Malcolm tipped his head back and laughed. "Oh, God, you're right! Which reminds me that we should get you downstairs before Riley thinks something's wrong and Jesse makes Stuart regret not hooking up with him and Cam that night."

"Pfft. Stuart wouldn't think that."

Malcolm drew his eyebrows together. "No?"

"Nope. You're the one he's looking at, Mal." Carter raised his own hands to the now finished knot while Malcolm turned him around again. "You know a guy is into you when not even the eye candy that is the speakeasy crew turns their head."

"You make a good point." Malcolm lifted Carter's jacket from the chair nearby and held it out. He tried not to feel too smug. "Thanks for that."

"No problem. Thanks for being here today." Carter slid his arms into the jacket, and together, they settled it over his broad shoulders. "And for the assist with my clothes. How do I look?"

"Perfect," said a familiar voice from the door. Only then did Malcolm notice that Jesse and Kyle had joined them at some point and were both smiling widely. Kyle took several steps forward.

"About time to get you downstairs, big man," he said, his dark brown eyes brighter than usual. "Ri and the kids are waiting."

"Oh, good!" Carter grinned. "I've been going stir-crazy cooped up on this floor with the cat for company and knowing that everyone else was downstairs. So lead the way, my good men."

Jesse held up a hand. "Yeah, I need a hug first or I'm going to start bawling my head off."

Catching Kyle by the elbow, he pulled him forward, and before Malcolm knew it, he'd been dragged into the hug, too. And while his eyes burned and his throat went tight, Malcolm was more than okay with that and squeezed his friend's back just as hard.

"You guys are really cutting it close," Stuart said a short while later as Malcolm dashed across the deck, now empty except for the speakeasy crew, with Jesse and Kyle close behind. "I think the senator and his boyfriend were about to do some recon."

"He's right," David called over Will and Cam's laughter.

"Everything's under control," Malcolm replied. "We've got about a minute to get out there or we're going to crash the processional, though. That won't be a good look on any of us."

"Oh, fuck six ducks." Jesse grabbed Cam by the hand. "Let's go!"

With a little hustle, the guys were seated by the time the acoustic guitar duo providing the music changed chords. Which was a good thing seeing Malcolm and his friends filled nearly every chair on the left side of the aisle alone. They handed around small baskets of rose petals while John Legend's *All of Me* filled the air and Malcolm thought he and the guys looked almost entirely together by the time Sadie and Dylan stepped off the deck. Of course, Will bobbled his basket of petals and a good number of them ended up in Malcolm's lap while the two of them and their dates tried to smother their laughter.

Sadie and Dylan made their way to the aisle and walked toward a silver-haired woman who stood beneath the gazebo with a pleasant smile, her demeanor welcoming and warm. Like his father, Dylan had dressed in silver-gray trousers and a pale-pink shirt, and he wore a gray bow tie and no jacket, a pink rose pinned to his breast pocket. Sadie's flower crown was in its rightful place, too, and she carried a basket of rose petals.

Moments later, the grooms appeared, hands linked and smiles bright, and Malcolm's throat ached again. His friends looked...radiant. Riley's gray jacket complemented the rest of his family's colors, though his trousers were white and his bow tie a deep rose. He looked dashing—because Riley always did—but Malcolm thought today he and Carter would have looked just as amazing in jeans and T-shirts. Both shone from the inside out, and a near-tangible happiness surrounded them. Malcolm swore he felt lighter just being present.

"Good afternoon, everyone," the woman beneath the gazebo said after the last bars of music had faded. She moved her gaze over those who'd gathered, then to Carter and Riley, who stood before her, with Sadie at Carter's side and Dylan at Riley's. "I am the Honorable Samantha Stone. I'm honored to have been asked here today to officiate a very special moment in the lives of

Riley Andrew Porter-Wright and Carter Ward Hamilton, one they've chosen to share with you.

"To all present, I say that today is a celebration. Of love and commitment, and friendship and family. Marriage is created in the hearts of two loving people, and Carter and Riley are two such souls. We gather here not to witness the beginnings of what will be, but rather what already is. In the years they've known one another, Carter and Riley's love has grown and matured into an unshakable union and they have decided that now is the right time to live their lives as husbands."

Justice Stone shifted her gaze to the Hamilton kids and smiled. "As I said earlier, today is also a celebration of family. To honor this uniting, Carter and Riley ask for their children's blessing. Sadie and Dylan, do you offer your dads your goodwill?"

Sadie and Dylan exchanged a glance, then nodded at the Justice. "Yes, we do," they said in unison.

"And do you welcome Riley as an honorary Hamilton and give him your love and affection?"

Dylan and his sister repeated, "Yes, we do," and Dylan flashed a thumbs-up at Riley, prompting gentle laughter from everyone.

"Thank you." Justice Stone shifted her focus again to the grooms. "Carter and Riley, true marriage begins well before the wedding day and continues far beyond the ceremony's end. A brief moment in time and the stroke of the pen are all that is required to create the legal bond of marriage. It takes a lifetime of love, commitment and compromise to make that union durable and everlasting."

She inclined her head beyond Carter and Riley to the crowd in their seats. "Today, you declare your commitment to each other before the people who love you. Your yesterdays were the path to this moment, and your journey to a future of togetherness becomes a little clearer."

A sense of wonder filtered through Malcolm. Just that morning, Stuart had described his future as having gone murky after leaving Utah. Malcolm's own future was still coming clear, too, in ways he'd never expected. A small part of him dared to hope he'd found a partner he could share that journey with, and even that Stuart might someday feel the same.

"The vows you are about to make share your love and commitment to each other," Justice Stone said. "They declare your promise to one another and your children, and to all those here who support you today." She gestured to Riley with a kind smile.

Riley turned toward Carter and gathered Carter's hands in his own. "It's hard for me to remember a time when I didn't love you, Carter, and there are still days that I can't believe we're here right now." He smiled, his throat working before he continued. "Today and every day, I promise to be your sympathizer and best friend, to always trust your judgment, and to love our kids with my whole heart. I promise to put you and Sadie and Dylan first and I will never forget how lucky I am to have your love in my life. I promise to be yours, Carter, and to be your husband for as long as you'll have me."

Carter nodded, but it was clear to Malcolm that he was struggling to keep it together. Heck, Malcolm's own eyes were smarting, too. Carter's voice sounded rough when he spoke, so Sadie took a step closer to her father and set one hand on his hip.

"Riley, you know me better than anyone and somehow still manage to love me, though I really don't know how." He paused as Riley looked skyward with a laugh and Malcolm saw them squeeze each other's hands tighter. "So today and every day, I promise to be your navigator and your sidekick, to always tell you the truth and to make our house a home. I'll do my best to never let you down. I also want you to know that Sadie, Dylan and I will stand with you always." A tear slipped down Carter's cheek, but he continued as if he hadn't noticed. "I promise you myself, Ri, and to always love you for who you are. Thank you for saying yes."

Sniffles were audible from both sides of the aisle as Dylan withdrew a pair of rose-gold wedding bands from his pants pocket and Malcolm had to swallow hard. Seeing his friends like this — the love shared with each other and their children — was a gift. Malcolm couldn't describe it any other way.

Raising his hands, Riley wiped the tears from Carter's cheeks and his own. He and Carter accepted the rings from Dylan, who looked as solemn as Malcolm had ever seen, and the Hamilton kids watched as their dads slipped the rings onto each other's fingers. In the next heartbeat, all four were grinning. Justice Stone waited for Carter and Riley to clasp hands again and set one of hers over theirs.

"Carter and Riley, you have declared your love by exchanging vows. You've symbolized your commitment by exchanging rings," she said. "So there's just one more question I need each of you to answer before I turn you loose to celebrate."

She met Carter's gaze. "Carter, do you take Riley to be your husband?"

"I do," he said with a grin.

"And, Riley, do you take Carter to be your husband?" she asked.

Riley barked out a gleeful-sounding laugh. "You bet I do."

Justice Stone brought her hands together with a chuckle. "Then by the power vested in me by the State of New York, I now pronounce you husbands. So kiss already, but keep it classy, and give your kids a hug!"

A roar burst from the crowd as Carter and Riley embraced. Malcolm got to his feet with the other guests, cheering as they threw handfuls of rose petals in the air, and Cam shoved two fingers in his mouth and blew the most ear-piercing whistle Malcolm had ever heard. Laughing, he turned toward Stuart. His heart sank as he caught something sad in Stuart's expression.

Stuart had tried so hard to find the same contentment only to have it go terribly wrong. Maybe watching two men exchange vows was more bitter than sweet for him, considering he'd lost his home and whole life simply for being gay.

"Hey." Malcolm wrapped his hand tight around Stuart's. "Are you okay?"

Stuart's eyes went wide. "Yes! Damn, I'm sorry." He squeezed Malcolm's fingers and seemed almost to shake himself. "It's a lot to take in, you know? Amazing. Overwhelming, too, and not in a bad way."

"You've no doubt figured out all of these guys are 'go big or go home' types." Malcolm offered what he hoped was an encouraging smile. The guitar duo had started up again, but now he ached with a need to make his man feel better. "Not sure they know any other way to be, so I hear you on the overwhelming part. I'm glad you're here. That you could see this with me."

So you could see what love looks like when the right people come together.

Understanding flashed in Stuart's eyes though Malcolm hadn't spoken those words. "I'm glad, too." He brushed a kiss to Malcolm's lips and the light touch sent warmth all through Malcolm when Stuart really smiled.

They paused then so they could cheer even louder as the grooms and kids made their way back down the aisle. The song the guitar duo had been playing became clear as the noise of the crowd died down, and when Malcolm looked at Stuart again, awe was clear in his face.

"Is that...are they playing Billy Idol's *White Wedding*?"

"Yep." Malcolm snickered. "Carter asked for two things on this day—that the kids be involved in the ceremony and that he be allowed to choose the recessional. He didn't tell Riley what song he chose, but I have a feeling Riley's so loved up right now he hasn't even noticed."

He held his arm out to Stuart, who'd started snickering, too. "Let's get in line for hugs with the happy couple, and then I want to grab a drink before the dancing starts."

"Dancing? You didn't tell me there'd be dancing."

"You're right, I didn't. And I can't wait to see you shake your ass."

The glower that settled over Stuart's features would have freaked Malcolm out only a month before. He really had gotten better at reading the man, though. He wasn't surprised at all when Stuart heaved a dramatic-sounding sigh and let Malcolm lead the way.

Chapter Sixteen

"Oh, my God, this cake is so good," Malcolm murmured. "I'm glad Riley decided to surprise Carter with his favorite flavor."

"It was good," Stuart agreed as he scraped his plate clean. He'd had a bite of the chocolate layer cake with peanut butter mousse and it was delicious, if a touch sweet for his tastes. "Still glad I got the passion fruit and lime. You said that was Riley's favorite?"

"Yes. I was torn between the two layers."

"Want me to get you a piece of this, too?"

"No," Malcolm said with a laugh. "All of the food was incredible today. I'd be stuffed if I had another bite."

"From what I saw, there will be plenty of leftovers," Stuart said. "You can always raid them later tonight or tomorrow."

"I like the way you think." Malcolm sat back with a contented sigh.

Stuart draped his arm across Malcolm's chair as Cam approached the deejay equipment set up on one side of the deck. Straightening the crown of flowers on his head, he picked up the microphone, then grinned at the crowd. Cam had been put in charge of the music for the reception and he'd set up playlists and worked as a low-key emcee, unobtrusively helping direct the flow of the events.

"I know you're all dying to get on the dance floor tonight," he said into the mic. "Before we kick this party into high gear, we have a few speeches. Dan, Max and Jesse, will you come up here, please?"

When Stuart rubbed his thumb against Malcolm's shoulder, Malcolm glanced over at him, a smile lighting up his face before he looked back at Cam. He'd been smiling nonstop since the reception began and the good mood around them was contagious.

Stuart had expected three things from Riley and Carter's wedding and reception: emotions running high, great food, and fantastic drinks. He'd been right about all three. He didn't quite know what to do with the former. The latter two he was enjoying the hell out of.

Kyle had, of course, helped Riley and Carter plan the drink menu. He'd brought in several staff members from Under to mix the cocktails so he could enjoy being a guest. The grooms had gone for passed hors d'oeuvres and an elegant buffet setup, similar to the CEC event, which worked perfectly for the small guest list and intimate feel. People were spread across the deck and the beach surrounding it and the mood was more joyous than any wedding he'd ever been to before. He knew Malcolm and all the speakeasy crew were determined to make it a good day for the grooms. So far, everything had gone off without a hitch.

After they worked their way through dinner and drinks, Stuart looked on with interest as Jesse gathered with Carter's brother-in-law, Max, and Dan, a friend Riley and Carter had known since their late teens. When Cam held out the microphone, Dan reached for it first. Stuart hadn't had many opportunities to talk to him yet today, but the man was handsome as hell with his light brown skin and small neat beard. His gray eyes twinkled as he smoothed down the lapel of his suit jacket, then smiled at the crowd.

"I'm not going to lie. When Riley and Carter said they wanted to limit the number of speeches tonight, I expected fistfights over who got to do the honors." The crowd laughed. "If there's anything I've learned about these guys over the years, it's that they inspire loyalty in their friends. As the person who was there from the very beginning when these guys met, I had a vested interest in saying a few words."

Out of the corner of Stuart's eye, he saw Riley lean in and whisper in Carter's ear, making him grin.

"Although at the time we all met, none of us could have anticipated ending up here. It was clear to me from the very beginning that Riley and Carter had something special together. The bond between them was different from the ones they had with anyone else. And while the road to get here hasn't been the easiest for either of them, I think it's clear that this is where they were meant to end up all along."

Stuart glanced over at Carter's ex-wife, Kate, sitting a table away, and wondered how she was taking all this. That had to sting. Yet Stuart saw only serene happiness on her face. Kate's blue eyes were bright, and her smile didn't waver as she snuggled into her boyfriend's embrace. She appeared content and happy for her ex-husband.

That blew Stuart's mind. If he put himself in Carter's shoes and considered how Becky would react to Stuart marrying a man, it was a far less pretty picture. While he deeply hoped that the hurt he'd caused her had faded over the years, he didn't think for a minute that she'd be happy for him. He did hope she was happy, however. That she'd found a good Mormon man who loved her and gave her the kind of relationship Stuart hadn't been able to. Who gave her the children she'd wanted. The life she'd dreamed of building.

He'd never considered the idea for himself before either. Not with any degree of seriousness. Outside of his marriage to Becky, he'd never met anyone he'd considered spending his life with, much less making it legal and permanent.

Being at a same-sex wedding had his head spinning, especially since he was here with the man he was dating. He glanced over at Malcolm, who was laughing at something Dan had said. Stuart and Malcolm were a long, long way off from considering anything like marriage, but could he imagine that someday? The idea made his heart beat faster in a mix of nerves and excitement. Maybe he could picture giving marriage a go again. With the right person. Someone he could be totally open and honest with. Except, that sent up that ever-present spark of fear. Because he still hadn't told Malcolm the truth about his kink. It would continue to hang over them until he did.

Despite the fear gripping his heart, Stuart was determined not to let it spoil their evening. This moment wasn't about him and Malcolm — it was about

Riley and Carter. With a shake of his head, Stuart tuned back into Dan's words.

"When I planned this speech, I considered all of the stories I could tell about the early days of the Riley-and-Carter duo. Like the many, many times people assumed they were a couple. Boy, are you two slow on the uptake!" The crowd laughed again, no one louder than the grooms. "You're here now, though, and, in the end, I decided not to focus on your past. Because today, we're here to celebrate your future. As a man who has been married to my wonderful wife, Melanie, for almost as long as you two have known each other, I want to offer you the best advice I have to give.

"Fall in love with each other continually. Every day, every hour, every minute you're together, continue to see the wonderful things that made you fall in love in the first place. If you're focused on being good to each other in the present, the future will work out for itself. View the other through that lens and your relationship will continue to grow and deepen over the years."

Dan's expression grew more serious. "Although, I suspect you two have already figured that out. So tonight, let's celebrate this new chapter of your lives. What began nearly twenty years ago in the dorm rooms of Harvard has led us to today and I wish them a lifetime of happiness together. Please raise a glass to Riley and Carter and their bright and happy future!"

The gentle roar of the waves in the background was drowned out by cheers and applause and the clinking of glasses. A deep, lingering kiss between the grooms led to even louder cheering and it took a while for everyone to settle down.

When the crowd had calmed, Max took the microphone from Dan with a rueful smile. "Well, that's not a tough act to follow or anything," he said. Stuart chuckled along with the rest of the guests. "As Carter's brother-in-law, and someone who is married to a Hamilton, I have one piece of advice for you, Riley. It's not as deep or as eloquent as Dan's, but it might save your life. When a Hamilton is having a bad day, just hand over some chocolate and get the hell out for a while."

"Oh, I learned that years ago," Riley called back to him, his tone dry. "Either that or bacon."

Everyone roared.

Max raised his eyebrows at his brother-in-law. "Carter, I suggest you figure out what Riley's thing is and do the same."

"It's gin!" Carter called back with a laugh, draping an arm around Riley's shoulders. "Definitely gin."

"And cheese!" Dylan piped up, prompting another laugh.

When the crowd settled down, Max continued with a smile. "All joking aside, I couldn't be happier that you are an official part of our family now. You've been in our lives for so many years and I've been truly happy to watch your relationship grow from friendship into love. I've been proud to call Carter my brother-in-law for years and I'm delighted to call you that, too, now, Riley. I wish you both only happiness together." He held up his champagne flute. "So let's toast the grooms and the lifetime of happiness that you both so richly deserve. To Carter and Riley."

Stuart lifted his own glass and echoed the toast. After he took a sip and set down his glass, Malcolm rested a hand on his thigh. Stuart leaned in, brushing his lips across Malcolm's hair. When he sat up straight,

Jesse was holding the microphone. This could get interesting.

"I think we all know we saved the best for last." Jesse flashed a big smile. "I'm not here to offer any advice on relationships tonight. You all know me and that the idea of getting married myself gives me hives. But I have never met anyone who should be married more than Carter and Riley. When Carter and I met, he was at a low point in his life. As I got to know him, I realized I'd never met a man more determined to dig himself out of that low point. The grit and determination he displayed were impressive. What impressed me more was the way he lit up when Riley came back into his life. It started a fire under him and has sustained him since. He became the best possible version of Carter Hamilton I could imagine.

"Since then, I've watched him and Riley build an incredible life together. Watching that has inspired me. You all know my partner Cam and I have a less traditional relationship than most. What you may not know is that Carter and Riley's relationship has inspired me." He smiled at the grooms. "You've taught me so much about how to be a good partner and how to make a relationship work. Your relationship has had a profound impact on me."

Surprised by the earnest and heartfelt toast, Stuart glanced at the grooms and saw both of them wiping their eyes.

Jesse smiled even wider. "So while I'll never stop reminding you two that if you ever do decide to open up your relationship, you better make sure I'm the first one you tell."

The crowd roared with laughter and Stuart saw Malcolm shake his head, his expression amused and fond.

"I couldn't possibly be happier that you two are getting married today. Despite your incomprehensible insistence on monogamy, I love you both and respect your choices. I know without a shadow of a doubt that the two of you will always love each other, no matter what the world throws at you. So I want to toast to your happy life together. No one deserves it more."

"Damn," Stuart murmured in Malcolm's ear after everyone had lifted their glasses. "That man has more depth than I gave him credit for."

"He does," Malcolm said quietly. "He may not see relationships the way most people do but he loves as hard as any of these people here, if not harder."

With a kiss for Jesse, Cam took back the mic. "Now, let's get this party started!" he said.

An upbeat tune Stuart didn't recognize filled the air and the small dance floor area quickly filled. Malcolm stood, grinning at Stuart. "Time to dance."

Stuart got to his feet with a groan.

"Hey now, no complaining. You promised to shake your ass for me!" Malcolm said, laughing. "Don't think you're getting out of it."

"Fine, fine." Stuart shrugged out of his suit jacket. "At least, let me get more comfortable first."

The moment Stuart had draped it over the back of the chair, Malcolm grabbed his hand and tugged him forward. Despite Stuart's initial reluctance, time flew by as he danced with Malcolm. They were surrounded by Malcolm's friends, who were all in high spirits. The grooms were in the thick of it and there was no shortage of partner swapping, though everyone kept it relatively tame since Sadie and Dylan were dancing alongside them, too. At one point, Cam spun Sadie and dipped her, making her shriek with delight, while Will and Dylan did something that vaguely resembled a foxtrot.

Eventually, the music slowed and became more mellow and romantic. While the grooms had skipped an official first dance, as they embraced and began to sway together, it was clear they didn't have eyes for anyone else. Malcolm touched Stuart's arm.

"Would you dance with me?" Malcolm asked. "To this?"

"I've never..." Stuart cleared his throat. "Yes. I would like to."

Malcolm stepped closer. "You can lead if you'd like." It took them a moment to figure out the hand placement and find a rhythm but soon it was as if Malcolm had melted against Stuart. Stuart hummed. This was nice. David offered him a small smile as he and Will danced nearby and Stuart closed his eyes. All he wanted right now was to focus on Malcolm. The scent of his cologne, the warmth of his body and the strength of his arms. Stuart lost himself in those sensations and he only reluctantly pulled away when the music segued and became more up-tempo again.

He pressed a brief, chaste kiss to Malcolm's lips before drawing back and saw Kyle watching them with a smile.

Someone pressed a drink into Stuart's hand and he sipped it while they continued dancing. Eventually, he grew warm enough to roll up his sleeves and loosen his tie. Malcolm had already done the same and the sight of his flushed cheeks and damp hairline made Stuart wish they were alone. But the music was good and when a familiar, favorite tune filled the air, Stuart threw his hands up in the air and swiveled his hips. Cam wolf-whistled while Jesse gave him a big grin.

"Now that's a sight I've been looking forward to," Jesse shouted over the music. Stuart just shook his head at them and rolled his eyes.

A few songs later, Stuart leaned in to speak in Malcolm's ear. "I'm going to sit for a minute."

Malcolm craned his neck and gave Stuart a questioning look. "You want me to come with you?"

"No, have fun."

Malcolm and Carter appeared to be having a dance-off and just because Stuart needed a breather didn't mean he wanted them to stop. Giving Malcolm a reassuring smile, he slipped through the crowd and dropped into his chair at the table. Stuart had never been much of a shake his ass kind of guy, but he'd done it for Malcolm. And had fun, too. Seeing Malcolm laugh and smile and let go of the stress he'd been carrying around lately made Stuart happy. He'd just taken a sip of water when Riley dropped into the chair next to him.

"He seems happy," Riley said. "Malcolm, I mean."

Stuart nodded. Riley's cheeks were flushed and his dark hair was in disarray. Stuart had never seen him so disheveled. Or so happy. "I think Malcolm is thoroughly enjoying your wedding reception," he said.

"I'm glad." Riley shot him a smile. "I meant he seems happy with you."

"Oh." Stuart glanced at Malcolm before looking back at Riley. "Well, I hope so. I want him to be happy."

"I'm glad you came with him this weekend."

"I appreciate you inviting me."

"Of course. As long as you're good to Malcolm, we want you here." Riley's expression was open and his words didn't sound threatening, but Stuart knew if he fucked up, there would be hell to pay from a lot of people who loved Malcolm. Which basically meant all the guests here.

"I'll do my very best," he said. "I really care about Malcolm."

"Hopefully, we haven't scared you off," Riley continued. "I know this group can be a lot to take."

"Ahh, yeah." Stuart raked a hand through his hair. "I'm not used to all this, I guess." He gestured to Kyle, Luka and Cam, who were dancing as a group. They weren't being inappropriate exactly, but they were getting there. Jesse slid in behind Kyle, placing his hands on Kyle's hips, and Stuart wondered if the four would end up in bed tonight, a little drunk and a lot horny from all the dancing. Not that he was judging. He simply wasn't used to seeing poly hookups at wedding receptions.

"This group can be a lot to take," Riley said, his voice light. "We do hope you'll stick it out. Everyone likes you a lot and we're glad to see Malcolm so happy."

"I don't have any plans to go anywhere," Stuart said as he watched Will and Malcolm cutting loose now.

"Good." Riley clapped a hand on his shoulder as he stood. "Glad to hear it."

"Congratulations, by the way," Stuart said. "I'm happy for you."

He meant that. Despite the strangeness of feeling a bit out of his element, Stuart liked these guys. He'd liked them when they took the cooking class he'd taught with Marisol years ago and he was truly glad they'd found a way to be happy together.

"Thank you." Riley beamed at him. When the song changed to a familiar late '80's rock tune, Riley laughed and held out a hand. "Want to join us out there again?"

"I'm good," Stuart said with a smile. "Go have fun."

Riley made a beeline for the dance floor and soon the entire speakeasy crew was singing along to *Pour Some Sugar on Me*. Even the typically strait-laced Senator Mori and his boyfriend were belting out the song and several of the guys had arms over each other's shoulders. Cam and Jesse were flat out diva singing, and as the song progressed, the group split into two, singing to each other with progressively louder voices and more exaggerated motions.

Astrid danced her way in between the two groups, out-diva-ing Cam and Jesse. Stuart laughed when the date she'd brought to the wedding — a stunning Latina woman whose name Stuart couldn't remember — shook her head in mock horror.

They were an interesting bunch, that was for sure.

After the sing-along, Cam and Malcolm headed Stuart's way. Malcolm paused beside him and set a hand on Stuart's shoulder. "I'm grabbing a drink. You want anything?"

"Nah, I'm good for now." Stuart held up his half-finished cocktail. He was feeling no pain at the moment, but he didn't want to overindulge and be useless later. It had been far too long since he and Malcolm had explored each other in the bedroom and if Malcolm was on board, Stuart was ready to pick that up again.

* * * *

"I'm glad you and Malcolm were able to work things out," Cam said several hours later. He draped an arm around Stuart's shoulders. "He seems so much happier with you."

"Thanks." Stuart managed a smile. Nearly every one of the guys had commented on his relationship with Malcolm in some way or another and it was starting to make him uncomfortable.

"You're kind of an enigma," Jesse said. "We'd all like to get to know you better. A lot better."

Stuart raised an eyebrow at him.

"Not like that!" Jesse waved his hand vaguely. "Being turned down more than once is bad for a man's ego and we all know you're Malcolm's and that neither of you share. I just meant we don't really know you yet. And I'm sorry, dude, but if you're going to hang around with us, you're going to have to open up."

Stuart sipped his drink. "I'm not used to big groups of friends like this. I had a lone-wolf thing going before I met Malcolm and I didn't realize he came as a package deal." Jesse frowned and Stuart was quick to amend his words. "Not that I'm complaining. You're all great. I just need time to adjust, okay?"

"Sure thing," Jesse said with an easy smile. "We'll be here whenever you're ready."

Stuart sighed as Jesse slipped an arm around Cam's waist and guided him toward the dance floor. Several people had left but Malcolm was happily dancing in the middle of a small crowd, so Stuart took the opportunity to slip into the much quieter house. It was late. The dancing had been going on for hours and even the kids had lost steam and allowed their mother to tuck them into bed upstairs.

The quiet stillness of the house was a relief. Stuart was used to the chaos of a kitchen but not to being a guest at this kind of event. Especially with a group as enthusiastic as the speakeasy crew.

Slowly, he walked up the stairs to the bedroom he and Malcolm had been sharing, intent on relaxing for a while before he headed downstairs again. Stuart could hear the muffled sound of music playing as he walked through the door, and he turned on the bedside lamps and plugged in his phone. He was debating stretching out on the bed when he heard a familiar voice.

"Hey there."

Stuart looked up and found Malcolm leaning in the doorway. He'd come in so quietly Stuart hadn't heard him open the door. "Hey."

"You okay?" Malcolm's brow furrowed with concern.

"Yeah." Stuart offered him a reassuring smile. "It was just…a lot. I needed to sneak away for a bit. I hope you don't mind."

"No, I understand. When these guys get together, it can be a lot. I came up to make sure everything was all right."

"Thanks for checking on me. I'm good. You can go back down if you'd like. I don't want to hold you back from enjoying the rest of the evening with your friends."

"Nah, I think it's winding down. I'm partied out, too." Malcolm pushed off the doorframe and walked over to Stuart. "I hope you had a good time."

"I did. I promise." When Malcolm slid his arms around Stuart, Stuart pulled him closer. "Um, can I be honest?"

"Of course. I always want you to be honest."

"Sometimes your friends are… a little overwhelming."

Malcolm gave him a lopsided smile. "I get that."

"Jesse called me out earlier. He said none of them felt like they knew me very well."

"I think David and Cam and Luka almost immediately fell in step with everyone, so they didn't expect it to take a while longer for you. Maybe they should have. It took Will time, too. I guess we all chalked it up to his lingering feelings for Riley."

"There's nothing wrong with how close you all are. I'm just not used to it," Stuart said. "I agree, though—I think they expected to pull me in right away."

"And you're not there yet?"

"I'm not." Stuart was relieved that Malcolm seemed to understand. "That doesn't mean I don't want to get to know them, but this feels like too much too soon." He grimaced. "That sounds awful. And I don't want to offend them."

"I can let them know they need to slow their roll. They won't be offended," Malcolm said. "These guys are big-hearted and can come across as pushy. They are respectful of boundaries if you make them clear, however."

"Thank you," Stuart said. He could do that himself, but it would be easier coming from Malcolm. He would know how to word things without accidentally causing offense.

Stuart rested his forehead against Malcolm's. "I really did have a good time tonight."

"I'm glad." Malcolm cupped his cheek and pressed his lips to Stuart's. Stuart let out a little groan as he kissed Malcolm back before pulling away.

"Did you have fun?"

A grin lit up Malcolm's face. "I did. I had a wonderful time. I'm glad you came with me. Tonight was even nicer with you here."

"Did you ever miss having someone?" A puzzled look crossed Malcolm's face and Stuart hastened to explain. "You're surrounded by couples. Did being the only un-partnered person ever get old?"

Malcolm shrugged. "No. Although I always enjoy it when I have one-on-one time with Carter. Or with Kyle when we go to yoga classes together."

"You didn't mind being the single person in the group?"

"No." Malcolm's expression turned thoughtful. "I never felt like I was lacking before. I did like having you here by my side tonight. It was a nice addition. Why do you ask?"

"I was just curious." For a while after his divorce, Stuart had felt lonely at times. Although his marriage to Becky had been lacking, he'd sometimes missed having that person to lean on. Being rejected for his kink had also led to periods of loneliness. In Malcolm's shoes, being constantly surrounded by couples would have been challenging. Malcolm had never felt that. Perhaps because he'd never experienced being in a serious relationship with someone before. Or maybe that was just Malcolm. "I'm glad to be a nice addition to your life."

"You are." Malcolm fitted himself closer to Stuart, sliding his hands along Stuart's waist until their bodies were flush against each other.

"I hope the photographer got some good pictures today," Stuart said.

Malcolm tilted his head. "What made you think of that?"

"I was thinking how gorgeous you look in that suit. It'd be nice to see some good photos of us together. Maybe get a copy."

"You're surprisingly sentimental."

"Sometimes." Perhaps all this wedding stuff was getting to Stuart's brain. He wanted to scoff, but truthfully, he'd always been rather sentimental. He'd simply buried that side of himself for a long time. Stuart didn't want to make Malcolm uncomfortable, so he changed the subject. "As gorgeous as you are in that suit, I know you look great out of it, too. How would you feel if I helped you out of it now?"

Malcolm smiled. "I'd be good with that."

"Mmm. Glad to hear it." Stuart loosened Malcolm's tie and slipped it from the collar. After placing it on the dresser, he worked each tiny button loose on Malcolm's shirt. When it hung open, he slipped his hands underneath. Rather than push the fabric off Malcolm's shoulders, he ran his hands across the undershirt Malcolm wore. Malcolm's skin was warm under Stuart's palms and Malcolm closed his eyes, letting out a hum of pleasure.

Stuart eased the shirt off Malcolm's broad shoulders and blindly tossed it on the nearby chair. After lifting his arms, Malcolm stood still as Stuart eased off the undershirt, leaving him naked from the waist up. Stuart took his time exploring Malcolm's shoulders and chest before he dragged a hand down Malcolm's smooth, firm abs. He was lean and defined. Malcolm let out a shaky breath as Stuart reached the waistband of his suit pants and teased along the edge of the fabric.

"Can I take these off you?" Stuart whispered.

"Yes."

Stuart went down on his knees and helped Malcolm step out of his trousers and underwear. After, Stuart pressed a kiss to Malcolm's thigh, feeling him shiver. When he stood, he held out a hand and tugged Malcolm over to the bed. He looked a little wide-eyed but there was no tension in his body as he stretched out on the sheets.

After Stuart undressed to his underwear, he settled next to Malcolm on the bed. He curled a hand around the back of Malcolm's neck before pressing their lips together. Malcolm's quiet moan encouraged him and as they kissed, their bodies twined together.

Stuart drew back, then brushed his thumb across Malcolm's cheekbone, staring into his eyes. "Now that we're back on solid footing, how do you feel about picking things up again? I'd like to keep exploring if you're feeling ready."

"I'd like that." Malcolm leaned in to kiss him. There was no mistaking the hunger in the kiss.

Stuart spent time finding the spots on Malcolm's neck and shoulders that made him squirm before he moved down to lap at Malcolm's nipple. He reached down and stroked Malcolm's cock. The skin was hot in his hand and Malcolm let out a breathless gasp when Stuart tightened his grip. Stuart slid up Malcolm's body and nuzzled his ear.

"How do you feel about me using my mouth on your cock?" he rasped. "No pressure to reciprocate, I'm just dying to taste you if you're ready for that."

"Okay." Malcolm's voice shook. Stuart wasn't sure if it was excitement or nerves.

Moving slowly, Stuart worked his way down again, leisurely exploring the flat plane of skin below Malcolm's navel and dragging his tongue along the crest of his hip bones. He teased Malcolm's thighs, gently biting at the muscles there until Malcolm writhed beneath him. His breathing was light and ragged as Stuart grasped his cock, and when Stuart looked up to check in with Malcolm, he was staring at

Stuart, his eyes brilliantly blue and full of need, even in the low light of the room.

"If you want me to stop at any time, let me know," Stuart said.

Malcolm nodded. A flutter of nerves in his own stomach, Stuart lowered his mouth over Malcolm's cock. He took it slow, teasing him with his tongue before he engulfed Malcolm with his mouth. The low, broken moan that escaped Malcolm when he bottomed out made Stuart so hard he ached. He had to change course before they both totally lost control. Sliding his mouth off Malcolm's cock, he moved lower and dragged his tongue across Malcolm's balls. Pleasure surged through Stuart as Malcolm's whole body quivered. He really wanted to rim Malcolm but that might be a step too far tonight. There *was* one other thing he'd been dying to do.

"Can I use a finger in you?"

"I — yeah." Malcolm's voice was breathless.

"I'm going to grab some lube." As Stuart rummaged through his bag to find it, he sent out a little thanks to himself for having had the foresight to pack some. He'd been hopeful.

Turning back to the bed, he stumbled at the sight of Malcolm watching him intently. His expression was heated and needy and it didn't escape Stuart's attention that Malcolm's gaze landed on the length between his legs. That look made Stuart's cock throb. He slid into bed beside Malcolm and settled between his thighs again.

"Open up wider for me," Stuart coaxed.

Malcolm spread his legs more, a flush staining his cheeks and chest.

"You have nothing to be embarrassed about," Stuart reassured him. "You are so incredibly hot right now." He propped himself up one elbow and kissed Malcolm's inner thigh. "So sexy."

He kept talking as he slicked his finger with lube and circled Malcolm's opening, just teasing the outside. "I love seeing you naked in front of me like this, trusting me to make you feel good."

Malcolm's breath hitched as Stuart applied gentle pressure and circled his hole again. "I'm going to use my mouth on you again and if you want to stop at any time, tell me, okay?"

"Okay." Malcolm's voice was reedy and when Stuart glanced up at his face, his pupils were blown wide.

Stuart dipped his head and ran his tongue along Malcolm's shaft. He worked his way down to lap at Malcolm's balls and when Malcolm let out a strained moan, Stuart gently pushed the finger forward.

Malcolm tensed around him and Stuart froze. Rubbing Malcolm's thigh, he gave him a moment to adjust to the feeling of fullness. Soon, Malcolm had relaxed and Stuart refocused his attention on Malcolm's cock. When Malcolm began to shift underneath him again, Stuart slid his finger back, then pushed inside again. This time, Malcolm didn't tighten up. In fact, he let his thighs fall open wider, and as Stuart slowly fucked him with one finger, Malcolm began to move his hips in time with the thrusts.

His hands landed on Stuart's head, holding tightly for several seconds before his grip relaxed. "I'm sorry—"

"No, I liked that," Stuart said. His voice was low and gravely from arousal and he couldn't remember the last time he'd been this turned on. "Guide my head if you want." He lowered his mouth down over Malcolm's cock again.

Malcolm threaded his fingers through Stuart's hair. While he didn't push Stuart down on his cock, he did guide him and the little tugs on Stuart's hair sent pleasure zinging through his body. Stuart took Malcolm deep and curled his finger.

Malcolm's grip tightened on Stuart's head and he let out a strangled gasp. "Stuart, I'm going to…"

Stuart sucked harder and gave another short, shallow thrust into Malcolm's hole. With a soft cry, Malcolm pulsed in his mouth. Stuart swallowed and Malcolm was still shaking as he eased his mouth off Malcolm's cock. Stuart's own orgasm had snuck up on him. The sheets were wet underneath and his cock was sensitive from where it had been rubbing against them.

Malcolm's willingness to let Stuart guide him to try new things made Stuart feel incredible. He pressed a kiss to Malcolm's thigh. The muscle there was still quivering and Stuart soothed it with his thumb as he gently worked his finger out from Malcolm's body.

As Stuart slid up his body and wrapped his arms around Malcolm, Malcolm let out a long sigh.

"Can I make you feel good?" he asked.

Stuart grinned. "You already did."

Malcolm tilted his head and gave Stuart a quizzical look. "I did?"

"Mmhmm. I got off on you enjoying yourself." Stuart sat up so Malcolm could see the wet spot on his boxer briefs.

Malcolm stared as Stuart settled back against the pillows. "Does that happen a lot?"

"Coming unassisted?"

"Well, yeah."

"To me, or men in general?"

"Both I guess."

"I don't think it's terribly common in general. It doesn't happen all the time for me. The connection we have is a lot deeper than I'm used to."

"For me, too, obviously." Malcolm gave him a sleepy smile.

For a few minutes, they just lay there, breathing. When Malcolm's body softened, Stuart gently shook him. "We should clean up."

"Mmhmm."

He chuckled. "Before you fall asleep. C'mon." Stuart climbed out of bed and held out a hand to Malcolm, who got up with a groan.

When they were under the warm, running water, Malcolm sighed and pressed close to Stuart.

"I'm glad you invited me this weekend." Stuart pulled their bodies more tightly together and brushed his lips across Malcolm's. He was falling hard for Malcolm and this weekend had been a big leap forward for both of them.

"I'm glad I did, too." Malcolm kissed him back. "Very, very glad."

Chapter Seventeen

"Hey, guys." Malcolm smiled down at his manager and Carter, who'd been seated beside her at Tara's workstation for most of the morning.

"Hey, Mal. What's up?" Carter briefly crossed his eyes then shook his head like he was clearing it. "Besides my retinas spontaneously detaching, I mean. Jeez."

"I'm headed to the printer to check on the merch order we placed last week, then downtown for a lunch thing." Malcom's stomach fluttered a bit at his own words, but Tara's sigh as she sat back in her chair caught his attention. "Everything okay?"

"Meh. I think my brain is broken." Tara and Carter had been reviewing reams of CEC membership data for hours and her dark eyes were bleary. "I'm not sure I even remember the last set of names we covered."

Malcolm frowned. "Do you need help? I can cancel my lunch if—"

"Don't even think it." Tara got to her feet. "Go, eat tasty food, and don't bother coming back to the office afterward, okay? Between last weekend and this week, you've worked a sick number of hours and I don't want you getting burnt out."

"Agreed," Carter said before Malcolm could protest. "The rest of us can hold down the fort." He glanced up at Tara from his chair. "But we should eat because, I swear, I just heard your stomach growl." Carter smiled at her laughter, and after she'd walked off, he turned back to Malcolm. "You're meeting your mom for lunch, right?"

"Yup." Malcolm hitched his bag higher onto his shoulder and grimaced. "It's been two weeks since Jackson sat her and my dad down to talk through the money problems. Feels like I've been waiting forever for the other shoe to drop."

Carter made a thoughtful sound. "She hasn't mentioned it at all?"

"Nope. We've talked on the phone a few times, but it's like the conversation with my brother never happened. I'd started to wonder if maybe she wasn't just blowing the whole thing off but she asked me to lunch and picked a place here instead of Staten Island," Malcolm said with a frown. "So now I have to assume she wanted to talk face-to-face. What if I'm wrong, though?" He sighed. "I hardly know what to say to her."

"Then maybe let your mom do the talking." Carter stood and gave Malcolm's shoulder a squeeze. "Give her a chance and see where she leads. That's all you can do, right?"

"You make a good point."

"Oh, before I forget, Will's in town this weekend — he's already over at our place with the dog," Carter said as they headed toward the exit. "He and Ri are heading out for dinner tonight and I know they plan to hit Under afterward. David will be there too, provided he can leave Long Island before the traffic gets bad."

"Sounds great. Stuart's off today, so he might be up for it. What about you—are you coming out, too?" Malcolm furrowed his brow when Carter shook his head.

"Nah, I'm wiped and too pooped to party. I figured I'd keep Mabel company instead, so Will doesn't need to worry about her. Which will be interesting when you consider how much my cat hates that dog." Carter gave Malcolm a smile. "Shoot Will a message, 'cause I know he wants to see you."

"Will do."

"And don't show your face around here until Monday or I'll be forced to do something passive-aggressive to express my displeasure. You know how much I hate that!"

Now Malcolm laughed. "Okay, okay, I'm going!"

He wondered about Carter's words as he looked over proofs for CEC T-shirts, mugs and other swag items. Will was Malcolm's friend, of course, and while they didn't often meet up outside of the speakeasy crew gatherings, Malcolm always enjoyed his and David's company. The idea that Will would express a specific desire to see Malcolm struck him though, particularly as it sounded like many of the crew was set to converge on Under anyway.

Malcolm's musings shifted from friends to family as he headed downtown for the Gopher's Parlour, a restaurant and bar located a few blocks from Whitehall Ferry terminal. He arrived a few minutes early and settled in a booth in the taproom with a pint of Gopher Red Ale, exchanging messages with Will and Kyle about meeting up later while also trying not to overthink his mother's invitation.

According to Jackson, his conversation with Kim and Stephen in the Staten Island house had been a total roller coaster ride, marked by reactions ranging wildly from outrage and disbelief to sorrow and regret. Kim had gone on the defensive and tried more than once to deny that she was in financial trouble, even storming out of the house at one point. Thankfully, she'd only made it as far as the end of the driveway before she returned, pale and shaken and finally willing to talk about ways to dig herself out of the hole.

The guilt on his brother's face as he'd described the scene had made Malcolm's stomach twist, but they'd known it had been the right thing to do. As much as Malcolm hated the idea of his family hurting, Stuart and the speakeasy guys had shown him that confronting his mother's financial problems head-on was the only sensible path. She had to be an active participant. And if it took Kim a while to find her footing on that path, the Elliotts were there to back her up and make sure she didn't fall even further.

"I'm not late, am I?"

A familiar voice dragged Malcolm back to the present. He stood, unable to help his grin at the way his mom was beaming at him. "Not at all," he said, then stepped away from the table so he could give her a hug. "I was early, thanks to the trains being oddly punctual today."

Kim rubbed Malcolm's back as they separated, her smile even bigger. "You know, it occurs to me that we could have met in Midtown. I had an appointment on 33rd and 6th and that would have been easier for you instead of coming all the way down here. I'm sorry."

"It's okay." Malcolm gestured to the seat he'd just vacated. "I was out of the office on an errand anyway and meeting here gets you closer to the terminal for the ride back. Unless you have other plans after this?"

"I don't but you're sweet to think of that." Kim settled into the booth and waited until Malcolm had taken the chair opposite. "I'm glad you could make time today, honey, considering I called you so last minute. You look great, by the way." She heaved a big breath, her expression going so serious that Malcolm's stomach tumbled.

"Um. Thanks?"

"I mean it." She patted Malcolm's hand where it lay on the table. "You've put on some weight since the last time I saw you and the color is back in your cheeks, which I hope means you're eating properly again."

Well, hell.

"Mom—"

"I can't tell you how sorry I am." Kim pressed her lips together in a tight line. "I really... I didn't realize how difficult I was making things for you and Jack and I know I should have. When your brother told me what the two of you have been going through to keep me afloat, you in particular..." She shook her head. "I knew you looked thinner but Jesus, Malcolm. I don't know what to say."

"I was happy to help." Malcolm swallowed against the lump that had risen in his throat. He wanted to say more—reassure his mother he really was okay—but stopped himself when the server, who'd introduced herself earlier as Isabel, approached the table.

"Good afternoon, ma'am," she said to Kim. "Can I get you something to drink?"

"I'd love a glass of white wine," Kim replied. Malcolm could see she was trying for friendly through her tight smile. "What would you recommend with your salads?"

Isabel clasped her hands behind her back. "The Trimbach Pinot Gris pairs well with the grilled salmon salad, and I like the Gruner Veltliner with the fresh burrata."

"Pinot Gris sounds nice, thanks. The salmon salad, too, if you wouldn't mind." Kim glanced at Malcolm's half-emptied glass. "How about you, honey?"

"I'm good with beer for the moment, thanks." Malcolm handed his menu to Isabel. "I'll go with a couple of the small plates, please — the sausage roll and truffled chips."

"Are you sure you don't want a sandwich?" Kim asked. A crease Malcolm had never noticed before worked its way between her eyebrows. "Small plates don't sound like all that much food."

"And I ordered two," Malcolm said. "That should be enough even for me and this way we can share."

"Excellent." Isabel's eyes twinkled as she collected Kim's menu, too. "I'll get the order right in for you."

A silence hung in the air after she'd gone, thick to the point of suffocating, and Malcolm fought not to squirm under his mother's gaze. It was a struggle to ignore his instinct to smooth things over and pretend nothing was wrong, but he and Kim needed to talk, even if it took them all afternoon to start.

"This is my treat," Kim said out of nowhere. "I know it would have been cheaper to have you to the house instead, but I wanted to do something nice for you. Your father helped me sell off those old motorcycles he's been keeping in the garage for the past twenty years, so I've got some money that I can spend on you for a change."

"Mom, stop." Malcolm held up a hand when Kim made to continue. "I appreciate the gesture, but you don't have to do that. My bank account is a lot healthier than it was a month ago, mostly because I'm back to splitting a lot of my expenses with Jack and Marissa. That said, I meant it when I told you I was happy to help when you needed it. I wouldn't change a thing about making sure you're okay."

"Of course, you wouldn't." Kim's throat worked, and she kept talking even as Malcolm tried to protest. "You and your brother are good men, Malcolm, and so giving, but it was my responsibility to deal with life after I lost my job, not yours. I'm not proud of the way I acted. In fact, I'm ashamed that I dragged you and Jack into my mess."

"You lost your job," Malcolm replied. "That's a blow that can knock anyone off their feet."

"It's still no excuse." His mom let out a quiet huff. "If I could go back, I would change some things. I never wanted to hurt you or Jack and I know I did. You most of all, Malcolm." Kim leaned forward in her seat and clasped her hands on top of the table. "Can you forgive me?"

Sadness and relief warred in Malcolm's heart. As much as he hated to hear his mother say those words, it was wonderful to know she was taking responsibility for herself.

"There's nothing to forgive," he said once he trusted his voice to be steady. "Jack and I wanted to help, so we did. I don't resent you for needing that help, Mom, and I'll never be sorry that we stepped in." He held his hand out and managed a smile when his mother took it.

"We're here for you. We may be more than a little dysfunctional, but you have to know that we love you just the same."

Kim actually scowled. "Don't say things like that, honey. You and your brother are perfect."

"So not true. I'm far from perfect, Mom. I'm working on being better, though."

"So am I. Starting with going back to work full-time." Kim sat back as Isabel arrived with her wine, then held the glass up toward Malcolm. "I've had three job interviews in the last two weeks and, today, I accepted an offer. I start in four days!"

The pride in his mother's expression sent a happy surge through Malcolm. "That's so great. What are you going to be doing? And where will you be working? Wait, is the job here in the city?" His rapid-fire questions made them both laugh. "Sorry, I'm being obnoxious. But tell me everything!"

He sat back, content to allow his mom to take over the conversation, warmth building in his chest as Kim told him about the job she'd taken with the Kinship Fund, a newly formed foundation dedicated to strengthening LGBTQIA communities in New York and New Jersey by investing in targeted organizations, projects and leaders.

"I'm working under the program director," Kim said, her eyes bright. "A large portion of Kinship's money goes to nonprofits and scholarship programs and we're setting up consulting and coaching opportunities for the leaders of those organizations that need them. Oh." She glanced down at her salad and laughed. "I just said 'we' and I only accepted the job offer two hours ago!"

Malcolm waved her off. "Pretty sure that means you're allowed to use 'we,' then. The office is in Midtown?"

"Yes, over near Penn Station. Not all that far from your neighborhood, now that I think about it. Gosh, it's going to be so interesting commuting into the city again!" Kim sipped her wine. "The funny thing is, I'm looking forward to it. I think…no, I know I was bored out there at the house because the job I had wasn't challenging and I never found anything substantive to do with my time. That's about to change, thanks to you and your friends."

Malcolm furrowed his brow. "Thanks to me?"

"Your friend Senator Mori is the Kinship Fund's executive director, honey. Didn't you know that?" Kim cocked her head. "He's only there part-time right now because he's still in office, but he's not running for re-election this fall. After his term ends, he'll be at the Fund full-time." She sat up straight in her chair then, eyes wide. "Crap, I'm not sure I'm supposed to say anything about that yet, so pretend you didn't hear it from me."

"Jesus, Mom." Malcolm spluttered into his beer, his thoughts spinning at the influx of information. He'd known David and Will were setting up a foundation and also that David had considered leaving office, but to get confirmation—from his mother of all people!—was a big deal. Malcolm really needed to catch up with his friends tonight. "Was David the one who contacted you about the job?"

"No. I spoke with his boyfriend, Will Martin, last week. He called about a position in administration at the college where he teaches. He gave me information about the Kinship Fund too, and said my experience might be better suited there. I applied for both jobs, but I knew from the start that Will was right—Kinship is the better match." Kim's smile softened then. "You really didn't know about any of this?"

"Not a thing." Malcolm ran a hand over his mouth. Honestly, did no one believe he was capable of handling his own life? "I'm grateful they helped you, but I'm not loving the fact that they did it without telling me. I'm sure that sounds petty."

"No, it doesn't. But you should blame me, at least in part." Kim bit her lip. "Will asked me to tell you that he and I had talked, and I didn't want to say anything until after I'd heard back about the job. I worried you might be disappointed if I didn't get it."

The apprehension in her expression shifted Malcolm's mood in a flash. "Hey, no. How could I be disappointed when I'm so proud of you for getting out there again?"

"Thank you. I just wish I'd done it sooner." Kim sighed. "I'm sure you know this, but your friends are good people. They helped Jack hook me up with a financial planner. And your brother told me about what they've been doing to help you too, and that Stuart stepped in first. You have a lot of people in your life who care for you."

Despite the fire in his cheeks, Malcolm bobbed his head. "I know. I care about them, too. Stuart especially." Just saying those two words made his heart swell. Malcolm more than cared about Stuart. He wanted to share absolutely everything with him. And Malcolm loved him, body and soul, even if he still didn't feel ready to say the words out loud.

"Really?"

"Yes, really." Malcolm swore his mother's smile could have powered the whole city.

"That's the best thing I've heard today. Even better than the job offer!" She speared salad greens onto her fork with gusto. "Can I say that you and Stuart are boyfriends when I tell my friends about him?"

"Ummm, yes?" In fact, Malcolm and Stuart hadn't talked titles or formalities or anything along those lines, but Malcolm didn't think they needed to. He had zero desire to see anyone else and felt confident Stuart was happy keeping things exclusive. "I don't know why your friends would care who I date, though."

Kim rolled her eyes. "My poor, oblivious boy. Of course, my friends care. And even if they don't, I do!"

Mystified at his mother's satisfaction but tickled all the same, Malcolm listened to her gush about Stuart and how happy the rest of the Elliotts were that he'd come into Malcolm's life. Which was funny, given Stuart hadn't even met them.

I could change that, Malcolm thought. While part of him cringed at the idea, a larger part loved thinking about Stuart meeting his father. *Christ, I'm in deep.*

After seeing his mom to the ferry terminal, he headed uptown on foot. Things had been so good in the weeks since the wedding in Southampton. They spent most nights Stuart wasn't working together, often hanging out with friends. Other times, they stayed in and simply enjoyed each other's company. Stuart maintained he liked coming home to Malcolm after work too, so if Malcolm didn't already have plans, he'd head for Little Italy after eating dinner at home. He'd bring along a tub of leftovers and use the spare key Stuart had given him to let himself into the apartment. And while Malcolm was often sleeping by the time

Stuart got home from King's, he'd rouse enough to exchange drowsy kisses before Stuart slipped away to clean up. There were usually more kisses after Stuart climbed into bed, and they didn't always stop at kissing, either.

Malcolm smiled to himself. Sex with Stuart was fun and hot, even at the slower pace Malcolm needed to set, and somehow that made him want to try new things far more than he'd ever have believed. Last night, Stuart had pinned Malcolm down and driven him to such distraction he'd literally begged to come. While Malcolm's body reacted in a very pleasant way to the memory, his mind and heart clung more so to what had happened afterward when Stuart had wiped Malcolm down and wrapped him up in his arms, so tight Malcolm had sworn he felt Stuart's heart thudding against his shoulder.

No matter what heights Stuart could drive him to, Malcolm wanted that connection even more. Didn't mean he'd stopped worrying from time to time that Stuart needed more when it came to sex. Malcolm had grown certain that Stuart also craved the connection between them. Whether or not they got off before they curled up together to sleep, Malcolm wanted anything Stuart was willing to give.

A mellow happiness made him feel light as he crossed from Chinatown into Little Italy. Stuart had invited Malcolm into his life. He'd gone out of his way to help Malcolm with his financial issues, even risking Malcolm's anger, and willingly stepped out of his comfort zone in an effort to know the speakeasy guys. Shit, Stuart had given Malcolm a key to his apartment, and if that wasn't a sign they were on the same page, Malcolm wasn't sure what would be.

He'd opened the outer door of Stuart's building when his phone buzzed with an incoming call from Will, who, oddly enough, sounded sheepish.

"Mal, I just heard from David. He told me the Kinship Fund has a new employee by the name of Kim Elliott."

Malcolm headed for the stairs. "She gave me the news about an hour ago. She's so excited, Will, you have no idea."

"Oh, great! You knew she'd applied, right?"

"Well, no. Today was the first I'd heard of it."

"Damn, I was afraid of that." Will sighed. "I'd been talking to some of the guys about needing staff and Carter mentioned your mom had experience with university admin, so I looked her up and things took on a life of their own. Clearly, since David and I had no idea she'd even interviewed at Kinship until today."

Smiling, Malcolm made his way up to the fifth floor. "It's okay. My mom said she wanted to wait until after she'd heard about the job before she told me, and I have to respect that."

"So we're cool?"

"Yes, we are. I appreciate that you guys thought about her in the first place."

"Well, Carter's the one who mentioned her name — things are usually his fault."

The teasing tone in Will's voice made Malcolm laugh. "Is my mom's job the thing you wanted to talk to me about tonight?"

"Actually, no. I need cookie recipes! I'm taking care of my niece and nephew next weekend while their parents are out of town and I figured baking up a batch or two of your favorites might be fun."

"Heck, yeah, that'd be fun." Malcolm stopped in front of Stuart's door. "How about I email some recipes and we talk them through when I see you tonight?"

"Sounds great, thanks. You bringing your boyfriend with you to Under?"

There's that word again, Malcolm thought. "Stuart's at the carpenters' workshop today. I'll know more later."

Knowing it could be a while before he even spoke to Stuart, Malcolm ended the call with Will and let himself into the apartment. He breathed in deeply as the now-familiar vibe of a space he'd started to think of as home fell over him.

As always, the aroma of spices hung in the air, cinnamon the most prevalent today followed by another, earthier note that Malcolm guessed was saffron. While most of the studio was as neat as a pin with everything in its usual place, Stuart hadn't made the bed that morning, and the sheets and comforter lay askew. That made it easy for Malcolm to spot something very out of place and drew his eye immediately to a streak of scarlet peeking out from under the pillows.

Frowning, Malcolm hung his bag on the hook by the door. He crossed the room, his gaze on the color glowing hot and stark against the cooler blues and whites surrounding it. He extended a hand as he got closer, but Malcolm stopped once he'd reached the bed, his fingers hovering over what he now saw was a loop of ribbon, as if the thing might be dangerous.

Whatever that is, you know it's not yours.

Heart in his throat, Malcolm slowly sat on the mattress. Grasping the loop with two fingers, he pulled, unaware he'd started holding his breath until it left him in a whoosh as a slip of fabric was revealed.

The panties were so...delicate. The satin was trimmed with lace and the ribbon that had caught Malcolm's eye was one of a pair of garters, the kind he knew could be attached to stockings. Malcolm recognized them because his ex, Liz, had worn a similar kind of garment on several occasions. Malcolm could picture her now, unhooking the garters with nimble fingers, her smile coy as she peeled the stockings off. Seeing Liz like that had piqued Malcolm's interest every time, and he'd found the sex they'd shared on those occasions deeply pleasurable.

I'm sure the woman who wears those panties makes Stuart feel good, too.

Malcolm clenched his eyes shut, his stomach twisting so tight it hurt. "No," he murmured to himself. "That can't be right."

Something was off. Stuart had always been upfront about his sexuality. He was a gay man, both out and proud, and he'd told Malcolm he preferred men. Except...that wasn't all he'd said. Stuart had also said that he'd found his ex-wife attractive. That maybe he was closer to bi, despite his preference for men. That he wasn't entirely gay, just like Malcolm wasn't entirely straight.

No big deal, right? So maybe Stuart enjoyed being with women as much as he liked being with men. That would mean he'd been lying to Malcolm about that preference from the very beginning, however. And maybe that wasn't all Stuart had lied about. Maybe he'd been lying about his feelings for Malcolm, too.

Malcolm's sinuses burned as the thought crashed through his head. Stuart had lied to him before. And Malcolm knew what he was looking at—what else could explain women's underwear tucked under the pillow he'd slept on just the night before? They belonged to someone. And what if Stuart loved her?

Before he truly knew he was moving, Malcolm was across the room and out of the door, slamming it closed behind him as he made for the stairs. He'd gotten two blocks east before his phone chimed in his pocket and when he forced himself to stop walking, his heart was pounding so hard his head spun.

Malcolm didn't need to check his messages to guess there was a new one from Stuart. Just like he knew he couldn't walk away, no matter how much he wanted to. Malcolm had walked away from Stuart once before and only ended up hurting them both, and god-fucking-damnit, he wanted an explanation. *Needed* it. Stuart owed him that much. If that meant knowing Stuart really had been lying to Malcolm all along? Then Malcolm would also know that all the fucking feelings he'd been trying so hard to hide for the past several weeks had just been a big waste of time.

Abruptly, his vision blurred. Great. Nothing like falling apart in broad daylight in the middle of the sidewalk.

Movements rough, Malcolm scrubbed at his eyes, then swore when he realized he'd left his bag behind in the rush to get out. Gaze on the ground, he forced one foot in front of the other and made his way back. And while it seemed like an eternity passed and everything he'd thought he'd known was changed, Malcolm found Stuart's studio as he'd left it, silent and still. No longer a place where Malcolm felt he belonged.

Chest tight, he shut the door, then stared at the scrap of red satin from across the room until his vision went blurry again. God, he felt so stupid. Especially now with nothing left to do but stay here until Stuart got back so they could talk or argue or whatever the hell people did when their whole relationship toppled down around their heads.

The fight that had been building inside Malcolm slowly faded, leaving him hollow in a way he'd never known before. He didn't bother wiping his eyes as he took his bag from the hook, then retreated to the window by the stove — as far away from the bed as he could get — and settled in to wait.

Chapter Eighteen

The odor of sawdust filled the air as Stuart jogged up the steps to his apartment. He'd enjoyed spending the day working in the shop, feeling the rough wood slowly turn silky smooth under his palm with repeated passing of progressively finer grades of sandpaper and, eventually, steel wool. The shelves he was finishing would look nice hanging on the wall beside the dresser. It would give Stuart some much-needed storage, too, especially since he planned to add a few baskets to corral smaller items. He'd have more space to offer Malcolm, who was spending more and more time at Stuart's place, something Stuart couldn't be happier about.

His lips curved in a smile as he thought about Malcolm. He'd stayed over last night, and Stuart had sent a text to Malcolm a short while ago to see if he would come over again after he was done meeting Will at Under tonight. Stuart had gotten used to sleeping with Malcolm's long, lean body pressed against his and there was nothing he liked better than waking up slowly, exchanging lazy kisses with Malcolm and sometimes stroking each other off. Arousal pulsed through him as he remembered the taste of Malcolm on his tongue this morning before Malcolm had to hurry off to work. Stuart had remained in bed for a while, eventually bringing himself to another explosive orgasm.

Stuart slotted his key into the doorknob and twisted it, his head filled with memories of Malcolm as he stepped into his apartment. He was so lost in those thoughts that it wasn't until he'd laced off his boots, removed them and walked toward the center of the studio that he spotted the very person he'd been thinking about perched on the deep windowsill beside the stove. That was somewhat odd, but Stuart was too pleased to see Malcolm to dwell on it.

"Hey!" Stuart grinned at the sight of Malcolm's face. His smile fell a little when Malcolm didn't return the greeting. "This is a nice surprise. What are you doing sitting over there?" He walked toward Malcolm, unease trickling through him as he took in Malcolm's stricken expression. As he got closer, he saw that Malcolm's eyes were red-rimmed.

"Malcolm?" Stuart slowed to a stop. Something was clearly very, very off and he let his messenger bag slip to the ground as he searched Malcolm's face for an explanation. "Did something happen? What's wrong?"

Malcolm swallowed and pointed at something behind Stuart. "That." His voice was hoarse and Stuart swiveled his head to see what in the hell Malcolm was pointing at. Stuart went lightheaded when he saw the scrap of red fabric draped over the edge of the mattress, shockingly bright against the white sheets.

Oh, no. No. Fuck.

Stuart pressed a hand to his eyes as if that would somehow make the underwear disappear. He would have sworn that after he'd masturbated this morning, thinking about Malcolm, he'd tucked the panties and garter under his pillow before he'd left the apartment. It had been careless of him to do that rather than put them in the drawer, but he'd been running later than planned and he'd been in a hurry to get out the door. He'd never expected Malcolm to show up here before he got back.

Stuart dropped his hand and turned back to face Malcolm, who looked like someone had sucker-punched him. Stuart licked suddenly dry lips, knowing how much hinged on what happened in the next few minutes. "Look, let's talk about this, Malcolm. Okay?"

Malcolm nodded once, jerkily, still looking shell-shocked. *Fuck.* "That would be good," he rasped. "I saw them under the pillow when I came in. I wasn't snooping. I swear."

"I didn't think you were," Stuart said quietly.

"To be honest, I left after I found them. I came back because I didn't want to run out without having a conversation with you about it."

"I'm glad you came back." Stuart held a hand out to Malcolm, who still looked chalky-pale. "Can we sit on the bed and talk?"

Malcolm's gaze darted to the bed again and he pressed his lips tightly together.

"Want me to put them away?" Stuart offered. Malcolm nodded.

Stuart's eyes stung as he gathered up the scrap of fabric. It hurt to see how much they bothered Malcolm. Stuart had hoped Malcolm might be more open-minded about them, but it was clear the sight of them disgusted him. *Fuck.* This was exactly what Stuart had hoped to avoid. He should have eased Malcolm into the idea. Maybe then it wouldn't have shocked him so much.

Once the lingerie was safely tucked back in the drawer, Stuart straightened the bedding and glanced at Malcolm again. Malcolm still stood by the stove, his arms tucked close to his body as if he were hugging himself. The sight of his expression and hunched posture sent another pang of regret through Stuart. He'd never hated his kink more. To think it bothered Malcolm so much. Maybe Stuart shouldn't be surprised. Malcolm was new to so many things and something like a panty kink had to be pretty jarring. This might be more than he could handle. Men with far more sexual experience than Malcolm had been disgusted, so it was hardly a new reaction. It had never hurt Stuart quite so much before.

Chest tight and heart aching, Stuart took a seat on the bed and patted the space next to him. "Sit with me?"

Slowly, Malcolm approached and sat near the foot of the bed, almost out of arm's reach. He didn't look at Stuart but stared down at his hands instead.

"So, I know it probably came as a shock for you to find lingerie in my bed," Stuart said slowly.

"You could say that." Malcolm's laugh was a hollow rasp.

"Um, I'll try to explain why."

"Okay."

Stuart took a deep breath, trying to put it into words. *Damn it.* Why hadn't he rehearsed this before? He'd tried but he really had no idea what to say.

"I've been trying to figure out how to tell you, but I kept putting it off. This isn't at all how I intended for you to find out." He didn't have a choice now. He had to find a way to explain it to Malcolm or risk losing him.

Even so, he might lose Malcolm anyway. Stuart's heart felt like it might crack in two.

"Right." Malcolm's expression had gone blank and very distant and he was hugging himself again. He kept looking at the door like he was tempted to bolt.

Panic rose in Stuart, the sour taste of fear in his throat as he imagined Malcolm leaving and never coming back.

"This is… It's something that I need," Stuart continued.

"You need to have sex with a woman?" Malcolm swallowed. "I thought we were on the same page about monogamy and… I just wish I'd known that was something you wanted. I wouldn't have… I wouldn't have fallen in love with you if I'd known you wanted to be with other people. Do I know her? Do you love her? There's no one I see the way I see you and I can't imagine feeling that way about anyone else. If you feel that way about her, I…" Malcolm looked like he was about to be sick.

Bewildered, Stuart stared at him blankly. "Sex with a woman?" Stuart frowned, trying to put together the pieces in his head. "Oh…oh, shit." His words came out on a shaky exhale as it finally sank in.

Of course, that was the conclusion Malcolm had leapt to, but it couldn't be further from the truth.

"No! Malcolm, I didn't cheat on you. You've got this all wrong. The lingerie doesn't belong to anyone else. I swear. I haven't had sex with anyone, man or woman, since before we met. And I'm certainly not in love with anyone but you. You have to believe that."

"Then why is there women's lingerie in your bed?" Malcolm's brow furrowed. "I want to believe there's some other logical explanation for this, but I can't think of any." He clearly seemed like he wanted to believe Stuart. That was something.

Stuart rubbed at his chest. Why was it so hard to breathe?

"They...the underwear..." Stuart's throat was so tight he could barely squeeze the words out. "They belong to... To me."

"To you?"

Stuart's heart beat double-time and, suddenly, his head swam. He had to put it between his knees to steady himself and, even then, he could feel the blood whooshing in his ears as he struggled to pull air in.

"Whoa, Stuart. Take a deep breath." Malcolm no longer sounded distant and Stuart felt a warm hand settle on his mid-back, rubbing softly. "Don't want you passing out on me."

"Just don't leave," he said tightly.

"I'm not going anywhere."

"Give me a sec." The words came out strained, but Malcolm's reassurance had helped. The vice around Stuart's chest slowly loosened, allowing him to pull in a few badly needed breaths.

"Take as long as you need," Malcolm said soothingly.

The gentle, steady pressure of Malcolm's hand on his back made Stuart's heart rate finally slow and, after a minute, he sat up straight. When he turned to look at Malcolm, he saw nothing but concern in his gaze.

"You okay?" Malcolm asked.

No. He nodded yes.

"The underwear belongs to you?" Malcolm prompted gently.

Stuart nodded again. "Yeah." He sounded hoarse. "I was trying to explain that. I...I'm into lingerie. Not seeing a woman in them but, uh, wearing them myself." The last few words came out in a rush.

"Oh." Malcolm's startled expression made Stuart realize he'd never considered that possibility. "Oh," he repeated as the words seemed to settle into his brain. "They're yours, meaning you dress in them?"

"Yes." Stuart licked his lips. "I find them...erotic to wear."

"Okay." A frown creased Malcolm's forehead. "Tell me more. If you can?"

"I will." Stuart took another deep breath. "Or at least, I'll do my best to explain it."

Malcolm sat back. Stuart reached out and grasped his hand and when Malcolm curled his fingers around Stuart's, he squeezed lightly. The touch sent a pulse of relief through Stuart, lifting the weight that had been sitting on his chest.

"It's going to take me a minute to pull my thoughts together," he admitted.

"It's okay." Malcolm gave him a small, reassuring smile. "I'll cancel my plans tonight with Will and the guys. So you and I can talk without being interrupted."

"You don't mind?"

"No. This is more important. I'm sure he won't mind rescheduling."

"That would be great." Profound relief swept through Stuart as Malcolm pulled his phone out of his pocket. He sent a message and Stuart leaned back against the wall, his focus on taking deep breaths to calm his racing heart and gather his thoughts.

He could do this. Malcolm knew and he hadn't run away. His reaction earlier had been horror at the idea of Stuart cheating on him, not disgust at the idea of Stuart's kink. He had to hold on to that.

When Malcolm's phone landed on the bed beside him, Stuart looked up. "All set?"

"Yes. We have as long to talk as you need."

"Thanks." Stuart licked his lips, trying to figure out what to say next. "Um, before I start, do you have any questions?"

"A few. Maybe."

"Go ahead, ask."

"How did you discover this...fetish?" An uncertain expression flickered across Malcolm's face. "Is that the right word for it?"

"I think it's more a kink than a fetish," Stuart replied. "A true fetish is something that's psychologically necessary for someone to orgasm, I think. I looked it up years ago and it didn't quite fit for me. Obviously, I can get off without wearing women's underwear. I mean, you've seen that."

Malcolm nodded.

"I enjoy sex without them. But wearing them definitely enhances things for me. It's more satisfying."

"Okay," Malcolm said slowly. "I can sort of understand that."

"It's a bit like when I lick that spot on your thigh and you respond really, really strongly," Stuart offered.

The tips of Malcolm's ears went pink and he ducked his head. "I didn't realize you'd noticed that."

"I noticed." Stuart smiled a little. They were talking about this rationally. Like adults. And Malcolm hadn't run off in disgust. Those were good signs, right? "Wearing lingerie is like that sensitive spot on your thigh. I mean, the sex is already good. The underwear just sharpens everything I'm already feeling."

"And is this something you've done with — with a lot of partners?"

Stuart let out a sad huff of laughter. "No. It's been a secret. My ex-wife didn't just find gay porn in that box. She also found my lingerie."

"Oh." Malcolm's eyes widened.

"Yeah. Becky was horrified. I've shared my kink with a few other partners since then, thinking they might be open to it…"

Malcolm's expression shifted to one of disbelief. "They weren't?"

"No. I've actually never been with anyone who really understands and accepts it."

Malcolm reached for Stuart's hand again. "I'd like to understand it."

"That means a lot to me." Stuart looked down at their clasped fingers for a moment. "Do you think it's something you might be able to accept eventually? I mean, even if it's not something you want to share with me, do you think you'd at least be okay with knowing it was something I'd do on my own?"

Surprise crossed Malcolm's face. "Would that be enough for you?"

Stuart shrugged. "I don't know. I'd be disappointed, I guess? I'd rather explore it with you. If the choice was between doing it on my own and losing you…"

"You'd be willing to compromise on that?"

"I'd try," Stuart said with a small sigh. "Knowing it wasn't a secret between us would help. That's been stressing me out a lot. I do worry that long-term it might not be a good choice. Not being able to share it with you, I mean."

Malcolm nodded. "I'd worry about that, too. And to be perfectly honest, I don't know that I can answer that question at this point. I have no idea how I'd feel about you wearing them. I'm still trying to wrap my head around all of it. One minute, I was convinced you were cheating on me and now I know you aren't, but I have absolutely no idea about a kink like this." He shrugged, worry etched across his face.

"No, I get that. That's how I felt about you telling me you were demisexual," Stuart said. "I needed time for it to all settle in my mind and be sure I understood it."

"Of course." Malcolm sounded grateful. "And, hey, we're still figuring that out."

"Yeah, we are." Some of the lingering tension eased out of Stuart at the reminder. They'd already dealt with big issues together and were stronger for it. Maybe this could be another one. He could only hope. "I'm sorry. I don't mean to push you or anything."

"I know."

"I'll give you as much time as you need."

"Thanks."

"Would you lie down with me?" Stuart asked. "It would be nice if we could just hold each other while we talk, if you're okay with that."

"Yes." Malcolm gave him a small smile.

When they were stretched out on the bed full-length with their heads next to each other on a pillow, another wave of tension ebbed from Stuart's body. Touching Malcolm like this helped. "Do you have any other questions?"

"Probably." Malcolm looked a bit unsure, but he twined their fingers together on the bed between them.

"You don't know what to ask or how?" Stuart guessed.

"Yeah."

"Why don't you just blurt out whatever pops into your head first and we'll go from there."

"Okay." Malcolm hesitated for a moment. "How did you realize you were into this in the first place?"

Stuart turned onto his back, unable to look Malcolm in the eye as he said this aloud. He didn't let go of Malcolm's hand. "Um, this is embarrassing, but for as long as I could remember, I've been fascinated by women's underwear," he mumbled. His face felt hot as Malcolm draped an arm across Stuart's chest, bringing their joined hands to rest against Stuart's side. The weight of his arm anchored Stuart. He stared up at the ceiling.

"I was really into the feel of the fabrics when I saw them at the store. It's not like most of it was even fancy or lacy. It was pretty utilitarian stuff for the most part but something about it intrigued me. Sometimes, we'd go to the bigger department stores and my mom would shop for nightgowns. Just the sight of the lingerie section made me feel all…" He struggled with how to put it into words. "It made me feel hot all over and when I got a little older, I'd get an erection if I brushed my arm against something with silk or lace."

"Interesting."

Stuart finally turned his head. "Is that good interesting or bad interesting? Are you horrified by all this?"

"I'm not horrified," Malcolm said. He gently petted Stuart's chest. "It's not like I'm unaware of kinks and fetishes. God knows Jesse, Cam and Kyle aren't shy about talking about all sorts of things. I just don't have any personal experience with them and I'm trying to absorb it all. I'm barely turned on by people—being turned on by an inanimate object isn't easy to wrap my brain around."

Stuart chuckled. "I can understand that." He leaned in and pressed a kiss to Malcolm's forehead.

"So you realized the underwear were a turn-on pretty early?"

"Yes. It didn't occur to me that I wanted to wear them at first. I assumed I was into the idea of women wearing them."

"Sure, that makes sense." Malcolm paused. "Do you think it has something to do with being Mormon? I mean, there's a big emphasis on underwear, right?"

"You mean the temple garments that Mormons wear? Maybe. I have considered the connection before," Stuart said. "The temple garments are basically a white undershirt and boxer briefs so the idea of something that's made of black lace does seem far more taboo and exciting by comparison. I don't know for sure."

"I was just curious."

"It's an interesting theory," Stuart said. He tucked that idea away for later to consider more. "I was a teenager when I finally realized that I wanted to wear lingerie." Stuart looked at the ceiling again. He'd never been this open with anyone before. "One of my sisters had a non-Mormon friend from college spend the night once. I went into the bathroom after she'd taken a shower. I found a pair of her panties on the floor. I remember they were purple. Silky with lace trim. They must have fallen out of her bag or something. I knew I shouldn't, but I grabbed them and stuffed them in my pocket. I figured she'd be too embarrassed at losing them to ask where they were. I remember lying in my bed that night, wrapping them around myself and jerking off. I'd never felt anything like it before."

"Wow."

Stuart smiled faintly at the ceiling. "I did that for at least a week. I'd wash them off in the bathroom sink and hide them in the back of my closet when I wasn't using them. Then one night, I was home alone. My sisters were both out and so were my parents and in the middle of jerking off, I got this urge to put them on. My hands were shaking as I slid them up over my hips. I was so hard and…" He gulped, feeling his cock begin to rise just thinking about it. "I've been wearing stuff like that ever since. When I was able to, anyway."

"Could I see?"

Stuart looked over at Malcolm wide-eyed. "See?" Did Malcolm mean what Stuart thought he did?

"The lingerie? Not you in them. Not yet. I'm curious to see what you own, if you're okay sharing?"

"Uh, sure." So, no, not quite what Stuart had thought but a good first step. "Come here."

Stuart got out of bed and held a hand out to Malcolm. Together, they went to the dresser and Stuart knelt beside it. Malcolm copied the motion, albeit more slowly. Stuart's hands shook as he slid the drawer open to reveal the pile of soft, silky fabrics, many of them edged in lace.

"May I?" Malcolm reached toward them, then paused, his hand a few inches from the fabric.

Stuart nodded. He watched, heart in his throat, as Malcolm lifted several of the pieces up, inspecting them closely.

"They're soft." Malcolm rubbed a black silky pair between his fingertips. "I can see why you would like that."

"Yeah?"

"Yeah, definitely." Malcolm offered him a smile. "I like textures, too. That part I know I'd be into."

"That's a good starting point," Stuart said, his voice hoarse. Could Malcolm actually be open-minded enough to explore this with him? Stuart wanted it so badly he could hardly think straight. He didn't want to push Malcolm, though.

"I used to like seeing Liz wearing lingerie."

Stuart blinked. Malcolm so rarely shared anything sexual or about his ex-girlfriend. This was good. He liked Malcolm opening up. And it was an encouraging sign that he didn't seem to see much difference between the idea of Liz wearing lingerie and Stuart doing it.

"Do you wear bras?" Malcolm continued.

"No, that's never been my thing," Stuart said. "Um, panties and stockings and garters mostly. Bras feel weird and I don't really find them sexy."

"Okay."

"I don't want to look feminine," Stuart blurted out. "I mean, I don't want to wear makeup or anything or be feminized—not that there's anything wrong with that—it's just..."

"Not you?"

"Exactly. I like that I'm a big, kinda hairy guy with a shitload of ink. I like that contrast with the underwear and—" Jesus, Stuart needed to stop talking before he really freaked Malcolm out. "Anyway, what's in here is the extent of it."

"Okay," Malcolm said. "I can work with that. I mean, it's something I'm willing to explore with you. I don't know how I'll feel about you wearing them, but I'll give it a try."

"So, we're okay?" Stuart croaked, hardly daring to dream that Malcolm might understand even a little.

"Yeah, we're okay." Malcolm smiled at him. "Let's take it one step at a time. I want to be with you, Stuart. And if that means figuring this out with you" — he held up a scrap of black lace and let it fall back into the drawer — "then I want to do that."

"Thank you." Stuart let out a sigh of relief that went clear down to his toes. He wrapped his arms around Malcolm and buried his head against his neck. His eyes stung with gratitude and love as Malcolm pulled him closer. "You have no idea how relieved I am to hear that. God, I love you, Malcolm."

"I love you, too." Malcolm pressed a kiss to his hair. The words sent a pulse of relief through Stuart's body. It occurred to him that this was only the second time they'd said those words to each other. And the first time they had both been panicking. "We'll figure this out. Together. I promise."

And for the first time, Stuart believed that might actually be true. Someone might really love him enough to accept every part of who he was.

Chapter Nineteen

Malcolm ran a hand over Stuart's hair. "We should probably eat."

"Not moving," Stuart muttered. "Too comfortable."

And hiding a little, Malcolm thought. He was struck by the seeming role reversal. Shyness was something Stuart so rarely showed. Not that Malcolm blamed him. Spilling a secret so big and complicated after literal decades of hiding had been gut wrenching, even to witness. Throw in the almost tortured nature of Stuart's past relationships, especially with Becky and…well, Malcolm's heart hurt for Stuart just thinking about it.

Now though, he bit his lip against a smile when Stuart's stomach rumbled loudly.

"Jeez." This time, he rubbed Stuart's back. "C'mon."

"Nope." Amusement colored Stuart's voice as he sprawled even farther over Malcolm, using the weight of his body to press him deeper into the mattress.

Malcolm couldn't help his groan. Stuart knew he liked being held down. Knew he liked a mouth on his neck too, and already, Malcolm's body was warm and thrumming. He swallowed a gasp when Stuart skimmed a hand along his ribs. Damn, he'd learned how to push all of Malcolm's buttons, some Malcolm had never even known he had. As much as Malcolm loved connecting with Stuart physically, he didn't feel right doing so now. Not when he knew there was still air to clear.

Moving one hand from around Stuart's shoulder, he slid it between them, so it rested against Stuart's chest then pushed, careful to keep the moment gentle. The last thing he wanted was for Stuart to feel rejected, and he knew his concern was valid when Stuart stiffened. Quickly, Malcolm pressed a kiss against his temple and used the arm still wrapped around Stuart to squeeze him tight.

"I'd like to talk some more," he said with another kiss, "and I think maybe you do, too. Also, I'd like it if you ate something so you're not tempted to eat my face while I sleep."

The laugh that rolled out of Stuart softened his tense muscles. "All right." Maneuvering onto his side, he propped his head on his elbow and while Malcolm missed the warmth and closeness, he'd needed to see Stuart's face again. Especially since Stuart's gaze kept skittering around the room like he wasn't sure where to focus.

Malcolm reached for Stuart's hand and twined their fingers together. "It's still okay if I ask questions, right?"

"Shit. Of course, it's okay." That worried line worked its way between Stuart's eyebrows. "I want to hear them."

"Okay. So why do you look like you're about to throw up?"

"Maybe because I still can't believe you're here after everything. Especially after the way you found out about the underwear."

"That sucked—I won't lie about that." Malcolm shared a wince with Stuart. "But I'm not going anywhere."

"Thanks." Stuart drew a deep breath in through his nose and sighed. "I guess I needed to hear that."

"I get it."

"I know you do." A thoughtful expression crossed his face. "And even when you don't get it, you try."

"I figure that's sort of the point of relationships. Romantic and otherwise." Malcolm sat up and tugged Stuart's hand until he followed suit. "Being there for one another. Learning about who we are. You've done a lot of work to figure out how to make a go of it with me, Stuart, and I want to do the same."

"I'm glad to hear that." Stuart leaned in and brushed a kiss across Malcolm's lips. "And I'm really glad that you're still here."

There were more kisses before they finally clambered out of bed and Malcolm stayed close as Stuart arranged a simple meal of cheeses, cured meats and fruit. Malcolm tasked himself with slicing bread, but set the knife down when he remembered one of the reasons he'd been so eager to talk to Stuart earlier in the day.

"I totally forgot to tell you—my mom got a job."

Stuart's jaw dropped. "Damn, I meant to ask you how it went. So lunch was good, I take it?"

"It was great," Malcolm said. "We talked—like, really talked—about Mom's money problems and her behavior and how she wants to do right by Jack and me. Honestly, it felt like the first truly adult conversation we've had in a couple of years."

"That's fantastic." Stuart gave him a huge smile. "Congratulations!"

Malcolm snorted out a laugh and went back to slicing bread. "I didn't do anything. Mom's the one who did all the hard work this time."

They set up another picnic on the braided rug by Stuart's bed and chatted about Kim and the Kinship Fund, which naturally led to talk of Will and David's involvement.

"I can't believe David's planning to leave office," Stuart said. He set his empty plate down, a slight frown on his face, and Malcolm cocked his head

"I thought you disapproved of his Republican-ness?"

"Oh, I do. David's a good man, though. Committed to doing what he believes are the right things for people and making their lives better. I liked knowing he was fighting the good fight from inside the GOP."

"He opened up a lot of people's opinions and minds," Malcolm said, "inside and outside of the Senate."

"And that right there is what I mean." Stuart ran a hand over his beard. "I also hate to think his seat could go to someone who doesn't have the best interests of people like us at heart. The next senator from District Eight may not care about our community the way David does."

"I've never considered it that way." Malcolm fixed his eyes on his socked feet. "In a way, I'm still getting used to the idea of being a part of the LGBTQIA community. Not everyone believes people like me have a place there."

"People who are on the ace spectrum, you mean?"

"Yes. Being with you changed everything, of course."

Stuart chuckled. "Relationships with the gays will do that."

Malcolm smiled in reply. The changes in him ran deeper than a simple switch from dating women to dating men. Malcolm had fallen in love with a man—this man—and couldn't imagine his life without Stuart in it. And that thought shifted Malcolm's focus from the tips of his toes to the bottom drawer of Stuart's dresser.

Malcolm had meant what he'd said—he wasn't going anywhere. If they were in this for the long haul, though, he needed to figure out how Stuart's kink figured into their relationship. Or if Stuart had other secrets that needed telling.

"I meant what I said."

Stuart's careful tone caught Malcolm's attention, and his expression was sober when Malcolm turned his way. "What do you mean?"

"It's okay to ask questions about my kink." Stuart tipped his head toward the dresser. "Since you were trying to burn a hole through that thing with your eyes for almost a minute, I'm guessing you've been thinking about what's in it."

Malcolm smiled. "You're right, I have. But I also wondered if there was anything else you're keeping from me."

"Anything else?" Stuart's brow furrowed.

"Secrets. Things you're not saying because you don't want to hurt my feelings." Malcolm drew his knees in so he could sit crossed legged. "When I found the...well, your underwear, my first instinct was to assume you'd been with somebody else. There's stuff I need to unpack there, but a big reason is because you'd lied to me before about not telling the speakeasy guys about my money problems.

"You weren't the only one bending the truth," he hastened to add when Stuart bit out a curse. "I gave you all kinds of bullshit reasons for not going out because I didn't want you to know I was broke."

"Not really the same thing, Mal."

"Maybe. The result was the same, though—we weren't truthful with each other. Some of my reaction today was about me, but a bigger part was about the lying. I don't want that for either of us. Suspicion and hiding things from each other—"

"—the way I hid things from Becky," Stuart cut in. His words sent Malcolm's stomach tumbling to the floor.

"I wasn't going to say that."

"I believe you." Stuart's expression was grim. "I'm saying it. I did lie and hide things from my ex. I'm not going to do that anymore. We won't do that to each other, okay?" He fell silent a moment, then frowned even more. "What did you mean when you said some of your reaction today was about you?"

"Oh." Malcolm grimaced. "I don't know if I want to talk about that right now."

"Malcolm, I think you should." Stuart ran a hand up and down Malcolm's arm. "What did you mean?"

"Nothing, really. Just..." Malcolm wet his lips with his tongue. "Being with me means going a lot slower than you would with other men. Sometimes, I wonder if maybe you want more."

"It's true we're going slower." Stuart gave a nod. "But I don't feel like I'm missing out on anything at all.

Because I'm going exactly the right speed with the man I want to be with — you."

The next thing Malcolm knew, Stuart had dragged him into a hug and he laughed softly as Malcolm was forced to untangle his legs.

"Holy ouch."

"Sorry." Stuart kissed Malcolm's cheek. "I mean it, though. I don't need or want anyone else. What I have with you is more than just mechanics and getting off and that's something I haven't had with anyone else."

Malcolm linked his arms around Stuart's neck. "I love that you said that."

"It's true. I've never felt like this about anyone." Stuart's dark gaze was so earnest. "I also don't want you to feel pressured into something you don't want out of some misguided belief that I'm not satisfied. I like what we do together, Mal. A lot."

"Mmm, I do, too. But making you feel good is important to me — sometimes even more so than getting off myself." Malcolm ran his fingers through the short hairs at the nape of Stuart's neck, tiny shockwaves of delight running up his arms as he did. "I know that probably doesn't make any sense, but it's all tied up in feeling connected to you and I need that. It's okay to push me a little. Sometimes, I need to be pushed. Want it too, even if it's just to hold you while you come."

"Okay. I can do that." Stuart set his hands against Malcolm's sides. His expression shifted in the next moment, however, and he slid his eyes toward the dresser, then back to Malcolm. "Do you want to talk about the lingerie?"

"I think we need to. Especially since you asked if I'd be okay sharing that part of your life."

"Yes. And you don't have to answer until you're ready." Stuart pursed his lips for a moment. "It wasn't fair of me to even ask you that question so soon after finding out about my kink."

Malcolm shook his head. "It's okay that you did. And obviously, I'm still trying to figure stuff out, like what my part would be. If the question is about me sharing your kink, then the answer is yes, I will."

The light drained from Stuart's eyes. "You should think about this some more."

Sitting back, Malcolm took Stuart's hand between his own. Unease fluttered in his gut at the hard line of Stuart's mouth. This wasn't at all the reaction he'd expected. "What's wrong? I thought you wanted me to know that part of you."

"I do, more than anything. But… Fuck, I don't know how to say this without sounding hostile. You really don't know what you're asking."

"That's fair. But I know that it wouldn't feel right to turn my back on something that's so important to you." Malcolm gave Stuart's fingers a gentle squeeze. "Or to ask you to keep the kink private and just to yourself."

"You have no idea how much it means to me that you'd say that." A pained smile crossed Stuart's face. "Now I'm even more sure we should go into this slowly. The potential for things to go pear-shaped is huge and that is the last thing I want."

"Okay, but—"

"Did you mean it earlier when you told me you loved me?"

"Yes." Malcolm's breath caught. "I've never said that to anyone before and meant it that way."

Meant it like forever.

Stuart drew him close, voice dropping to a near whisper as he pressed his forehead to Malcolm's and closed his eyes. "Okay. Maybe you can understand how afraid I am of losing that, then. Of you hating me because that one part of my life fucks everything up."

"Oh, Stuart." Malcolm brought a hand to Stuart's cheek. "I didn't fall in love with parts of you. I fell in love with all of you. And if kink is a part of who you are, I want to know it just as much as the rest of you."

The tight sigh that rose from Stuart's chest set his whole body trembling. His hold on Malcolm tightened, though, so Malcolm gathered him up and just held on until the storm of emotion had passed.

"How about I follow your lead this time?" he asked when Stuart seemed calmer. "I want you to feel comfortable about how and when you share your kink."

"You know, from anyone else, that could be a dangerous proposition." Sitting back enough to meet Malcolm's eye, Stuart shot him a smile, and yes, there was the impish side Malcolm liked so much. "I appreciate you letting me drive. The underwear has always been a very private thing for me, obviously. I think it'll take time to open up to someone about it."

Malcolm pushed down a tiny flare of disappointment. Of course, Stuart needed time to adjust. Hell, Malcolm did too, so he could truly understand what he was getting into.

"Whenever you're ready," he said and meant it, though once more, his eye was drawn to the dresser's bottom drawer.

What the hell was he getting into, anyway? Obviously, his man liked to wear lacy things. Craved the sensations of tiny scraps of fabric against his skin.

Intellectually, Malcolm knew lots of men shared the same kink. The idea of wearing something so delicate and lacy himself was something Malcolm couldn't imagine at all, especially when he glanced down at himself.

"Stuart?" He tried to ignore the heat flooding his face when he lifted his gaze back up. "Is the lingerie a thing you like your partner to wear, too? I'm game to talk about it if that's something you need, but I'm not sure it'd be a good look for me."

Stuart's eyes went so wide Malcolm almost laughed. "I've never thought about it before. Holy shit, I'm thinking about it now, though. And damn."

"Oh, God." Now Malcolm did laugh. That set Stuart off too, and it was a moment before either of them could form coherent words.

"I'm sorry." Stuart knuckled tears from his eyes. "You caught me off guard. Put some incredible images into my head, too."

"Happy to help." Malcolm snorted. Bless this man and his lack of filter. "It was a serious question, however. I don't think this" — he waved a hand at himself — "belongs in anything so fragile."

"For what it's worth, I think you're selling yourself short. I'm not exactly a delicate flower by any means and that's part of the appeal as far as I'm concerned." Stuart ran a hand over Malcolm's thigh, his touch raising prickles of sensation right through Malcolm's gray chinos. "The idea of those long legs in a pair of stockings is an unbelievably tantalizing image, too.

"I like you buttoned up and neat. That is a great look on you. My favorite in fact." The promise in his low voice pinged Malcolm's insides just right. "So, no, I don't expect you to wear lingerie. If you ever want to try a walk on the wild side, though, I'd be more than happy to help you out."

The simple delight in Stuart's face made Malcolm's heart squeeze. "I'll keep that in mind."

* * * *

Despite the unexpected drama of that Friday afternoon, the dust settled quickly in the days that followed and life continued. Malcolm imagined it would appear that nothing had changed to anyone on the outside of his and Stuart's relationship. However, things were changing on the inside, in very quiet ways that broke new ground and told him that Stuart was finally putting his past to rest.

For one, Stuart went out of his way to offer Malcolm space of his own within the confines of the tiny studio and make it feel like his home, too. A bigger boot tray appeared by the door to hold their shoes, just like handmade shelves were hung on the wall and a space opened up inside Stuart's old wardrobe, all gestures that offered Malcolm places to store his things.

Stuart got bossier in bed, too, in ways that worked perfectly with Malcolm's very specific wiring. While he'd always shown an instinctive understanding of Malcolm's need to surrender control, Stuart leveraged that knowledge more and coaxed Malcolm into trying new things that made his body hum. Even better, Stuart chased his own pleasure without apology, so each touch he shared became a connection Malcolm craved, regardless of whether he came or not.

Though Stuart rarely mentioned his kink, Malcolm didn't find the behavior all that surprising. Stuart had been very plain about not needing it to get off. He started leaving the dresser drawer of lingerie open, however, a move Malcolm knew was an unspoken invitation to explore its contents if and when he wanted. Malcolm did just that on occasion, indulging his love of color and texture by running his hands among the pieces of silk, satin, velvet and lace. He returned to a particular pair of boyshorts more than once, drawn by the contrast of black lace against ice-blue satin, especially when paired with the matching garter belt. He thought their sheen and color would suit Stuart quite well.

He almost dropped a stack of plates one night when he spotted a gleam of that same pearly blue peeping out from under the waistband of Stuart's jeans. They were cleaning up after dinner and Stuart had bent to pick a platter up from the floor, the motion causing his Pixies T-shirt to ride up just enough to flash some skin and a bit of something extra. Malcolm set the plates on the wooden counter that covered the bathtub with a clatter.

Was that…?

A half-smile crossed Stuart's face as he and Malcolm stared at one another, followed by a rush of color in his cheeks. "Everything okay, Mal?"

Malcolm wanted to roll his eyes. Like the jerk didn't already know. He played along anyway, just in case Stuart still felt nervous. Something Malcolm didn't feel at all.

"I'm great. I also think maybe you've figured out I like that color blue." He offered Stuart a smile and stepped forward, hands out and palms up, asking without words if his touch was welcome.

Stuart's smile grew wider. "You made it easy. I found this pair on the top of the pile more than once and connected the dots." He reached out, circling

Malcolm's wrists with his fingers, and drew him in. "I didn't wear the garter belt, though. I figured we should start out slow and maybe work our way up to that. If you still want to, of course."

"Of course."

Stuart set Malcolm's hands on his waist. Without breaking eye contact, he lifted the hem of the T-shirt up and over his head, pulling it off in one smooth motion. A quiet sigh worked its way through Malcolm as the heat of Stuart's skin seeped into his palms. He followed Stuart's hands with his gaze, almost holding his breath as Stuart reached for the fly on his jeans and eased the buttons open. Slowly, the weathered denim slipped down, exposing skin and ink and the tiny blue boyshorts that had so captured Malcolm's fancy.

"Whoa." Heat swept through Malcolm in a wave. The contrast of satin against the hard planes of Stuart's body was... Fuck, he couldn't look away. Swallowing hard, he ran the fingers of one hand along the waistband of the shorts, the pads of his fingertips prickling under the rasp of the stiff lace. "Oh, wow."

A low noise rumbled through Stuart's broad chest. "Yeah?"

Malcolm forced himself to meet Stuart's gaze, but he went still at the storm he saw there. There was heat in those dark eyes but something wary too, and whatever nerves Stuart was feeling sent a fine tremor through his body. Heart in his throat, Malcolm slid his arms around Stuart, then rested his palms against the small of Stuart's back, the waistband of the boyshorts teasing his fingers.

"I'm sorry," he murmured. "I should have asked before I touched."

Stuart shook his head once and threaded his arms around Malcolm's neck. "You're fine. You never have to ask me that." His voice was gruff. "I like the way your hands feel on me. Especially right now." He paused and swallowed, the movement making his nostrils flare. "Do you like it?"

Rather than answer, Malcolm slid one hand lower, running it over the swell of Stuart's ass. The sensation of satin over muscle sent a shock of arousal crashing over him so intense his head actually spun.

"Oh, Jesus." The words came out of him on a raspy moan that made Stuart's breath hitch in his chest. "Yeah, I like it. I mean, I knew I'd be okay with it because it's you. But seeing you like this. Touching you. God, Stuart."

Stuart cupped Malcolm's face with his hands. "Baby."

"They feel so good."

"Yeah, they do. I like wearing these — you know that." Stuart smiled. "Wearing them with you, though…fuck. I feel like I'm high."

Malcolm knew exactly what he meant. The buzz that always came when Stuart touched him had filled Malcolm head to toe, so intense he could hardly speak. Malcolm was hard, too, his boxer briefs already uncomfortably tight. And he needed more. Needed to see and taste and feel, thirst exploding within him and turning his knees to jelly. Malcolm slowly sank down, pulling Stuart's jeans lower with him as he moved.

Stuart's jaw sagged. "Malcolm —"

"It's okay," Malcolm whispered. Because it was. Malcolm didn't know what he was doing. Had never done this before. But he wanted it so, so much.

Acting on instinct, he pushed Stuart's jeans off the rest of the way. Once Stuart had stepped out of them, Malcolm trailed slow kisses along his thighs, delighting in the zing of soft skin and crisp hair against his lips. He closed his eyes at Stuart's low groan, the need in his core expanding even more.

Settling onto his knees, Malcolm kneaded Stuart's skin with his fingers. He pressed his face against the blue satin and breathed in wood and sweat and man. His groan mixed with Stuart's and Malcolm shifted closer.

"Mmm."

He wound his arms around Stuart's hips and nuzzled him through the boyshorts, reveling in the hardness of the cock barely hidden behind them. A shiver ran through Malcolm as Stuart's hands came to rest on his head. He opened his mouth over the fabric, tonguing the satin, shivering at the goosebumps that rose up all over him as Stuart moaned Malcolm's name.

Pleasure swept Malcolm with the force of a bonfire. Peeling his eyes open, he stared up at Stuart, pride slashing through him at the lust that made Stuart's eyes glow. He loved making Stuart feel good.

"I imagined this," Stuart rasped out. He twined his fingers into Malcolm's short hair. "You on your knees. Eyes on me, just like this."

Dropping a hand to Malcolm's mouth, he dragged his thumb over Malcolm's lips, over and over, pulling a whine from him that became a gasp when Stuart twitched against his lips. Malcolm's fingers shook as he pulled the waistband of the boyshorts over Stuart's groin.

"Oh, fuck." Stuart bit his lip. With deft movements, he guided Malcolm's fingers so they pulled the underwear down together, tucking the front beneath Stuart's balls while they still clung to his hips and ass.

"You're the hottest thing I've ever seen, Malcolm." Stuart's voice was a rough croon of praise. "So gorgeous on your knees for me. I love this. Love that you're mine."

Yes.

Malcolm's eyes fluttered closed once more. Wrapping one hand around the shaft of Stuart's cock, he slowly licked the tip, bitter and salt exploding on his tongue. Above him, Stuart swore. Malcolm licked again and hummed, loving the combination of hard heat and velvet softness, his own dick throbbing.

Before he could think too hard, he took Stuart between his lips, the need for more making him brave. He couldn't take Stuart very deep, but he suspected it didn't matter because Stuart was moaning steadily now, his thigh muscles trembling against Malcolm's shoulders. His hands were back on Malcolm's head, his touch firm but never rough as he guided Malcolm's movements, showing him how he liked to be sucked. Too soon, Stuart was moving, carefully pushing Malcolm back, and Malcolm couldn't stop his frown as he let Stuart's cock fall from his mouth.

"What is it?" Malcolm's insides went tight as Stuart hauled him to his feet. "Did I do something wrong?"

"Not a fucking thing—you're perfect." Stuart's kiss scorched Malcolm from the inside out. "I was about to blow my load," he said, panting now that they'd come up for air, "and I need to touch you more before that happens. Can I make you feel good?"

He waited for Malcolm's nod, then kissed him again and guided Malcolm backward out of the kitchen and toward the bed, the command in his touch unmistakable. The buzz inside Malcolm grew stronger as he was stripped down to his boxer briefs, and he felt floaty and almost drunk by the time he'd been laid out on the bed.

Stuart's eyes shone as he ran them from Malcolm's head to his toes. "Gorgeous."

He peeled off the blue boyshorts, then skated his fingers over Malcolm's torso, tickling his ribs and tweaking his nipples so Malcolm shivered. Craving more contact, Malcolm pulled Stuart down beside him and snuggled into his embrace, almost drowning in their deep, drugging kisses. He writhed and gasped as Stuart palmed Malcolm through the cotton of his underwear, the desire rattling around his body, almost too much to bear.

Malcolm still wanted more. *Everything. All.* He shuddered as Stuart slid his fingers under the waistband of his boxer briefs.

Stuart wrapped his fingers around Malcolm's cock and kissed him again. "I love being with you like this."

"Me too. I need you." The waver in Malcolm's voice caught Stuart's attention, and their gazes locked, the air between them crackling with new energy. "Need you inside me."

Stuart brought a hand to cup Malcolm's cheek, his expression grave despite the fire in his eyes. "Is that what you want?"

"Yeah." Certainty pulsed through Malcolm, buoying him up high. "I want that with you, Stuart. I'm sure."

Whatever Stuart saw in Malcolm's face made him smile. His next kisses were softer, almost reverent, and they made Malcolm's heart hurt in the best way.

A hand still on Malcolm, Stuart turned to the nightstand and only let go when he had to. His eyes rarely left Malcolm's as he rolled on a condom and slicked his fingers with lube, and he made a soft noise of approval when Malcolm let his thighs fall open. Cradling Malcolm close, Stuart kissed him until Malcolm lay boneless and panting and only then did he reach between Malcolm's legs. He trailed cool lube over Malcolm's balls and the sensitive skin behind them, his touch teasing as he fingered Malcolm's rim. Malcolm swore his whole body was on fire by the time Stuart pushed a finger inside.

Spreading his legs wider, Malcolm grasped at Stuart, his fingers spread wide and digging into Stuart's muscles. Sweat broke out over his skin and he lost himself in the sensations washing over him. Hot skin against his. The rasp of beard on his cheek. The achy-good burn of being stretched. He moaned when Stuart pushed a second finger in, filling him up and yet not enough.

"Want it," he murmured, throat going tight when Stuart hugged Malcolm tighter and pressed a lingering kiss against his temple.

"I've got you."

Stuart pumped his fingers slowly, driving the need inside Malcolm higher and higher until he thought sure he'd lose it. Then Stuart slid a third finger home and curled them just right, reducing Malcolm to a trembling, gasping mess. He groaned loudly when Stuart finally slipped his hand away.

"Oh, God. Don't stop, Stuart. Need more."

Stuart kissed the corner of Malcolm's mouth. "Okay."

He slicked them both up with more lube before climbing over Malcolm, and as he lined their bodies up, he smiled. Malcolm could do nothing more than hold on and breathe. Stuart brushed the head of his cock against Malcolm's ass.

His gaze didn't waver as he breached Malcolm, pushing so, so slowly past the tight ring of muscle. He paused, murmuring sweet nothings to Malcolm, then sank deeper, still at that achingly slow pace and love written all over his face. Malcolm brought a hand up to twine in Stuart's hair, his nerves alight as he stretched and burned.

"So full," he whispered. "Fuck. I didn't know. Didn't know it could be like this. It's — " His voice broke. "I feel you."

Stuart wrapped Malcolm up tight in his arms. "You're unbelievable," he choked out, then pressed kisses against Malcolm's face.

He rocked in and out of Malcolm, his movements gradually gaining speed until they found a rhythm that transformed the razor edge of Malcolm's pain into a deep, delicious ache. Malcolm lost all sense of time, consumed by the man who held him, filled him, loved him.

His bones turned liquid when Stuart wrapped a hand around Malcolm's cock. Desperate to get closer, Malcolm clung to him, raising his knees to Stuart's hips. He jolted hard when Stuart shifted just so and lightning raced through Malcolm, the sensations so intense he sobbed.

"Fuck, Mal," Stuart rasped out. "You're gonna make me come so hard."

Yes.

A fierce joy lit Stuart's face. He gasped, his thrusts turned erratic, and came, his hold on Malcolm like iron. Malcolm fell apart without warning. Chest twisting hard, he soared, the world a blur around him and pleasure piercing him through. Time stretched, shining and perfect as his cock pulsed, marking his and Stuart's skin. Distantly, he was aware of Stuart's movements slowing and his tender kisses, and Malcolm gladly let himself fall. With Stuart beside him, Malcolm would be just fine.

* * * *

"Any chance you can play hooky tomorrow?"

"What did you have in mind?" Sprawled on his stomach with his arms wrapped around his pillow, Malcolm threw a lazy smile at Stuart, who waggled his eyebrows and grinned. "Nothing that involves the motorcycle, right? I'm not sure I'm up for that kind of ride."

"Ah, no." Stuart laughed. "I wouldn't do that to you." Rolling closer in the bed, he made a contented sound when Malcolm snuggled in. "Your body needs at least a day before you go climbing on the bike."

Stuart ran a hand over Malcolm's ass, petting him gently through the sheet. He'd taken good care of Malcolm in the aftermath of their lovemaking, grounding Malcolm as he'd come back to himself and wiping him down as he'd dozed. And while Malcolm was indeed a little sore, he'd loved it. Loved letting go and that Stuart had owned him utterly. Truth be told, Malcolm suspected he might still be sex-stoned, and he was glad he didn't have to go anywhere until morning.

And particularly not having to go anywhere on the back of the motorcycle.

"I'm not on until three and I'd like to take you out to the wood shop in Brooklyn," Stuart said. "I did some work on the table that goes with those bar stools and thought you'd like to see it."

"If the table looks anything like the stools, it'll be stunning. But sure, I'd love to go with you. As long as you don't mind taking a train or boat." Malcolm paused as a thought occurred to him. "Are you planning to sell the set?"

"No. I'm sure it'd fetch a good price, but I always meant to keep it. And now that you're here, it'll be nice to have somewhere to sit that isn't the floor."

Malcolm angled his head up for a kiss. "I like that idea. I like our picnics too, though. I'd miss them if we gave them up entirely."

"Then we won't." Stuart pressed his lips to Malcolm's again. "It doesn't matter to me where I eat as long as the food and company are good."

"That's nice. You're such a sap." Malcolm knocked his knuckles against Stuart's chest. "Hey, would you let me cook for you sometimes? My food won't be as cheftastic as yours, but I'd like to do it anyway."

"That word you just made up does not describe the meals I make here. Heck, I still skip plates and eat out of the pan when the mood strikes me." A laugh rolled out of Stuart. "Every meal you've made for me has been great, plus your cookies are some of the best I've ever put in my mouth."

"Okay." Malcolm smiled. "I want to do something nice for you for a change."

"What do you mean, 'for a change'?" Stuart cocked his head. "Like you don't do nice things for me on the regular?"

"I suppose that's true. I also feel like I could do more. Make you happy, the way you do me." With a sigh, Malcolm brought a hand up and smoothed Stuart's hair back from his forehead. "You've given me so much. Helped me understand myself. Showed me what love can be. You changed my life and I'll never forget that."

The intensity in Stuart's gaze made Malcolm shiver, but his voice was quiet as he laced their fingers together. "You've done the same for me, Malcolm. Don't you know that by now?" He settled down against the pillows beside Malcolm and wrapped him up tight. "You give me everything, just by being you."

Chapter Twenty

January 2017

"You need anything before I head out?" Stuart stuck his head in Marisol's office. It was his day off, but he'd come in to catch up on some paperwork from a recent catering gig. Stuart had seen a definite uptick in interest since the first CEC event last spring. The CEC had hired him for another fundraiser last fall and the annual holiday party. He was also booked for an upcoming fundraiser in May and it was only late January now.

Marisol looked up from her laptop screen. "Nope, I think we're good. I'm just going over the books."

"How're we doing?"

"Pretty fucking well." She leaned back in her chair with a pleased smile. "We had a record number of sales in the last quarter of the year and profits are up."

"Glad to hear it."

She lowered her voice. "Don't share this with the rest of the crew yet but I'm planning to announce raises for everyone."

Stuart offered her a grin. "I'm sure that will go over very, very well."

"Hey, you know I'm committed to making this a good place to work. For everyone. I want you guys to have some quality of life."

"I do know that, and you've done a hell of a job with it," Stuart said. "Don't think I don't realize how lucky I am to work here every day I come in."

"Yeah, yeah. Cut that shit out. I'm not looking to get my ass kissed here."

"Apologies, Chef." The corners of his mouth quirked up in a smile.

Marisol gave Stuart a look that told him she'd picked up on the teasing note in his voice. "And I don't need your sarcasm either."

"You like my sarcasm. It's why you hired me."

"True. It certainly wasn't for your handsome face." She briefly dragged her hands across her own face and yawned, prompting a spike of concern in Stuart.

"And what about your quality of life? Are you looking out for that?"

"Hmm?" Marisol rubbed at her eyes again.

Stuart dropped into the seat across the desk from her. "You look exhausted. And you deserve a break. Have you considered taking a vacation?"

A ghost of a smile crossed Marisol's face and she looked more like her usual self. "I'm fine, just a little tired. And I have actually considered a vacation. Beth and I have been discussing it. Probably just a long weekend upstate or something." She shrugged.

"It would at least help you recharge your batteries."

"Exactly." Marisol drummed her fingers on the desk. "You good with filling in for me while I'm gone?"

"Sure. As long as it doesn't overlap with any catering gigs I have lined up, I'd be happy to."

"I checked to make sure you weren't otherwise occupied so I'll email you the dates I was considering in the next day or two," Marisol said.

"Sounds good."

Marisol looked at the clock and rose to her feet, shutting the lid of the laptop. "We're about to open for dinner so I need to get my ass in the kitchen."

"You like these days I have off, don't you?" he teased.

"When I have a chance to get my hands dirty on the line? You bet I fucking do. Now get out of here. I know for a fact you have a handsome man to go home to."

Stuart grinned. "I sure do."

* * * *

Twenty minutes later, Stuart pulled his bike up to the curb and parked. A sense of contentment stole over him as he chained the bike and pulled the cover over it. He and Malcolm had recently moved, and while he occasionally missed living in Little Italy, it was mostly because he missed the food. Parking was actually easier around their new place here on the border of Kip's Bay. He and Malcolm had searched high and low for an apartment around Little Italy and K-Town. They'd also weighed renting versus buying before finally settling on buying a studio on the edge of the NoMad district.

Stuart nodded at the doorman, who held the door and greeted him with a friendly, "Good evening, Mr. Morgan."

"Hi, Dominick." He tucked his helmet under his arm as he nodded his hello. A woman glanced his way as he strode through the lobby, eyeing him up and down with an appreciative glance. Stuart didn't recognize her so he figured she must be waiting for a tenant to come down. Some of his neighbors had given him wary looks for a while—especially when he wore his riding leathers—so he'd gone out of his way to introduce himself and greet them warmly until their wariness faded.

A jog up several flights of stairs brought Stuart to the apartment he lived in with Malcolm and he hummed to himself as he fitted the key in the brand-new lock. The building was on the small side, it was well maintained, and their unit had been recently renovated. Their apartment made him smile every time he stepped inside of it and today was no exception. Although it was already dark out thanks to the early hour of sunset, the space felt light and airy.

At just over five hundred square feet, the studio was easily twice the size of Stuart's old place and was laid out much better. A large closet and roomy bathroom were off to one side, but the majority of the space was an open rectangle with the kitchen at one end. The sight of it had made him gasp audibly one night when he and Malcolm had been online browsing real estate listings.

Malcolm had glanced over at him. *'You love that kitchen, don't you?'*

'I do.' Stuart had groaned and leaned in to inspect it more closely. Although still compact, it had been well laid out with an excellent workflow. He had liked the cabinets that went all the way up to the ceiling and the stainless-steel gas cooktop and range, but they hadn't been what drew him in most. Even the solid stone countertops and dishwasher—unheard-of luxuries for him—hadn't outshone the vision Stuart had of himself

cooking breakfast on weekend mornings while Malcolm worked on his laptop at the narrow breakfast bar nearby. Stuart had pictured the table he'd build with hidden leaves that would expand to seat their friends. And after he'd explained that to Malcolm, Malcolm had given Stuart a soft smile and kissed him lightly on the lips.

'*That sounds amazing.*' Malcolm had scrolled up to look at the price. '*Oof. It's definitely at the top end of the range we discussed.*'

Stuart had stolen a peek and frowned. '*It is. You'd have to be okay with me putting the bulk of the down payment down and I know that's not ideal for you.*'

Malcolm had nodded and bit his lip. '*It's not. We do have one other option.*'

'*What's that?*'

He'd leaned back in his chair. '*Well, when I mentioned we were shopping for a place, both Kyle and Carter offered me a loan. Separately. I'm not even sure they talked about it with each other at all. They just know how expensive Manhattan real estate is and that it's a tight market.*'

Stuart had raised an eyebrow in surprise. '*You're considering it?*'

'*Do you think I shouldn't?*'

'*No, I didn't say that at all,*' Stuart had replied, his words coming out slowly as he considered how to phrase what he wanted to say. '*I'm just surprised…*'

'*Given the way I reacted when they bought me groceries?*'

'*Yeah.*' Stuart had rubbed Malcolm's shoulder.

'*I guess I learned from that whole situation,*' Malcolm had said with a little sigh. '*There's no good reason for me to be so stubborn. It's one thing to have pride, it's quite another to let it keep me from being happy. From doing something that would make you happy. And this place would make you happy, wouldn't it?*'

Stuart had shrugged. *'I like it a lot, yes. The kitchen is definitely a selling point and I can see us living there. None of that is worth causing you stress, though.'*

'I appreciate that. But I think it would be worth accepting the help,' Malcolm had said slowly. *'Now that my mom's financially stable, my savings are building up again, but it's going to be a while before I have enough to make much of a contribution to a down payment. I don't want to wait a year or two to move in with you and I want it to be a place we can stay in for a long while. If borrowing some money from friends allows me to do that sooner rather than later…why not? I know I'll be able to pay them back, and a loan will let us do it now rather than having to wait.'*

'If you're comfortable with it, I say go for it,' Stuart had said. *'And let's call the real estate agent immediately because this place will go fast.'*

Thanks to a loan from Carter and Riley and a good chunk of Stuart's savings, they'd managed to put in an offer that snagged them the studio and now they were settling in nicely. Moving had been easy enough because neither of them owned a lot and they were slowly furnishing it with items they'd found together at thrift stores and the belongings Stuart had tucked away in storage.

Stuart's favorite spots—apart from the kitchen— were the two deep windowsills. They held small pots of greens and a variety of herbs. They didn't compare to what he had planned for next summer, however. Their fire escape had enough space and direct sunlight that Stuart was going to try growing potted strawberry and blueberry plants along with patio tomatoes. He had plans to build planters that would hang from the railings and the grates above. Luka had cringed when Stuart mentioned it, but Stuart had shown him the small landing area out of the way of any foot traffic, Luka had agreed the garden wasn't a fire safety hazard.

Stuart was both amused and appreciative of the way the speakeasy guys looked after one another. He was officially one of the crew.

Now, Stuart brushed his fingers across the tender basil leaves in one of the windowsill pots, releasing a cloud of spicy-herbal fragrance. Every time Malcolm caught Stuart trimming off dead leaves or carefully watering the soil in his herb garden, he gave Stuart a small, fond smile.

The whole apartment made Stuart happy. From the customized Murphy bed that tucked up into the wall to the kitchen island Stuart had built to give them more prep space, the place was theirs. Some days he had to pinch himself to believe that he'd finally found the home he'd been searching for since he left Utah.

It wasn't the space Stuart had moved into that made the place a home, though—it was the man he'd moved in with.

And the dog, Stuart thought as he felt a wet nose nudge his hand. He looked down with a smile. "Well, hello there. You must have been snoozing hard not to wake up when I got home." He scratched behind Chase Barksdale's fawn-colored ears and was rewarded with a thump of Chase's tail on the floor as the dog wiggled happily at the attention.

They'd gone to the shelter with no particular breed in mind and Stuart had fallen in love with Chase the moment he'd laid eyes on his intelligent expression and saw his friendly nature. When Malcolm had expressed concern that the dog might not have the right temperament for a small apartment, the person on staff had assured them that the Whippet-Lab mix was perfect for them. Slightly bigger and broader than a typical Whippet due to his Labrador blood, Chase had the calm, low-maintenance temperament of the Whippet breed.

They had both bonded with the dog and now Stuart couldn't imagine a life without him. He and Malcolm often spent evenings on the couch with Chase between them, his head stretched out on Stuart's thigh while his tail whapped against Malcolm's legs.

Debbie—one of Stuart and Malcolm's neighbors—worked from home and loved to go on afternoon runs. When she'd met Chase, he'd taken to her immediately, and she'd enthusiastically offered to take Chase with her on those runs. It gave him a chance to stretch his legs and burn off energy. Most days when Stuart or Malcolm got home from work, they found Chase snoozing in his bed on the floor.

The sound of a key in the lock made Stuart look up. He'd been lost in his thoughts far longer than he'd realized. He glanced at the clock on the wall to see it wasn't quite as late as he'd imagined. Perhaps Malcolm had left work early today.

"Hey!" he called out as Chase trotted over to the entrance to greet Malcolm. Stuart heard laughter and Malcolm's soft greeting, and a few minutes later, Malcolm and the dog appeared in the main living area.

"I have a surprise for you." Malcolm sauntered toward Stuart with a smile, a bag dangling from his finger. Stuart recognized the black bag with the gold logo immediately and a jolt of excitement went through him.

"When did you stop there?" he asked, intrigued as he met Malcolm halfway.

"Carter sent us all home a little early, so I stopped on my way home from work."

"What's the occasion?" Stuart leaned in and brushed his lips across Malcolm's.

Malcolm shrugged and gave him another quick kiss. "Do I need an occasion to buy my man sexy lingerie?"

"No, no, you don't." Stuart's smile stretched so wide it almost hurt his face. Malcolm's acceptance of his kink had meant the world to Stuart. But this, Malcolm's eager participation in it, meant even more. It filled him up in ways he hadn't even known he was lacking and soothed the hurts from every previous person who'd dismissed or belittled his kink. It made Stuart feel comfortable and proud of who he was, not ashamed. They'd come a long way in the past six months.

Stuart was still smiling as he took the bag from Malcolm's hand and pulled out the black tissue paper.

They'd stumbled upon the boutique lingerie store one day while exploring the neighborhood. Stuart had lingered near the window and Malcolm had been the one to finally coax him inside.

They'd both been nervous. Stuart because, in the past, he'd mostly shopped online for anonymity's sake and Malcolm because he was generally a very private person, especially when it came to anything to do with sex. But the salesclerk had been kind and understanding and hadn't batted an eye when they'd finally, awkwardly, admitted they were shopping for Stuart. She'd merely measured his hips, gave him a once-over and asked which styles he preferred.

Now, Stuart slowly flipped over the pieces of tissue paper, savoring the moment as he stared down at a scrap of peacock-blue fabric. He set the paper aside and held the material up, inspecting the sheer mesh overlaid with matching lace. It would cup his ass and wrap around his hips and he could already picture how it would look stretched over his cock as Malcolm kissed him through the fabric…

"Wow." It came out hoarser than he'd intended, and his body filled with heat at the idea.

"That's what I thought when I saw it." Malcolm wrapped his arms around Stuart's hips. "I imagined them on you and…" Malcolm stole another kiss, then rested his forehead against Stuart's.

Stuart rubbed his thumb across the lace, feeling how soft and finely woven it was. "It followed you home?"

"Something like that." Malcolm sounded like he was smiling.

"You spoil me." Stuart was smiling, too. And it wasn't a complaint. He enjoyed when Malcolm surprised him like this.

"Would you wear them tonight?" Now Malcolm was the one whose voice sounded husky.

"To drinks at Under?" Stuart leaned back to look Malcolm in the eye. He'd never worn lingerie when they hung out with Malcolm's friends.

"You don't have to if you're not comfortable with the idea. I just thought it might be something we'd both enjoy." Malcolm gave him a small shrug. Stuart knew if he said no, Malcolm would respect it. He wouldn't push and Stuart would never feel any pressure from him. The idea intrigued him though.

"I could give it a try. Any ideas about what I should wear over them?" He didn't have a lot of options. Jeans, a few pairs of trousers…

"I was thinking leather pants."

Stuart raised an eyebrow. "You've thought about this a lot, haven't you?"

"Maybe?" Malcolm gave a sheepish shrug. Stuart set the underwear and bag on the nearby couch, then stepped forward, sliding his arms around Malcolm's waist to pull their bodies tightly together. "Like...maybe the whole walk home. And I might have almost walked past our building because I was so distracted."

Stuart chuckled. "I can't imagine why."

Malcolm let out a little grumbling noise of disagreement. "Liar. You're hard right now just thinking about it."

Stuart rubbed gently against Malcolm's hip. "So I am."

"Maybe I should do something about that before we leave for Under..."

"Mmm." Stuart let out a rumbling noise of approval at the idea before he caught a glimpse of the clock. "I'm afraid it'll have to wait until after. We need to get ready and grab a bite to eat before we head out or we'll be cutting it close for time."

"Damn it."

"It'll be worth it. I promise. Now, go get changed while I heat up leftovers from last night." Stuart lightly smacked Malcolm's ass. "I'll get ready after we eat if you'll clean."

"Don't I get to watch you get dressed?"

"No." Stuart grinned. "One, if you do, we'll never get out of here on time. And two, it'll heighten the anticipation for both of us."

"I hate it when you're right."

"No, you don't." Stuart gave Malcolm a deep, lingering kiss and smacked Malcolm's ass again. "Now go."

* * * *

As Stuart descended the stairs to Under, he wondered if he'd made a terrible mistake. He felt a little self-conscious as he trailed after Malcolm, highly aware of the soft rub of lace against his cockhead. Malcolm had assured him the texture of the lace couldn't be seen underneath the supple leather, but he was starting to regret his choice to prolong the torment. Trying to keep his erection down was a challenge.

Malcolm greeted Jim at the door and Stuart nodded a distracted hello to him. The group of men who stood up to greet them diverted Stuart from his thoughts long enough for him to regain his composure. He got a warm greeting from Riley, Carter, Will and David, and a moment later, Jesse and Cam appeared.

"Hey, good to see you." Jesse kissed Malcolm on the cheek. "I've missed you, Maleficent."

"I've missed you too, Jes. We've been busy getting settled into the new place. Stuart's been at the workshop, building us some amazing custom furniture. The dining table is almost done."

"I can't wait to check it all out. Thanks for inviting Cam and me over for dinner next weekend. I'm looking forward to sampling some of Stuart's scrumptiousness." He waggled his eyebrows in a way that should have been utterly ridiculous but somehow came off as charming.

Malcolm laughed as he hugged Cam. "Always innuendo with you, Jes, isn't it?"

"Always." Jesse gave Malcolm a dazzling grin, then leaned in to hug Stuart.

Cam asked about Chase Barksdale and he and Malcolm chatted about him as Stuart made a beeline for the bar.

"Goddamn, do I approve of your boyfriend wearing leather pants. You are a lucky, lucky bitch, Mal." Jesse's words floated above the murmur of voices and Stuart smiled to himself. He caught a glimpse of Kyle, laughing and shaking his head as he mixed another drink.

Stuart tried to imagine what Jesse and the rest of them would say if they knew what he had on underneath the leather pants. Actually, he was pretty sure he knew what the reaction would be. Some friendly teasing, a few wolf-whistles and a whole lot of acceptance. His kink wasn't something he wanted to share with these guys. At least, there was zero chance they'd ever be judgmental if they did find out.

They'd been nothing but supportive of Malcolm as he'd figured out his sexuality and came to understand who he was. It would be the same for Stuart.

"Hey there." Kyle came around the end of the bar to enfold Stuart in a warm hug. "I mixed up a batch of something called a Fennel Countdown. It's rum, calvados, citrus-clove infused liqueur, fennel syrup and apricot puree. You interested in trying it?"

"Oh, wow. That sounds great. You're definitely giving me recipe ideas."

Kyle chuckled. "You say that like it's a bad thing."

Stuart grinned. "Not at all. I'm thinking about roast pork with a fennel-citrus rub and an apricot-clove sauce."

"Hell, Stuart. I will happily let you experiment on me any day if you're making that."

Stuart laughed heartily. Of all the guys, he and Kyle had meshed the most easily. They'd bonded over their love of booze and food and he felt their humor generally aligned well. He liked them all, but Kyle was the one he was most likely to socialize with one-on-one. Stuart and Kyle had gone hiking a handful of times throughout the fall and winter, and once the snow began to melt, Stuart hoped they'd get out again.

As Stuart sipped the delicious cocktail and planned recipes in his head, Luka arrived. Kyle greeted his boyfriend with a kiss and Stuart gave the handsome fireman a firm hug.

"So I hear congratulations are in order?" He looked between Kyle and Luka.

"They are." Luka offered him a smile as he fingered the silver band on his left ring finger. "Kyle finally agreed to make an honest man of me. I think he'd be happier going to a courthouse and keeping it very quiet, but I have a huge family who would murder us both if we went that route. Not to mention Jesse."

"You could always get married at the courthouse first," Stuart suggested. "Tell no one else. Then there would be less pressure on the day of the big ceremony and reception."

"Now that's some sensible advice," Kyle said in a thoughtful tone. "We're thinking of doing the reception upstairs here, actually, which takes some of the pressure off."

"At The Over Under? That's a great idea."

"I've been meaning to talk to you about catering, actually."

"Oh, man, I'd love to." Stuart grinned, delighted to be asked.

"I am glad to hear it. It'll be a load off my mind, knowing it's in your capable hands."

Stuart glowed a little at the praise and the other guys crowded around as they chatted about the upcoming wedding. Riley and Carter chimed in with their advice on how to keep the planning from getting too out of hand while Stuart contemplated the idea that he and Malcolm might head down that road at some point in the future. After his marriage with Becky, Stuart never would have considered the idea. But now...

Malcolm caught his glance and smiled in a way that sent butterflies surging through Stuart's chest. Goddamn, he loved Malcolm.

"Cam has some big news, too!" Jesse announced, breaking Stuart's focus on Malcolm. He glanced over to see Cam's face turn pink as he ducked his head.

"Yeah? What's that?" Will asked, his tone curious.

"I kissed a girl." Cam's muttered words were almost quiet enough to be missed but Stuart caught them.

"Tell them the rest!" Jesse teased, wrapping his arm around Cam's waist.

"I liked it," Cam admitted with a huff.

Behind him, Kyle hummed the familiar Katy Perry tune under his breath and Stuart let out a deep belly laugh in response.

"Hey, this isn't funny," Cam protested but he was laughing too. All of them were. There was nothing malicious about it, however. Only good-hearted humor at the situation and Cam's uncharacteristic shyness about it.

"It's a little bit funny, babe," Jes said, pressing a kiss to Cam's temple. "And you totally gave me permission to tell them all, so I know you aren't actually mad."

"Yeah, yeah."

"So how did this happen, exactly?" Carter asked, still chuckling.

"The same way they usually do," Jesse said. "We went out one night and met an interesting couple."

"Okay, but it's usually two guys, right?" Riley asked.

"Well, Cam's watched me with a woman before. The man was bi and very into Cam. They had fun while I got to enjoy his girlfriend. It worked for us."

"So what made this time different?" David asked.

"I don't know. The vibe was just right, I guess. Something just...meshed. I've never felt that for a woman before but..." Cam shrugged. "I asked her if she was into me experimenting some and she was all for it, so I gave it a go. No one was more surprised than me when I enjoyed it but I'm not one to turn down an opportunity like that if it feels right."

Jesse grinned. "It didn't go any further with Cam and her that night—we needed to talk more about it first—but we got their number and we may see them again. So, that's fun." He shot Cam a sly grin and stole a kiss.

"Huh," Malcolm said. He exchanged a glance with Stuart.

Polyamory would never work for them, but it clearly made Jesse and Cam happy, so who were they to judge? Malcolm and Stuart had their own kinks. Stuart thought briefly of the blue panties he had on and arousal tickled at the edge of his consciousness. He had a lot to look forward to when they went home tonight.

"Who knows, maybe there's still hope for me hooking up with Riley and Carter eventually," Jesse teased.

Will hooted. "In your dreams, Jes."

"Mmmhmm." Jesse looked off into the distance. "Filthy, filthy dreams."

Riley leaned over and whispered something in Carter's ear. Carter rolled his eyes at Riley, then leaned over and planted a kiss on Riley's cheek.

The conversation segued into other topics as they settled into the seating area with their drinks. As everyone laughed and caught up on all the new things happening — Riley and Carter reveling in happily married life, Will and David running their foundation and living in Manhattan part-time now that David had left office and become an Independent — a sense of completion settled over Stuart.

When he'd left Utah on a bike, with tears in his eyes and nothing but a wild hope of building a new life in Manhattan, he'd never dreamed it would look like this. He'd never imagined it would include a partner he loved, a thriving career and a hell of a lot of people who accepted and welcomed him into their lives.

Seeing how unfailingly supportive these men were made Stuart realize how lucky he was, not only to have met Malcolm but to be a part of this strange and wonderful group. They could still be overwhelming at times, but Stuart had come to realize that he'd mostly been scared to trust them. Scared to get close to anyone who could reject him. He'd lost his family and everyone else in his life when he'd come out. Now, he'd finally begun to believe that these guys weren't going anywhere.

Stuart reached out and snagged Malcolm's elbow, pulling him closer. Malcolm looked over at him with love and laughter in his eyes.

"I love you so much," Stuart said, his voice husky with emotion. "And I am so damn glad that other caterer canceled on you last year."

"I know exactly what you mean." Malcolm closed the distance between them and brushed their lips together.

As he drew back, Stuart knew with bone-deep certainty that whatever happened in the future, he had everything he needed right here.

Life was good.

A Note from the Authors

Dear Reader

If you've followed us on this Speakeasy journey, you already know how much our characters mean to us. Malcolm Elliott introduced himself even before the speakeasy Under even existed, and though he was always rather quiet and unassuming compared to some of the men who became his family, we grew to care about him. After he made it clear he identified as gray ace/demisexual, we realized Malcolm also had a story.

Not every gray ace/demisexual reader who picks up this book will recognize themselves in Malcolm. No two people experience the world or romance in the same way, and that is very much the case with people on the asexual spectrum. If you do recognize yourself in Malcolm, we hope that seeing some of you on these pages is a happy experience. Your feelings are real, and you are loved and valid.

K. Evan Coles and Brigham Vaughn

Want to see more from these authors? Here's a taster for you to enjoy!

Wake
K. Evan Coles and Brigham Vaughn

Excerpt

August, 1996
Cambridge, Massachusetts

"These rooms always look so much bigger online."

Carter Hamilton flinched in surprise at the smooth voice behind him. Blinking slowly, he drew a breath to quiet his heart, then turned to meet a pair of lively blue eyes.

"Sorry." A guy Carter's age stepped inside the door, his expression sheepish. A smile lit his handsome face and an intriguing flush colored his cheeks. "I didn't mean to startle you."

Carter shrugged before standing up from the couch where he'd been reading. "I'll live."

"I knocked, but no one answered. The door wasn't bolted, so I assumed no one was here."

"Ah, that's my bad." Heat crept up Carter's neck. "I got caught up in my book and didn't hear you. I'm Carter and I'm guessing you're one of my suitemates — are you Riley or Daniel?"

"Riley Porter-Wright."

Riley walked forward with a grin. Riley was lean and tall, though still an inch or two shorter than Carter, who stood six foot three. His stylish black shirt and trousers were immaculate compared to Carter's T-shirt and jeans and his dark hair fell forward onto his forehead as he shook Carter's hand.

A small smile crossed Carter's face. He'd been exchanging messages with his suitemates for weeks. Daniel, who had yet to show himself, hailed from Philadelphia, while Riley, like Carter, lived in Manhattan, though the two had never met. They'd coordinated basic furnishings for their Harvard University rooms and agreed to fill in gaps later.

"I'm Carter Hamilton," Carter told him with a laugh, "which you know. And since I was the first here, I guess it's okay for me to say it — welcome to Wigg."

Riley rolled his eyes, making Carter smile wider. He'd been amused by the freshman dorm's nickname, too, but Wigglesworth was highly desired, with large suites and convenient placement for the university libraries. Carter watched Riley approach the window and frowned upon noticing he carried only an overnight bag and nothing more.

"You planning on staying?" Carter eyed Riley's bag when he turned and cocked his head in question. "I know from your email messages that you're not big on decorating, but one bag seems like taking traveling light to new extremes. You said you'd bring a fridge, too, in case you forgot."

Riley glanced down at himself and laughed, the clear boyish sound echoing through the sparsely furnished common room.

"I didn't forget. I did bring a fridge and more boxes and bags, too — they're in a moving van stuck in traffic on Storrow Drive. One of the movers called me twenty minutes ago," he added, drawing closer to set his bag against the side of the couch. "I'm not sure I buy their story, though. They probably got here hours ago and found someplace to have lunch and a couple of beers before they drop my shit off.

"Nice couch, by the way." Riley nodded at the charcoal-colored couch Carter and his father had carried in earlier. "You picked out a bedroom already?" he asked, taking a seat.

"Not really. I got here late this morning, so we moved everything in and pushed it out of the way." Carter sat down too, waving at the boxes and suitcases lining the wall to their left. "The way I see it, once Dan shows, we can figure out who's going to share and who's got the single."

"Someone had a productive day," Riley teased, raising his brows and making Carter laugh.

"Yeah, well, my parents wanted to stay and meet you guys, but I didn't want them hitting rush hour on their way home. You'll meet them soon, anyway — they're already talking about their next trip up.

"I bought them lunch before they left," Carter added, unsure why he was sharing so much information with a guy he'd just met. "I figured that was the least I could do after they helped me drag my stuff up three flights."

Riley blinked several times, appearing vaguely surprised. "Your parents helped you move in?"

"Sure," Carter replied with a shrug. "My dad's an alumnus and my mom graduated from Wellesley — they enjoy visiting Cambridge." He chuckled. "They were definitely excited to help me settle in, even if it meant manual labor."

Riley's expression became thoughtful. Looking down, he traced a frayed spot on the right knee of his jeans with his finger. In a flash, Carter understood Riley was on his own.

Riley glanced up at Carter again. "My parents couldn't make the trip," he said, his voice light. "They're having dinner with friends tonight and didn't want to be late. I took the car up from the city."

Carter nodded. The idea of his parents choosing to socialize over seeing him off to school seemed utterly alien. Did it bother Riley that his parents were uninterested in what had to be an exciting day for him?

An impulse struck Carter to make Riley comfortable. "You know, you never told me where you live in the city."

Riley smiled, though a trace of melancholy flickered in his eyes. "West 86th Street. That's where my parents live, and I suppose I'll be there for a while longer. What about you?"

"East 63rd Street." Carter grinned. "That's funny."

"Funny?"

"We live in the same city separated by twenty-three blocks and the Park. Doesn't seem like much when you consider we had to come to Cambridge, Massachusetts, to meet."

Riley's eyes brightened. They chatted easily about their trips from New York until the door banged open, then watched a figure shoulder its way in with a stack of boxes. The boxes landed on the floor with a thump, revealing a cheerful-looking guy with a wiry build, golden-brown skin and inquisitive gray eyes.

"Dan Conley," he said, flashing a smile. "My dad's parking the car. You guys want to arm wrestle now or later to settle the whole double vs. single room thing?"

After a quick discussion, it became clear Dan and Riley preferred the single room, while Carter was willing to share the double. He sat on the couch with

Dan's parents, watching his new friends flip a coin. Dan won the toss and celebrated with an exaggerated touchdown dance, complete with slo-mo action that made Riley roll his eyes.

Riley's movers arrived then and made short work of bringing his load of boxes and bags upstairs. The trio started arranging furniture and unpacking, with Dan's parents providing useful — if unsolicited — feedback.

After the rooms were in some order, the Conleys insisted on taking all three suitemates to Grendel's Den for dinner. They got to know each other better over sandwiches, while Dan's parents asked Carter and Riley about their families. They had a pleasant evening, though Riley shared little about himself and even less about his parents. He talked easily about New York and the traveling he'd done during school vacations but shut down personal questions. He wasn't rude — if anything he seemed the opposite, with his open expression and bright gaze, but spent more time listening to the others than talking about himself.

It was late when Carter finally dropped onto his bed with a grunt. Dan had already been asleep for an hour and Riley had headed for the shower while Carter closed his eyes and took mental inventory of his sore muscles.

The sound of the bathroom door opening roused Carter from his dozy thoughts. He peeled an eyelid open to peer up at his roommate, who was moving around the bedroom and taking pains to be quiet. Like Carter, Riley wore a pair of dark sleep pants, though he had forgone a T-shirt. Droplets of water fell from his still wet hair, shining in the low light as they rolled over his bare shoulders and back. Carter was still trying to understand why he'd even think such a thing when

Riley turned, looking pensive. Carter rolled onto his side and propped his head on one hand.

Riley jumped, startled by the sudden movement. "Jesus, Carter!"

"Um, just Carter will do—no need to get formal." Carter bit his lip against a smile.

"You scared the shit out of me. I thought you were asleep, you sneaky bastard."

Riley's words were sharp, but the glint in his eyes told Carter his irritation was mostly for show.

"Sorry. Consider it payback for scaring me earlier today."

Carter pushed himself up to pull back the bedding and slip underneath the duvet and sheet. He watched Riley puttering about, getting ready for bed and his amusement faded. Despite his roommate's smile, Carter sensed Riley had something on his mind. He lay quietly, worrying his lower lip with his teeth until Riley sat on the edge of his own bed.

"Is this bothering you?" Carter asked, waving one hand in a vague circle. Riley eyed him blankly. "The room-sharing thing, I mean. I know you've never had a roommate before, so I can sort of see where you'd be feeling weirded out."

"No, I'm—" Riley began before pausing, his lips pressed into a thin line. He blew out a slow breath before he spoke again, his voice low and calm. "I'm okay. It is a little weird sharing a room. I mean, my room at home is bigger than the whole suite." He grimaced a bit at Carter's laugh, and shrugged. "But you probably guessed that already. You come from the same world."

Carter reached up to fold his hands behind his head. "It does seem like culture shock in a lot of ways. I have almost a full floor at my parents' and now I'm sharing three rooms with strangers. In the middle of freaking Red Sox country, no less." Both guys laughed. "I like it, though. Yeah, it's small and all bricks and ivy but it feels…I don't know, right. At least to me."

"I get it." Riley ran his hands over his damp hair with a sigh. He was quiet for so long Carter wondered if he would speak again. "My parents aren't the warmest people in the world. You probably gathered that when I told you they couldn't be bothered to even meet me here."

Carter nodded, Riley's words settling over him.

"I'm used to it," Riley added, rubbing his forehead. "I've never known any different. Oh, my parents have always taken care of me and they'll give me almost anything I ask for. Except for their attention. They leave that to the nannies and minders and secretaries, who give me attention because they're paid to."

The air grew heavy, charged with emotion Carter understood Riley didn't want to acknowledge.

"My parents aren't interested in me." Riley held up a hand when Carter opened his mouth to protest, though he didn't meet Carter's eyes. "They're not, trust me. I've known it for a long time and I can't remember when I last sorry for myself about it. My parents aren't interested in each other, to be honest — they can't even drum up enough feeling to fucking fight with each other."

Riley's words came more slowly as he continued, dropping his fingers to trace a spot on the right knee of his sleep pants. Carter had watched him do the same thing a few times already, always when he seemed to be masking some emotion.

"Watching the Conleys today," Riley said, "listening to you talk about your parents and to them after they called… I started thinking, Carter. I'm so used to the way my parents behave I'm almost at a loss to understand how normal families function."

"I'm not sure my family is what you'd call normal, Riley." Carter's voice was quiet. "They're certainly not average compared to Dan's parents. The Conleys are pretty well off, but we both know Dan's here on a partial music scholarship."

Riley made a dismissive noise. "Over half of the students here are on some kind of scholarship. It's not like that's particularly unusual. Sure, your family has a lot more money than the Conleys. I'm talking about the connections, though, between people. Between you and your parents, between Dan and his. Hell, between your mom and your dad, and Dan's mom and —"

"I get it."

Something in Carter's gentle interruption caught Riley's attention. Suddenly, he met Carter's gaze and held it.

"I don't know why I'm telling you this. No, that's a lie—I do know. I don't want to be like that. Like my parents, I mean. Frozen with this hard shell wrapped around me." Riley's eyes flashed with something raw. "I don't want to be one of the Porter-Wrights and make my life about the job and the parties and how many cars and houses and boats I can buy."

Carter pursed his lips, struck by Riley's choice of words. "Your focus doesn't have to be about the material things, man. But unless you plan to cut ties with your family, parties and cars and houses and boats are going to be part of your life."

"You're right. Possessions shouldn't be anyone's focus, or at least not all the time." Riley closed his eyes for a moment, fatigue written across his face. "I'm glad I'm here. Away from them and that life."

"At least until Thanksgiving, anyway," Carter teased. He didn't know why Riley was suddenly opening up, but he wanted to offer his roommate some cheer. "You can come to my house for dinner. We'll show you how the Hamiltons party like the Founding Fathers."

Riley grunted, then stretched out, pulling the bedding over himself before he spoke again. "I'm down. My parents usually go away for Thanksgiving. They're partial to Grenada. My mother works on her tan and my father works on his golf swing. I used to go with them, but last year I decided to hang out in New York."

"Was it weird?" Carter couldn't imagine Riley's parents leaving him to rattle around a huge apartment alone while they went on vacation.

"No — it was fantastic."

Riley turned his head and the genuine warmth in his expression made Carter feel lighter.

"Some of my friends from school came over. We bought a ton of Thai food for dinner and smoked some weed and just sat around on the balcony for a while. The party went on for a couple of days."

Carter raised an eyebrow. "Sounds pretty debauched."

"Oh, you know it. I still hear stories about what happened in my own house. Fucking animals." Riley rolled onto his side. "The best day, though, was Sunday. I took the car uptown to this church in Harlem that one of my father's secretaries attends. They put on a Thanksgiving Gospel Concert every year, so I hung out and listened to music. Amazing."

Carter smiled at the awe on his roommate's face. "It sounds it."

"Come with me this year," Riley urged suddenly, propping himself up on one elbow.

"Sure. If you come to dinner at my house," Carter bargained, "assuming your parents will be out of town."

"Fuck it." Riley grinned. "I don't care where my parents are, Car—I'll be at your door for dinner whenever you want me."

"I've never been to a Thanksgiving concert before," Carter mused. "No one's ever called me Car before, either."

Riley's eyebrows shot up. "Really? Not even your parents or friends?"

"Nope."

"I can stop, if you want."

"Doesn't bother me." Carter smiled lazily. "Anyone call you Ri for short?"

"Sure. The nannies and the minders and the secretaries call me Ri. Kids at school. My teachers. Anyone who's known me for more than a couple of hours." Riley's laugh was rueful. "Basically, anyone but my parents."

"Sounds like I'm in good company then." Carter rolled over with a yawn and closed his eyes. "Night, Ri."

* * * *

Carter, Riley and Dan fell into their lives at Harvard with ease. Dan was a music major minoring in French, while Carter and Riley were both business majors. The time the friends spent together each day increased after all three gained membership to the same club, Phoenix-SK.

The final clubs were Harvard's version of Greek fraternities. They promised networking opportunities after graduation but also provided social outlets away from the dorms. Carter's and Riley's fathers had also belonged to Phoenix-SK but had missed knowing one another by a few years.

Carter was pleasantly surprised to find himself comfortable with Riley's almost constant presence. They shared many of the same interests, including cyberpunk novels and Quentin Tarantino movies, and even had similar tastes in food and music. The more they talked and spent time together, the more firmly their friendship cemented.

The one activity Riley refused to consider was heavyweight crew. Carter had rowed with a junior club during high school and was eager to use his height and powerful build as part of the Harvard Crimson. Riley thought Carter was out of his mind.

"I don't understand you." He cocked an eyebrow after Carter explained rowing was a Hamilton family tradition. "What kind of person voluntarily sits in a boat with a bunch of other meaty guys while someone screams at them through a bullhorn?"

Carter rolled his eyes as Dan joined in chuckling with Riley.

"A me kind of person, I guess. You should at least try it before making a decision, guys."

"You know, it sounds fun," Dan said. He held up a placating hand while Riley made an outraged noise. "But I'm an inch under six feet and we both know that's too short for heavyweight crew."

"True. You could try out for lightweight, instead," Carter offered, narrowing his eyes at Riley's snort. "Shut it, you."

Dan gave Riley the finger. "I could, but I need to spend time in the music rooms downstairs, anyway. If you and I were on the same team, that'd be one thing, but..."

"I get it, man," Carter replied and he did. Dan's academic schedule was busy enough before club activities—add time at the piano composing and he needed every spare minute he could find.

Carter aimed a beady eye at Riley. "What about you, funny guy—you up for a free workout with a view? The river's awfully pretty, especially first thing in the morning."

Riley laughed. "Yeah, you lost me at 'first thing in the morning.' Look, you say rowing crew is Hamilton family tradition. Fine, that's your business. The Porter-Wrights have traditions, too. They include not getting up at the crack of ass every morning to risk drowning in a muddy river. Thanks, but no thanks."

Despite the teasing, Riley and Dan seemed genuinely pleased when Carter came home with soggy shoes and a place on the team. Carter suspected they were just being polite, but he appreciated their efforts nonetheless.

Carter enjoyed rowing for the Crimson and losing himself in the simple physicality of the task and feeling part of a team. He looked forward to the quiet hush of the river, the lap of the waves against the side of the boat and the collective breaths and grunts of the team as they worked together.

There were negatives, of course, starting with practice at dawn and the feeling he just didn't have enough hours in the day. Carter focused on being grateful when Riley helped him bandage his blisters and smiled at the protein bars Dan stuffed into his coat pockets. Riley and Dan attended races when they could, sharing thermoses of Irish coffee and cheering while the Crimson's boats slipped by on the river.

As the weeks passed, Riley lost the shell he'd confessed to hating. Carter doubted anyone outside himself and Dan saw the subtle difference in their friend. Riley's dress grew more casual, as did his speech. He talked more about himself, which gave people a chance to get to know him better. He still didn't say much about his parents and when he did, he often dropped his right hand to his knee to draw circles on his pant leg with his fingers. Riley didn't glance away anymore, though, and he met the gaze of whoever he was speaking to unwaveringly.

It was during a Halloween party in one of the dorms that Carter became aware of how others perceived his friendship with Riley. He'd been chatting with Susannah, a pretty girl from his calculus class, and had been about to ask her out for coffee when she put a hand on his forearm and sighed.

"What's that about?" Carter peered under the brim of Susannah's midnight-blue witch's hat and gave her a smile.

Susannah grimaced slightly. "Don't take this the wrong way, Carter—you know I like you. If you were straight, I'd be really, really interested in you."

Carter frowned, the word *straight* still sinking into his brain while Susannah continued.

"I don't understand why the only guys who ever talk to me at parties are gay. You know?" Susannah twisted strands of her long, dark hair around one finger. "Honestly, I've basically despaired of finding a man of my own. I'll have to hang out with you and your boyfriend and pray people think we have some kind of polyamorous arrangement going on."

Carter shook his head slowly, Susannah's words beginning to make a kind of strange sense. She wrinkled her brow as Carter stood silent and she stepped closer, to squeeze his arm gently.

"Dude, I'm sorry. Did I... Was the poly thing too much? I was just joking, I swear."

"Susannah, are you under the impression I'm gay? That Riley and I are together?"

Susannah cocked her head. "Well, yes. Aren't you? Gay, I mean. And Riley's boyfriend?"

"No, I am not. Gay or Riley's boyfriend." Carter fought conflicting urges to be angry and amused. "Riley's not gay, either. Where the hell did you get that idea?"

"Oh, my God, I'm so sorry." Susannah's face flushed deep red and she put her fingers over her mouth. She looked so stricken that Carter gave in to the impulse to laugh. "Jesus, I'm so embarrassed!"

"You should be," Carter scolded, though he laughed harder at the expression of horror on her face. "Why would you think that, woman?"

"You're always together!" she exclaimed. "I've never seen either of you with a girl and you told me Riley is your roommate. I assumed it all added up to the two of you being, you know, together."

Carter laughed hard enough he had to put down his drink. "What about Dan? He lives with us and we hang out all the time. Is he one of the boyfriends, too?"

"Dan goes on dates, Carter. He dates women. Okay, one woman," Susanna clarified, turning to search the crowd, and pointing when she found the right faces. Carter craned his neck to follow her gesture. He nodded at Dan with his arms around Melanie Howard, another music major who often came by their suite. They'd coordinated their costumes, with Dan dressed as a devil and Mel an angel, and come to the party with a group of friends.

"Everyone knows Dan and Mel are dating," Susannah said. "They've been together practically since the first day of classes."

Dan and Mel really were inseparable. She was double majoring in music and psychology and planned to go into music therapy. Mel was a petite beauty, with dark hair, creamy golden skin and greenish-gray eyes. Carter appreciated her bright and sarcastic brand of humor and knew Dan really liked her.

"Okay, I see your point." Carter glanced back to Susannah with a steely expression. "Making assumptions about Riley and me, though, is not cool."

Susannah gulped, and dropped her gaze to the drink in her hands. "You're right. You should know I'm not the only one who thinks you're together, by the way."

Carter frowned, trying to understand how to feel about what Susannah had told him. He'd grown up with a diverse group of friends and he didn't much care whom a person spent their time with. As far as Carter was concerned, whatever and whomever made a person happy was fine by him, provided everyone involved consented. The idea people thought he was someone's boyfriend, however... That didn't fit into Carter's world. It certainly did not fit into his family's, either.

"People really think Riley and I are together?"

"Well, girls, mostly," Susannah replied, "and that's because they're trying to figure out what's going on with you and Riley."

"Nothing is going on, Susannah."

"I know." Her voice dropped low as she tried to smooth Carter's ruffled feathers. "I'm sorry we gossiped. Two good-looking guys, in each other's company more than anyone else's…a girl's gonna try to put the pieces together."

"Uh-huh. Put the pieces together incorrectly, you mean," he replied. Carter imagined his parents' reaction to the rumor and his stomach knotted.

The dejection on Susannah's face softened his annoyance, however. He'd really wanted to take her out for coffee before she'd let her 'secret' slip. And his heart beat a little faster as he understood taking Susannah out would nip the 'boyfriends' rumor in the bud, too.

"Are you very angry?" she asked quietly, concern visible in her green eyes.

Carter smiled. "No. You surprised me, that's all. I might have been a little offended, too, but only because you could have asked me instead of gossiping. That shit's not okay, Susannah. Especially because I planned on asking you out."

Susannah's mouth dropped open. "You did?" she squeaked, then cleared her throat, obviously working to recover her composure. "You could still ask me, you know. Or, maybe you should let me take you out. So I can apologize for being a gossipy shrew."

Her words warmed Carter and his grin slowly widened. "Sure. I think I can handle that."

PUBLISHING

Sign up for our newsletter and find out about all our romance book releases, eBook sales and promotions, sneak peeks and FREE romance books!

About the Authors

K. Evan Coles

K. Evan Coles is a mother and tech pirate by day and a writer by night. She is a dreamer who, with a little hard work and a lot of good coffee, coaxes words out of her head and onto paper.

K. lives in the northeast United States, where she complains bitterly about the winters, but truly loves the region and its diverse, tenacious and deceptively compassionate people. You'll usually find K. nerding out over books, movies and television with friends and family. She's especially proud to be raising her son as part of a new generation of unabashed geeks.

Brigham Vaughn

Brigham Vaughn is starting the adventure of a lifetime as a full-time writer. She devours books at an alarming rate and hasn't let her short arms and long torso stop her from doing yoga. She makes a killer key lime pie, hates green peppers and loves wine tasting tours. A collector of vintage Nancy Drew books and green glassware, she enjoys poking around in antique shops and refinishing thrift store furniture. An avid photographer, she dreams of traveling the world and she can't wait to discover everything else life has to offer her.

K. and Brigham love to hear from readers. You can find their contact information, website details and author profile page at https://www.pride-publishing.com